...pocket to pull out his wallet, extracting a gold-embossed business card he pressed into her hand.

Mia read the elegant lettering with a lift of her brows. "ARES Security?"

"It's a company I started with a few friends. Trust me. We have the expertise and technology to find out exactly what Tony was doing."

Mia's lips parted to demand what had happened to his career as a diplomat, only to hastily swallow the words. There was no way in hell she was going to reveal her seething interest in what he'd been doing since he'd returned from the Middle East.

He'd cut her out of his life.

So be it.

"Why?" she instead demanded.

His brooding gaze slid down to the stubborn tilt of her chin. "What do you mean?"

"What's your interest in any of this?"

"Tony was coming to see me," he said. "I want to know why."

"And that's the only reason?"

"No." Reaching up, he cupped her face in his hands. "I'm here for you, Mia. . . ."

**Published by Kensington Publishing Corporation**

# KILL WITHOUT SHAME

## ALEXANDRA IVY

ZEBRA BOOKS
KENSINGTON PUBLISHING CORP.
http://www.kensingtonbooks.com

ZEBRA BOOKS are published by

Kensington Publishing Corp.
119 West 40th Street
New York, NY 10018

All Kensington titles, imprints and distributed lines are available at special quantity discounts for bulk purchases for sales promotion, premiums, fund-raising, educational or institutional use.

Special book excerpts or customized printings can also be created to fit specific needs. For details, write or phone the office of the Kensington Sales Manager. Attn.: Sales Department. Kensington Publishing Corp., 119 West 40th Street, New York, NY 10018. Phone: 1-800-221-2647.

Zebra and the Z logo Reg. U.S. Pat. & TM Off.

First Printing: January 2017
ISBN-13: 978-1-4201-3757-6
ISBN-10: 1-4201-3757-3

eISBN-13: 978-1-4201-3758-3
eISBN-10: 1-4201-3758-1

10 9 8 7 6 5 4 3 2 1

Printed in the United States of America

# Prologue

The worst part of being held in a Taliban prison was the recurring nightmares. At least as far as Lucas St. Clair was concerned.

No matter how many years passed, his nights were still plagued with memories of being trapped in the smothering darkness of the caves. He could smell the stench of unwashed bodies and undiluted fear. He could hear the muffled sounds of men praying for death.

He knew his parents assumed that his biggest regret was the derailment of his political aspirations. After all, his military career was intended to be the first step in his climb to a position as a diplomat.

From there . . . well, his family was nothing if not ambitious. They'd no doubt seen the White House in his future.

But there were few things that could make a man view his life with the stark clarity of five weeks of brutal torture.

By the time he'd managed to escape the caves, he'd known he was done living his life to please the precious St. Clair clan.

Instead he'd banded together with his friends—Rafe Vargas, a covert ops specialist; Max Grayson, who was trained in forensics; Hauk Laurensen, a sniper; and Teagan Moore, a computer wizard—to create ARES Security.

He'd wasted too much of his life.

He intended to leave the past behind and concentrate on his future.

Of course, there was an old saying about "the best laid plans of mice and men. . . ."

# Chapter One

The Saloon was the sort of bar that catered to the locals in the quiet Houston neighborhood.

It was small, with lots of wood and polished brass. Overhead there was an open beam ceiling, with muted lights that provided a cozy atmosphere, and on the weekends a jazz band was invited to play quietly on the narrow stage.

Lucas spent most Friday evenings at the table tucked in a back corner. It was unofficially reserved for the five men who ran ARES Security.

The men liked the peaceful ambiance, the communal agreement that everyone should mind their own business, and the fact that the table was situated so no one could sneak up from behind.

Trained soldiers didn't want surprises.

At the moment, the bar was nearly empty. Not only was it a gray, wet Wednesday evening, but it was the first week of December. That meant Christmas madness was in full swing.

Perfectly normal people were now in crazy mode as they scurried from store to store, battling one another for the latest have-to-have gift. It was like Thunderdome without Tina Turner.

Currently Lucas and Teagan shared the place with a young couple seated near the bay window at the front of the bar. Those two were oblivious to everything but each other. And closer to the empty stage was a table of college girls. Already at the giggly stage of drunk, they were all blatantly checking Lucas out. At least when they weren't gawking at Teagan.

No biggie.

Both men were accustomed to female attention.

Teagan was a large, heavily muscled man with dark caramel skin, and golden eyes that he'd inherited from his Polynesian mother. He kept his hair shaved close to his skull, and as usual was dressed in a pair of camo pants and shit-kickers. He had an aggressive vibe that was only emphasized by the tight T-shirt that left his arms bare to reveal numerous tattoos.

Lucas St. Clair, on the other hand, was wearing a thousand-dollar suit that was tailored to perfectly fit his lean body. His glossy black hair was smoothed away from his chiseled face, which he'd been told could easily grace the covers of fashion magazines. As if he gave a shit.

His eyes were so dark they looked black. It wasn't until he was in the sunlight that it became obvious they were a deep, indigo blue.

Most assumed he was the less dangerous of the two men.

They'd be wrong.

But while the girls became increasingly more obvious in their attempts to attract their attention, neither man glanced in their direction.

Teagan because he already had a flock of women that included supermodels and two famous actresses.

And Lucas because . . . He grimaced.

To be honest, he wasn't sure why. He only knew that his interest in women hadn't been the same since he'd crawled out of that hellhole in Afghanistan. Not unless he counted the hours he spent brooding on one woman in particular.

The one who got away.

Lucas gave a sharp shake of his head, reaching for his shot of tequila. It slid down his throat like liquid fire, burning away the past.

Nothing like a twelve-year-old vintage to ease the pain.

Lucas glanced toward his companion's empty glass. "Another round?" he asked.

"Sure." Teagan waited for Lucas to nod toward the bartender, who was washing glasses, at the same time keeping a sharp eye on his few customers. "I assume you're picking up the tab?"

Lucas cocked a brow. "Why do I always have to pick up the tab?"

"You're the one with the trust fund, amigo, not me," Teagan said with a shrug. "The only thing my father ever gave me was a concussion and an intimate knowledge of the Texas penal system."

Lucas snorted. It was common knowledge that he would beg in the streets before he would touch a penny of the St. Clair fortune. Just as they all knew that Teagan had risen above his abusive background, and temporary housing in the penitentiary, to become a successful businessman. The younger man not only joined ARES, but he owned a mechanic shop that catered to a high-end clientele who had more money than sense when it came to their precious sports cars.

"I might break out the violins if I didn't know you're making a fortune," Lucas told his friend as the bartender arrived to replace their drinks with a silent efficiency.

"Hardly a fortune." Teagan downed a shot of tequila before he reached for his beer, heaving a faux sigh. "I have overhead out the ass, not to mention paying my cousins twice what they're worth. A word of warning, amigo. Never go into business with your family."

"Too late," Lucas murmured.

As far as he was concerned, the men who had crawled out of that Taliban cave with him were his brothers. And the only family that mattered.

"True that." Teagan gave a slow nod, holding up his frosty glass. "To ARES."

Lucas clinked his glass against Teagan's in appreciation of the bond they'd formed. "To ARES."

Drinking the tequila in one swallow, Lucas set aside his empty glass. There was a brief silence before Teagan at last spoke the words that'd no doubt been on the tip of his tongue since they walked through the door of the bar.

"Are you ever going to get to the point of why you asked to meet me here?" his friend bluntly demanded.

Lucas leaned back in his chair, arching his brows. "Couldn't it just be because I enjoy your sparkling personality?"

Teagan snorted. "If I'd known this was a date I would have worn my lucky shirt."

"You need a shirt to get lucky?"

"Not usually." Teagan flashed his friend a mocking smile. "But I've heard you like to play hard to get."

Lucas grimaced at the direct hit. Yeah. Hard to get was one way to put it.

"I want to discuss Hauk," he admitted, not at all eager to think about his lack of a sex life.

Teagan leaned forward, folding his arms on the table. "Did you pick up any intel from your overseas contacts?"

Lucas didn't ask how his companion knew he was quietly reaching out to his diplomatic associates in an effort to track down whoever was stalking Hauk. They were each using their various skills to discover who was responsible for leaving the creepy messages that were increasingly threatening in nature.

"Yeah." He'd received an updated report earlier that morning. "There's been no chatter that includes Hauk or anything about our escape from Afghanistan."

Teagan nodded. Each of them had managed to make enemies during their time in the Middle East. It was war. But Hauk was a sniper who'd received a very public Medal of Honor for taking out three powerful terrorist leaders during his time in service.

That was the sort of thing that pissed people off.

"Then this isn't the work of an organized cell?"

"Nope." Lucas gave a decisive shake of his head. He'd contacted everyone he knew, including those at Homeland Security. If Hauk's name had been floating around as a potential target, someone would have heard it by now. "It's more likely some independent whack job."

Teagan's jaw hardened with frustration. "I don't know whether to be relieved or disappointed. If it was a cell we could keep an eye on them, but how the hell do we find some lone nutcase?"

"I have word out that I'm looking for information on anyone who's shown an interest in Hauk." Lucas studied his companion's grim expression. "What about you?"

Teagan reached for his beer. "I'm doing a computer search on anyone who served with Hauk during his tour in the Middle East and has left the military in the past six months."

Lucas arched a brow. Teagan was talented. Maybe even the best hacker in the world. But he wasn't a miracle worker.

"That's a long list."

"It's going to take a while," Teagan admitted, taking a deep drink of his beer.

"Shit. I hate this waiting," Lucas muttered. The thought

that some unseen enemy was hunting Hauk was making them all twitchy. "What about Max?"

"He's . . ." Teagan slowly lowered his beer as his gaze narrowed. "Did you forget to pay your taxes?"

Lucas frowned. "What the hell are you talking about?"

Teagan nodded across the room. "There's a government employee who just flashed a badge at the bartender and is now heading in our direction."

Lucas glanced over his shoulder, his gaze trained on the middle-aged man strolling in their direction.

The stranger had thinning blond hair that looked like his wife had trimmed it. A suit that was in dire need of a good pressing. Cheap shoes. And a face that had a hint of a bull-dog in the features.

Yep. Definitely a government grunt.

Lucas turned back toward his friend. "How do you know he isn't looking for you?"

"I'm too clever to get caught."

Lucas rolled his eyes. "Christ."

"Lucas St. Clair?"

Halting next to the table, the man instantly locked his attention on Lucas. Which meant he knew exactly what Lucas looked like.

So, had he recognized Lucas because of his ties to the St. Clair clan? Or because he'd done a background check before entering the Saloon?

Lucas was betting on the background check. The stranger didn't look like the sort of man to take an interest in politics.

"Yes."

The man flashed a badge that identified him as Houston Homicide Detective Sergeant Sam Cooper. "I have a few questions for you."

Lucas remained relaxed in his chair. There was no reason to get his panties in a twist. If there'd been a death in his powerful family he wouldn't be contacted by a midlevel bureaucrat.

And he hadn't killed anyone. At least, not lately.

"Concerning?" he asked.

The man glanced around the nearly empty bar. "Do you want to do this here?"

Lucas shrugged. "Unless we need to include my lawyer."

"That won't be necessary."

The "yet" hung in the air between them, and suddenly Lucas was a lot less nonchalant about the encounter.

Narrowing his gaze, he nodded his head toward the chair across the table. "Have a seat, Detective." Waiting until the man lowered his solid form into the chair, Lucas waved a hand toward his friend, who glowered at the lawman with a menacing frown. "This is Teagan Moore."

"Detective Cooper," Teagan muttered, folding his arms over his chest to make it clear he wasn't leaving.

Lucas hid his smile. In his work as a negotiator, he'd learned the art of subtlety. It was easier to coerce people to do what he wanted, rather than trying to force them.

Teagan, on the other hand, was a sledgehammer.

Returning his attention to the detective, Lucas tapped an impatient finger on the table. He had a dozen things he needed to take care of before he could return to his elegant town house in the center of Houston.

ARES Security might be a relatively new business, but they were already swamped with demands for their services. And to make matters more insane, Rafe had taken off with his new bride to Hawaii for a well-earned honeymoon.

Lucas wanted to be done with this cop so he could get back to work. "You said you have some questions," he prompted.

The man offered a self-deprecating smile, but Lucas didn't miss the cunning intelligence in his blue eyes. He was a man who liked to be underestimated.

Taking the time to pull a small notebook and pen from an inner pocket of his jacket, Sam Cooper laid them neatly on the table.

Precise. Careful. Meticulous.

"What's your relationship to Anthony Hughes?" he at last asked.

Lucas frowned. "There is no relationship. I've never heard of—" He bit off his words as an ancient memory floated to the surface of his brain. "Wait. I went to prep school with a Tony Hughes. I don't know if that's the same guy."

"Where was the school?"

Lucas shrugged. "Hale Academy in Shreveport."

The detective's face remained impassive, but something flashed through his eyes that told Lucas they were speaking about the same person.

"So Tony is your old high school friend?"

Lucas hesitated. In truth, the two couldn't have been more opposite.

He was the son of Senator St. Clair. He'd lived in a fancy mansion on the edge of town with a nanny while his parents spent most of their time in DC. On the other hand, Tony was the youngest of five brothers who grew up in a shack that had barely been habitable. If Tony hadn't been a six-foot-two behemoth who excelled at football he would never have been admitted into the exclusive private school.

And even that wouldn't have made them more than classmates.

It was only their mutual friendship with Mia Ramon that'd thrown them together.

"Not really," he said. "I haven't seen him in fifteen years."

Sam scribbled on his notepad, his gaze never leaving Lucas's face. "You're sure? He hasn't tried to call or contact you?"

"I'm sure." Lucas felt a stab of dread. "What's going on? Is he in trouble?"

The detective instantly pounced. "Why would you say that?"

Lucas arched a brow. "Beyond the fact a homicide detective is asking me questions about him?"

"Yeah, beyond that."

"It was no secret that Tony was doing drugs from the time he arrived at Hale," he admitted, not bothering to add that Tony was also dealing to make enough money to support his deadbeat dad. It wouldn't take much of a detective to dig up that old dirt. "He was kicked off the football team when he tested positive for weed our senior year. If some unknown donor hadn't come up with his tuition he would have been forced to leave school."

More scribbling on the pad. "Were you close growing up?"

"I didn't really know him until he transferred to the academy."

"But you were friends?"

"We both played football and occasionally hung out together." Lucas made a sound of impatience. "Are you going to tell me what your interest in Tony is?"

"He's dead."

"Dead?" Lucas blinked at the blunt response. Somehow he'd already leapt to the conclusion that Tony had been arrested for murder. And that he was now desperately trying to call in favors from the powerful acquaintances he'd acquired during high school. With an effort, he readjusted his thinking. "An overdose?"

"He was shot three blocks from your office building."

A stab of regret sliced through Lucas even as he lifted his brows in surprise. "Tony was in Houston?"

The detective gave a small nod. "He was."

"Did he live here?"

Sam Cooper shrugged. "He was carrying a Louisiana driver's license. We're checking the address that was listed."

The air pressure dropped as Teagan leaned forward, his

expression hard with annoyance. Despite his years in the military, the younger man harbored a deep distrust of authority figures.

"Why are you here?"

The detective turned his head to meet Teagan's glare. "Excuse me?"

"If you have a body, shouldn't you be out looking for who made it dead?" Teagan demanded.

"I find it's quicker to discover the killer when I know my victim."

Lucas studied Sam Cooper. The authorities were clearly treating this as a targeted murder, not a random drive-by shooting.

Interesting.

"Then you came to the wrong guy," Lucas informed the detective. There was no point in letting the man waste his time. He felt bad as hell that Tony was dead, but it had nothing to do with him. "Like I said, I haven't seen or heard from Tony since high school."

Sam Cooper ignored the unmistakable cue to bring the interview to an end. "Odd that he was shot so close to your building, don't you think, Mr. St. Clair?"

"What do you mean 'odd'?"

The detective shrugged. "You supposedly haven't seen Tony Hughes in years, but he manages to get shot just a few blocks away."

"Enough." Lucas abruptly shoved himself to his feet, vaguely aware that Teagan was rising at the same time. "I've tried to be polite and answer your questions, but you're starting to piss me off." He held the detective's steady gaze. "Are you trying to imply I have some connection to this crime?"

Sam Cooper remained sitting, remarkably nonchalant as both Lucas and Teagan glared down at him. Of course, they would have to be idiots to attack a member of the Houston Police Department in the middle of a bar. Plus he was probably carrying. Hard to detect beneath the sports jacket that should have been burned in the seventies.

"I think Tony Hughes was coming to see you," Sam said in a calm voice.

Lucas scowled. "Why?"

"Because of this." Reaching into his pocket, the detective pulled out a clear baggie and set it on the table.

Lucas leaned forward to study the wrinkled piece of paper that had his name and address scribbled on it.

"Where'd you get that?" he demanded.

"Tony had it in his front pocket."

"Shit," Lucas breathed in shock.

"Still no idea why he was in the neighborhood?"

"No." A chill inched down Lucas's spine. Why the hell had Tony been looking for him after fifteen years? And who would shoot him on the street? Questions that needed answers, but not until he shook off the tenacious lawman. It was never a good idea to chat with a homicide detective when he had a connection to the dead body. "And we're about to take this to my lawyer's office."

"About damned time," Teagan muttered.

Sam Cooper lifted his hand, trying to look harmless. "I just have one more question for now."

"What?"

The detective reached into his pocket to pull out another baggie. This one held a photo of a dark-haired woman with the words—"Kill her or else"—scrawled across her face.

"Do you recognize this woman?"

Lucas reached to snatch the baggie off the table, holding the picture toward the muted light. He barely heard Teagan's low curse or the detective's protest at his rough handling of evidence.

Even at a distance he'd easily recognized the image of a stunning young woman.

Oh, her features had matured from the soft prettiness of

youth into elegant lines. And her body had filled out with curves that made his mouth water.

But he'd recognize the thickly lashed dark eyes and soft, kissable mouth anywhere.

His stomach was fisted with a stark sense of horror that wrenched the air from his lungs.

"Mia," he rasped.

"Mia?" With a surge, the detective was on his feet, snatching the baggie from Lucas's fingers. "Last name?"

"Ramon. Mia Ramon," Lucas said even as he was turning away from the table.

On some level he understood that he wasn't thinking clearly. Shock did that to a man. But his primitive instincts didn't give a shit. All he knew was that Mia was in danger.

Nothing else mattered.

"Wait," Detective Cooper commanded as Lucas headed toward the door. "Where are you going?"

Lucas's long strides never faltered. Not even when he sensed Teagan moving to walk at his side.

"What can I do?" his friend asked.

That simple.

No aggravating demands for an explanation. Just a sincere desire to help.

"Tell the guys I'm headed to Shreveport," he said, his subconscious making a list of tasks that had to be finished before he could leave Houston. "I don't know when I'll be back."

# Chapter Two

Despite the chilly temperatures, the humidity in the air was the stuff of nightmares. Only in Louisiana could a person shiver with cold at the same time they were sweating like a dog.

Entering the recently constructed brick building on the northern fringe of Bossier City, Mia barely resisted the urge to peel off the fitted black jacket that matched her A-line skirt. It wasn't just the fact that the expensive material was sticking to her skin. She always felt like a fraud in designer clothes.

At heart, she was a jeans and sweatshirt kind of gal.

Unfortunately her corporate accounts expected the owner of Ramon Landscaping and Nursery to look like a professional. Especially when they were expecting a normal, middle-aged Caucasian male to show up for the contract signing, not a thirty-two-year-old woman with lush curves that regularly made men turn to watch her walk past.

She'd already decided she would return to her small house just a mile down the road during lunch so she could change. For now she was in dire need of a hefty dose of caffeine and a few minutes' peace.

To say her morning had been stressful was like saying a tsunami was a little wave.

With impeccable timing, Taylor Price rose from behind the reception desk to study her with open concern.

The woman had been Mia's best friend throughout high school, and when Mia finally managed to stabilize her business to the point she could afford a full-time secretary, she'd pleaded with Taylor to leave her job as a waitress to help her.

Mia might have a talent for creating a thriving business with satisfied customers and five full-time gardeners, plus another five part-time workers during the summer months, but she desperately needed someone to keep her organized.

Taylor had been an answer to her prayers. The single mother of a sixteen-year-old son had taken charge of the office, along with keeping the employees on task with a brisk efficiency.

Now she watched as Mia lifted a hand to pull out the pins that held her hair into a bun at the nape of her neck, releasing the glossy black strands to fall in a smooth curtain down her back.

"Crap," Taylor muttered, studying Mia's strained expression. "You didn't get the contract."

Mia managed a weary smile. She'd worked for weeks to convince Fox Construction to accept her bid. Getting the contract meant that her crew would be in charge of landscaping the new subdivision being built near Wallace Lake.

"It's signed, sealed, and will be delivered by Monday."

"Sweet." Taylor tilted her head to one side. Despite having a teenage son, she looked like she was barely out of high school. She was as slim as a reed, with honey-brown hair that she kept cut short and green eyes that could sparkle with amusement or flash with fury. She'd gotten pregnant by a local bad boy who'd taken off the second Justin was born, but that had never slowed her down. She worked, coached her son's baseball team, and took care of her aging mother. Not to mention keeping Mia somewhere in the vicinity of sane. "So why do you look like you lost your puppy?"

Mia rolled her shoulders, trying to ease the stiffness. "I'm sweating, my feet hurt, the owner of Fox Construction couldn't take his eyes off my boobs despite the fact they were covered in two layers of clothing. And some idiot nearly ran me off the road." She shook her head, her pulse still unsteady from the memory of the large SUV that'd swerved into her lane, clipping her bumper. It was a miracle she'd avoided going into a ditch. "I swear, trained monkeys could drive better than most people."

Taylor took efficient control. "What do you want first? Coffee? Or a maple cream donut?"

Mia glanced toward the reception desk across the simply designed room with white tiled floors and walls painted a soft apricot. Currently it was decorated with a large Christmas tree set in one corner and festive holly that was draped from the drop ceiling.

Behind the office building she'd constructed long sheds where she stored the equipment her landscaping company needed, and next door was a lot where she'd built rows of greenhouses. But in here, she'd demanded a hint of feminine charm.

It was her eye for design that had taken her business from just another lawn-mowing company to a full-service landscaping business worth millions.

This morning, however, her attention was laser-focused on the full coffeemaker and lovely pink box from her favorite bakery.

"You are a saint," Mia murmured.

"True." Taylor reached out to give her a light push. "Go into your office and put your feet up."

Mia didn't have to be told twice.

Coffee. Donuts. A few minutes' peace . . .

Priceless.

Entering her office, which was decorated in the same apricot and white as the reception room, only without the Christmas decorations, she tossed aside her briefcase and eased herself into the chair behind her desk.

Taking in a deep breath, she released it with a slow exhale, already feeling the knots in the pit of her stomach unraveling. Minutes later Taylor bustled in, setting a large mug of black coffee and a massive donut on the desk.

"Ah. Bless you," Mia said, reaching for the coffee. "Any problems while I was gone?"

Taylor shrugged. "When isn't there a problem?"

True. There were enough moving parts in her business it was inevitable there would be daily disasters.

"Hit me."

"Not until you finish your donut."

"Okay, Mother." Mia rolled her eyes, but she picked up the donut and took a bite. When Taylor put on her bossy pants it was easier to do as she commanded. Savoring the sinfully decadent pastry, Mia at last wiped the sticky maple from her fingers and took another sip of her coffee. "Done," she said as she leaned back in her chair.

Taylor reached for the crumpled napkin, throwing it in the trash before starting the daily list of glitches.

"First up, the garage called and said they had to order a part for the flatbed."

Mia nodded. It wasn't entirely unexpected. The flatbed truck was nearly twelve years old. Unfortunately, they needed it to haul the larger pieces of equipment and a new one wasn't in the budget until after the holidays.

"How long?" she demanded.

"Next week."

"Call the rental company and tell them we'll need the truck until next Friday. What else?"

"Sonny stopped by to say that the Richardsons didn't pay him yesterday. They claimed they sent a check last week."

Sonny had actually worked with her father mowing lawns and trimming hedges for the rich. Now he was her most trusted employee.

"How far are they behind?" she asked.

"Three months."

Mia made a mental note. The Richardsons owned two small strip malls that were struggling to survive in the depressed economy. She'd tried to be patient. They'd once been a big deal around town and it was possible they'd be able to refinance their business to avoid bankruptcy. But enough was enough.

They would either come up with a payment plan or she would have to cancel their contract.

"Tell him I'll deal with them," she promised. "Next."

"We added three new orders for Christmas decorations."

"That's not a problem. That's fantastic news."

Taylor planted her hands on her hips. "It was a brilliant idea, sweetie, but next year we're going to have to hire more help."

Mia smiled. It'd been her brainchild to offer a new service that would install Christmas lights and even decorate homes for a substantial fee. And it had been a startling success. The perfect Christmas was in high demand in the suburban "upwardly mobile" fancy homes. Thankfully, these home owners had more money than time. Which meant a lucrative profit for Mia.

"See who's willing to put in some overtime, and make sure you schedule the work when I can oversee the project," she said.

Taylor frowned. "Mia—"

"No lectures," Mia interrupted. She didn't need anyone to tell her that she worked too hard.

Taylor rolled her eyes. "Stubborn bitch."

"Anything else?"

"Nothing that can't—" The chime from the front door interrupted the secretary's words. "Hold on." Leaning back, she peered out the open door, her lips pursing in a silent whistle. "Well, hello, tall and dark and why-aren't-you-in my bed," she murmured.

Mia chuckled. "You really have to stop ogling the customers."

"Hey, I might have forgotten what my hoo-ha is used for, but that doesn't mean I'm dead."

"Good Lord," Mia muttered, even as she ruefully acknowledged her friend wasn't the only one who hadn't used her hoo-ha for far too long. "Maybe you should see what he wants."

Taylor ridiculously waggled her brows. "I can do that." About to step forward, the secretary halted, her smile fading. "You know, he looks familiar."

"Who doesn't? This town is too small to—"

"Shit."

Mia blinked in surprise. Her friend was usually unflappable. So who the hell could make her hands clench into tight fists and her face flush with fury?

"Taylor?" She rose from her chair. "What's wrong?"

"I can't believe that bastard would show his face here."

"Who?" Mia demanded.

Usually only Taylor's ex-husband could make her look like she was contemplating murder.

Not surprising. The bastard periodically showed up in town, hoping for an easy handout from his ex-wife. Mia had tried to convince her friend to slam the door in his miserable face, but Taylor insisted that she never wanted her son to realize his father was a total schmuck.

She would endure the visit for Justin's sake, even as she was no doubt wishing she could castrate the jackass.

But while Mia tried to imagine who could be worse than Danny Price, the stranger strolled into her office.

No. Not a stranger.

Lucas St. Clair.

Slamming her hands flat on her desk as her knees threatened to give way, Mia studied the tall, dark-haired man. Disbelief shuddered through her.

It'd been fifteen years since she'd last seen him in the flesh, but nothing had changed.

He was still indecently gorgeous. Maybe even more so. His features were more finely chiseled, emphasizing his male beauty. His hair was still a glossy black and smoothed from his face. And his body was honed with sleek muscles beneath his white dress shirt that he wore with the sleeves rolled up, and pressed black chinos.

He reminded her of a predatory cat.

Sleek. Lethal. Ruthless.

Even worse, the mere sight of him managed to set off the shivers of explosive awareness that no other man had ever managed to create.

Damn him to hell and back.

"Hello, Taylor," he murmured, ignoring the secretary's glare of death as he stepped toward the center of the office, his gaze locked on Mia's face. "Mia."

Pain sliced through her heart.

Once she'd loved this man with every fiber of her being.

She'd been young and passionate and unable to contain her vulnerable emotions. Why would she? Lucas had made her believe they were perfect soul mates, destined to be together for all of eternity.

*Jackass.*

And then he'd left Shreveport to attend military school and she'd been forgotten as easily as if she was something he'd scraped off the bottom of his shoe on his way out of town.

"What are you doing here?" she said between clenched teeth.

His lips twitched. "I'm fine, thanks for asking. It's good to see you too."

"'Good' and 'seeing you again' shouldn't be in the same sentence," she said between clenched teeth.

"Do you want me to get my stun gun?" Taylor offered.

Tempting. But probably not wise.

"Not yet." Mia's lips tightened as the phone abruptly rang. "Will you get that, Taylor?"

For a second the secretary hesitated, clearly wanting to zap the hell out of Lucas. Then, as Mia sent her an impatient frown, she held up her hands in defeat.

"Yeah, yeah," she muttered, heading out of the office.

A few moments later the ringing stopped and Mia returned her attention to the man watching her with a disturbing intensity.

She felt a burst of anger. Dammit. He didn't have the right to look at her like that.

Not anymore.

"I asked you a question," she snapped.

"You look good, Mia." He stepped forward, his indigo gaze moving slowly down the stiff lines of her body. "More than good."

Her stomach clenched, tingles of anticipation racing through her blood, which pissed her off.

What was wrong with her? She should be longing to kick him in the nads, not wondering how fast she could strip off his clothes so she could lick him from head to toe.

"I don't have time for this," she said. "If you want to hire a gardener I suggest you call one of my competitors. We only take care of commercial properties."

He folded his arms over his chest—an unspoken warning he wasn't going to be easily dismissed.

"Ramon Landscaping and Nursery," he murmured. "I'm

impressed, Mia. I always knew you would make a success of yourself, but you've taken your father's small business and turned it into the beginning of an empire."

A glow of pride filled her heart even as she pointed toward the door.

"Morgan's Mowing Service is just down the road. I'm sure they'd be happy to help you."

"I'm not here for a gardener."

"We don't have anything else to discuss." She turned back toward the desk, silently willing him to leave.

She was a strong, independent woman, but having Lucas standing so close made her feel . . . vulnerable.

"Tony Hughes," he said softly.

She froze before slowly turning to meet his grim gaze. "Tony?"

"You remember him, don't you?"

She unconsciously unbuttoned her jacket and shrugged it off. It felt like it was strangling her.

And when the hell did her office get so warm?

Had Taylor turned up the heater?

"Of course I remember him, but I haven't seen him in months," she said, tossing the jacket on the chair where she'd left her briefcase. "If you're looking for him—"

"He's dead."

"What?" Mia blinked, suddenly feeling light-headed as she swayed forward.

Straight into Lucas's waiting arms.


Lucas tugged Mia tightly against his chest, briefly savoring the feel of her soft body and the sweet scent of honeysuckle.

This was what he'd wanted from the minute he'd walked into the office. The sight of her had been like a punch to his gut, the regrets and aching need suddenly as raw as they'd been the day he'd driven away from Shreveport.

At the time he'd convinced himself he was doing what was best for Mia. Best for both of them.

Now he knew he'd been full of shit.

He'd been a coward. And he'd paid for it every day since leaving this fabulous, passionate woman.

But while he was happy as hell to hold her in his arms, he realized he'd been a jackass to share the news about Tony's death without easing the blow.

"Crap, I'm sorry," he murmured, running a soothing hand up and down the curve of her spine. "I didn't mean to tell you like that."

"Mia?" Taylor charged back into the office, taking in Mia's pale face before she was glaring at Lucas. "What the hell did you do to her?"

"It's okay, Taylor," Mia assured her friend, pushing her hands against Lucas's chest until he reluctantly allowed her to step back. "Can we have some privacy?"

Taylor scowled. "Are you sure?"

"Yeah."

"I'm going to be at my desk." She deliberately glanced toward Lucas. "Where I keep my stun gun. Just yell if you need me."

Her warning delivered, the woman turned to leave the office, while Lucas chuckled.

"I've always liked her," he said with perfect sincerity.

Taylor was fiercely loyal to Mia. He admired that in a friend.

Mia shoved a shaky hand through her hair, her face still pale with shock. "What happened to Tony?" she demanded. "Was he in an accident?"

"No." Lucas grimaced. There was no easy way to say it. "He was shot."

She bit her lower lip. "A drug deal?"

*Ah.* So his first instinct hadn't been wrong. Tony hadn't changed over the years.

"It's being investigated," he said. "But the cops aren't treating it like a random crime."

"God, this is horrible." She shivered. "Why wasn't it on the news?"

"It happened in Houston."

"Really?" Her brows pulled together in confusion. "What was he doing in Houston?"

"The cops think he was coming to see me."

"You?" Her confusion deepened. "Why would they think that?"

"He had my name and address scribbled on a piece of paper."

"You live in Houston?"

His lips twisted. What had he expected? That she'd kept track of his career? Just because he'd remained obsessed with her didn't mean she was equally fascinated with him.

Hell, she'd probably shoved all thoughts of him from her life years ago.

"I don't crawl beneath a rock every night," he said in dry tones.

She hesitated, then cleared her throat. "I heard that you were"—she struggled for the word—"captured in Afghanistan. I'm sorry."

He stiffened. Of course that would be the one part of his past she would know about.

The part he never discussed. Not with anyone but his ARES brothers.

"I survived," he muttered.

Easily sensing his discomfort, she backed away.

Regretting his inability to accept even a polite show of sympathy for what he'd endured, Lucas swallowed a sigh. No one could understand, so there was no point in trying to explain.

"Do you know why Tony was coming to see you?"

"No idea," he said with a shrug. "I haven't seen or talked to him in fifteen years. Is there any reason he'd be in Houston?"

She took a minute to actually consider his question. "Not that I can think of," she finally said. "His brothers have stayed in the area and he never mentioned having friends or distant family in Texas."

His gaze slid over her delicate features, the past briefly colliding with the present. It'd been Tony who'd brought them together.

Granted, Lucas had caught brief glimpses of Mia on the rare occasions when she was helping her father during the summer. George Ramon had been the gardener for his parents as well as several other families in the exclusive subdivision of Shreveport.

But it wasn't until Tony had invited Lucas to a party deep in the wetlands that he'd finally had a chance to meet Mia face-to-face.

He'd been stunned by her beauty.

Hell, he was *still* stunned.

With an effort he forced himself to concentrate on the reason he'd spent the night tying up loose ends so he could leave Houston at the crack of dawn.

Right now nothing mattered but ensuring that this woman wasn't in danger.

"How well did you know Tony over the past few years?" he asked.

She gave a lift of her shoulder. "I hired him when he needed extra cash."

"You always did rush to take care of the underdog," he murmured.

Mia shrugged aside his soft words.

"Unfortunately, last summer he was busted in one of my vehicles with a bag of weed." Regret darkened her velvet brown eyes. She'd always had a soft spot for their mutual friend, even when he was acting like a complete idiot. "I told him he couldn't work here anymore."

He reached to brush the silky dark hair from her cheek, his body clenching at the feel of her warm skin. Thankfully, she was too distracted to notice that he allowed his fingers to linger.

"So you wouldn't know if someone wanted him dead?"

She flinched. "No."

Lucas squashed his instinct to back away from his questioning. Mia was still reeling from the shock of Tony's death and in no place to discuss the gruesome details of why someone might have murdered him. But once again he reminded himself that the sooner they found the killer, the sooner he could be certain Mia was safe.

"No ex-wife?" he pressed.

She shook her head. "Tony never married."

"Girlfriend? Mistress?" He paused. "Secret male lover?"

"I didn't keep up with his private life." She wrinkled her nose. It was a habit she'd had when she was young. He swallowed a sudden lump in his throat. "To be honest, I never saw him date anyone," she admitted.

Lucas frowned, trying to think back. It was true. Tony had always been the life of the party. And he'd occasionally walked off into the swamps with a girl. But Lucas couldn't remember seeing him with a steady date.

Of course, he hadn't really paid attention.

"Odd," he muttered.

There was a short silence before Mia was sucking in a deep breath, as if trying to clear the fog from her mind. Then, she studied him with a growing puzzlement.

"Are you with the police?"

"No."

"Then why are you investigating his death?"

"I want to know why he was coming to see me."

Her eyes narrowed. There was more than one reason why he'd been fascinated by this female.

Her beauty, of course.

Her passionate heart.

And her incisive intelligence that had kept him on his toes whenever they'd debated an issue.

There was something deeply sexy about a smart woman.

Unfortunately it meant that she easily sensed that he was keeping something from her.

"And?" she prompted.

"And why he was holding your picture when he was shot," he grudgingly added.

"That's exactly the question I was about to ask." The unexpected male voice intruded into their private conversation.

Turning his head, Lucas cast a frustrated glance toward the intruder. "Who the hell are you?" he demanded.

"Detective Brian Cooper." The man offered a self-depreciating smile. "I believe you met my uncle in Houston."

Lucas scowled, easily picking up the family resemblance to Detective Sam Cooper. The same dark blond hair, although this man's was still thick and currently in need of a cut. The same solid body and bulldog features. He even had the same taste in clothing. An off-the-rack jacket, khakis, and cheap shoes.

"Damn," he muttered beneath his breath.

# Chapter Three

Mia frowned, staring at the stranger in confusion.

She was still reeling. How was she supposed to process Lucas's startling appearance, followed by the news that Tony was dead? That didn't even include the last bit of information—that her old friend had been carrying a picture of her.

Now she struggled to clear her fuzzy thoughts as she ran her gaze over the intruder.

He looked harmless enough with his dark blond hair rumpled from the breeze and his guileless brown eyes. Certainly he was handsome, but in an engaging, non-threatening way.

At least until she caught sight of the gun holstered beneath his unbuttoned jacket.

"What's going on?" she demanded.

The man reached into his pocket to pull out a slender wallet. "I'm Detective Brian Cooper from the Caddo Parish Sheriff's Office," he said, flashing his credentials.

Taylor muscled her way past the lawman, her face tight with frustration. First Lucas had snuck past her, and now this stranger. The younger woman was clearly in the mood to knock some heads together.

"I'm sorry, Mia, I tried to stop him," she said through gritted teeth. "He was very insistent."

"It seems to be a theme today," Mia muttered, trying to muster a smile for her friend. "Why don't you make some fresh coffee, Taylor?" Waiting until her secretary had stomped out of the office, Mia turned her attention to her latest visitor. "I suppose this is about Tony."

"It is. I have a few questions," the detective said, glancing toward the silent Lucas. "You'll excuse us, Mr. St. Clair?"

Lucas folded his arms over his chest. "No."

The detective's jaw hardened, hinting at a ruthless temperament below his facade of just another good ol' boy. "That really wasn't a request."

Lucas gazed down his nose with all the arrogance that came from being born into a family that considered themselves a part of some superior species.

"Aren't you out of your jurisdiction? Tony was murdered in Houston."

"My uncle asked me to help with the investigation. Tony lived here, after all," the lawman smoothly answered. "It's important to retrace the steps of the victim. Now, if you don't mind—"

"I do mind," Lucas interrupted. "I'm staying."

Detective Cooper didn't budge. Suddenly Mia's respect for him inched up a notch.

"That's not up to you."

Lucas turned toward her, his expression impossible to read as he held out a hand. "Mia?"

"I . . ." She bit back her instinctive desire to kick him the hell out of her office. He hadn't been around when she'd needed him for the past fifteen years, had he? But if she was being honest, she was still reeling from the thought that her childhood friend was dead. Right now she'd take any support she could get. "Yes." She reached out to allow him to wrap his fingers around her hand. "I'd like for Lucas to stay."

Something flared through the deep blue of his eyes. "Thank you."

Detective Cooper thinned his lips, but he seemed to decide this wasn't a battle he was willing to fight.

"Very well." He glanced toward the desk. "Do you want to have a seat?"

She shook her head, just wanting to get it over with. "No."

Tucking away his badge, the detective pulled out a small notepad and pencil. Then, with a smile that was intended to put her at ease, he began asking her the usual questions.

Mia answered with as much information as possible.

Yes, she'd known Tony since grade school in Bossier City. Yes, they'd stayed friends despite him going to a fancy prep school across the river in Shreveport. She admitted they'd briefly lost touch after high school, but that she'd hired him when he showed up at her door five years ago.

She also admitted that Tony had been caught with weed and that she'd fired him the past summer.

Then Detective Cooper's questioning became far more pointed. Did she have a relationship with Tony? Did she have any enemies?

Mia unconsciously shifted closer to Lucas, allowing his heat to combat the chill that was shivering through her body.

"I think that's enough, Detective." Lucas immediately took charge, his arm wrapping around her shoulder to pull her tight against his side. "Ms. Ramon has had a shock. If you have more questions you should speak to her lawyer."

"Lawyer?" Mia blinked in shock, for the first time realizing there might be more to the detective's visit than to gain info on Tony. "Do you think I'm involved?"

"Mia—"

She interrupted Lucas's protest. "I want to know."

Detective Cooper reached into the pocket of his jacket to pull out a photocopy of a picture. "We found this clutched in

Tony Hughes's fingers," he said, holding it out so Mia could see the enlarged black-and-white picture.

Her stomach clenched as she recognized the image of herself walking into the office building, with the words "Kill her or else" scrawled across her face.

*What the hell?*

"Tony had this?" she breathed.

"Yes."

She lifted her gaze to find Cooper watching her with a piercing intensity.

"Why?"

"That's what we intend to find out." The detective nodded toward the photo. "Do you know when this would have been taken?"

She licked her dry lips. "No, but it had to be within the last few weeks."

"How can you be sure?"

"The construction on this building wasn't finished until the end of October."

Cooper tucked away the photocopy and scribbled in his notepad.

"Was Tony angry that you fired him?"

"Not really." Mia abruptly stiffened, belatedly realizing what the man was asking. "Wait. You can't think that Tony wanted to hurt me?"

"It's one possibility."

"Enough." This time there was no mistaking the authority in Lucas's tone. "Any further questions will be asked in the presence of a lawyer."

The detective flashed Lucas a glare of frustration before sliding his pen and paper in his pocket and pulling out a business card. Then, smoothing his expression, he cast Mia a reassuring smile.

"I'll be in touch," he murmured, handing her the card with his name and number printed on it. "Call me if you think of anything, no matter how small. You'd be surprised how many cases have been solved by a clue that was initially dismissed as inconsequential."

"You don't think he was killed because of a drug deal?" she demanded, unable to imagine Tony involved in anything more sinister than an encounter with a pissed-off junkie.

Her old friend might have been a burnout who'd wasted what little potential he'd possessed as a jock, but he'd never been involved in serious crime.

"I like to keep an open mind," Detective Cooper said in noncommittal tones, giving a nod of his head. "Ms. Ramon. St. Clair."

She was vaguely aware of the detective leaving the office, and even the fact that Lucas was staring at her with an increasing concern, but she was lost in a heavy sadness.

*Poor Tony.* He'd come from a crappy family who'd barely noticed he was alive unless he was on the football field. He'd never managed to find a purpose in life. Or at least, none that he'd shared with her.

For the first time, she realized just how private Tony had been.

Oh, he was always up for a party, but he'd never truly shared his thoughts or feelings. She didn't know any more about him than she had when they were both six years old.

"Mia?" Grabbing her by the shoulders, Lucas turned her to meet his worried gaze. "Talk to me."

With an effort, she pulled herself out of the dark hole that threatened to suck her in.

"This doesn't make any sense," she said, forcing herself to concentrate on the questions buzzing at the edge of her mind. She couldn't change her friend's death, but maybe she could help catch whoever was responsible. And at the same time, figure out who the hell had written that horrible message on her photo. "Why was Tony in Houston? And why did he have a picture of me?"

"I don't know yet, but I promise I'll find out."

She stilled, studying his grim expression. "You said you weren't working for the cops."

"I'm not." A fierce smile curved his lips. "I'm better."

She rolled her eyes. "I see you haven't lost any of your arrogance," she muttered.

"It's not arrogance, it's fact."

Stepping back, he reached into his pocket to pull out his wallet, extracting a gold-embossed business card he pressed into her hand.

Mia read the elegant lettering with a lift of her brows. "ARES Security?"

"It's a company I started with a few friends. Trust me. We have the expertise and technology to find out exactly what Tony was doing."

Mia's lips parted to demand what had happened to his career as a diplomat, only to hastily swallow the words. There was no way in hell she was going to reveal her seething interest in what he'd been doing since he'd returned from the Middle East.

He'd cut her out of his life.

So be it.

"Why?" she instead demanded.

His brooding gaze slid down to the stubborn tilt of her chin. "What do you mean?"

"What's your interest in any of this?"

"Tony was coming to see me," he said. "I want to know why."

"And that's the only reason?"

"No." Reaching up, he cupped her face in his hands. "I'm here for you, Mia."

ARES Security had chosen to open their business in a newly constructed office building in an upscale Houston neighborhood. The faded redbrick building with large windows and ornamental molding looked more suited for a financial service. Or a law firm.

But Lucas had wisely argued that the sort of customers who would be able to afford their highly exclusive services would be comforted by the feel of Old World charm.

It was a theme that was carried through the large reception area and front offices. The carpets were plush ivory, the walls were darkly paneled, and the furniture made of sturdy wood with crimson cushions. The hushed atmosphere, however, was decidedly absent on the top two floors. The second floor was dedicated to the high-tech lab where Max Grayson worked his forensic magic. The top floor had been claimed by Teagan.

Unlike Max, who liked to work in brightly lit rooms with white tiled floors, Teagan preferred to keep the curtains pulled to protect his equipment. The series of darkened offices were filled with sleek computers, four separate servers, and a line of monitors that kept constant watch on the companies that hired them, as well as the area around their building.

They were still hoping to catch the bastard who was leaving Hauk threatening notes.

At the moment, Teagan was settled behind his massive desk, wearing a Henley that was tucked into a worn pair of fatigue pants, and his feet were covered by a pair of motorcycle boots.

Entering the office, Max gave a slight shake of his head at the sight of the empty pizza boxes tossed in a corner and the garbage can filled with beer bottles. No one, not even the cleaning staff, was allowed in Teagan's private space.

Period.

Teagan ignored his friend's expression of disapproval.

Max was a neat freak who bordered on OCD. Thankfully, he was also a brilliant forensic whiz who was constantly being badgered by the FBI to join their lab at Quantico. The feds didn't seem to care that Max's parents were currently lodged in prison for a Ponzi scheme that'd earned them millions of dollars before they were caught.

Teagan didn't care either. Hell, his own father spent more time behind bars than on the street.

Max strolled toward the desk. Over six feet, he carried himself with a military bearing that was emphasized by his crisp white shirt and black slacks. His dark blond hair was cut short and brushed away from his chiseled face. His gray eyes were rimmed with black and were unnervingly piercing as they rested on Teagan's face, reminding Teagan that he needed a shave after his long night.

"What are you doing here?" Teagan demanded.

His friend shrugged. "Hauk was busy with a client when he got your message."

Teagan frowned. Max was supposed to be clearing up his backlog of work so he could spend Christmas in Switzerland enjoying a long overdue vacation.

"No, I meant what are you doing out of your lab?" Teagan asked. "You only have a week before you take off."

"I cancelled my trip when I heard that Lucas might need our help."

Boom.

That was it.

Someone needed him, so Max was there.

It was the foundation of their friendship. And what'd drawn them together to open ARES Security.

The time together in the Taliban prison had been the starting point, but that was only a small part of why they'd connected to form a family.

"Lucas is going to kick your ass when he finds out," Teagan warned.

Max settled on the edge of the desk, his attention shifting to Teagan's computer. "Tell me what you've got."

Teagan didn't bother to argue. Max was calm, methodical, and stubborn as hell. Like a bulldog with a bone.

He turned the monitor so Max could see the birth certificate he pulled up.

"Anthony Gerald Hughes. Thirty-three years old. Born and raised in Caddo Parish." He clicked the mouse, pulling up a new screen. "Goes by the name Tony. The youngest of five boys. His father was a roughneck on an oil rig until he was injured on the job when Tony was ten years old. The seven of them survived on disability checks and whatever the boys could poach in the swamps."

Max leaned forward. "Abuse?"

"More neglect," Teagan said. He'd done a thorough check of all local hospitals and free clinics to see if there was a pattern of broken bones or mysterious injuries. "The boys ran wild, but there was no record of violence."

"Were they in trouble?"

"Petty shit." Another click of the mouse to pull up Tony's rap sheet. "Trespassing, theft, recreational drugs. Nothing that earned them more than a few days in jail."

Max grimaced. They'd all hoped there would be a criminal link between Tony and his killer that would be easy to follow.

"Did you find any connection to Houston?"

"None." Teagan leaned back in his chair, running a hand over the stubble on his jaw. He needed to go home so he could shower and shave, but first he wanted to pass on what he'd learned. He didn't doubt that Lucas would be calling for an update. "His car was found less than a block from his body."

"North or south."

"North."

Max gave a slow nod, his razor-sharp brain easily focusing on the pertinent revelation. "So if he was coming to speak with Lucas, then he must have arrived before four o'clock or he would have parked closer to the office," he murmured.

Teagan smiled. They'd all learned during the past months that parking was a premium in the neighborhood. If you didn't arrive early you would be leaving your car in one of the community lots that were blocks away.

"There's no formal time of death yet," Teagan added. He didn't mention that he'd hacked into the Houston coroner's office to see if there'd been a report issued. Sometimes his friends weren't as willing to bend the rules as he was. "But I talked with a cabbie who did a pickup just down the street at three. He didn't see anything then."

Max nodded. "So after three and before four."

"That would be my guess."

"Any security cameras?"

"Nothing that I could locate." Teagan shook his head in disgust. Tony had been shot in front of an expensive dress shop and a home decor firm. They both had cameras inside, but nothing aimed at the street. Worse, there wasn't a damned ATM within three blocks. "I'm running a trace now on both Tony Hughes and any other murders in the area. I'll have more tomorrow."

Max nodded, far more patient than Teagan. "What about the woman?"

"Ah." Teagan leaned forward to click on the mouse. Suddenly the image of a dark-haired beauty with soft brown eyes and proud features filled the screen. "Meet Mia Ramon."

Max released a low whistle. "Nice."

Teagan nodded in agreement. Mia was more than just a pretty face. There was a compelling sensuality in her features that promised all sorts of sinful pleasure.

"She's the daughter of George Ramon, the St. Clair family's gardener," he told his companion. "Now she runs her own landscaping business."

"Beautiful and smart." Max glanced toward Teagan. "Married?"

"Nope."

Max's lips twitched. Of course they were sorry as hell that Lucas's old friend was dead, but they were all fascinated by his reaction to the picture of Mia Ramon.

Lucas was always cool and in control under pressure. The perfect diplomat. They'd never seen him so rattled.

Certainly not when it came to a woman.

"Interesting," Max murmured. Then, folding his arms over his chest, he was all business. "Anyone want her dead?"

Teagan shook his head. His background check hadn't finished running, but he'd learned enough to know that Mia Ramon wasn't the sort of woman to attract enemies.

"She hasn't filed any restraining orders and the only employee she fired was Tony," he said. It would take time to finish his search on the employees, but no one stuck out as a potential suspect.

"Any family drama?" Max asked.

"Not the kind you mean," Teagan said. Teagan and Max were both casualties of "family drama." "Her mother died when she was ten. No siblings. At sixteen she started dating Lucas. He was her first serious boyfriend."

Max arched a brow. He didn't ask how Teagan had uncovered the information about her relationship with Lucas.

Wise. His hacking skills had once again come in handy.

"Does she work with her father?" Max instead asked.

Teagan shook his head. "He died a little over six months ago from cirrhosis."

"An alcoholic?"

"Most likely," Teagan said. His background search on George Ramon had been harder than expected.

The older man had been a legal immigrant, but he'd clearly distrusted the government and lived off the grid as much as possible.

That included avoiding hospitals and any doctor office that would have kept a record of his medical history.

"Did he owe anyone money?"

Teagan grimaced. Financial institutions were another thing that George Ramon shunned. He ran a cash gardening business that managed to elude the IRS, and he'd clearly bought his property without taking a loan.

"I'm still trying to unravel the money trail," he said.

Max grimaced, his gaze returning to the image of Mia. "Being raised by an alcoholic father, with no mother, must have been tough on a young girl."

Teagan nodded. Mia had used the hurdles life placed in her path as stepping stones to success instead of an excuse to fail.

"She didn't let it halt her," he said. "She started helping her father when she was just a kid, and by the time she was a teenager she was working almost full-time."

Max smiled. "I would have hired her to trim my hedges."

"No shit." Teagan easily understood Lucas's continued attraction toward the woman, although there was no obvious explanation for why he'd ever left her. "At the age of twenty-one she'd taken over her father's customers and expanded to hire two extra employees. When she was twenty-seven she expanded again to purchase equipment and a large plot of land on the northern edge of Bossier City. She also hired three more employees."

"Damn." Max arched a brow, looking suitably impressed. "Clearly she has a talent for business."

Teagan smiled, about to get to the good part. He'd been itching for hours to share what he'd discovered.

"She does, but she had trouble acquiring a loan for her rapid growth from a traditional bank."

"Did she?" Max shifted his attention to Teagan, sensing his amusement. "I assume she managed to get her money from another source?"

Teagan handed his companion a sheet of paper he'd printed off around four in the morning.

"Shreveport Development Center approached her with an open line of credit."

Max frowned as he studied the copy of what looked like an official pamphlet.

"A government program?"

"That's what I assumed. Turns out it's a shell company."

Max stilled. A shell company always meant there was something dodgy going on.

"Do you know who set it up?"

"I do." Teagan's smile widened.

"Who?"

"Lucas St. Clair."

# Chapter Four

Taylor Price had done her best to squash her motherly instinct to hover over Mia. Her friend had shared what little information she knew about Tony's death and the fact that he'd been clutching her picture in his hand, with a threat written on it. But she'd clearly not been in the mood to dwell on the tragedy.

Or the fact that the man who'd broken her heart was suddenly back in town.

Taylor had respected Mia's desire to concentrate on work, but by five o'clock she was done pretending that this was just another day.

Clearing her desk, she headed into Mia's office, finding her friend staring at the computer, although it was obvious that her thoughts were miles away.

"Are you okay?" Taylor asked, leaning her shoulder against the doorjamb.

Mia jerked her head up, revealing the pallor of her face. "Yeah." She grimaced at Taylor's look of disbelief. "No," she ruefully admitted. "But I will be."

Taylor believed her. Mia had endured the death of her mother, the abandonment of the boyfriend who'd claimed to love her, and a father who'd retreated into a bottle to avoid life. And still she'd come out on top.

"Can I get you anything?" Taylor offered. "Coffee? Tea? A shot of bourbon?"

Mia leaned back in her chair. "I might borrow your stun gun."

"Good choice," Taylor said in approving tones, not at all opposed to the thought of the arrogant Lucas St. Clair taking a few volts to the ass. Then she abruptly sighed as she recalled the reason the man had returned to town. "Tony. God." She gave a shake of her head. She'd never been as close to Tony as Mia, but it was still painful to think of him being shot to death. "I can't believe it."

"I know what you mean." Mia shoved her fingers through her hair, her hand not entirely steady. "I wish I knew what he was doing in Houston."

"And why he had your picture." Taylor felt a shiver inch down her spine. She was genuinely worried for her friend. "I hate to admit it, but I'm glad that Lucas is back in town."

Mia blinked in surprise. "I thought you wanted him castrated?"

"I do." Taylor felt a pang of guilt. When Lucas had left Shreveport fifteen years ago she'd been so wrapped up in her own miserable relationship she hadn't been able to offer Mia the support she should have. Now she intended to do everything in her power to help her friend. "He was a lowlife bastard who broke your heart. But if he has the skill to keep you safe, then he has my full approval."

Mia grunted. "I just want him to stay the hell away from me."

Taylor bit her tongue. She'd seen how Lucas was looking at Mia. As if he'd just discovered a rare treasure that he thought he'd lost forever.

Mia had enough on her mind without sharing that little tidbit.

"Once we figure out who killed Tony, we can run him out of town," Taylor assured her friend.

Mia forced a weary smile to her lips. "It's late. Go home and feed your son."

"Why don't you come over?" Taylor impulsively offered. Justin loved having Mia come for dinner. It meant he could let the two women talk so he didn't have to actually communicate in more than grunts and nods. "I'll order a pizza and open a bottle of wine. I think we can both use it."

Mia wrinkled her nose. "Thanks, sweetie, but I just want to go home and put up my aching feet."

"Fine, party pooper." Accepting she'd done everything she could to ease Mia's stress, she turned to leave, only to come to a sharp halt as she recalled the message lying on her desk. "Oh, before I forget, Vicky Fontaine's lawyer called again."

"Christ." Mia gave a shake of her head. The wealthy socialite had made her first offer to purchase George Ramon's land just a few days after his death. Since then she'd called or had her lawyer call at least twice a week. "How many times do I have to tell them I'm not ready to sell?"

Taylor held up a hand. "I warned him you weren't interested, but he claimed he has an offer you can't refuse."

"I don't get it." Mia made a sound of irritation. Not unusual when someone was discussing the older woman. Vicky Fontaine was the wife of a wealthy financier who could trace her ancestors back to one of the original French settlers in Louisiana. Something she droned on about with nauseating frequency. "Why the heck would she want twelve acres of swampland?"

That was a question that Taylor had asked herself more than once. Vicky owned a sprawling mansion south of Shreveport as well as a condo in New Orleans. She certainly wasn't the type who would want a decaying cabin or bunch of wetland that was overrun with the junk George had collected over the years.

"Who knows?" Taylor said with a shrug. "It's probably

sitting on a fortune in oil. Or maybe Vicky wants to start an alligator farm. The coldhearted bitch would fit right in with the reptiles."

"Just keep telling them no," Mia told her. "I don't have time to deal with them."

"You got it."

Mia gave a wave of her hand. "Now go."

Taylor hesitated. "I don't like leaving you here alone."

"Alone?" Mia gave a short, humorless laugh. "Have you looked outside?"

Curious, Taylor moved across the office to glance out the window. Darkness had already cloaked the parking lot in shadows, but the streetlights revealed a boring midsize car that she'd bet good money belonged to Detective Cooper and a silver Porsche Cayman that only Lucas could afford.

Turning back, she sent Mia a small smile. "Nice."

"Nice?"

Taylor shrugged. "There are worse things than two handsome men stalking you."

Mia arched a brow. "You think Detective Cooper is handsome?"

*Well, crap.*

Taylor hadn't intended to share that little tidbit. So what if she'd felt a ridiculous tingle of awareness when the detective had strolled into the office? She'd sworn off men after her dickwad of a husband had walked out.

Even if they did have warm brown eyes and the sort of face that made a woman think of solid dependability and . . .

*No, no, no.*

"Don't do anything I wish I was doing," she forced herself to say in light tones, ignoring Mia's speculative gaze as she headed out of the office.

She paused long enough to pull on a light jacket and grab her purse before she left, double checking the front door was locked, then heading toward her black Jeep.

Once in her vehicle, Taylor glanced toward the Porsche where Lucas was slouched in the driver's seat, his focus locked on the office building. Clearly he wasn't going anywhere until Mia left.

Detective Cooper, on the other hand, fired up his engine even as she backed up the Jeep and pulled out of the small lot. Taylor frowned, caught off guard when Detective Cooper's headlights appeared in her rearview mirror, his car following her as she traveled over the bridge into Shreveport.

He remained on her tail as she turned into a small residential area just off Market Street. Once it'd been filled with middle-class families who took pride in mowing their yards on Saturday afternoons and repainting their shutters. Now it was fading into rental homes for college students and abandoned lots.

Thankfully the crime rate remained low, and her grandfather had built the house Taylor shared with her mother and Justin.

It wasn't fancy, but it was constructed to last.

Pulling into the driveway, she automatically checked to make sure her son's light was on in the upstairs window before stepping out of the Jeep. Once assured Justin had made it home from school, she climbed out of the vehicle and walked to the end of the driveway.

Within seconds the car following her pulled to a halt near the curb and Detective Cooper crawled out to meet her narrow-eyed glare.

"What the hell are you doing?" she demanded.

The lawman offered a reassuring smile. Did he practice it in the mirror?

"I hoped we could have a chat."

She ignored the tiny zing of pleasure at the sight of his clean-cut features and the dark eyes that seemed to study her with an interest she hadn't experienced in years.

Dammit. What was wrong with her?

Aggravated by her unwelcomed response to the man, Taylor did what was familiar. She went on the attack.

"Shouldn't you be keeping Mia safe?"

He stepped closer, almost as if he was trying to block the brisk breeze that was whipping down the street.

"She already has a watchdog," he said, his lip twisting.

Clearly he wasn't a big fan of Lucas St. Clair.

No doubt because it was the St. Clair name that had prompted the Shreveport authorities to get involved. The lawman could say whatever he wanted about helping out his uncle, but there was no way in hell the department would put a lot of tax dollars into solving the case of an unemployed druggie who'd managed to get gunned down on the streets of Houston.

Only the powerful St. Clairs and their terror of having any hint of scandal attached to their precious family could have forced them to start an all-out investigation.

"What do you want?"

He glanced over her shoulder. "Wouldn't you be more comfortable inside?"

"No." There was no compromise in her tone. "My son is home."

"Okay." He stepped back. "We can talk in my car."

She rolled her eyes. He obviously wasn't going to go away until he'd asked his stupid questions.

"You're a pain in the ass, you know that?" she muttered, stomping toward his car and yanking open the passenger door.

"I might have heard that a time or two," he said in dry tones, rounding the hood to take a seat behind the steering wheel.

"No shit." Taylor settled in her seat and slammed shut the door. She was relieved to discover the heater was running and the interior was surprisingly tidy. Not at all like the cop cars she'd seen on television. She glanced at the detective's shadowed profile. "What do you want to know?"

"You've been friends with Ms. Ramon for some time?"

"Since we were six."

He turned his head to meet her impatient gaze. "Then you would know anyone who might want to hurt her."

"No one," Taylor said in fierce tones. "Everyone loves Mia."

"I appreciate your loyalty, Ms. Price—"

"Taylor," she interrupted his soothing words. "I hate to be called Ms. Price."

There was a short silence as he studied her with a searching intensity that made her want to squirm in her seat. Had he already run a background check on her? Probably. Which meant he knew she'd gotten pregnant in high school and promptly been abandoned by her husband.

For no reason at all, the knowledge bothered her.

"Taylor," he at last said in soft tones. "Your friend might be in danger. It's not unusual that she wouldn't want to think she has enemies, but we all do. You would know them better than anyone."

She bit her bottom lip, silently chastising herself. This was about Mia, not her hang-up with men.

"I suppose," she muttered.

"I really am trying to help, Ms. . . ." He held up a hand of apology. "Taylor."

Taylor forced herself to take time to truly consider his question.

"There are a few men in the landscaping business who aren't thrilled by Mia's success," she admitted. "The 'good ol' boy' system is still alive and well in this area. It hurts their tender pride to be beaten out of contracts by a young woman."

Cooper nodded, reaching beneath his jacket to pull out his notebook. "Can you get me a list of names?" he asked.

"Yes, but I don't think any of them would threaten her."

"You'd be surprised," the detective said.

Taylor hesitated before she gave a slow nod. He was right. It was always amazing what could make some people snap.

Still, it seemed a long shot.

"Fine. I'll get you a list," she promised.

"Anyone else?" he prompted. "Any ex-boyfriends?"

She released a short, humorless laugh. "Lucas St. Clair."

He lifted a brow. "Are you implying—"

"No," she hastily denied. "Lucas was a jackass when he walked out on Mia fifteen years ago, but he's always been fiercely protective," she told her companion. "He might break her heart but he would give his life for her."

"War can change a man."

Taylor tensed at the soft warning. It was true that Lucas had not only served in the Middle East, but had also been held prisoner by the Taliban for weeks.

That could unhinge anyone.

"Do you think he's a danger?" she breathed.

"No." The denial came without hesitation. "He just annoys the hell out of me. Any other exes?"

She squashed her instinctive urge to smile at his honesty. Detective Cooper was trained to lower people's defenses. How else could he get the information he needed?

"None that were ever serious."

"Any men who were hoping for more than she was willing to give?"

Taylor thought back to the various men who'd pressed Mia for dates. There were quite a few. Mia was a woman who attracted male attention.

But for the most part they accepted her refusals with good grace.

Although . . .

She furrowed her brow. "Mia does have a neighbor who shows up without invitation," she told her companion. "She's said a couple of times that she's caught him peeking out his window when she was walking around her yard. Nothing threatening, but he gives her the creeps."

Cooper pressed his pencil to his notepad. "Name?"

Taylor dredged the name out of the recesses of her tired brain. "Carl. Carl Greene." She shrugged. "He's the only one I can think of."

"What about employees?"

"We have five full-time gardeners who've all worked with Mia for years." She waited while he continued to write in his notebook. She didn't bother to waste her breath telling the lawman that the employees all adored Mia. Taylor was beginning to suspect that Detective Cooper wouldn't be happy until he'd interviewed each and every person who might be connected to her friend. "Our part-time workers change, but none of them have ever been violent."

"Can you get me a list?"

She heaved an impatient sigh. "Yeah, I can get you a list. Anything else?"

"I'll need a list of anyone who owes her money."

Taylor widened her eyes. Okay. Now he was making sense.

"We do have customers who are well behind on their payments," she admitted. "Some of them owe several thousand dollars. I've told Mia we should hand them over to a collection agency, but she insists on dealing with them personally, even when the client becomes downright nasty." She wrinkled her nose, recalling the times she'd heard the raised voices and occasional threats coming from Mia's office. "I'll get you the names."

His lips twitched, as if sensing she finally accepted he might be capable of doing his job. "Thank you."

Tilting her head to the side, she studied his solid features. "Do you think you'll find Tony's killer by investigating Mia?"

"It's one angle," he murmured in dismissive tones.

And that was all he was going to give her. Period.

She pointedly reached to open the door. She still had dinner to make for a hungry sixteen-year-old boy and her mother, who would be waiting for Taylor to give her an insulin shot.

"Any other questions?"

He tucked away his notebook, briefly holding her gaze.

"I'll be in touch."

"Awesome."

Crawling out of the car, Taylor slammed the door shut.

She didn't want Detective Cooper to be "in touch." Not when he reminded her that she was still a woman with the sort of needs that weren't going to be fulfilled by a homicide detective whose only interest in her was catching a killer.


Mia had intended to linger in her office. It seemed like poetic justice to make Lucas sit in his car waiting for her.

For hours. Days. Years . . .

But by six o'clock, Mia accepted that she was being ridiculous.

Why punish herself by sitting in her office? Especially when she was in dire need of a hot bath and a very large glass of wine?

It wasn't like forcing Lucas to sit in a hundred-thousand-dollar car for a few hours was actually going to make up for being dumped like yesterday's news. The damned Porsche probably made him coffee, gave him a pedicure, and turned into a Transformer when he was bored.

Powering down her computer, she did a walk-through of the office to make sure everything was locked up tight before switching on the alarm and leaving the building. Then, crossing straight to the silver sports car, she waited for Lucas to lower his window.

"I'm heading home," she abruptly announced.

The overhead security lights revealed the twitch of his lips. "Okay."

She glared at him, her heart squeezing at the sight of his fiercely handsome face. Would there ever come a day when she could look at this man and not feel as if she was being struck by lightning?

"There's no need to follow me."

"Okay."

She clenched her teeth. He might be gorgeous, but he was annoying as hell. A good thing to remember.

Turning on her heel, she crossed the cement lot, climbed into her car, and started the engine. Then, without a glance toward the sleek Porsche, she pulled onto the street and headed the short distance to her home, which was tucked at the end of a quiet street.

It wasn't much.

The small house was covered by a weird white stucco that'd been in fashion during the fifties, with a narrow, covered porch. Inside, there was a living room that was barely large enough to fit a couch and TV, two bedrooms that shared one bath, and an eat-in kitchen. But she'd used the bulk of the unexpected money she'd inherited from her father as a down payment on the new office building for Ramon Landscaping and Nursery. What she had left over she'd used as a down payment on the house.

It was certainly a step up from the shabby Shreveport apartment she'd lived in since leaving home at eighteen. Plus it was within walking distance of work.

Pulling into the driveway, she crawled out of the car and muttered a curse as the Porsche pulled in behind her. Not that she'd expected anything else.

She waited as Lucas slid out of the car with a grace that always made her feel like an awkward klutz.

"I told you there was no need. . . ." Her words trailed away in disbelief as he boldly moved forward and snatched her key chain from her hand. "Hey. What the hell do you think you're doing?"

Stupid question. Even an idiot could see that he was using her key to open the front door and step inside. She hustled to join him in the living room as he flipped on the lights.

"Making sure the house is clear," he told her.

"Clear of what?"

"Anything. Wait here," he commanded, heading toward the nearest bedroom.

"Obnoxious ass," she muttered, tossing her purse on the couch and kicking off her heels.

"I heard that," he called back.

"Good."

She stepped to the middle of the room, watching as he peeked under the bed and in the closet before checking the lock was secure on the window.

He repeated the process in the next bedroom, making her cringe as he hesitated at the end of the bed where she'd tossed her lace nightgown. So sue her. She might be a tomboy, but she liked girly negligees.

At last done with his intrusion into her privacy, he moved back through the living room and into the kitchen. She followed behind him, sliding off her jacket and hanging it on the back of the chair that matched the three others set around the wooden table.

She might have been worried about him if she hadn't already noticed the gun he had visibly holstered around her waist.

Clearly he wasn't the same man—the one who believed the pen was mightier than the sword—that she'd known when they were young.

He crossed the tiled floor to enter the attached pantry where she kept her washer and dryer, peering out the window of the door that offered a view of her spacious backyard and the empty field beyond the rickety shed.

Her neighbors were cramped on either side of the house, but the open view behind her gave a sense of space that appealed to Mia.

Finished with his self-imposed task, Lucas returned to the kitchen and leaned against the white-painted cabinets.

Slowly he allowed his gaze to roam up and down her rigid body. "Aren't you going to offer me a drink?"

"No."

Expecting some smart-ass comment, Mia was caught off guard when he shoved away from the counter and gently brushed the back of his fingers over her cheek.

"Mia, let me stay," he said in low, pleading tones. "Please."

# Chapter Five

Lucas knew he was pushing Mia.

As far as she was concerned he was nothing more than the bastard who'd broken her heart.

She certainly hadn't taken one look at him and allowed the fifteen years to fade away. And she wasn't desperately hoping to give their relationship a second chance.

But there was a ball of dread lodged in the pit of his stomach with Mia's name on it. He needed to be close to her. At least until they discovered why Tony had been shot.

Perhaps sensing it was going to take far more energy than she currently had to dislodge him, she rolled her eyes and headed back into the living room. Minutes later she returned with her cell phone.

"I'm ordering dinner." She sent him a challenging glare. "What do you want?"

Pretending he didn't notice her blatant lack of enthusiasm, he said the first thing that came to mind.

"Is there any place that delivers a good po' boy?"

Like any respectable Louisianan, Mia had the restaurant on speed dial.

"Anything with it?" she asked as she pressed the phone to her ear.

"Coleslaw," he answered, heading across the linoleum floor. "Do you have any beer?" Opening the fridge, he smiled in satisfaction. A six-pack from a microbrewery. "Perfect," he murmured, pulling out two beers and twisting off the tops.

He made his way back to Mia, handing her one of the bottles before taking a deep drink. He sighed as the crisp ale slid down his throat.

"Make yourself at home," she muttered.

He took another drink before he set the bottle on the table and studied Mia's pale face. He wished he had the right to demand that she crawl into bed and let him take care of her.

"I noticed a scratch on your bumper," he said instead. He'd used a part of the long day to do a thorough inspection of the long sheds filled with equipment and the neat rows of greenhouses adjacent to her office building. He'd been impressed with the scope of her operations. He'd known she'd been doing well, but this . . . It wasn't until he'd walked past her car that he'd seen the dent in her bumper. It looked recent. "What happened?"

"Nothing."

"Mia." He narrowed his gaze. "Tell me."

She took a drink of the beer. No doubt it was that or hitting him over the head with the bottle.

"An SUV swerved into my lane and tapped my bumper," she at last informed him through clenched teeth.

"It was more than a tap."

"Accidents happen."

"When?"

"This morning."

*Shit.* A cold chill inched down his spine.

It wasn't a coincidence. No matter what Mia wanted to believe.

"Did you get a license plate number?"

She cast him a glance of disbelief. "Of course not. I was trying to avoid the ditch, not playing detective."

He ignored the jab. "Did you at least notice if it was from Louisiana?"

She hesitated, biting her bottom lip as she tried to remember.

"I think so."

"Describe the SUV."

"Big." She shrugged. "Black."

"That's it?" he demanded.

"That's it."

He pulled out his phone, hiding his frustration with her lack of details as he sent a quick text to Teagan.

It wasn't like she could have known she would need to describe the vehicle that rammed her. And anyone would be rattled by such a close call.

Still, a plate number would have given them their first tangible lead.

Sending the message, he looked up from the phone to meet Mia's narrowed gaze. "Any other near accidents?"

She set down her beer, her face hardening with that stubborn expression he remembered when they'd just been teenagers.

"What are you doing here, Lucas?"

He pocketed his phone, unable to resist the urge to reach out and tuck a silky curl behind her ear. His fingers slid down her neck before lingering on the pulse beating at the base of her throat.

"You know why I'm here."

"No." She smacked his hand away, but not before he felt her pulse leap. "As a matter of fact, I don't."

"I'm worried you're in danger," he said without hesitation.

"Why would you be worried?" she pressed.

"You saw the picture—"

"No," she interrupted in a hard voice. "Why does my safety concern you?"

Lucas frowned. "Is that a joke?"

"There's nothing funny about this." Her jaw jutted to an aggressive angle. She was spoiling for a fight he had no intention of giving her. "Fifteen years ago you walked away with some stupid note that said I was better off without you, and then nothing until you suddenly reappear in my office with the pretense of caring whether or not I'm in danger."

Regret scalded through him. Not only for the pain he'd inflicted all those years ago, but for the realization that his past screwups meant she didn't trust him.

It was going to be a constant battle to try and keep her safe.

"There's no pretense." He squashed his instinct to pull her into his arms. She was more likely to break his nose than snuggle against his chest. "I do care. I always have."

She made a sound of disgust. "Are you trying to drum up business?"

He stiffened. What the hell?

"Business?"

"Am I going to get a bill from ARES Security for your services?"

"Shit, Mia," he growled, stung by her accusation.

She hunched a shoulder. "It's a fair question."

It wasn't fair. He'd dropped everything, including several lucrative contracts, not to mention a friend who was being harassed by a dangerous stalker, to rush to her side.

But maybe she deserved the opportunity to give one or two shots below the belt.

"I'm here because you're important to me," he said, reaching to grasp her shoulders as he leaned down until they were nose to nose. "And yes, I'll use every asset that I can get my hands on, including my friends and their considerable expertise. But no, I have no intention of billing you." He deliberately paused. "Satisfied?"

She pushed him away, color staining her cheekbones as she sucked in a deep breath.

His touch disturbed her. Good. It meant that she wasn't as over him as she wanted to pretend.

She wrapped her arms around her waist. "Are you staying with your parents while you're in town?"

He winced. Another low blow. She better than anyone knew that he had a shitty relationship with his family. And since his return from Afghanistan it'd been nonexistent.

They'd assumed that once he was back home he would eagerly cash in on his brief moment of fame to demand a position in the State Department. When he'd instead chosen to open a security business they'd all but washed their hands of him.

Thank God.

"They spend December in Saint-Tropez," he reminded her in soft tones.

Her blush deepened, something that might have been remorse darkening her eyes.

"Of course."

His male instinct was to pounce while she was feeling guilty at having deliberately tried to hurt him, but his training as a negotiator warned him that he might gain a temporary advantage, but in the end lose the war.

An unacceptable outcome.

Instead he grabbed his beer and glanced around the kitchen. "When did you move here?"

He could see her visibly relax as she followed his lead.

"About four months ago. My father left me a small inheritance and I used it for a down payment on this house as well as the new office building."

"I didn't know he'd passed until this afternoon," he said.

She arched a brow. "Were you running a background check on me?"

His lips twisted. What would she do if she knew he'd been keeping a distant eye on her for the past fifteen years? He still wasn't sure how he'd missed the death of George Ramon.

"Gathering intel," he corrected, silently promising to make sure she never caught sight of the detailed report that Teagan had e-mailed just an hour ago.

She rolled her eyes. "Intel."

"I'm sorry for your loss," he said in gentle tones.

She heaved a faint sigh. "Me too, but to be honest I lost my father years ago. He always drank, but after I took over the business he retreated from the world and into a bottle," she admitted, an edge of pain in her voice. "In the past few years he wouldn't let anyone come visit him. Including me."

He took a swig of his beer. "Families," he muttered.

They shared a mutual look of resignation. Their childhoods had been polar opposites, and yet remarkably similar.

A sudden knock on the door had Mia jumping and Lucas instinctively reaching for the gun he had holstered at his side.

He felt like a cowboy, but in Louisiana he didn't have the necessary permit to carry a concealed weapon.

Then, giving a shaky laugh, Mia pressed a hand to the center of her chest. "That's probably the delivery boy."

"I'll get it," he muttered, taking a step forward.

Instantly Mia was standing in his path. "It's my house. I can answer my own door."

He cupped her face in his hands. "I'm wound a little tight right now, Mia," he warned.

"So you get to be a pushy bastard?"

"Yes."

He kissed her.

Just like that.

It wasn't intentional. Hell, he'd planned to play it cool.

Like he was just an old friend in town to help out.

But the thought of her opening the door to some random stranger had triggered every male instinct he possessed.

Including the one that said this woman belonged to him.

And it was about damned time he claimed her. . . .


For a crazed moment, Mia melted into Lucas's kiss.

God, she'd missed this.

The sizzling heat. The leap of her heart. The flutters of excitement in the pit of her stomach.

No one else had ever managed to create such a frenzy of need inside her. No one had ever left her aching with a hunger that woke her in the middle of the night.

Her lips parted, allowing the tip of his tongue to dip in her mouth. He tasted of tangy beer and raw male lust.

A perfect combination.

Her hands lifted, her fingers sinking into the luxurious satin of his hair. At the same time, her body arched to press tight against his chiseled muscles.

Her toes curled in pleasure.

He was leaner, harder than he'd been at eighteen. And maybe an inch taller. Somehow the small changes only intensified her desire to rip off his clothes and do a more thorough inspection.

There was another rap on her door, yanking her out of her fog of passion.

Good God, what was she doing?

Yeah, Lucas could make her toes curl. But he also was the jerk who'd dumped her.

She pulled back her head, her heart missing a beat as his lips skimmed down the arch of her neck.

"The food," she breathed, pressing her hands against his chest. "Lucas."

She heard a groan wrenched from his throat before he was reluctantly lifting his head.

"You're lucky I haven't had a decent po' boy in years," he murmured, giving her lower lip a sharp nip.

"You're lucky I couldn't reach the steak knives," she retorted, shuddering as he pulled away and headed out of the kitchen. Her heart continued to race and there was a throbbing deep inside her that she feared wasn't going to go away anytime soon. "Dammit, Mia, get it together," she muttered in a low voice.

Five minutes later, Lucas returned, spreading out the food on the table while Mia automatically moved to gather plates, forks, and two fresh beers.

There was a tiny voice in the back of her head that warned this was a very, very bad idea. Playing house with Lucas St. Clair was bound to stir up emotions that she didn't want stirred.

There was another part, however, that wasn't opposed to having company for dinner. Even if it was Lucas.

She was still shaken by the news of Tony's murder. She didn't want to be alone to think of the life he'd wasted. Or who might want him dead.

After they were done eating she would put on her big-girl panties and kick Lucas out.

Picking up his sandwich, Lucas took a bite and promptly heaved a sigh of pleasure. "Damn, I've forgotten how good food tastes in Louisiana."

Mia picked up her own sandwich. Lucas was right. There wasn't anywhere that made a better po' boy. Fresh oysters drenched in cayenne-spiced cornmeal and deep fried before being piled on a buttery homemade bun with rémoulade sauce.

Scooping a second helping of coleslaw onto her plate, she ate with a surprising appetite, considering the circumstance. But even as she hoped that she could just forget about the shitty day and relax, Lucas was pushing aside his empty plate and studying her with a renewed sense of purpose.

*Crap.*

"You didn't answer my question," he abruptly reminded her.

"Which one?"

He leaned his elbows on the table. "Have there been any other accidents?"

"No."

"You're sure?"

"I'm sure." She rose to her feet. Dinner was over. Time to get back to reality. "Now, it's late. So if you don't mind I'd like to have a hot bath and get ready for bed."

Shoving himself upright, Lucas squared his shoulders. "I suppose we might as well get this argument out of the way."

"What are you talking about?"

"I'm taking your spare room."

She blinked. What the hell? Did he just assume he was staying the night?

Staring at him in disbelief, she gave a sharp shake of her head. "No. No way."

He folded his arms over his chest, his expression grim. "I use the bed in the spare room or we sleep together." He held her narrowed gaze. "Your choice."

"Forget it."

"I'm not leaving you alone, Mia," he insisted.

She planted her fists on her hips. "It's not your decision, Lucas."

His mouth parted, no doubt to insist he was going to stay, but the words died on his lips as there was a loud squeak on her back porch.

They both froze; then, reaching to his side, Lucas pulled out his small handgun.

Leaning down, he spoke directly in her ear. "Stay here."

"No." She touched his arm, a surge of panic clenching her heart. "Lucas, don't."

"It'll be fine." He brushed a light kiss over her lips. "Lock the door behind me."

# Chapter Six

Lucas gently tugged out of Mia's tight grip, heading to the living room and quietly out the front door. Then, pausing until he heard Mia lock it behind him, he slid silently through the shadows along the side of the house.

He didn't have the same skills as Hauk or Rafe, but he'd been taught to move with enough stealth to get a jump on whoever had been lurking on the back porch.

Reaching the corner, he pressed his back tight against the house and peeked around the edge. He narrowed his gaze, still trying to adjust to the darkness, when there was a rustling in the hedges that lined Mia's property as the intruder made a swift retreat.

"Shit."

Giving up on the hope he could sneak up on the bastard, Lucas dashed toward the hedge, discovering a narrow opening into the neighboring yard. He peered through, but he wasn't stupid enough to walk into a trap.

Instead he headed toward the end of the bushes where he had a clear view of the yard.

No big surprise that there was nothing to be seen.

The intruder had plenty of time to disappear between the row of houses, or even into the empty field that stretched behind them. He paused to study the darkened windows of the small home next door.

There were no lights on inside, but he'd been almost certain he'd seen a curtain twitch.

Yanking out his phone, he called Teagan. "I'm going to need some extra manpower," he said, without bothering with social niceties. Someone had been either spying on Mia or trying to get into her house. He wanted to make sure he had someone watching her 24/7. Without hesitation Teagan agreed to send backup. "Thanks, man," Lucas breathed, absently retracing his path. "Oh, and would you run a check on Mia's neighbors?"

Jogging up the back steps, he knocked on the door, pleased when Mia cautiously peered through the window before she was turning the lock and pushing it open.

Lucas stepped inside, closing and locking the door before slipping his gun back into his holster.

Mia bit her bottom lip, trying to hide the fear that smoldered deep in her eyes.

"Did you catch them?"

He grimaced. "No. Whoever it was disappeared through the hedge."

"You know, it could just have been someone cutting through the yards," she said.

He didn't bother to respond to the ridiculous suggestion. They both knew that a person cutting through yards didn't creep onto back porches.

Instead, he shrugged off his jacket.

"Which room is mine?"

Max watched Teagan tuck his phone back in his pocket. The two had stopped at a local restaurant that looked like a dive, but served the best enchiladas in town.

"Lucas?" Max demanded.

"Yeah, he has a situation," Teagan said, finishing off his beer, preparing to return to the office.

"And?" Max prompted.

Sometimes his companion had the communication skills of a caveman.

Teagan shrugged, rising to his feet to pull on his leather coat. "And he wants me to run a few names through the computer and then head to Shreveport to give him some backup."

Max felt a surge of anticipation, grabbing his own coat as he followed his friend past the cramped tables and out the door. The damp night air felt chilly after the heat of the restaurant, but Max barely noticed.

Until this moment, he hadn't realized how stifled he'd felt over the past few weeks.

It might have been a reaction to the adrenaline rush they'd all experienced when Rafe had faced off against a serial killer. Or maybe it was some lingering PTSD symptom.

Or, more likely, it was his inner need to be constantly occupied.

His childhood had been a chaotic mess. Even before his parents had been charged with investment fraud, they'd hauled him from town to town, their flamboyant lifestyle matching their temperamental natures. He'd existed in a war zone long before he'd ever joined the military.

In response, he'd developed a calm, cool, and always logical approach to his days. It was the only way to feel in command of his life. Unfortunately, in an effort to maintain that facade of control, he had to stay constantly busy.

"I'll go," he offered, as they reached Teagan's recently remodeled '69 Camaro Z28.

Teagan shook his head. "No need. I got this."

"You're more use in the office," Max pointed out. "I finished up the last of my reports for our clients yesterday." He'd been working around the clock to make sure his desk was clear for his vacation. "Until we get forensic evidence from Lucas to test I'm just sitting around with my thumb up my ass."

Teagan arched a brow. "Aren't you working on the shit we've collected on Hauk's stalker?"

A familiar sense of frustration twisted his gut. "I've done all I can. Which isn't much." He'd gone over the threatening notes a hundred times. "But for now all I can say is that the paper came from Turkey and that whoever wrote the messages was smart enough to wear gloves. No fingerprints, no spit, no sweat, no stray DNA . . ." He shook his head, his jaw tight. "Nada."

"What about the satellite image?"

Max shrugged. "Anyone could have pulled it off Google. And whoever hired the courier company to deliver it to the office used a stolen credit card."

Teagan grimaced. The computer whiz had run into his own difficulties trying to trace surveillance cameras in the hope of spotting the stalker.

"The bastard is clever."

"Or watches *CSI*," Max said in dry tones.

"True." The dark eyes narrowed. "Eventually the son of a bitch is going to get sloppy."

Max nodded. "Until then, you concentrate on playing your computer games and I'll go watch Lucas's ass."

Perhaps sensing Max's need to get out and do something, Teagan flashed a mocking grin. "I think he'd prefer the beautiful Mia watch his ass, but hey . . ." He reached up to punch Max in the shoulder. "Knock yourself out."

Lucas was up and dressed long before the sun rose. Not tough to do when he'd spent the night tossing and turning.

His restless night had nothing to do with the narrow bed in Mia's spare room. He'd slept on worse. No, his insomnia was entirely due to the knowledge that she was lying only a few feet away, wearing nothing more than that scrap of lace he'd seen in her room when he'd done his sweep.

Christ, the tiny negligee would cling to her with a mouth-watering perfection. The soft, rose-tipped breasts. The narrow waist. The lush ass.

His body felt fevered, burning up one minute and shivering with hunger the next. And worse, the walls were so thin he could hear each time she shifted on her mattress.

No, wait. Nothing was worse than the fact that the very air was saturated with her feminine scent. With every breath she seemed to seep deeper beneath his skin.

But even as he envisioned the pleasure of breaking down the thin wall and dragging her into his arms, he'd recalled her barely concealed frustration when she'd led him to his room.

She might hate him, but she wasn't stupid.

The lurker had spooked her enough to make her accept she needed his protection.

That didn't mean, however, that she had to like it.

Or that she was going to do anything in her power to make him feel he was a welcomed guest.

Thankfully, at six o'clock he'd received a text from Max saying that he was waiting for him in front of the house.

Slipping out the back door, he joined his friend long enough to tell him to keep an eye on Mia before he headed out. He needed time to clear his brain, which was clogged with lustful images.

Last night had only solidified his belief that Mia was in danger. Shit, if he hadn't been there . . .

With a shudder he slid into his car and revved up the powerful engine. He needed to get his damned head in the game.

Confident that Max would do whatever necessary to protect Mia, Lucas drove around the neighborhood, looking for any sign of a black SUV. Then, stopping by her office, he punched in the alarm code he'd stolen from her phone that she'd left on the table, and easily dealt with the locks.

A quick sweep ensured that the place was empty and that there weren't any hidden bugs or cameras that could be used to spy on Mia. Well, except for the camera that he installed in the corner of her office. He'd tell her about it later.

Much later.

Once he was finished he slipped out and reset the alarm. Then, returning to his car, he headed across the bridge into Shreveport.

Parking in front of the Caddo Parish Sheriff's Office, he glanced at his watch. Seven o'clock. He climbed out of his car and headed toward the small diner across the street.

Detective Cooper struck him as a creature of habit.

For most cops that meant a cup of coffee and breakfast to start the day. It was usually the only meal they didn't have to eat on the run.

He pushed open the glass door and stepped inside, instantly hit by the scent of coffee and bacon grease.

Clearly the diner had seen better days. There were half a dozen tables spread across a cracked linoleum floor, with a long counter at the back that had an open view of the kitchen. Two aging waitresses tended to the handful of customers, their pace slow but efficient.

Lucas smiled as he caught sight of the man wearing a dark suit and brown shoes sitting in the corner. If ever a man needed a wife it was Detective Cooper. Not only did he need someone to coordinate his suit and shoes, but he'd left his house with a dollop of shaving cream just below his ear.

Walking forward, Lucas waved away the waitress and took a seat across the table from the lawman.

Cooper remained intent on his breakfast, proving he'd been aware of Lucas since he'd entered the diner. Or maybe from the minute he'd parked in front of the station. It wasn't like his Porsche was made for stealth.

Reaching for the Tabasco sauce, Cooper shook a few drops on his scrambled eggs.

"How did you find me?" he demanded.

"It's the closest restaurant to your office," Lucas said.

Cooper at last glanced up, his eyes hard with suspicion. "And how did you know that I don't eat breakfast at home?"

Lucas shrugged. It seemed best not to pass along the info that Teagan had done a thorough background check on the detective that revealed he didn't have a wife or kids. Which made it easy to assume he wasn't spending a lot of time in his kitchen.

"Lucky guess."

The detective's lips flattened. Was he thinking about the gun that was holstered at his side?

Clearly deciding he couldn't shoot a civilian, even if he was interrupting his breakfast, Cooper sat back in his seat.

"What do you want?"

Lucas got straight to the point. "There was an intruder at Mia's house last night."

"Intruder?" Cooper stilled. "Did you get a look at him?"

"No. We were standing in the kitchen when we heard footsteps on the back porch." Lucas didn't try to hide his frustration. "By the time I managed to get around the house, the person was running through the hedges. I lost sight of them."

Cooper's expression was impossible to read. "Person."

"Yeah, person."

"You're not sure if it was a man or woman?"

Lucas arched a brow. The detective was sharp. Until he'd pointed it out, Lucas hadn't realized his mind had hesitated to place a gender on the intruder.

"No. I just caught a glimpse," he admitted. "It could have been anyone."

"Did you hear a car?"

"No, but I didn't stay outside for long."

Cooper narrowed his eyes. "I assume you called it in?"

"Call what in?" Lucas snapped. His temper was on a short leash. "A dark figure darting through the hedge?"

Cooper studied him in silence, processing the information.

"Then why are you sharing it with me?" he at last demanded.

Lucas scowled. "Because we both know she's in danger."

"We don't know anything beyond the fact that the victim was holding her picture."

Lucas surged to his feet. Enough. He didn't have time to play power games with the man.

"Fine."

He was walking away when Cooper called out. "St. Clair."

Halting, Lucas glanced over his shoulder. "What?"

The detective's bulldog face was hard with warning. "I can't stop you from staying in town, but if I catch you poking your nose in my investigation we're going to have words."

Lucas made a sound of impatience. "Let's not play games, Detective. We both know the only reason you're on this case is because a St. Clair is involved."

The man's expression hardened. "What's your point?"

"Let me make it easy for you. You've done a background search on me, so you know I have resources that can help." His lips twisted. "Not to mention the fact I don't have to follow the same rules that you do."

"That's my point," Cooper growled. "If you go rogue there's a good chance you'll do something stupid that will either screw up any hope of prosecuting the perp, or worse, spook him into fleeing."

Somewhere inside, Lucas knew the man was just trying

to do his job, but that didn't stop him from wanting to grab him out of the chair and give him a shake.

Mia was in danger. That's all he cared about.

"I don't know what you mean by going rogue, but I do intend to do whatever necessary to protect Mia," he stated in firm tones. "Period."

Cooper glanced toward the window, where a light drizzle had started to dampen the streets. "Shouldn't you be doing that right now?"

Lucas shrugged. "I have a friend keeping an eye on her."

"Shit." Cooper grimaced. "Another one of you?"

"You're going to love Max," he taunted, giving the detective a wink before heading out of the diner.

He shivered at the cold rain that smacked him in the face, jogging across the street to crawl into his car and flip on the heater. Then, without hesitation, he pulled away from the curb and headed back to Bossier City.

He'd done what he wanted. The authorities would soon be aware that Mia was at risk. No matter what Detective Cooper might say, the lawman would consider it his duty to insist that the police department do a few drive-bys to check on Mia.

The more eyes keeping track of her, the better.

Stopping once to pick up coffee and Max's bran muffins that looked like horse food to Lucas, he drove to Mia's office and parked. Then, climbing into Max's silver SUV, he took one of the coffees and handed the bag to his friend.

"Anything?" he asked, his gaze locked on the window that gave him a shadowed view of Mia seated at her desk.

Max leaned against the door, his smile wry. "A few lethal glares from your woman in the rearview mirror on the drive here, but nothing since she went inside."

"No black SUV?"

Max nodded toward the main road. "A few that passed by, but none that parked in the area."

Lucas sipped his coffee. He'd known it was too much to

hope that the vehicle would follow Mia so they could get a plate number.

Still, not all criminals were the sharpest knives in the drawer.

Max demolished one of the muffins, his jaw shadowed with an early morning beard. He'd obviously driven all night to arrive in town at such an early hour. A knowledge that tightened something in Lucas's chest.

"I didn't have the opportunity to say it earlier, but thanks, man," he said.

Max shrugged. "It's what we do."

"It is, but I hate like hell that I interfered in your plans." Lucas studied his friend's profile.

Max hadn't shared his reason for traveling to Switzerland. Or whether he'd intended to travel there alone. And Lucas wasn't about to ask.

The five men of ARES might be as close as brothers, but none of them pried into the intimate details of each other's lives.

"Switzerland isn't going anywhere," Max said, his expression impossible to read. "I can reschedule for the new year."

Accepting that the subject was closed, Lucas slipped his hand into his pocket to pull out a thin card. "Here's the key to my hotel room." He tossed the card onto the dash. "I'll stop by later to get my stuff."

Max glanced, nodding toward the window where Mia was currently standing, her arms folded over her chest as she glared at the two men.

"Are you sure you want to stay in the same house with a woman who looks like she's contemplating the pleasure of slicing off your balls?"

Lucas felt excitement jolt through him at the sight of her

dark, sultry beauty. Even giving him the stink-eye, she was the most beautiful thing he'd seen in fifteen years.

"She can't stay mad forever," he murmured.

Max snorted. "You don't know much about women."

Lucas couldn't argue. There'd been a few relationships since Mia, but they'd been too transitory to give him much insight into the female brain.

He'd told himself he was too focused on his career to make room for a woman in his life. Now he knew he'd been waiting for the *right* woman.

"I know Mia," he said with utter confidence.

Eating another muffin, Max took a sip of his coffee. "Just how well do you know her?"

"We dated in high school."

"And that's it?"

Lucas hesitated. He'd never been comfortable talking about his feelings. The St. Clairs were very much a family of stiff upper lips. But if he hoped to change things this time around, then he'd have to learn to . . . what was the word?

Share?

Some shit like that.

"No. I loved her," he admitted. "I still love her."

Max cleared his throat, as if astonished by the sudden heart-to-heart. Lucas smiled wryly. His friend wasn't the only one shocked.

"Then what went wrong?"

"The St. Clair curse."

"I'm sorry, man. Hit you kind of young, didn't it?" Max drawled, a teasing glint in his gray eyes. "Still, they have little blue pills that can help . . . ow." Max rubbed his shoulder where Lucas slugged him.

"Not that kind of curse, you prick."

Max's smile faded, his expression suddenly somber. "Tell me what happened."

Lucas's gaze moved to the battered pickup that pulled into the lot, closely followed by a car. Both vehicles drove past the office to the sheds at the back.

It was clearly time to start the workday at Ramon Landscaping.

"My family is . . ." His words trailed away as he tried to find a polite way of describing his parents.

Max released a short, humorless laugh. "Hey, my family is currently residing in prison. No judgment."

Lucas nodded, his gaze monitoring the next car that pulled in the lot and headed toward the back. Until he was familiar with the employees, he intended to consider each of them a threat.

"My father's a cold, distant bastard who barely acknowledged that he had children unless it was to express his deep disappointment in us," he at last said. "My mother plays the perfect Stepford wife, aided by large doses of Prozac. And my older brother shot himself to escape the expectations that were dumped on him from the day he was born."

Max sucked in a shocked breath. "Shit, man. I didn't know that about your brother. I'm sorry."

Lucas was sorry too. Not only that his brother was dead. But that he'd been gone before Lucas ever had a chance to get to know him.

"I hate to say it, but I barely remember him. He was ten years older than me." Lucas had a vague memory of the house being shrouded and the servants speaking in whispers. Then his father had led him into his private office that no one was ever allowed to enter so he could explain Lucas's role as the new St. Clair heir. "I had just turned five, but I was quickly taught that I was expected to fill his shoes."

Max nodded. No doubt he'd been groomed by his own parents to maintain a facade of a perfect family.

"And Mia Ramon didn't meet your parents' requirements as your future wife?"

Lucas rolled his eyes. His parents had been obscenely horrified when they discovered that their son was dating the gardener's daughter. It was one thing to bang her in the backseat of his car. That's what rich boys did with unsuitable girls. But to actually be seen in public with her had been unacceptable.

"Not even close, but that wasn't the reason I walked away," he said.

Max arched a brow. "Then why?"

A bittersweet emotion clenched his heart. Being near Mia had been like standing near a raging fire after being locked in ice for years.

"Mia was always so passionate. So full of life. Like a beautiful red rose blooming in a field of white lilies."

"That's very"—Max cleared his throat—"poetic."

Lucas shrugged. Mia made him feel poetic. His friends were just going to have to suck it up.

"There was no way in hell I was going to watch her become an emotional zombie like my mother," he continued.

Max studied his grim expression. "What made you assume that's what was going to happen?"

"I could already see Mia trying to change to please my parents. She bought new clothes and cut that glorious hair after my darling mother informed her that she looked like a homeless gypsy." He shuddered at the memory of watching her walk toward him with her bland beige dress and her hair chopped off. Suddenly she hadn't been his warm bundle of sunshine. Instead she'd been . . . muted. The knowledge he was responsible for the change in her had run like acid through his veins. "And that would only have been the beginning," he muttered.

Max nodded. "I get it."

Lucas sucked in a deep, cleansing breath. The past was done. All he could do was try and change the future.

"I was an idiot. I walked away from Mia when I should have walked away from the St. Clair clan and taken her with me."

"And now?"

"Now I fight," he said without hesitation.

Max smiled. "Good enough."

# Chapter Seven

Mia was doing her best to be reasonable.

Lucas St. Clair was only trying to protect her, right?

That was why he'd returned to Shreveport. Why he'd bullied his way into staying at her house. And why he had some strange man following her to work.

Granted, she'd nearly gone ballistic when she found the small camera planted on the edge of her window frame. She'd even considered the pleasure of stalking out to the parking lot and zapping the intrusive bastard with Taylor's stun gun.

The only thing that helped to ease her violent urge was that Lucas had made no effort to hide the fact that he was spying on her.

Still, by lunchtime, she was too itchy to pretend she was working.

She'd spent the entire night tossing and turning, so acutely aware that Lucas was sleeping in the next room she could barely breathe. Then she'd entered the bathroom, which was still filled with the scent of his soap and the unfamiliar sight of shaving cream in her sink.

She wanted to be pissed off, but instead she was aching with a need that made her want to scream.

At last deciding to channel her locked-up frustration into something more productive than staring out the window at the man who was currently driving her nuts, Mia grabbed her purse.

She avoided Taylor's searching gaze as she headed out of the office with a vague promise she'd be back in an hour. Then, making a dash through the rain to her car, she covertly noted that the SUV was gone and Lucas was sitting alone in his car.

Starting her vehicle, she pulled out of the lot, doing nothing to try and avoid the Porsche that was tailgating her as she drove toward the mechanic shop outside town.

She might feel the need to be proactive when it came to discovering who might want her dead, but she wasn't stupid. She needed someone watching her back. Hell, if she thought that Lucas wouldn't try to forbid her from becoming involved in the investigation, she would have included him on her current mission.

Unfortunately, she knew him too well. If he even suspected she was asking questions about Tony, he would have her locked in her house.

At last reaching the shop that was built behind a pawnshop, Mia pulled into the muddy lot.

In front of her the long, metal building was overflowing with wrecked vehicles, used auto parts, and tires. The roof was a rusty mess and may have looked like a junkyard to a passerby. But Mia had gone to school with Pete Young and knew he was a wizard when it came to anything with a motor. Which was why she'd contracted him to take care of a wide variety of equipment.

Today, however, she wasn't there to discuss her flatbed.

Sliding out of her car, Mia grimaced at the chilled rain that continued to drizzle from the overcast sky. She didn't mind the cooler weather—it was winter after all—but she hated the gray clouds and damp air.

She was walking through the back door to the shop when the Porsche slid to a halt beside her car. She caught sight of Lucas pressing his phone to his ear, no doubt running a check on Young's Automotive. He'd soon discover that she regularly did business with Pete. Which hopefully would give her time to do her questioning before he came in to butt his nose in what she was up to.

With a tug, she pulled open the door and stepped into the cramped office that held a couple of chairs and a long desk. Or at least she assumed there was a desk buried beneath the stacks of paperwork, empty coffee mugs, and greasy rags.

The walls were equally messy, with invoices stapled to warped wood paneling. Overhead, the drop ceiling was missing several tiles and at least one fluorescent lightbulb was burned out.

At her entrance, Pete glanced up from a stack of bills he was studying as if they were written in a foreign language.

"Hey, Mia." He lifted his tall, skinny body out of the chair, flicking back his shoulder-length brown hair. "I thought I told Taylor it would be another week on the truck."

"You did." Mia smiled, silently wondering if Pete ever wore anything besides his worn jeans and the stained blue shirt with his name embroidered on the pocket. "I'm here to see Burt."

Pete heaved a small sigh, glancing toward the door where the sound of hammering filled the air. "I told him to stay home, but he said he needed the hours," he told her. "Penny's pregnant."

Mia blinked in surprise. Penny was twenty-five and already had six children.

"Again?"

"Yep."

Mia shared a grimace with Pete before giving a shake of her head. None of her business.

"I just want to give him my condolences," she said.

"He's taking a break in the breezeway," Pete said. "Tell him to take his time."

With a nod, Mia made her way into the shop, ignoring the lingering looks as she made her way past the men working beneath the car lifts. After years of running a male-dominated business, she'd discovered that no reaction was the best reaction when it came to unwanted interest.

At last reaching the back of the shop, she opened the door and stepped onto the cement walkway that led directly to the pawnshop that was owned by Pete's ex-father-in-law.

Seemed like an awkward setup to Mia, but whatever.

Thankful the walkway was covered, she stepped away from the door even as the dark-haired man turned around to face her.

All the Hughes boys looked alike. Big, powerful bodies with thick chests. Square faces with light brown eyes. And skin that easily darkened in the hot Louisiana sun.

"Hey, Burt," she murmured in soft tones.

He tossed aside his cigarette. "Mia."

She offered a sympathetic smile. "How are you holding up?"

He shrugged, blinking away his tears. "Shit happens."

"Yeah, it does." She reached out to lightly touch his arm. "But that doesn't make it any easier."

"I suppose not." Burt clenched his jaw. "Tony was always wild, but I never expected . . ." He allowed his words to trail away.

"Me either." She paused before gently asking the question that had been troubling her since learning that her friend had been shot. "Do you know why Tony was in Houston?"

Burt shook his head, regret etched on his face. "Like I told the cop, I haven't seen or heard from Tony in months."

Cop? Did he mean Detective Cooper?

"I hadn't seen him either." She grimaced. Would Tony

still have gone to Houston if she hadn't fired him? "I wish I'd done more to stay in contact with him."

"Yeah, me too," Burt muttered. Then, with hands that weren't quite steady, he lit up another cigarette. Mia didn't protest. Burt was clearly in pain. "When we were all young we were inseparable," he abruptly said.

Mia nodded. "I remember."

Her father had called the Hughes boys a bunch of hooligans.

"We didn't have anyone but each other," Burt continued. "But after Tony started going to that fancy school, he changed." He gave a slow shake of his head, his expression unbearably sad. "I always thought it was because he thought he was better than us. He was always gone, you know. Hanging around kids who lived in the big houses and staying out all night." He paused, his gaze shifting toward the lot behind the shop where they parked the cars waiting to be serviced. "But now I'm not so sure."

Mia frowned. "Why not?"

"After talking to the cop I started thinking back." He took a deep drag on the cigarette. "I realized that it wasn't just that Tony pulled away from us. He became secretive. Like he was hiding something from us."

Mia nodded. She'd sensed the same thing, although she'd always dismissed it as Tony being Tony. Now that he was dead, she was trying to find answers to the doubts that had niggled in the back of her mind.

"His drugs?" she suggested.

Burt gave a decisive shake of his head. "Naw. He never hid his weed," he said. "Not even when he was selling."

"Did he deal a lot?"

Burt shrugged. "Just enough to keep himself supplied. Why?"

Mia chewed her bottom lip. She'd loved Tony. The last thing she wanted was to hash through his habit of breaking the law. But how else was she going to get the info she needed?

"He usually worked for me a few weeks out of the year, but that wasn't enough to pay his bills," she pointed out.

Burt gave a slow nod, his brow furrowed. "I asked a few times, but he never gave me a straight answer. I know that he must have had some extra source of income, and that it started in high school. Sometimes he would stop by Ma's house with a wad of bills." He gave a short, humorless laugh. "Everyone was so happy to know we would have food in the fridge for a few weeks we never demanded to know how he got the money."

Mia could sense Burt's guilt. As the older brother he no doubt assumed he should have done more to protect Tony.

Mia felt the same guilt.

"Could he have been dealing something more lucrative than weed?"

"I suppose it's possible, but I really don't know." Burt made a sound of disgust, crushing his cigarette beneath the heel of his boot. "And now it's too late."

Realizing that she'd intruded into Burt's mourning long enough, Mia got to the last point of her visit.

"Can I ask a favor?"

Burt nodded. "Sure."

"Tony gave me the key to his condo when he moved in," she said. "Do you mind if I look around?"

Burt raised his brows. "Look around for what?"

Mia wrinkled her nose. She didn't know. It was simply the only thing she could think of that would make her feel like she was *doing* something.

"I suppose I want a reason for why he was in Houston," she said, careful not to mention the picture that Tony had been clutching in his hand. She had no idea what she was allowed to say about the investigation. "It bothers me."

"Knock yourself out," Burt muttered before giving a sudden frown. "Wait. That cop said he was going to search the condo today, so you might want to wait until tomorrow."

She nodded. Would the condo be sealed off? Surely not. It wasn't a crime scene.

"Thanks." She once again reached out to touch Burt's arm. "Is there anything I can do?"

"Naw." He heaved a deep sigh. "The funeral will be on Sunday."

"I'll be there," she promised.

He flashed a sad smile. "You were a good friend to Tony."

"I'll miss him." She stepped back. "Take care of yourself, Burt."

"You too."


Taylor stifled a yawn as she finished printing the billing invoices.

She wanted to blame her lethargy on the gray December day. Or even the fact that it was Friday. It had, after all, been a long, stressful week.

But if she'd learned anything from her wild-child years, it was that sticking her head in the sand was a recipe for disaster.

The reason she was tired today was because she'd spent the night fantasizing about a blond-haired detective with gentle brown eyes.

It was ridiculous. He wasn't at all her type. She'd always fallen for the bad boys who were custom-designed to treat her like shit.

She didn't do nice, solid guys who stuck around when times got tough.

Almost as if her dark thoughts had made Detective Brian Cooper materialize in front of her, the man stepped through the front door.

Taylor felt a sizzle of excitement race over her skin as he headed across the floor and settled in the chair that was set at the corner of her reception desk.

Once again he was wearing a suit jacket that was in need of a good tailor, with a crisp white shirt and blue tie. His shoes were scuffed and his hair was ruffled from the breeze.

He should have been completely unremarkable to a woman who liked leather and tats.

But the zing of awareness at his handsome, clean-cut features warned Taylor that he was far more dangerous than any other man she'd known. Including her jackass ex-husband.

Annoyed with herself, and even more annoyed with the man who was no doubt going to disrupt her dreams again tonight, she sent him a glare.

"You again."

Brian arched a brow even as a small smile curved his lips. "I hoped for a warmer reception."

"I hoped I would win the lottery," Taylor countered in sweet tones. "Seems like we're both doomed to disappointment."

"I come bearing gifts."

He held up his hand to reveal the small pink box from her favorite bakery.

*Shit.* Had he noticed the box she'd had on her desk yesterday? Clearly this man wasn't only intelligent, he was dangerously observant. She'd be a fool to forget that.

She reached for the stack of invoices and efficiently began to stuff them in envelopes. "You think I can be bought with pastry?" she asked.

"I think you're a loyal employee and a devoted friend." He leaned forward to place the box in the center of her desk. "Both qualities I admire in a person."

She hesitantly reached to flip open the top, already knowing what she'd find inside.

Maple cream donuts. *Yep. Dangerous.*

"You really are pulling out the big guns," she muttered, frowning at him with blatant suspicion. "What do you want?"

He studied her for a long minute, his dark gaze unnervingly intense.

"Do you dislike me because I'm a cop, or because I'm a man?"

"I . . ." Her words trailed away. She wasn't about to tell him that she disliked him because he was making her remember what it was like to be a young, vibrant woman.

"Taylor?" he at last prompted.

She reached to grab a donut, willing back her urge to blush.

"I don't dislike you."

"Good. I really am trying to help," he said in soft tones. "Not only to find Tony's killer, but to keep your friend safe."

He was right. She was a selfish bitch not to be delighted such a dedicated detective was involved in solving Tony's murder.

She grimaced, rising to her feet to cross to the counter that ran beneath the window. "Do you want coffee?"

"Yes, thank you," he murmured. "Black, please."

Pouring two large mugs of the coffee she'd made in an effort to survive the day, she returned to the desk and waved a hand toward the box.

"Donut?"

Sipping his coffee, Brian glanced over the edge of his mug, something dark and delicious simmering in the velvet depths. "Thanks, but sweets aren't my weakness," he said in a low voice that shivered down her spine. "I prefer my indulgences to have more substance."

*Oh.* Was he flirting with her? It felt like flirting.

But what the hell did she know?

Her last boyfriend had considered romance a quickie in the back of his pickup.

"Are you going to tell me why you're here?" she demanded, nervously taking a bite of her donut.

He watched her lick the sticky maple from her lips.

"I spent the morning at Tony's condo," he finally said.

"Did you find something?"

His jaw tightened with frustration. "Nothing that would explain why he was in Houston. Or why someone would want to shoot him."

Her brows drew tighter. She'd assumed he had some new lead that he was following. "Then why are you here?"

He smoothed his features to the polite mask that she was beginning to suspect was his "cop face."

"Ms. Ramon said that Tony was a part-time employee."

"So?"

"Where else did he work?"

Taylor blinked in confusion. "I don't know. I never heard of him working anywhere else."

He paused, as if considering his words. "He didn't do any extra jobs for your employer?"

"What are you asking?"

"You know." He gave a casual shrug, the corner of his mouth curling up in a smile of faux innocence. "The sorts of jobs that are easier to keep off the books."

Taylor stiffened, tossing aside the donut as she glowered at the aggravating man. "Are you accusing Mia of being a tax cheat?" she demanded.

His smile remained. "I'm just saying that a lot of landscaping businesses prefer to pay their employees in cash."

"Not this one," Taylor snapped.

"You're sure?"

"That's it." She scooted back her chair, preparing to kick

Detective Brian Cooper out the door. She didn't give a damn if he was a cop or not. "I've tried to be polite, but I'm done."

"Wait." He lifted a hand. "Please, Taylor."

"No," she said, although she remained seated. As much as she longed to use her stun gun to prod him out of the office, she wasn't going to let him get away with tarnishing her friend's reputation. "Mia isn't like her father," she ground out between clenched teeth. "She's done everything necessary to make sure she's running a legitimate business. Even when it meant she had to take out additional loans to meet those stupid regulations for her nursery. She even paid a tax lawyer to go over her accounts to make sure she was doing everything right."

An emotion that might have been regret softened his features. "Okay, I didn't mean to insult Ms. Ramon."

She sniffed. "Well, you did."

"I'm just curious."

She hesitated, well aware that his casual, good ol' boy manner was all nothing more than an act. He was a master manipulator who was playing her like a fiddle.

If she had a brain in her head she'd tell him to take his ugly insinuations and get the hell out of the office.

Instead, she stepped into his trap with her eyes wide open.

"Curious about what?"

"How a man who worked a few months a year could afford to pay rent on his condo, not to mention buy a brand-new Ford pickup."

She rolled her eyes. "I'm sure you've managed to uncover the not-so-secret fact that Tony was dealing drugs on the side."

"I heard," he said with a brief nod. "Which was why I checked with the narcotics unit. They recognized Tony's name, but they assured me he was nothing more than a small-time user who occasionally made deliveries for free weed." He took another sip of his coffee, giving her time to process his words. "Nothing that could possibly keep him in condos and new vehicles."

Taylor tapped her finger on the desk, realizing she'd never given much thought to how Tony managed to live without a full-time job.

"When he was young he used to get into trouble for petty theft," she at last said. "I think all the Hughes boys spent some time in juvie for having sticky fingers."

"Did he ever steal from your employer?"

Taylor widened her eyes, genuinely surprised by the question. "I doubt it," she instantly said. "Mia was the only one Tony could turn to when he was in trouble. I don't think he'd ever do anything to hurt her."

He looked unconvinced. "People will do all sorts of things when they're desperate."

It was true. Taylor had seen firsthand what panic could do to people. Still, she truly believed that Tony would lay down his life for Mia.

And maybe he had. . . .

Her heart twisted with pain.

"I'm not saying that Tony wouldn't break the law. I just don't think he'd hurt Mia," she clarified, forcing herself to rise to her feet. The thought of Tony lying dead on the street was a dark cloud on an already crappy day. Besides, she wanted the detective gone before Mia returned to the office. She had enough to worry about. "Did you have any other questions?"

He took a long minute before he answered. "None that can't wait."

"I should get back to work. . . ." She let her words trail away, watching as he rose to his feet.

Expecting him to turn away, Taylor was caught off guard

when he instead took a step toward the desk. His gaze skimmed over her face, examining each feature with a fierce concentration that made her heart miss a beat.

"I've seen you before, you know," he abruptly said.

She studied him in confusion. "Excuse me?"

He smiled, this one genuine enough to warm his brown eyes. "My brother works with juvenile offenders. During the summer months he organizes a baseball team to keep them off the streets. I help out when I can."

It took a second for Taylor to sort through the various summer league teams she coached against.

Then she recalled the team that had won the pennant last year. Some of the kids had laughed at the players who couldn't afford official uniforms or expensive cleats. At least until they were on the diamond, getting their butts tromped.

"Oh." She gave a nod. "The Cajun Bombers."

Brian wrinkled his nose. "My brother's name for the team, not mine."

She shrugged. "He's a good coach."

"He is," her companion readily agreed. "He has a talent for working with kids." There was a deliberate pause. "Just like you."

A renegade excitement fluttered through her stomach. An enticing, dangerous sensation that she hadn't felt in years.

She squared her shoulders. "Now what do you want?"

"Nothing." He held up his hands in a gesture of peace. "I swear, Taylor. I just think you do an amazing job with your son."

Heat touched her cheeks. Nothing mattered more to her than to be a good mother. Something this man was sure to have sensed.

"Right," she muttered.

He studied her for a long beat, then with a rueful shake of his head, he headed across the room. He glanced over his shoulder as he pushed open the door. "Someday you'll trust me," he murmured.

She tilted her chin. "Doubtful."

"We'll see."

He strolled out the door, his words hanging in the air.

A promise or a threat?

Taylor licked her dry lips, wondering why the gloomy day suddenly seemed so much brighter.

# Chapter Eight

Lucas stood at the side of the building, waiting for Mia to make a dash to her car.

His first instinct had been to follow her into the grimy shop. He didn't like her being out of his sight. Not even if it was a public place in the middle of the day.

Besides, he was quite certain she was trying to do some secretive snooping.

Mia had many fine qualities, but she would never earn a living as a spy. His lips twitched with amusement. She couldn't have been more obvious as she'd strolled to her car with an exaggerated nonchalance. Even her refusal to glance in his direction had warned him that she was up to something.

But while he'd been unable to resist the need to hover near the door where he could hear if she shouted for help, he'd grimly forced himself to stay outside.

It'd been fifteen years since he'd lived in Shreveport, but he hadn't forgotten what it meant to carry the name of St. Clair. Either people were embarrassingly eager to please him, or they clammed up and eyed him with blatant suspicion.

No one was actually comfortable in his presence. Just one of the many reasons he hadn't returned home after the war.

Now he understood the only way Mia was going to get any information was if he stayed out of her way.

Something that had become more vital when Teagan had called after running a background check on the auto shop to say that Tony's older brother worked there as a mechanic.

Shivering at the sharp breeze that easily sliced through his leather jacket, he breathed a sigh of relief as Mia at last appeared around the side of the building. With three long strides he was standing directly in her path.

"Done?" he asked.

She came to a reluctant halt, her hand lifting to brush back the curl that danced over her cheek.

"I run a business, I'm never done."

"Okay." He refused to react to her sharp words. She was clearly angling for an argument. Instead, he offered a coaxing smile. "Are you ready for lunch?"

"I usually have a yogurt at my desk."

"Not today."

She scowled. "Not your decision to make."

He folded his arms over his chest. She was stubborn. But he was devious. And he was fully prepared to use whatever weapons necessary.

"I have info on the shooting, but I absolutely refuse to share it watching you eat yogurt at your desk," he said in tones that warned her that there would be no negotiation.

Her eyes narrowed. "Blackmail?"

He shrugged. "Whatever works."

A tense silence pulsed between them as Mia visibly battled between her urge to tell him to go to hell and the urgency to discover what he'd learned.

At last she heaved a resigned sigh. "There's a diner—"

"We should go back to your house," he smoothly interrupted. He knew she was busy running her small empire, but he was selfish enough to insist on having some time alone with his woman. "We need privacy for this discussion."

Clearly annoyed, she sent him a warning glare. "I'm not cooking for you."

"No problem. I'll stop and pick something up."

He glanced down at her cheeks, which were flushed a light pink. The cold? Or excitement? He was hoping for excitement. "Deal?"

"Fine," she muttered, accepting she'd been outmaneuvered.

He waited until she was sliding into her vehicle before he called out. "Mia."

She frowned at him with seething impatience. "What now?"

"When you get home, wait in your car with the doors locked until I can do a search of the house."

Mia clenched her teeth, no doubt wishing she had her friend's stun gun handy, but astonishingly she didn't argue. Instead she slammed shut the car door and backed out of the lot with a tiny spray of mud.

With a wry smile, Lucas jogged back to his sports car, easily finding a nearby drive-through where he picked up a salad and a large muffuletta they could split, along with two sweet teas.

Then, gunning his engine, he managed to make it to Mia's before she could convince herself that she didn't have to wait for any stupid male.

Parking behind her, he grabbed the bags of food and crawled out of his car. Mia was already at the front porch by the time he crossed the yard, using her key to open the front door.

"Stay here," he commanded, dumping the food in her arms as he pulled his gun and headed into the house.

Moving room to room, he checked the windows and in

the closets, making sure no one had been in the house. Only when he was convinced that it was safe did he return to the living room to face a smoldering Mia.

"You're even bossier than you were fifteen years ago," she muttered, stomping into the kitchen to place the food on the table.

Lucas followed behind her, putting away his gun before taking a seat.

"I'll do whatever's necessary to protect you," he said without apology.

With a roll of her eyes, she poured the tea into glasses and collected real silverware to replace the plastic. Then, taking her seat, she ignored her salad and sent him an expectant glance.

"So, what did you discover?"

Lucas divided the sandwich, sliding a small portion in her direction. It was a game they'd played since high school. Mia would insist all she wanted was a salad, and then would grab whatever he was eating. Pizza. French fries. Hamburgers.

Watching as she absently picked up the sandwich and nibbled at the edge, he leaned forward. "First I need your promise."

She stiffened, her jaw clenching as if sensing she'd been set up. "What promise?"

He took a large bite of his sandwich, sighing in pleasure at the tart taste of olive salad mixed with freshly baked bread. Swallowing, he took a drink of the tea before he answered.

"If I include you in my investigation, then you have to share with me what you learn."

Her eyes widened before she was trying to pretend that she didn't know what he was talking about.

"How could I learn anything?"

"Okay." He took another bite of his sandwich. "You don't want to work together. . . ."

He allowed his words to trail away, not surprised when she muttered a low curse.

"You are such a pain."

He held her gaze. "You'll share?"

"Yes," she snapped. "Now tell me what you know."

Lucas took another bite before giving in to her command. Not to be an ass. He was genuinely hungry.

*Odd.* He'd had thousands of meals since leaving Shreveport, but somehow sharing the simple lunch with Mia stirred his appetite as nothing else could.

And not just for food, he acknowledged, feeling himself hardening in response to being so close to Mia.

Just the sweet scent of her shampoo was enough to set him on fire.

With an effort he forced himself to concentrate on what he'd learned from his recent conversation with the ARES office.

"The official coroner's report hasn't been issued, but the cause of death was a gunshot to his chest," he told her. "It went straight through his heart."

"God." Mia squeezed her eyes shut, forced to accept the full horror of Tony's death. Lucas wished he could protect her, but he knew that if she discovered he was holding back information she would poke around without him. This morning had already proved she wouldn't stay in her office and let the professionals take care of the investigation. "How awful."

"At least it was quick," he assured her in low tones. It'd been the first thing he'd asked. "He didn't suffer."

"I'm glad for that," she murmured, blinking back her tears. "Tony suffered enough."

Lucas nodded. He'd never fully understood the demons that seemed to haunt the younger man, but he'd always sensed them beneath Tony's bluster. "Agreed," he said.

With an effort she regained command of her composure, wiping away her tears.

"We know how he died, but it doesn't really help us," she pointed out. "Anyone could have shot him."

He leaned forward, situating the salad directly in front of her.

"Actually it does help."

Absently she resumed eating. "How?"

He polished off his sandwich before he answered.

"Tony was shot point-blank," he said. "Which means he knew who murdered him."

She sent him a surprised glance. "You can't be sure."

"Tony might not have been well educated, but he was street smart." He held her wide gaze. "He would never have let anyone get that close to him unless he trusted them."

She gave a nod, conceding his point. "Who could he know in Houston?"

"Besides me?" Lucas shrugged. "I have Teagan checking on any connections."

"Teagan?"

He smiled at the thought of his friend. From the amount of files he'd been sending Lucas, it was obvious he'd been at the office 24/7 gathering intel. The cunning hacker had the tenacity of a bloodhound when he was focused on a goal.

Not for the first time Lucas sent up a prayer of thanks that Rafe had managed to convince the younger man to join ARES.

"One of my partners," he said.

Mia blinked in confusion. "How is he checking?"

"Family relations. Phone records. Credit card transactions."

Her confusion became astonishment. "You have access to those things?"

"Yeah, but it's better if you don't mention that to the

detective," he said in dry tones. "Sometimes Teagan works in that gray area outside the law."

She studied him with raised brows. "And you?"

He leaned back in his chair. There would have been a time in his life when he would have said there was no excuse to break the law. Now he understood that nothing was ever black-and-white.

"I respect the rules," he said, sending his companion a wry grin. "As long as they don't get in my way."

For a brief second her lips twitched, almost as if she'd forgotten that she was supposed to hate him. Then, all too soon, the shadows returned to her eyes.

"Did you learn anything else?"

He swallowed a sigh. It would take time to rebuild the trust he'd destroyed.

"The cops found a receipt in Tony's truck from a gas station in Corrigan he was at a few hours before he was shot," he said.

"He was driving from Shreveport," Mia murmured. Corrigan was on Highway 59 between Shreveport and Houston.

Lucas nodded. The receipt proved that Tony hadn't been staying in Houston.

"That would be my guess," he said, not pointing out that Tony was probably followed by his killer. She was smart enough to figure it out by herself.

She reached for the sandwich he'd shared, taking a large bite as she silently considered what he'd revealed.

"It must have been an impulsive trip," she finally said.

Lucas studied her with a lift of his brows. "Why do you say that?"

"His brother Quinn manages a gas station in Shreveport," she said, wrinkling her nose. "Tony keeps an open tab there."

Lucas nodded. An "open tab" meant that Tony never

bothered to pay his bill. Which meant that he would never leave on a planned road trip without filling up with free gas.

"Very clever," he murmured, eyeing Mia with open appreciation.

She shrugged, a blush staining her cheeks. "I have my moments."

Not giving her time to realize what he was doing, Lucas was out of his chair and moving around the table.

"I remember," he murmured in husky tones, reaching to grasp her upper arms and tug her to her feet. Lowering his head, he buried his face in the curve of her neck. "And your moments are glorious."

Mia shuddered in pleasure.

It felt so good to have him tug her against his hard body. The heat. The brush of his lips. The wet touch of his tongue over her racing pulse.

She swallowed a moan as a sizzle of raw arousal zapped through her.

She'd agreed to this lunch to learn what Lucas had discovered about Tony's murder. Not to . . .

Her thoughts evaporated in a haze of bliss as he nibbled a path of kisses along the neckline of her dark green sweater that she'd matched with a pair of black slacks.

Reaching up, she grasped his shoulders. Her knees were threatening to buckle as his hands skimmed up her sides, gently cupping her breasts, which were heavy with need.

She wanted him to rip off her sweater. She ached to feel his lips against her bare skin and his fingers tormenting the sensitive tips of her breasts.

It'd been so long.

He murmured something beneath his breath, his head lifting so he could seek out her mouth in a kiss that demanded surrender. Her nails dug into his arms, her lips parting to allow his tongue to slip between them.

The taste of him was achingly familiar.

With lethal ease the years faded away. In this moment she was once again the young, eager Mia who embraced life, and Lucas, without fear.

His thumbs stroked the soft mounds of her breasts before moving to circle the hardened nipples. Mia trembled, her moan lost in his heated kiss.

Increasingly restless, Lucas pressed the growing length of his arousal against her lower stomach.

The delicious image of being perched on the edge of the table with Lucas between her spread legs seared through her mind.

It would be so easy. . . .

The sudden sound of a dog barking next door jerked Mia out of the fog of erotic sensations.

God. Was she out of her mind?

Pressing her hands against his chest, she arched back. "No. Lucas," she breathed, ignoring the stinging frustration that raced through her body. "We can't do this."

He trailed his lips down the side of her neck, his thumbs continuing to caress her nipples.

"Why not?" he demanded.

*Yeah, why not?*

The question whirled through her fuzzy mind as her body continued to quiver with unfulfilled need. It would be so easy to give in. To allow the exquisite passion to overwhelm her.

Then the memory of fifteen long, empty years without a damned word from this man blasted away her lingering desire.

"You had your chance and you blew it," she said, as much to remind herself as Lucas.

Lifting his head, he studied her flushed face with a brooding gaze.

"Would you believe me if I told you that I never meant to hurt you?"

She gave a sharp shake of her head. "No."

He grimaced at her stark refusal to listen to his excuses for dumping her.

"I thought I was doing what was for the best," he insisted.

"You don't have to explain, Lucas." Batting away his hands, Mia took a step back. "I knew from the start that the daughter of a gardener was never going to be good enough for a precious St. Clair." She shrugged. "If my heart broke, I don't have anyone to blame but myself."

His hands lifted, as if he intended to pull her into his arms, only to drop back to his sides when she stiffened in rejection.

"You have it completely backward, Mia," he said, the words clipped. "We were the ones who weren't worthy of you."

She rolled her eyes. The old "it's not you, it's me" excuse. "Yeah, right."

"It's true," he insisted, gazing down at her with a fierce intensity. "You were so gloriously innocent."

"Not for long."

He sucked in a sharp breath, as if she'd managed to land a direct hit.

"Damn, Mia."

She grimaced. Okay, that was below the belt. Lucas hadn't done anything to her that she hadn't begged him to do.

"It doesn't matter," she muttered.

He eased forward, his thumb tracing the line of her clenched jaw.

"You're right," he admitted, regret darkening his eyes. "I

took your innocence, but I wasn't going to steal your joyous nature."

"What's that supposed to mean?" she asked before she could halt the words.

"I wasn't going to let the St. Clair clan turn you into a plastic model version of Mia Ramon," he said, his fingers skimming down her neck while he studied her with a somber expression. "They would have destroyed you in an effort to make you the proper daughter-in-law."

Her breath tangled in her throat. Dammit. She didn't want to listen to his soft, persuasive words.

"I'm not completely spineless," she snapped.

His lips twisted. "No, but you were young, and worse, you didn't have a mother who would have told my parents to go screw themselves." He thankfully didn't point out that her father wasn't interested enough in his daughter to care how she was being treated by the St. Clair family. "Eventually you would have been molded into someone you didn't want to be." His hand slid beneath her hair to cup her nape in a possessive gesture. "Trust me, I know."

Mia glanced away as the memory of Nora St. Clair's crushing disapproval seeped through her. For a young, impressionable girl it'd been unnerving to know that she'd been condemned as unworthy without ever being given the opportunity to prove how much she loved Lucas.

So maybe she had been anxious to show the older couple that she could be exactly what they wanted in a daughter-in-law. And maybe she had tried to conform to their expectations. . . .

Abruptly realizing that he was forcing her to question the bitterness she'd deliberately harbored for the past fifteen years, she returned her gaze to his impossibly beautiful face.

"As I said, it doesn't matter."

"It does to me." He lowered his head until his lips were

brushing against her forehead. "There hasn't been a day that's passed when I don't regret my decision not to take you with me when I left."

A voice in the back of her head told her to walk away. What was the point in dissecting their painful past? But now she had to know.

"Why didn't you?"

"I was an idiot." There was an edge of self-disgust in his voice. "I was still hoping I could somehow earn my parents' approval."

"And now?"

His lips nuzzled over her temple and down to her ear. "Now I don't give a shit."

Despite her best efforts, she believed him.

She believed that he had truly thought he was doing what was best for her. And that he'd left in an effort to protect her from his parents.

That didn't mean she intended to forgive him, she swiftly assured herself. He should have explained why he was leaving. Instead he'd let her believe that he'd abandoned her because she was unworthy.

The fear had left wounds that'd never fully healed.

Still, it did make it even more difficult to resist the warm kisses that moved over her upturned face.

She wanted to lean forward and feel his arms wrap around her shivering body. She wanted to bury her fingers in his hair and kiss him until they were both drowning in pleasure.

It was the sheer intensity of that need that had her stumbling backward, her hand lifting to touch her cheek that still tingled from the heat of his lips.

"I need to get back to work," she breathed.

Lucas grimaced, as if he was in pain. And maybe he was.

If he was even half as sexually frustrated as she was, then he no doubt felt like punching something.

"Wait, Mia," he demanded.

She eyed him warily. "What?"

"You haven't told me what you discovered."

*Oh.* She swallowed a sigh. She really didn't want to share, but she'd made a deal.

"Not much." She rolled her eyes as his expression tightened with suspicion. "Seriously. I asked Burt if he knew how his brother made his money, but he claimed that Tony had never told any of them. Burt did say that Tony had been helping his mother out since high school."

"High school?" Lucas frowned. "Interesting."

"Burt also agreed to let me use my key to check out Tony's condo tomorrow."

"That's it?"

"That's it," she said. "I didn't want to press him while he's still grieving. Besides, he wasn't very close to Tony. I doubt he knows anything that can help."

Lucas planted his fists on his hips. "Damn."

A trickle of fear inched down her spine at his blatant disappointment. His reaction reminded her that there was more than Tony's murder to worry about.

"Why do you think he had that photo of me?" she demanded.

His eyes darkened, his features tightening with a grim concern. "I don't know, but I think it worried him enough to come to Houston and ask for my help."

"I do too." She wrapped her arms around her waist, her mouth suddenly dry. "God."

Lucas reached to cup her cheek in his palm. "Mia?"

She put her worst fear into words. "He might have been killed because of me."

Lucas's brows snapped together. "He was killed because some ruthless bastard put a bullet in his heart."

"But—"

"No," he interrupted, his fingers tightening on her face. "You have no responsibility for this. Period."

# Chapter Nine

Lucas glared down at his companion, barely resisting the urge to give her a small shake. How the hell could she waste even a second blaming herself?

When he'd known Tony, the younger man had been a drug user, a petty thief, and a habitual liar. He doubted that the years had changed him much.

The odds had always been that he'd end up dead. Or in jail.

Of course, Mia was too stubborn to simply accept his assurances.

"That's not true and we both know it," she muttered.

Lucas made a sound of impatience. "What are you talking about?"

"I've tried to tell myself that Tony was killed because of his connections to drugs." She shivered. "Or because he owed the wrong person money."

"Both legitimate assumptions," he said.

"But neither explains why he had my picture or why it had a threat written on it," she pressed. "This has something to do with me."

There was no way to argue. The picture proved the crime

had to have some connection to Mia. But he wasn't going to let her assume that she was responsible for Tony's death.

"It could still be because of something Tony was involved in."

"Lucas—"

He pressed his thumb against her lips. "No. Hear me out," he insisted. "It's very likely that Tony was messed up in illegal activities. The fact he could afford to work a few months out of the year proves that he had an alternative source of income." He held her gaze, willing her to believe him. "It's quite likely whoever shot him was afraid that Tony either shared some detail about his secret life with you or you saw something that you weren't supposed to see. They wanted to make sure you could never talk."

Mia took a long moment to consider his words. It was a habit she'd had even when she was just a teenager.

She would never leap to conclusions or simply give in to whatever everyone else believed. She would listen to an argument, then make her own decisions.

At least she did until his mother managed to undermine her self-confidence.

Yet another reason he'd gone away.

"Why not just kill me themselves?" she at last demanded.

It was a question that had haunted Lucas since he'd seen the photo.

"Maybe to make a point," he said. It was the most reasonable explanation. "Forcing Tony to kill one of his few friends would teach him to keep his mouth shut."

She furrowed her brow. "But instead, he went to see you."

"Yes." Lucas still didn't know how Tony knew that he was in Houston. Or why he'd chosen him to help. He could only assume that Tony was smart enough to know that Lucas was the one person in the world who would do whatever necessary to protect Mia. "They underestimated his loyalty to you."

"So they killed him," she said in pained tones.

He allowed his fingers to skim over her cheek, tucking a satiny curl behind her ear.

"Can you think of anything Tony might have said?"

She bit her lower lip, obviously searching through her mind for anything that might help.

"No," she finally said, heaving a frustrated sigh. "I haven't seen or spoken to Tony in months."

"He didn't send you anything, or ask you to keep anything safe for him?" he asked. If Tony was spooked he might have turned to Mia for help.

She shook her head. "No."

"Not even at the office?"

"I don't think he was ever at the new offices," she told him. "But I can check in the sheds and the truck he used."

"I'll have Max take care of that," he said, tapping her nose when she jutted her chin to a stubborn angle. Not surprisingly, she didn't like the thought of a stranger poking around her property. "He's a forensic expert," he informed her. "More importantly, he's OCD when it comes to the most miniscule detail. We might overlook something important, but he won't."

"Okay," she grudgingly conceded. "What do you want me to do?"

He gazed down at her wide, velvet brown eyes. What he wanted was to take her to his elegant condo in Houston. Or better yet, to get on a plane that would whisk them to some remote, tropical island.

Unfortunately, he knew she didn't trust him enough to leave Shreveport until they found Tony's killer.

Not yet.

"Are there any other friends whom Tony might have confided in?" he forced himself to ask.

"None that I know of." Her eyes grew distant, as if she was remembering Tony when the two of them had been young and left to run the streets without supervision. "He was acquainted with everyone in town, but I don't think he actually had any friends."

"I—" A sharp knock on the front door interrupted Lucas's words. He instinctively reached to touch his holstered gun. "Were you expecting company?"

"No. I'm never home during the day."

She was moving before he could halt her, heading into the living room so she could peek around the edge of the curtain. Lucas was quickly posed directly behind her, catching a glimpse of the man who was standing on the porch.

"Do you recognize him?" he asked, his gaze moving over the brown hair that was sprinkled with gray and the pudgy body that was stuffed into a hand-tailored suit.

"Frazer Hart," she muttered. "He's Vicky Fontaine's lawyer."

Lucas's attention shifted to Mia's tense profile. Clearly she wasn't happy at the arrival of the unexpected visitor.

"Why would Vicky Fontaine's lawyer be knocking on your door?"

"She's been trying to buy my dad's house and land since he died."

Lucas easily recalled the older woman. She'd been a friend of his mother. Or rather, they pretended to be friends while each of them tried to outdo each other in the small, highly competitive social scene. Then, while Lucas was still in high school, Vicky's husband had run off with millions of dollars that he'd embezzled from the pension funds of the state of Louisiana. It was rumored he was living in Belize with a lover half his age.

The scandal had tarnished the older woman, but she'd refused to retreat into her mansion and lick her wounds. No. Vicky Fontaine had continued to maintain the same opulent, exceedingly public lifestyle that she'd always enjoyed. And within a few months, she'd managed to overcome her faithless husband and the nasty gossip that would have destroyed a lesser woman.

"Why would she want a patch of swampland?"

"I have no idea," Mia muttered. "All I know is that she's been driving me crazy."

Lucas frowned. It was a long shot that Vicky's interest in the land had anything to do with Tony's death, but he intended to check it out.

Hell, right now he was desperate enough to follow any clue. No matter how ridiculous.

"Has anyone else shown an interest in your dad's property?"

Mia shrugged. "Not really."

There was more pounding on the door. "Ms. Ramon?"

Mia tensed, and Lucas ran a soothing hand down her back.

"Don't worry. I'll get rid of him."

"Good. I need to get back to work." She straightened, jerking away from his lingering hand.

Lucas hid his smile as he pulled his phone from his pocket and sent a quick message to Max. Obviously his touch bothered Mia more than she wanted to admit.

Good.

He wanted her bothered.

And hot. And aching.

And willing.

His phone pinged as Max swiftly answered his text. Sliding the phone in his pocket, he walked Mia to the kitchen and waited while she gathered her purse before they moved toward the back door.

"Wait at the side of the house," he commanded, grabbing a jacket that was hanging from a hook and wrapping it around her shoulders. He didn't care if she glared at him or not. The light rain continued to fall from the gray clouds, adding a chill to the air. "Max is on his way to pick you up and take you back to the office."

"That's not . . ." Her words trailed away as he glared down at her. His expression must have warned her that she wasn't going to win this argument. She heaved a faint sigh of resignation. "Fine."

Grasping the lapels of her jacket, he coaxed her forward, his entire body clenching with need as the soft swell of her breasts hit his chest.

It seemed crazy, but he was beginning to suspect that his libido had been running on autopilot, simply waiting for this woman to turn it back on.

Now it was making up for lost time.

"We'll finish our conversation over dinner," he said.

Her dark eyes heated with a ready response, her tongue peeking out to wet her dry lips. But even as he watched the tiny pulse at the base of her throat race with desire, she was pretending she didn't recognize the heat that sizzled between them.

"What conversation?"

He wanted to lean down and cover that fluttering pulse with his lips. He wanted the warm, sultry taste of her skin on his tongue.

Better yet, he wanted to lick a path down her body to discover the sweet honey between her legs.

"The one where you tell me that you forgive me for the past and agree to give me another chance," he murmured, his voice thickening.

She trembled even as her hands lifted to press against his chest.

"Why would I do that?"

He held her gaze. "Because you've missed me."

"I've done just fine since you left."

His lips twitched. She hadn't denied his accusation that she'd missed him.

"Are you happy?"

"Of course."

His gaze lowered to her mouth. Over the years he'd devoted a lot of time imagining those lush lips.

"I could make you happier," he assured her with a slow, wicked smile.

"Sex?"

"It's much more than that," he swore. And it was true.

Did he want this woman in his bed? Hell, yeah. But much more importantly he wanted her trust, and her friendship, and her heart.

He wanted to earn a place back in her life.

"Yeah, I bet," she muttered, not quite able to hide the hint of vulnerability that softened the tense line of her mouth.

Regret sliced through him. Lifting his hand, he cupped her cheek. "Mia. I'm not too proud to say it," he murmured in soft tones. "I've missed you."

She released a shaky breath, swaying forward as he lowered his head. His lips barely brushed over her mouth when the sound of pounding resumed.

"Lucas," she muttered. "The door."

He nuzzled a line of kisses along the edge of her jaw. "He'll go away."

"Trust me, he won't," she said, a low moan ripped from her as he found a sensitive spot just below her ear.

He nipped the lobe of her ear. "I could shoot him," he offered, not entirely kidding.

In this moment he'd do just about anything to get Mia naked.

But as if the fates were determined to give him a serious case of blue balls, Lucas heard the sound of a car pulling around the garage and directly into Mia's backyard.

Max.

Dammit.

With a muttered curse, he stole a fierce, all-too-brief kiss before he was stepping back to pull open the door.

"Tonight," he warned as Mia scurried past him.

Mia spent the rest of the afternoon in the sheds with Sonny, finishing up the inventory forms her accountant demanded were necessary to close out the end-of-the-year accounts.

Usually she waited until the last minute to complete the tedious task, but today she eagerly latched onto any chore that kept her mind occupied and her body moving. If she'd been stuck behind her desk there would have been no way in hell she could have kept herself from wasting her time with thoughts of Lucas.

There was, after all, something comforting about touring through her small but growing empire. It reminded her that she was no longer the young, overly impressionable girl who'd been desperate to become the next Mrs. St. Clair. Instead she was a strong, capable woman who could stand on her own.

Thank God.

It was almost four by the time she returned to her office. Not bothering to turn on the computer, she pulled out a sketch she intended to include in her bid for one of the local casinos, not surprised when Taylor entered her office less than five minutes later.

"Prince Charming is here with his very flashy carriage," the secretary informed her.

Tossing aside her charcoal pencil, Mia rolled her eyes. She'd known Lucas wouldn't allow her to find her own way home. Or even wait until five o'clock to pick her up.

"Hardly Prince Charming," she muttered, rising to her feet.

Taylor studied her with a knowing expression. "Are you sure about that?"

Mia's lips parted to tell her friend that Lucas St. Clair was as far from Prince Charming as a man could get, but instead she heaved a deep sigh.

"No."

Taylor wrinkled her nose. "He's getting to you again, isn't he?"

"He claims he left because he was afraid his mother was turning me into a carbon copy of herself."

"Carbon copy?" Taylor blinked in puzzlement. "What does that mean?"

"A plastic model."

"Oh."

Mia rose to her feet and rounded the desk. She hadn't missed the strange emotion that'd rippled over her friend's face.

"Taylor?"

The secretary gave a small shrug. "As much as I hate to agree with Lucas about anything, I can't deny I was worried at the time that the woman was going to turn you into a well-trained zombie."

Mia ground her teeth. Had everyone secretly been worried she was acting like an idiot?

The thought made her cringe.

"He should have talked to me," she muttered. "Not run off."

Taylor gave a short, humorless laugh. "He was an eighteen-year-old boy. Their specialty isn't talking."

They exchanged rueful glances.

"True," Mia agreed, a tendril of excitement curling through the pit of her stomach.

She suspected that while Lucas had obviously improved his communication skills, his other talents were still spectacular.

"What are you going to do?"

Mia slowly shook her head. "I have no idea."

Taylor reached out to lay her hand on Mia's arm. "Whatever you decide, you know I have your back."

"Thanks." Mia tilted her head, regarding her companion with a searching gaze. She didn't doubt Taylor's sincerity. The younger woman had always been a loyal friend. Mia, however, was beginning to suspect that her secretary was more than a little distracted. "What about you?"

Taylor raised her brows. "Me?"

Mia leaned against the edge of the desk, not fooled for a second by Taylor's overly innocent expression. "Sonny told me that a certain detective arrived with a pink box earlier today."

"Detective Cooper is investigating Tony's murder," Taylor said.

Mia didn't bother to hide her smile. "Sonny said he stayed for nearly half an hour and didn't ask to speak to anyone else. That doesn't sound like investigating to me."

"Sonny needs to mind his own business."

Mia didn't miss the sudden heat that stained the efficient secretary's cheek. The soft pink color emphasized the fact that Taylor was still a young, beautiful woman. It was no wonder the detective was stopping by the office with donuts.

"Are you blushing?" Mia teased.

"Would you stop?" Taylor growled, her cheeks going from pink to bright red. "He was only here to ask questions."

"Hmm." Mia felt a prick of astonishment. She'd never seen her friend so . . . what was the word? Flustered. Definitely flustered. "But you wish it could be more?"

"I barely know him," Taylor protested, then she bit her

bottom lip, her eyes softening with an unexpected regret. "And even . . ."

"What?" Mia prompted as her friend allowed her words to trail away.

Taylor sucked in a deep breath. "And even if there was a possibility that he wanted to spend time with me that didn't include a murder investigation, he's O-O-M-C-Z."

Mia frowned. "O-O-M-C-Z?"

"Out of my comfort zone."

It wasn't what Mia had been expecting. Taylor was always so poised and self-assured. Hell, Mia only wished she had her friend's natural confidence.

And while Detective Cooper was a nice-looking man with a charming smile, he wasn't Channing Tatum.

"Because he's a cop?" she at last demanded.

"Because he's a good guy," Taylor corrected her. "A really good guy."

*Ah.* Mia suddenly got it.

Her friend made a habit of choosing men who would eventually walk away. It was as if she protected her independence by dating losers.

Detective Cooper might be a pain in the ass, but he most certainly was not a loser.

"Taylor—" She bit off her words as Lucas stepped into the room.

As always, the mere sight of him was enough to make her shiver with a sizzling sense of anticipation.

It was more than just his impossible beauty. Or the chiseled perfection of his body. Or even the rich, enticing scent of his male cologne.

It was the way his gaze landed on her and never wavered, no matter who else was in the room. As if she was the only person in the world.

His dark blue eyes shimmered with the same excitement

that fluttered in the pit of her stomach as he reached to grab the jacket she'd tossed on a chair across from her desk.

"Ready?" he asked.

Mia briefly considered telling him that she never left the office before five. It was a source of pride that she was the first to arrive and the last to leave.

But before she could surrender to the cowardly impulse to hide behind her work, Taylor was reaching out to give her a small shove toward the door.

"Go," she commanded. "I'll lock up."

Glaring at her friend, who mysteriously appeared to be encouraging Lucas, Mia allowed Lucas to wrap the jacket around her shoulders.

"Traitor," she muttered.

Taylor gave a rueful shrug. "Have a good weekend."

"We'll discuss this Monday," Mia warned, grabbing her purse and following the smugly smiling Lucas out of the building.

# Chapter Ten

Mia gave a lift of her brows as Lucas led her to the silver SUV while his friend peeled out of the parking lot in Lucas's expensive sports car.

Still, she waited until she was safely strapped in to the passenger seat and Lucas was sliding behind the steering wheel before she asked the obvious question.

"What's going on?"

Lucas pulled out of the lot and turned in the opposite direction of her house.

"I thought we would take a side trip," he told her.

She frowned as they continued past the edge of town. "Where?"

"To your dad's place."

A familiar combination of pain and regret sliced through her heart at the mention of her father. Her relationship with George Ramon had been difficult at best and nonexistent at worst.

Things might have been different if her mother had lived. But her grieving father had no idea what to do with a vulnerable young daughter, and instead of trying to forge a bond between the two of them, he'd done his best to forget she even existed. It was only when she was helping him mow yards or trim hedges that he acknowledged she was worthy of his attention.

"It's almost dark," she inanely pointed out, glancing toward the gray sky.

He shrugged. "I just want to have a quick look around. There has to be a reason Vicky Fontaine wants to buy it."

"I assume that means you spoke with Frazer," she said, not at all sorry she'd left Lucas to deal with the slimy, relentless lawyer.

Lucas made a sound of disgust, merging onto the main road that would lead them around the edge of Barksdale AFB.

"As much as you talk to a lawyer," he said. "He refused to say anything beyond the fact that his client was looking to invest in land."

"For what?" Mia shook her head. Her father's land was surrounded by bogs. It would cost a fortune to try and develop it into anything of value.

"He refused to say." Lucas picked up speed as they melded into the heavy Friday traffic. "I spent the past few hours trying to discover more about Mrs. Fontaine."

"That must have been fun." Mia grimaced. The older woman had never hidden the fact that she considered George Ramon and his daughter as lesser beings. There were times Mia even thought that the woman might hate them, although she didn't know what they'd ever done to piss her off.

"Not really," he muttered.

"Did you find anything of interest?"

"She does have a large stock portfolio that she took charge of after her husband disappeared with his lover, but none of it in real estate."

"No land?"

"Not on the surface."

Mia frowned in confusion. "How could land not be on the surface?"

He gave a low chuckle. "Not on the surface of her investments," he clarified. "It actually took some digging to discover that her husband secretly bought a company called Vernon Recycling in the early eighties."

"Why would he want it to be secret?"

"Because it didn't actually recycle anything. It's a shell company used to buy land for toxic waste dumps," Lucas said. "Vicky has been slapped on the wrist several times by the EPA, but the profit she makes far outweighs any fines."

"I suppose she might be thinking of buying my dad's property to expand her toxic waste business," Mia murmured.

"I'm having Teagan continue the search on Mrs. Fontaine," Lucas said. "He can dig a lot deeper than I can."

Mia nodded, about to warn Lucas that they were nearing the exit. To her astonishment, however, he automatically veered off the highway onto the narrow road that quickly turned into a dirt pathway.

How had he known where she lived?

When they were young she'd never invited Lucas to her home. It wasn't that she was ashamed. . . . No, that wasn't true. She was desperately ashamed of the small shack she'd shared with her father. Not because they were poor. Everyone in town knew that they barely scraped by. But because of the piles of trash left in the backyard to rot and the dozens of junk cars that her father collected with the belief he would someday fix them up.

Who wanted their boyfriend to see that she lived in a pigsty? Especially a boyfriend who lived in the biggest mansion in Shreveport.

But Lucas's ease in turning from one dirt road to another proved he'd been well aware how to find her. And that he'd driven out to the house more than once.

Something that couldn't be accidental, considering that the house was set in the wetlands, miles from civilization.

Hell, there wasn't even a nearby neighbor.

"You've been out here before," she said, belatedly realizing the words came out as an accusation.

He pulled into the short drive and parked in front of a stack of old tires. Flicking off the engine, he shifted in his seat to regard her with an unreadable expression.

"I couldn't force you to let me take you home after our dates, but I sure as hell wasn't going to let you drive these roads in the middle of the night without being close enough to help if something happened."

Mia widened her eyes. "You followed me?"

"Yeah." He reached out to stroke his thumb over her lower lip. "I would turn off my car lights and stay far enough back you couldn't see me."

"I had no idea," she murmured.

He shrugged. "I couldn't have slept without being sure you were safely tucked in your bed."

The low words were said in an offhand tone, but they managed to melt yet another layer of ice that surrounded her heart.

For years she'd convinced herself that Lucas hadn't truly loved her. How could he, if he'd walked away so easily? Now she was being forced to accept that he had cared. Perhaps even more than she ever realized.

Unnerved by the thought, she abruptly turned her head to peer out the side window. Instantly, she grimaced.

*God.* It was even worse than she remembered. During her brief trip after the funeral to clean out the fridge and make sure the windows and doors were locked, she'd been in shock. It didn't matter that her relationship with her father had been nearly nonexistent. His passing had still been a blow. It wasn't really surprising that she'd barely noticed her surroundings.

With a shudder she allowed her gaze to skim over the dozens and dozens of cars that were left in a haphazard pattern along the back of the property. Some were nearly hidden by the tall grass and others were covered in the Spanish moss that draped from the trees. It gave the impression of a creepy old graveyard.

"Are you okay?" Lucas demanded, clearly sensing her distress.

"Yeah." She wrinkled her nose, her gaze turning toward the house, which was made of warped boards that had long ago lost any paint, and a sagging roof. It'd never been a palace, but the damp Louisiana weather had taken its toll over the past few years. "I came here after my father died, but I really didn't pay attention to the place." She gave a rueful shake of her head. "I didn't realize how bad it'd gotten since my father stopped allowing me to visit."

Lucas immediately reached for the key he'd left in the ignition. "If you want to leave—"

"No." She grabbed his arm, sucking in a deep breath. The air of neglected sadness was nearly tangible, but she couldn't continue to ignore the mess. Eventually she'd have to face it. What better time than when Lucas was at her side? "I'm okay," she assured him, forcing herself to continue to survey her childhood home.

"This was a stupid idea," Lucas muttered. "I thought maybe we could see why Vicky Fontaine would be so interested in the land, but—" His words cut off as her fingers dug in his arm. "Mia?"

She leaned forward, her gaze locked on the unmistakable footprints she could see in the mud.

"Someone's been here."

She was turning to push open her door when Lucas abruptly grabbed her by her shoulders and yanked her back to meet his deep frown.

"Where the hell are you going?"

She glanced at him in surprise. "This is my property. I need to make sure there hasn't been any damage."

"You're not stepping out of this vehicle until I'm sure there's no one lurking around."

Her lips parted, but before she could protest he was out of the SUV and closing the door behind him.

Mia smiled wryly and settled back in her seat as she watched him jog toward the back of the house.

She might as well make herself comfortable. Until Lucas was certain that it was safe, there was no way she was going anywhere.

Lucas grimaced at the gloomy darkness that was swiftly closing in.

He'd been a fool to bring Mia out here. Unfortunately, it was too late to regret his impulsive decision. Now that she'd spotted the footprints she wasn't going to be satisfied until she'd assured herself there'd been no damage done by the trespasser.

*As if any stray vandal could do anything to make matters worse*, he wryly acknowledged.

The entire place needed a good bulldozing.

Following the tracks toward the line of cars, Lucas abruptly slowed his pace.

Even in the fading light he could see that there'd been more than one person rummaging around the property. And what was more unexpected, someone had busted the windows on several of the cars. Moving forward he could see the shattered glass still shimmering on top of mud. Which meant the damage had been recent.

But why?

It could be a group of kids looking for a place to drink and smoke weed. Or even thieves who were searching for anything of value in the cars. But Lucas suddenly had a bad feeling.

Completing his sweep, Lucas took a mental note of the tire tracks that headed deeper into the wetlands, and one of the nearby sheds that had a door hanging open, before he returned to the SUV.

She was out of the vehicle before he could halt her. "Well?" she demanded, moving to stand directly in front of him.

He shrugged. "Whoever was here is long gone."

"It's probably poachers," she suggested. "When my father was alive no one was stupid enough to try and sneak past his shotgun. Now I'm sure most locals know that no one is staying here. They can come and go without worrying about being seen." She grimaced. "I need to check inside the house."

"We can do that when it's light," he hastily suggested, fully intending to return with Max before he allowed Mia to enter the house.

Naturally, she refused to listen to reason, brushing past him on her way up the narrow pathway.

"The electricity is still on, so we might as well do it now," she said.

He clenched his teeth. Mia would no doubt claim that she was determined. He would say stubborn as a mule.

Accepting he wasn't going to change her mind, he hurried to walk at her side, his gaze scanning the gathering darkness for any hint of danger.

"What do you intend to do with the land?" he asked.

"First I need to have it cleared." She waved a hand toward the piles of junk. "Later I might put up some new sheds to store my equipment and even expand my nursery."

"You aren't tempted to sell it?"

She didn't hesitate. "No. This land isn't much, but it was in my mother's family for years." A sad smile touched her lips. "It's really about the only thing I have left that belonged to her or my grandparents."

Lucas was sharply reminded of how tough it'd been for Mia growing up. The death of her mother. Her father's drinking. The stuck-up bastards who treated her like shit because she was George Ramon's daughter.

The fact that she'd become such an amazing woman was a testament to her sheer determination.

They rounded the back of the house, the singsong sound of frogs filling the air.

"It's isolated," he said, not at all happy with the thought of her using the land for her business. A young, beautiful woman shouldn't be alone in such a remote location.

"Yes," she agreed, unaware he intended to do his best to halt her plans. "There used to be an old trapper who lived down the road. He died almost ten years ago."

"Who owns the land now?"

"A nephew, I think." Mia gave an absent lift of her shoulder. "I've never seen him out here."

Lucas frowned, glancing toward the tangled undergrowth and mossy ground. If Vicky Fontaine wanted a toxic waste dump, why didn't she buy the neighbor's land? It sounded as if no one was particularly attached to it.

He pulled out his phone to send a quick text to Teagan to have him check out the neighbor. He was just finishing when he heard Mia's soft gasp.

Instantly he had the phone shoved back in his pocket and was jogging up the back steps.

"What's going on?"

"The lock is broken," she whispered.

"Let me look around," he commanded, pulling his gun out of the holster as he stepped into the house.

Flipping on the lights, he made his way through the kitchen, which was little more than a stove, a fridge, a sink, and two cabinets. The living room was equally small, with the windows heavily covered by drapes, as if afraid that a peek of sunlight might manage to penetrate the shadows. He continued into the two bedrooms, which clearly hadn't been used in years. He assumed that George had preferred to sleep on the threadbare couch in front of the ancient TV.

Within a few minutes he'd assured himself there were no hidden intruders and returned to gesture to Mia that it was okay to come inside.

"It's impossible to say if anyone was in here," he said. "Do you want to see if anything is missing?"

"It's doubtful," she murmured, slowly walking through the kitchen and into the living room. She heaved a sigh at the meager belongings shrouded in dust. "My father didn't have anything of value."

Lucas studied her tense profile, considering his words. He preferred not to admit that he'd had her father fully investigated.

"He might not have expensive furniture or electronics, but I remember my mother always paid your father in cash," he said. "I assume that's how he asked most of his clients to pay him."

She nodded. "He was paranoid that the government was spying on him. Or at least that's what he always claimed." Her lips twisted in a humorless smile. "I think he wanted to avoid paying taxes."

"Which means that it was probably well known that he kept a large amount of cash in his home."

Her eyes widened, belatedly realizing the danger of a drunk old man living in the middle of nowhere with a ton of cash lying around.

"True," she breathed. She shivered, moving toward the couch.

He watched as she pulled off the old cushions. "You said that he left you an inheritance?" He asked the question that'd been nagging at him since he'd entered the barren shack.

It seemed impossible to believe that a man who lived in this place could afford to leave money to his daughter.

"A few days before he went into the hospital he called Sonny and asked him to come out here to pick up the hope chest that he'd made for me when I was a little girl," she said, her tone distracted as she unzipped the ratty fabric that covered the cushions and reached her hands inside. Clearly that was where George hid his cash. "When I opened it up I found fifty thousand dollars in cash."

Lucas released a slow whistle. "That's a lot of money."

She jerked her head up, a flush staining her cheeks. "I declared it on my taxes before I used it as a down payment on the new office and my house."

He held up a hand, hating the fact that she felt the need to defend her morals. Yet another legacy that came with being the daughter of George Ramon.

People like Vicky Fontaine could shrug off the scandal of having a husband who embezzled millions, but Mia would always have to prove her integrity.

"I just mean that it's a considerable fortune for a gardener to be able to save," he said in soft tones.

She searched the last cushion before returning them to the couch with a faint sigh.

If there had been any money, it was obviously gone.

"As you can see, he didn't spend much on himself." She shrugged. "And I think he said something about my mother having a life insurance policy. I assume that's where most of the inheritance came from."

"Is there anyone who would know about the insurance money?" he demanded.

She wrinkled her nose. "I suppose the lawyer who set up my mother's will and . . . oh."

Lucas moved forward as Mia suddenly bent over to pick up something that was half hidden beneath the couch.

"What is it?"

Mia held up the shiny object. "Tony's lighter."

He stood close beside her, his brows pulled together. "You're sure it's Tony's?"

"Yeah." She turned it over to reveal the ornate etching on the back. "It's inscribed with his initials." She lifted her head to regard Lucas with a somber expression. "He never went anywhere without it."

Lucas reached to take the lighter, slipping it into his pocket. He would have Max take a closer look at it.

"Would he have a reason to visit when your father was still alive?" he asked when Mia obviously intended to protest his bossy behavior.

She rolled her eyes, seemingly accepting she wasn't going to change him.

Smart woman.

"No," she at last said. "My father never hid his opinion of the Hughes brothers. He said they should all be locked up and the key thrown away."

"Which means he came here after your father's death," Lucas said, trying to imagine Tony slipping through the shack.

Certainly he would have known that George kept money here, but it was doubtful he would have known about the life insurance policy. And if he had been looking for petty cash, why waste his time driving all the way out here on the vague hope there would be some lying around?

It would have been easier to ask Mia for a loan. She would never have said no.

"Probably," Mia said, looking troubled.

"So, the question is . . ." Lucas glanced around the cramped room. "Did he come here to look for something? Or to hide something?"

# Chapter Eleven

Mia was silent on the trip home.

*God.* She hated to visit her father's house. It not only brought back memories of her grim, lonely childhood, but it was a nagging reminder that she couldn't pretend that the mess would simply go away. At some point she had to actually take a few days off work to clean out the house and hire people to haul away the junk.

Now she had to add in the baffling realization that Tony, and God knew who else, had been sneaking onto the property.

What was he doing out there?

Was he looking for money? Or hiding from whoever killed him? Or was he using the abandoned shack to conceal some mystery item that the murderer wanted to get back?

The questions scurried around her brain like a hamster on a wheel, spinning faster and faster with no answers.

It was a relief when they pulled into her driveway. She had to concentrate on jumping out of the SUV and digging through her purse for the key as they crossed the yard to climb the steps onto the narrow porch.

Shoving open the door, she was firmly tugged aside so Lucas could enter the house in front of her. Ignoring her companion's slow and thorough inspection of each room, Mia pulled off her jacket and tossed it on the couch along with her purse. At the same time she kicked off her shoes.

It'd been a long day and she intended to make herself comfortable.

Crossing the room, she was intent on discovering if she had any beer left in the fridge when Lucas wrapped his arm around her waist.

"Lucas," she breathed, shivering when she felt him tugging her hair out of the braid she'd used to keep the heavy strands out of her face while she was doing inventory.

"Are you hungry?" he asked, his lips skimming her cheek as his arm tightened around her.

Was she? Mia found it impossible to think as his tongue traced the shell of her ear.

All she knew was that the tiny tremors that shook her body were no longer from the chilled air. Or the aftereffects of being at her father's house.

Nope. They were entirely due to the lips that were pressed to a spot just below her jaw.

"Not really," she managed to mutter.

"Good."

He brushed her hair over her shoulder so he could trail a path of kisses down the line of her throat. Another shiver raced through her. The feel of his lips brushing against her skin was setting off tiny explosions of pleasure.

She swayed until her back was pressed against his broad chest, trying to remember why this was a bad idea.

"Lucas." Her mouth went dry as his hand slid beneath her sweater, skimming up the tense muscles of her stomach before he was cupping her breast. "Shouldn't we be doing something?"

He chuckled, pressing the thick ridge of his erection against her behind.

"We are."

"I meant we should be looking for Tony's murderer," she tried to insist.

His thumb found the tip of her breast, stroking it to an aching peak. Acute pleasure streaked through her. Did he remember how sensitive she was there?

"There's nothing more we can do tonight," he assured her, licking the pulse that was fluttering at the base of her neck.

Her heart slammed against her ribs as he blew a soft breath over the damp skin, his fingers moving to efficiently deal with the tiny clip that held her bra together.

Instantly her breasts tumbled free, and she felt a tiny pang of panic.

"The investigators will be done with Tony's condo," she forced herself to say, making a last stab for sanity. "We could go check it out."

With one smooth motion, he was skimming the sweater up and over her head. He had it tossed aside along with her bra before she could protest. Then, grasping her shoulders, he turned her to face him.

"Tomorrow," he said, his voice husky as his gaze moved over her face and down to her bare breasts.

His fingers dug into her shoulders as his eyes darkened at the sight. She heard his low moan before he was slowly lowering his head, his lips closing around a pink nipple that was already beaded to a hard point.

Her hands instinctively lifted to press against his chest as jolts of electric excitement threatened to overwhelm her.

"Lucas," she groaned, her nails digging into his flesh.

Reluctantly lifting his head, he studied her flushed face. "Do you want me to stop?"

Stop? She did, didn't she? After all, she'd decided she wasn't going to let this man get to her again.

He'd hurt her. Betrayed her. Abandoned her.

Of course, he'd explained he'd only been trying to protect

her, the voice of temptation whispered in the back of her mind. And besides, this didn't have to mean anything, right?

It was just sex.

Fantastic, mind-blowing sex with the one man who could make her burn with need.

After the crappy few days she'd had, she deserved this.

"I don't know," she breathed.

Any other man might have been offended by her mixed signals. Or at least frustrated. But not Lucas. His wicked smile revealed the arrogance of a man who knew how to get exactly what he wanted.

"Then let me see if I can help you make up your mind," he murmured.

Allowing his hands to slide down her back, he cupped her butt as he grazed her lips with a light, teasing kiss. Over and over he tormented her with the butterfly caresses, giving her a hint of paradise only to pull away.

Frustrated, Mia wrapped her arms around his neck and parted her lips, silently urging him to deepen the kiss.

He didn't hesitate.

With a slow, drugging perfection he consumed her. There was simply no other word for it. His kisses were hot, demanding, utterly possessive. In this moment he owned her, body and soul.

Making tiny sounds of anticipation, she allowed herself to melt against his hard body. She didn't know why it was only Lucas's kisses that could set her on fire, but right now she didn't care.

She simply wanted to savor the heat curling through the pit of her stomach and the frantic beat of her heart. And his amazing ability to make her feel as if she was beautiful and desirable and gloriously alive.

Time lost all meaning as he continued to kiss her, the troubles of the day temporarily forgotten. In his arms, the real world was far away.

At last, his mouth moved to stroke over her flushed cheeks, allowing her to suck in a deep breath.

"God, I've missed the taste of you," he groaned, burying his face in her hair. "Your smell."

She blinked. "Smell?"

"It's like summer," he whispered in her ear. "Rich earth. Sun-kissed roses."

She shivered as his warm breath brushed over her skin. "I was working in the sheds."

"No. It's you," he said. "Just you."

Skimming his lips over her cheeks, he captured her lips in a kiss that seared a path of pleasure to the tips of her toes. At the same time, he wrapped his arms around her so he could scoop her off her feet.

Mia pulled her head back as he smoothly carried her across the floor and into her bedroom. That panic was once again fluttering at the edge of her mind.

"Are you sure you know what you're doing?" she demanded.

His lips twitched, a sinful amusement burning in the depths of his indigo eyes.

"It's been a while, but I think I can figure it out," he assured her in low tones.

She didn't doubt that for a second. There was an unmistakable skill in the ease with which he lowered her onto the mattress and skimmed his fingers along the curve of her midriff to hook in the waistband of her slacks. With a gentle tug the silky pants were being pushed off her hips and down her legs.

She was left wearing nothing more than her white lace undies.

"This is going to complicate everything," she muttered.

His brooding gaze took a slow, thorough survey of her

near-naked body, a hint of color highlighting his chiseled cheekbones.

"Yes," he said.

She blinked in surprise, watching as he shrugged out of his coat and dropped it onto the floor.

"What?"

He held her wary gaze, unhooking his holster and carefully placing the gun on her dresser before swiftly shedding the rest of his clothing.

"I know you want me to say this is just sex," he said.

She blushed, wondering if he could read her mind. "I didn't say—"

He interrupted her stumbling words. "You didn't have to. I can see it in your eyes." He moved to place a knee on the edge of the mattress, his hand reaching out to trail a finger along the top of her panties. "You want to pretend that this is nothing more than a meaningless hookup."

Mia licked her lips, silently studying his lean, beautiful features before her gaze moved down to his perfectly sculpted body.

God. He was spectacular.

The broad shoulders. The chest that was lightly sprinkled with dark hair that arrowed down his flat stomach. His hips were narrow and his legs were long and surprisingly muscular. Even his feet were flawless.

She'd always been a bit amazed that such a man could be interested in her. Which was no doubt a part of the reason she continued to protect herself from his persuasive charm.

What had Taylor said? O-O-M-C-Z? Lucas St. Clair was out of the comfort zone of any normal woman.

She would be an idiot to believe she was more than a brief moment of madness.

"I won't let you hurt me again," she said, more to reassure herself than to warn Lucas.

He leaned forward, planting his hand on the mattress next to her head.

"I intend to make you the happiest woman in the world," he assured her.

Against her will, her lips twitched. "You still have the arrogance of a St. Clair."

He gave a slow shake of his head, heat smoldering in his eyes.

"Not arrogance, just a promise that I'm going to do everything in my power to please you."

Mia's breath was wrenched from her lungs as his finger dipped beneath her panties. Instinctively she let her legs part, allowing him to explore the slick heat.

"That's a good start," she rasped, her hips lifting off the mattress as he found her clit and teased it with feathery brushes of his fingertip.

"Just good?" he demanded, his finger moving so it could slide deep into her body. "What about this?"

Her body quivered with anticipation, the feel of his finger thrusting in and out of her unbearably erotic.

Still, she wasn't going to feed his ego. It was quite large enough, thank you very much.

"Not bad," she managed to croak, the restless movement of her body easily giving her away.

"Hmm." Lucas brushed his lips over her cheek, her brow, and down the length of her nose. "I see I'm going to have to work at this."

He claimed her mouth in a searing kiss, then brushed his lips along the line of her jaw. Mia released a soft sigh of pleasure, relishing the slow, sinfully delicious seduction.

He nipped the lobe of her ear, taking time to trace the delicate shell with the tip of his tongue before he was moving his lips down the curve of her throat.

Her hands instinctively lifted so she could thread her fingers through the soft silk of his hair. She desperately wanted to prolong the moment. To make it last the entire night.

But her body was already trembling with a need that was becoming downright painful.

As if sensing her fierce desire, Lucas abruptly grabbed her delicate undies to rip them off. Her lips parted to protest, but she forgot what she was going to say when his lips closed over the tip of one nipple.

*Oh . . . yes.* Her eyes slid shut as she arched her back in silent encouragement.

Using his teeth and tongue, he tormented her, at last moving to pleasure her other nipple before he was headed downward.

Her stomach clenched as he kissed a path of destruction ever lower. Allowing his hands to slip under her legs, he tugged them farther apart as he sank to his knees next to the bed.

She moaned, her nerves so sensitized to his touch that the scrape of his whiskers against her inner thigh nearly made her come.

"Sweet summer honey," he murmured, his hands holding her still as he licked his tongue through the center of her pleasure.

Her breath was released on a soft hiss as her fingers tightened in his hair. He was pure magic as he stroked over her tender clit, swiftly driving her toward an explosive climax that made her entire body shake with the shocking force.

Easing her through the cataclysmic orgasm with short, teasing licks, Lucas at last lifted his head to study her with a smug smile.

"Good?" he asked.

Mia rolled her eyes. Good? It had been stunning, and gloriously decadent. As if she'd been shattered with a bliss that she didn't even know existed.

"I think my scream was enough to prove how good it was," she said in dry tones.

Placing a last, lingering kiss on her inner thigh, Lucas reached for his wallet and extracted a condom. Then, crawling onto the mattress, he stretched out beside her.

"It's only going to get better," he assured her.

"Yes." She leaned forward to brush a light kiss over his mouth as she wrapped her fingers around his cock. "It is."

He sucked in a startled breath. "Mia."

"You never let me do this before," she murmured, marveling at the texture of soft skin that was pulled tight over his rock-hard cock.

With a low groan, he buried his face in her hair. "I was barely capable of getting your clothes off before I came."

She pressed her fingers down the length of his cock, feeling him swell beneath her touch.

"And now?"

He lifted his head to reveal his eyes, which smoldered with a dark, aching need.

Mia shuddered. In this moment she couldn't deny that he wanted her. Desperately.

"You still have the power to make me embarrass myself," he said in a gruff voice.

Unnerved by the emotions that sizzled between them, Mia busied herself with planting tiny kisses along the strong line of his jaw before moving down the length of his body.

Lucas made a strangled sound, his hands fisting in her hair as she wrapped her lips around his cock. Using the tip of her tongue, she explored the blunt tip, allowing her fingers to stroke up and down.

A shudder shook through Lucas, the musky scent of his arousal filling the air.

"Shit, Mia. That feels amazing," he breathed.

The knowledge that she could make this man tremble sent a thrill of excitement tingling down Mia's spine. Widening her lips, she took him deep inside her mouth, allowing her teeth to lightly graze his tender flesh.

She was just finding a steady rhythm when he was grabbing her shoulders and ruthlessly pulling her upward.

"No more," he growled.

"Unfair," she pouted.

"You can play next time," he muttered, reaching for the condom and hurriedly rolling it on. Then, moving on top of her, he released a small groan as they were pressed skin to skin. "Tonight I need to be inside you."

She wrapped her arms around his neck, their gazes locked as he allowed the head of his cock to slip into the entrance of her body.

"Now," she urged, lifting her hips upward even as he thrust home with a low groan of satisfaction.

Glad they'd left the lights on, Lucas studied Mia's delicate profile as she nestled against his side, her head tucked on his chest.

It was a familiar position. As was the peace that filled him.

Usually after sex he was already thinking of how soon he could leave. It was no reflection on the lovely women who'd welcomed him into their beds. He simply hadn't been able to connect with them when his heart belonged to Mia.

Now he simply took the time to appreciate the sensation of just how . . . right this felt.

Unfortunately, he could already sense Mia beginning to stiffen. No doubt she was trying to remind herself of all the reasons she was supposed to hate him.

Which meant that he had to find a distraction. Quickly.

"Do you know how many nights I dreamed about you?" he murmured softly.

She made a sound of disbelief. "Yeah, right."

His lips twisted. She truly had no idea of how often she haunted his thoughts over the years.

"When I was in Afghanistan I used to imagine wrapping you in my arms," he said, tightening his hold on her slender body. "I think that was the only thing that kept me sane."

Her tension eased as she tilted back her head to study him with a sudden curiosity. "How were you captured?"

Lucas kept his expression unreadable. He detested talking about the war. And even more about his time spent in the Taliban prison.

But if it kept her warm and willing in his arms, then hell, he'd talk about whatever she wanted.

"I was negotiating the release of an Afghan leader who was friendly to our government," he said, grimacing at the memory of how often loyalties changed among the enemy. One day a leader would be offering help to allied forces and the next they would be shooting them in the back. "It turned out to be a trap. The soldiers with me were killed outright and I was taken hostage."

Sympathy flared through her dark eyes. She knew him well enough to be certain that he tortured himself with guilt over the deaths of the young men who'd traveled deep into enemy territory with him.

"That's where you met the friends you work with at ARES?"

"Yep." His fingers absently stroked through her hair, breathing deep of her floral scent. It helped to keep him grounded. Something that was important when he allowed the painful memories to surface. "We formed a bond plotting our escape."

Almost as if sensing how much it cost him to discuss the war, she smoothed her hand across his chest, lingering over the steady thud of his heart.

"How did you get away?"

"Rafe did the planning," he said. It'd been an easy choice.

Rafe Vargas had not only been trained in special ops, but he was a natural leader. "I befriended a guard who was willing to trade the keys to our cells for my watch, which I'd managed to hide during my capture," he continued.

Mia gave a short laugh. "Why am I not surprised it was your charm that helped you escape?"

He shrugged. He couldn't deny the fact that he readily used his skills in interpersonal relationships to convince the susceptible young guard to help them.

His parents had been masters in manipulation.

That particular skill was the one thing he'd been happy to inherit.

"Hauk took out the guards at the entrance to the prison," he continued, not mentioning the fact that Hauk was one of the top snipers in the world and that both guards had been neatly shot in the head before they realized they were in danger. He had enough nightmares for both of them, thank you very much. "And Teagan managed to send our coordinates after he hacked into the DMS—"

"The what?" she demanded in confusion.

"Sorry." He shook his head. Sometimes he forgot he was using soldier-speak. "The Defense Message System."

"How'd he manage to do that?"

"With a laptop we found in a nearby village." His lips twitched. "No one but Teagan could have done it."

She continued to rub her hand over his chest, no doubt hoping to soothe him. Instead, her light touch was sending erotic sparks of pleasure through him.

His cock hardened, ready and eager to enjoy round two.

How the hell had he ever thought he might be losing his sex drive?

Right now he was certain he could spend the next few months in this bed doing nothing but making love to Mia.

"You make it sound so easy," she said.

"No." He grimaced. "It wasn't easy."

"Does it still bother you?" she asked.

He pressed his lips to the top of her curls. He didn't resent her questions. Not like he usually did.

She was asking because she was genuinely concerned, not out of some morbid curiosity.

"I have nightmares," he readily admitted. She needed to know since she was going to be sharing his bed. "And there are times when a small space can make me panic. But I'm far luckier than many others who served."

With a low sound of distress, Mia lowered her head to press a kiss against his shoulder. "Thank God it's over."

"Let's hope," he muttered, growingly distracted.

How was a man supposed to think when his skin felt branded by her soft kiss and her fingers continued to create chaos as they trailed a path of fire down to the tense muscles of his stomach?

"Why do you say that?" she demanded.

"I'm afraid there's something from Hauk's past that's haunting him," he said, his lips brushing over her forehead to linger against the soft skin of her temple.

"I know the feeling," she muttered.

Lucas rolled onto his back, using the arm he had wrapped around her waist to tug her on top of him. Instinctively her legs draped on each side of his hips, arranging her pelvis to rest with sheer perfection against the hard ridge of his erection.

"We're going to figure this out, Mia," he murmured in low tones.

Her hands pressed against his chest as she gazed down at him with darkened eyes.

"How?" she demanded.

One hand lifted to push the thick curls over her shoulder, allowing him an uninterrupted view of her face. His heart clenched as he took in the wide, velvet eyes that were so heavily fringed she never needed to paste on fake lashes. The slender nose. The full, utterly kissable lips.

He'd lost this woman once.

There was no way in hell he was going to lose her again.

"My friends are very good at what they do," he assured her, his palm cupping her cheek. "It doesn't matter how deeply Tony tried to bury his secrets, they'll find them."

Something eased deep inside him as she gave a hesitant nod. She might not be ready to forgive and forget his betrayal, but she was learning to trust him.

That meant as much as her eager response to his kisses.

He didn't just want her in his bed.

He wanted her at his side, planning a future together.

Clearly incapable of reading his mind, she cleared her throat, futilely attempting to look nonchalant.

"You said it'd been a while."

His lips twitched. He was getting to her. Slowly but surely.

"A while?"

"Since you'd . . ." A charming blush touched her cheeks as she struggled for the words.

"Made love?" he helpfully offered.

Abruptly realizing she was giving away just how vulnerable she was, Mia gave a sharp shake of her head.

"Forget it."

"I'm sorry, Mia," he said, grabbing her hips when she would have pulled away. "The truth is that when I left Shreveport I thought I could make myself forget about you. And I tried." He held her gaze, allowing her to see his regret. "But since I returned from the Middle East I haven't been interested in sharing my bed. To be honest, there were times when I worried that my libido had been destroyed in that Afghan hellhole." Slowly he skimmed his hands up her rib cage until he could cup the lush softness of her breasts. He swallowed a moan as the pink nipples instantly hardened into tiny buds of invitation. "Thankfully I have been utterly reassured there is nothing at all wrong with me." He strummed his thumbs over her nipples, smiling at her throaty groan. "It wasn't that I didn't want a woman. I simply was waiting for the *right* woman."

An emotion that might have been fear rippled over her face before she was deliberately forcing a smile to her lips.

"It's no wonder you were supposed to become a diplomat," she teased. "You always know the perfect thing to say."

Lucas narrowed his gaze. *Oh, hell no.* He wasn't going to let her dismiss his words as if they were empty platitudes.

"I mean what I say, Mia," he warned. "This isn't just sex."

Her brows drew together. "Lucas."

"It's messy and complicated and—"

His words were cut short when she suddenly leaned forward to kiss him with a fierce need.

"Shut up, Lucas," she muttered against his lips.

Heat blasted through him, making it impossible to think. Later he would convince her that this was only the beginning of a very long life together.

For now, he was much more interested in getting his aching cock buried deep inside her.

"And you call me bossy?" he teased.

She nipped his bottom lip. "You have better things to do with that mouth."

With a low chuckle he flipped her flat on her back, kissing his way down her shivering body.

"I do indeed."

# Chapter Twelve

Taylor stood just outside the diner, staring through the large window.

She didn't need the flutters in the pit of her stomach to tell her that this was a very bad idea. Or the realization that she'd been standing on the street staring at the man with dark blond hair and the clean-cut features that had haunted her dreams.

But when she'd awakened early that morning, she'd suddenly recalled the last time that she'd seen Tony. Still groggy from sleep, she'd reached for the card that Detective Cooper had left on her desk and dialed his number.

Now she had to wonder if the urgency to see him had more to do with helping to discover who murdered Tony, or a personal desire to spend time in his company.

Shivering as the early morning wind tugged at her coat, she forced herself to pull open the door and step into the welcomed warmth. It would no doubt be wiser to turn around and walk away. But she'd been the one to set up the meeting. It would be rude to drag the man out of bed at the crack of dawn and then not even bother to show up.

Right?

Crossing the linoleum floor, she weaved her way past

the surprising crowd that already filled the diner. The place might look like a dive, but it obviously had the sort of food that attracted a large number of repeat customers.

Or maybe it was just its proximity to the sheriff station house, she wryly acknowledged, belatedly noticing the large number of people in uniforms.

Reaching the table in back, she watched as Detective Cooper rose to his feet and circled the table. He was dressed in a pair of black pants and a white shirt that Taylor itched to properly starch and iron.

Not that the wrinkles distracted from his quiet good looks.

"Good morning, Taylor," he murmured, politely pulling out a chair and waiting for her to take a seat.

"Detective," she murmured.

Holding on to the back of her chair, the lawman leaned down to speak softly in her ear. "Brian."

A shiver of pleasure raced through her. "Excuse me?"

"My name is Brian," he insisted in low tones.

"Okay," she breathed, another delicious shiver making her back arch with an excitement she'd almost forgotten existed.

His fingers brushed over her shoulders, tugging off the leather jacket she'd pulled over her favorite jade sweater and faded jeans that her mother said were too tight to be worn in public.

"Thank you."

She felt a blush touch her cheeks as he carefully folded her jacket and set it on an empty chair before he returned to take his seat. She'd pulled her clothes on without really thinking about what she was doing. Now she realized that she'd dressed as if this was a date.

And it wasn't. It absolutely, positively wasn't.

Studying her with an unreadable expression, Brian leaned his arms on the table. "Where's your son this morning?"

She licked her lips. Why were they so dry?

"He has a part-time job stocking shelves at the local grocery store. He usually works all day on Saturday when he doesn't have practice or homework."

Brian slowly smiled. "Good."

She blinked in confusion. "I think so, but why do you?"

"It means we don't have to rush through breakfast," he said with unhidden satisfaction.

Her blush deepened. Dammit. This was ridiculous.

"I just want coffee."

"Have you already eaten?"

"No, but—"

She forgot how to speak as he reached across the table to touch her hand.

"You have to try the grillades and grits. They make them with slices of pork in tomato sauce. It's the best in town."

So that's what smelled so good. Taylor's mouth watered. Still, she tried to pretend that she was only there out of a sense of civic duty.

"I'm really not that hungry."

He gave her fingers a small squeeze. "Indulge me. I get tired of eating alone."

Her heart lurched. Although she had her son and mother, she understood being lonely.

"You're not married?"

"Nope." With a last squeeze of her fingers he sat back in his seat, thankfully acting as if he was unaware that she was blatantly fishing for his relationship status. "Not now, not ever."

"A confirmed bachelor?" she asked.

"Not by choice," he instantly informed her. "I've always wanted a wife and family."

Her heart missed a beat. Was he serious?

"Really?"

He held her gaze. "It's true. Unfortunately not many women want a husband who is a detective."

"I can't imagine why not," she said before she could halt the words.

They were true, after all.

This was the sort of man whom women wanted in their lives after they'd gotten over the whole "bad boy" phase.

"My hours are crappy. My pay is even crappier." He shared a teasing grin. "It might help if I looked like Charlie Hunnam, but I'm not delusional enough to think that's ever going to happen."

Once again her words slipped out before she could halt them. "A woman who loved you wouldn't care about any of those things."

Their gazes tangled, the noisy diner briefly fading away as a dangerous awareness pulsed between them.

"You give me hope," he said, a fierce intensity in the words.

Taylor instinctively scuttled back behind her safe, emotional shields. Hope was a dangerous, dangerous temptation that she couldn't afford.

"I suppose you're wondering why I called," she said in firm tones.

"I'm just glad you did." Brian continued to hold her wary gaze until he turned to smile at the approaching waitress. "Two of your specials and another coffee," he ordered.

Taylor rolled her eyes. "You don't listen very well for a cop."

He shrugged. "Another failing, I'm afraid."

A part of her wanted to be annoyed. She wasn't the sort of woman who needed a man to tell her what she should or shouldn't want.

In fact, her independence had run off more than one date by the end of the night. That and the fact she had a teenage son and dependent mother waiting for her at home.

She swallowed a sigh.

"Do you want to know why I wanted to get together or not?" she demanded.

He sipped his coffee. "Tell me."

Laying her palms flat against the table, Taylor silently organized her scattered thoughts before she spoke. Her awkward flirtations with this man might be meaningless, but she was dead serious about keeping Mia safe.

"I've been trying to remember anything that struck me as odd about Tony."

Brian was instantly all business. "You thought of something?"

She wrinkled her nose, understanding that it was a long shot.

"It's probably nothing, but I stopped by his condo after Mia fired him," she said.

"Was there a particular reason?"

"I delivered his last paycheck so he wouldn't have a reason to come back to the office." She grimaced. "Mia felt awful that she had to tell him he couldn't work for her anymore. They'd been friends since they were both in grade school." She accepted the cup of coffee the distracted waitress set in front of her before hurrying off to another table. "I didn't want him to pester her."

Brian studied her with an odd expression. "Does she know how lucky she is to have you working for her?"

"She's not just my employer. She's my friend."

"We should all have a friend like you."

Warmth spread through her heart as she poured a dollop of cream into her coffee. Did he sense how much pride she took in caring for those people she considered her family?

The thought made her feel strangely vulnerable.

"Anyway, when I arrived at Tony's place he was already drunk as a skunk," she continued in a gruff voice.

She thought she heard him heave a faint sigh, but he didn't press her.

"From what I've heard about Anthony Hughes that wasn't all that unusual," he said.

"No," she agreed. "I don't think Tony was an alcoholic, but he definitely used drugs and booze to self-medicate."

"What happened?"

Taylor absently sipped her coffee, her mind drifting back to the brief confrontation.

"I wasn't nearly as close to Tony as Mia was, but I felt sorry for him," she said, giving a shake of her head. "When he opened the door he looked like he hadn't slept in days. His eyes were bloodshot and his skin was a weird shade of gray, and to be honest, I don't think he'd had a bath in days." She gave a small shudder. "I asked him if there was anything I could do to help."

"What did he say?"

"He asked me if I had a time machine."

Brian arched a brow. "Time machine?"

Taylor had been equally baffled by the strange words.

"I assumed he wanted to go back in the past so he could make sure he didn't get caught with weed in Mia's truck."

"Did he say anything else?"

She nodded. The words had returned to her at five o'clock in the morning, waking her from a restless dream.

"He said the body refused to stay buried."

Brian stilled, his attention fully captured. "What body?"

"I asked him and he started to babble about vipers in his bed." She lifted her hands. "I assumed he was too drunk to know what he was saying, so I left."

"A body that won't stay buried and the desire to change the past," Brian murmured, his expression distracted.

"It's probably meaningless." Taylor wrinkled her nose, more than a little afraid she was making a mountain out of a molehill. Tony had said a lot of stupid things when he was drunk. "But I thought you should know," she muttered lamely.

Brian leaned forward, a smile that could melt the Arctic curling the edge of his lips. "I'm glad you came to me, Taylor."

Her heart skipped, abruptly reminding her of the danger of spending more time with this man.

"I should be going, I—"

Her words came to an abrupt end as he reached across the table to grab her hand.

"Stay, Taylor," he said in low tones. "Please."


Lucas stomped out of the house, barely noticing the sharp chill that edged the early morning breeze. He should be feeling on top of the world. After fifteen long years, he at last had Mia back where she belonged.

In his bed.

What could be better?

But instead of waking to find Mia snuggled in his arms so they could celebrate their reunion with a few hours of slow, delectable lovemaking, he'd opened his eyes to find himself alone.

Hearing running water, he'd put aside his disappointment and headed out of the bedroom. He wasn't opposed to starting the day by sharing a shower with Mia. In fact, the mere idea of their wet, naked bodies pressed together as the hot steam filled the room was enough to make him so hard he hoped he wouldn't embarrass himself.

But even as he was wondering how long it would take to get Mia ready, he turned the doorknob only to discover it wouldn't budge.

Mia had locked him out.

Frowning in disbelief, he'd rapped his knuckles on the door, not entirely surprised when Mia ignored his knocking.

For a crazed minute he'd actually considered kicking down the door. Not because he was angry. Okay. He was a little angry. But because he couldn't bear the knowledge she was once again trying to put walls between them.

Dammit.

Thankfully the sound of his phone buzzing managed to distract him long enough to regain command of his senses. Mia obviously didn't want him to join her.

He would only push her further away if he forced his way into her private space, he grimly told himself.

So instead he walked back into the bedroom and pulled on a pair of jeans and a cream cable-knit sweater. Then, shoving his feet into a pair of leather loafers, he headed out of the house.

Max was waiting in his silver SUV, which was parked in the driveway. Climbing into the warmth of the vehicle, Lucas glowered at his friend's freshly shaved face and hair that was still damp from his shower. He looked well-rested and as fresh as a fucking daisy.

"Morning, sunshine," the younger man murmured, his lips twitching at the dark whiskers that shadowed Lucas's jaw and his dark hair that he hadn't bothered to comb.

"This had better be good," Lucas warned.

"You're a little testy," Max teased. "Do you want to talk about it?"

Lucas narrowed his gaze. When did his friend develop a death wish?

"Do you want your face rearranged?" he asked.

Max chuckled. "Easy, amigo." He shifted in his seat to study Lucas's tense expression. "Is there anything I can do?"

Belatedly realizing that he was taking out his frustration on his friend, he gave a shake of his head.

"No. It's going to take patience. Something I have in short supply." With an effort he forced himself to concentrate on the reason Max had texted him. A task that would be easier if he didn't keep visualizing a warm, wet, naked Mia standing in the shower. "What did Teagan find?"

"He did a background check on Carl Greene."

It took a minute for Lucas to connect the name to the next-door neighbor.

"And?"

Max glanced toward the small house that was only a few feet from Mia's.

"Greene worked on the docks loading and unloading barges until he was injured on the job," he said. "Since then he's been collecting disability."

"No criminal record?"

Max turned his attention back to Lucas. "Nothing that stuck."

"He was suspected of a crime?"

"His girlfriend claimed that he tried to run her over with his car." Max shrugged. "Nothing was proven and she dropped the charges before it was ever investigated."

Lucas gave a low whistle. Was it just a coincidence that someone had tried to run Mia off the road?

It was difficult to imagine what the man could hope to gain by hurting Mia. Maybe she'd shot down his advances. Or maybe he was just a garden-variety psycho who liked hurting women.

It was worth finding out.

"Anything else?" he asked.

Max grimaced. "Over the years, more than one neighbor has complained that he's a creeper who likes to watch pretty women. Unfortunately, as long as he stays on his own property that isn't a crime."

The mere thought of the man peeking at Mia made Lucas's gut twist with fury. "It might not be a crime, but I'm sure I can convince him that it's a habit that's bad for his health," he said in dark tones.

"True." Max allowed a humorless smile to curve his lips. "And if he doesn't get the message the first time, I'd be happy to do my own convincing."

The men shared a glance of mutual understanding. They were born protectors who wouldn't hesitate to punish a pervert who was bothering an innocent woman.

Lucas made a mental note to visit Carl Greene before the day was over.

"Is that all?"

"The Houston PD is still waiting on the official autopsy, but Teagan managed to hack into the inventory that listed Tony's belongings when he was shot."

For once Lucas didn't consider the risk his friend had taken. Teagan was going to do what the hell he wanted to do.

Besides, Lucas would willingly break any law if it kept Mia safe.

"Was there anything interesting?"

"Beyond his clothing he had a wallet that had almost fifty dollars in cash," Max revealed.

Lucas frowned. "So this wasn't a robbery."

"It doesn't look like it," Max agreed. "Although there weren't any credit cards."

"Hard to believe a mugger would take the cards and leave the cash," Lucas muttered.

Max grimaced. "I agree."

"Any drugs?"

Max shook his head. "Nope. Not even a joint."

"Weapons?"

"A small pocketknife."

"Anything else?"

Max gave a lift of his shoulders. "Keys to his truck, the paper with your name and address, and the picture of your woman."

"Shit." Lucas balled his hands into tight fists. When he'd gotten Max's text he'd allowed himself to hope that there would be a break in the case. Now frustration twisted his guts into a tight knot. "There's nothing that can help tell us who killed him."

"Actually it's what was missing that caught Teagan's attention," Max told him.

"The credit cards?" Lucas wasn't impressed. Tony Hughes came from a family who had probably never qualified for credit. Whether it was cards or a bank loan. "Not everyone carries them."

"No." Max deliberately paused. Like some damned drama queen. "His cell phone."

*Ah.* Now Lucas understood Teagan's interest. Tony might not have credit cards, but he damned sure had a cell phone.

"Maybe he left it in his truck," he suggested.

"It wasn't listed in the inventory," Max said.

Lucas tried to consider the various possibilities. He quickly decided there weren't a lot of them.

"So either he was shot and someone stole his cell, or he gave it to someone before he was shot," he concluded.

"That's the theory," Max agreed. "Teagan decided to do some poking around to see if he could find out if Tony had a phone and where it is now."

Lucas smiled. "Remind me to give Teagan a pat on the back when we return to Houston."

Max snorted. "Teagan will expect a twelve-pack of his favorite beer and a weekend at your parents' home in Saint-Tropez."

Lucas released a sharp laugh. The thought of releasing Teagan on the hapless citizens of Saint-Tropez was an image he was going to savor.

Then, with a shake of his head, he met Max's amused gaze. "Did he find the phone?"

Max shook his head. "Turns out Tony didn't have a landline or a contract for a cell phone. Which means he probably used a burner."

Another dead end. Lucas released a hiss between his clenched teeth. He wanted to punch something. Really, really hard.

*Dammit, Tony, what were you into?*

"Shit," he growled.

"That's exactly what Teagan said," Max said in dry tones.

"Tony clearly didn't want anyone able to trace who he was talking to," he muttered. "It has to be drugs."

"It gets better." Max turned to the side, reaching into the backseat to grab a stack of papers. With a flick of his wrist he tossed them into Lucas's lap.

"What's this?" Lucas automatically straightened the papers, skimming through the bank balances, tax returns, and car loans.

"Teagan had them scanned and e-mailed to my computer at the hotel," Max explained.

Lucas lifted his head to send his companion a puzzled frown. "I assume these are Tony's financials?"

"Yeah." Max reached over to pull out one of the sheets of paper. "Check out his rental payments."

Lucas studied the neatly typed receipts that were signed by the manager of his condo.

"He paid in cash." Growingly convinced that Tony was more heavily involved in the drug trade than anyone had ever suspected, Lucas pulled out his phone. He wanted to talk to Hauk. The older man was creating an extensive list of shady contacts who were willing to trade information for money, or occasionally for a favor.

Before he could complete the call, however, Max reached out to grab his arm in a punishing grip.

"Lucas."

Lucas jerked his head up, his senses on full alert. "What?"

"Look." Max nodded toward the black SUV that was pulling out of the narrow alley and shooting into the street with a squeal of its tires.

What the hell? Had the SUV come from the empty field behind Mia's house?

Lucas's heart squeezed with sudden fear.

"Try to follow it," he ordered his friend, pushing open his door and leaping out of the vehicle that Max had already shoved into reverse. "I'm going the check on Mia."

# Chapter Thirteen

Something was wrong.

Terribly, horribly wrong.

Mia blinked, her coffee mug dropping from her suddenly lifeless fingers.

It'd come on without warning. One minute she was leaning against the kitchen counter and feeling fine, and the next her mouth was dry and her head so fuzzy she could barely form a coherent thought.

Was she having a seizure? Or worse, was it a stroke?

Struggling to stay upright, she stumbled into the living room. Where was Lucas? She'd peeked into the bedroom after her shower to discover the bed empty. She assumed he would be in the kitchen, but he hadn't been there either.

Had he left?

Not that she would blame him.

Still, she needed to find her phone. Whatever was wrong with her wasn't going to go away on its own. She needed a doctor.

Managing to reach the middle of the room, she struggled to clear her vision. The sofa was no more than a blurry smudge. She turned, holding out her hands as she tried to find the wall. She could use it to lead her around the room to the side table where she'd left her phone.

And hopefully it would help keep her from falling on her face.

Trying not to panic, she inched her way to the side. She'd taken less than two steps when she heard the sound of the door opening and her name being called.

*Oh, thank God. Lucas.*

Turning toward the door, she tried to answer but her tongue wouldn't work. Instead her knees gave way and she found herself tumbling forward.

*Crap.* With a heavy thud she hit the floor, for once thankful for the thick carpeting she'd promised herself she would replace once she'd saved up the money. It might be butt-ugly, but it kept her from cracking open her head.

She felt gentle hands grabbing her shoulders to turn her onto her back.

"Mia."

A dark shadow fell over her. Lucas. But his face remained obscured by a darkening mist.

"What happened? Are you hurt?"

She tried to swallow. "Tongue," she managed to slur.

His hands moved to smooth her tangled hair from her face, his touch unbearably tender.

"You hurt your tongue?"

She released a sigh. It was too hard to explain. In fact, it was too hard to even keep her eyes open, so she let them slide shut.

Lucas was here now. He would take care of her.

She trusted that knowledge with every fiber of her being.

"Tired," she breathed. "So tired."

"Shit, Mia." He gave her a small shake. "Stay with me."

She moaned. Why wouldn't he let her sleep? "I . . . can't."

He gave her another shake, this one even more rough. "Look at me," he snapped. "Mia, look at me."

*Damn.* He wasn't going to leave her alone until she obeyed his command.

Fiercely concentrating, she managed to force her eyes open a small slit.

"Lucas."

He leaned down until they were nose to nose. "Did you eat something?"

Had she? It seemed a ridiculous question, but she tried to remember.

She'd gotten out of bed. She felt a pang of regret. That'd been her first bad decision. If she'd simply stayed in Lucas's arms they might be making glorious love instead of her being near comatose on her ugly carpet. Then what had she done? Oh yeah, she'd gone into the kitchen to turn on the coffeemaker, but she hadn't eaten anything, had she? No. She'd gone into the bathroom and locked the door. Her second bad decision. She should have left the door open so Lucas could join her in the soapy spray of the shower. . . .

"Mia." He sharply intruded into her ambling thoughts. "Did you eat?"

"No." The word was so low it was a miracle he heard her.

"What about something to drink?" he insisted. "Water? Juice? Coffee?"

*Ah.* This question was easy. "Coffee."

There was the sound of another male voice as the door slammed. "I lost the damned—" Footsteps pounded across the carpet. "What happened?"

Mia felt strong arms scooping her off the floor.

"Call Detective Cooper and get him over here," Lucas commanded as he straightened, keeping Mia cradled close to his chest.

"What about you?" the other male voice asked.

Who was it? Max? Yes, that was his name. Max.

"I'll take her to the hospital," Lucas said even as Mia felt herself being carried across the room.

"You should call for an ambulance," Max said, walking beside them.

There was the squeak of the door opening.

"I'll be faster," Lucas said, his voice not quite steady.

He sounded so . . . worried. Strange. No one ever worried about her. Certainly not her father.

Mia tried to tell him that she was going to be fine. How could anything bad happen when she was in Lucas's arms?

But her mouth refused to open. She was going under. She could feel the darkness rising like a tidal wave. And this time there would be no fighting.

She must have made some small sound of distress. His arms tightened and she felt the brush of his lips against her forehead.

"Shh. I've got you, Mia," he murmured in a soft voice. "And I'm not letting go."

Lucas would have sworn that there could be nothing worse than his days in the Taliban prison.

The heat. The stench. The pain. The relentless, gnawing fear.

But pacing outside the doors of the emergency room had taught him that there was more than one sort of torture.

At least it hadn't taken long for them to cleanse her of the toxins that were making her sick. Within an hour she was in a private room with a nurse whom Lucas had hired to watch over her 24/7.

Nothing was going to happen to her on his watch.

Not again.

Seated beside the bed, Lucas did his best to ignore the various machines that were hooked into her fragile body and concentrated on the steady rise and fall of her chest.

There was no point in brooding on the knowledge that he'd failed her.

She was alive. And the doctors assured him she would be fine. And eventually he would track down the person responsible and rip them into tiny, painful shreds.

Later he would worry about the nightmares that were sure to haunt him.

Almost on cue Mia stirred and slowly opened her eyes. Lucas leaned forward, the invisible bands around his chest easing as he met her sleepy gaze.

She was still dazed, but her color was good and she instantly recognized him.

"Lucas," she breathed.

"I'm here," he assured her. "How do you feel?"

She wrinkled her nose. "Thirsty."

The nurse bustled forward to pour a glass of water, but before she could reach the bed, Lucas was taking it from her.

He needed to be the one giving Mia comfort.

"Here," he murmured, sliding an arm beneath her shoulder to lift her off the mattress as he pressed the cup to her lips.

Taking several small sips, she pulled back her head to indicate she was done. Lucas handed the cup to the nurse and gently settled Mia back on the narrow mattress. Then, perching on the edge of his seat, he studied her with a worried frown.

"Better?"

She reached to grasp his hand, clinging to him as if he were a lifeline. Savage pleasure jolted through him at the feel of her tight grip.

Was she aware of what she was doing?

Or was it sheer instinct?

Both possibilities pleased him.

"Where am I?" she asked, her voice husky but strong.

"The hospital."

She was silent for a long moment, her brow furrowed.

"Did I have a seizure?" she at last demanded.

Lucas hesitated. His first instinct was to protect her from

the truth. She was weak, and the last thing he wanted was to frighten her. But he logically understood that was only putting her in more danger.

Mia needed to know what had happened so she could protect herself.

Or better yet, let him protect her.

"You were poisoned," Lucas at last admitted.

She looked confused. "Food poisoning?"

"No, it was deliberate."

The monitors beeped as she struggled to sit upright. "Are you serious?"

The nurse hurried forward, pressing the button on the controller that lifted the top of the bed so Mia could lean back and still hold Lucas's steady gaze.

He squeezed Mia's fingers, wondering how long it was going to take before the doctor released her. He needed to have her home so he could hold her tight in his arms. And more importantly, he wanted her somewhere he could control the environment.

She was way too exposed in this hospital room.

"Trust me, I would never joke about you being hurt," he rasped.

She gave a slow, disbelieving shake of her head. "How?"

"I'm assuming it was the coffee," he said. "You said that was the only thing you'd had this morning."

"It was the coffee," Max said as he stepped into the room. Although the younger man was immaculately dressed in gray slacks and a cashmere sweater, his blond hair was ruffled as if he'd been running his fingers through it, and his expression was grim. "Or at least that's the preliminary report."

Lucas rose to his feet. "I'll be back," he assured Mia.

She tightened her grip on his fingers.

"No. Someone tried to hurt me," she reminded him. "I need to know what's going on."

She was right. Lucas might not like it, but she needed to be included in the investigation.

"Have you talked to the detective?" he asked Max.

"Briefly." Max looked disgusted. "He's not giving much away."

No big surprise. The authorities didn't like people butting in to their cases. Even people who clearly had the talent and the resources to help.

"But you're sure it was the coffee?" Lucas pressed.

Max nodded. "I took a few specimens before the cops arrived. I tried to make sure I swabbed most of the obvious things she might have eaten or drank."

"I didn't have anything but the coffee," Mia insisted.

"Some poisons can take several hours to work," Max pointed out in quiet tones.

Mia shuddered. "Oh."

Standing close to the bed, Lucas laid a protective hand on her tense shoulder. Her attention, however, was focused on Max.

"And you already have the results?"

"I used my contacts to find a local lab," he said, sending Lucas a wry glance. "And dropped your name to make sure they understood it was a priority."

Which meant that he would be expected to repay the favor at some point. Not that he cared. He'd give every penny in his trust fund to discover who was trying to hurt Mia.

"What did they find?" he asked. The emergency room doctor had refused to discuss Mia's medical condition, claiming that Lucas wasn't family.

Of course, he'd given Lucas a long lecture on how Mia would physically recover in a matter of hours since she was treated so quickly after swallowing the pills, but that her mental stability would be delicate for weeks, so he'd already concluded that she'd overdosed on prescription drugs.

He didn't try to correct the doctor. Detective Cooper

would eventually arrive and everyone would know that someone had tried to kill her.

Until then Lucas didn't want to attract unwanted attention.

"A concoction of painkillers and antidepressants," Max revealed, giving a shake of his head as Lucas parted his lips to demand if there was a way to trace them to a source. "All of them are easily prescribed and could have been bought on the streets or a hundred other places."

It was more or less what Lucas had expected, but that didn't keep him from muttering a curse of frustration. It was Mia who asked the obvious question.

"But how did they get into the coffee?"

Lucas frowned, trying to picture her kitchen. "I didn't notice—do you have a coffeemaker with a timer?" he demanded.

She gave a careful shake of her head. "No, it's just a cheap one I picked up at the thrift store," she answered. "Usually I wait to have coffee once I get to the office. I only make it at home on the weekends."

Max leaned against the doorjamb, studying Mia with a focused intensity. "Walk me through your morning," he commanded.

"I got up . . ." Her words briefly faltered, a blush staining her cheeks as she no doubt realized that Max was well aware she'd shared her bed with Lucas. She cleared her throat. "And then I took a shower."

Max offered an astonishingly gentle smile and Lucas realized his friend wasn't just doing this for him. Max was determined to find the killer because he genuinely liked Mia.

The knowledge warmed his heart.

The men of ARES had become his family. It was important that they accept the woman he intended to keep in his life.

"Did you make the coffee before or after your shower?" he pressed.

Mia hesitated, as if trying to remember her movements during the morning.

"I started it and then went into the bathroom," she at last said.

Max glanced toward Lucas. "The coffee was already brewing when you left the house?"

Lucas gave a decisive nod. He distinctly recalled the scent of coffee filling the air as he walked out the front door.

"Yeah."

"So." Max studied Lucas. "The time that someone could have put the pills into the pot was after you left the house, until Mia got out of the shower." He folded his arms over his chest. "That's a short window of opportunity."

Lucas frowned. Unless the intruder managed to sneak in while he was still in bed, he would have had less than ten minutes to get in the house, poison the coffee, and get away.

He glanced toward Mia. "Was the back door locked?"

"Yes . . ." Mia's words trailed away as she suddenly bit her bottom lip.

Lucas studied her tense face. "What is it, Mia?"

"I lost my keys a few weeks ago," she admitted, tilting her head to meet his worried gaze. "Or at least I assumed that I lost them."

"Someone could have stolen them?"

"Yes."

There was a sudden movement near the door. Lucas stiffened even as Max subtly shifted to block the man's path into the room.

Neither man had been allowed to carry a gun into the hospital, but that didn't mean they weren't without weapons. Both of them were fully trained to kill with their hands.

The tall man in a white coat came to a startled halt, his expression wary even as he pointed toward Mia.

"I need to check on my patient."

Lucas gave a jerk of his head, and with a slow step Max moved out of the way. As the doctor approached, however, Lucas glanced toward the nurse he'd hired and she moved to stand next to the bed. He wasn't leaving Mia alone with anyone he hadn't fully vetted.

Once assured the woman would keep a careful eye on the doctor, Lucas turned his attention to Mia.

"I'll be back," he assured her in low tones. Fear flashed through her eyes. He bent down to brush his lips over her forehead. "Trust me," he murmured.

He waited for her small nod before he turned and forced himself to leave the room with Max.

*God.* The sight of Mia's fragile vulnerability made his gut twist with fury.

It was one thing for her to be told someone might want her dead. It was another to actually know someone snuck into her house and filled her coffee with pills that were intended to kill her.

The intruder stole something precious from her. . . .

A sense of comfort in her own home.

The mystery person was going to pay for that. Hopefully in blood.

Moving across the hall, Lucas leaned against the wall where he could still see into the room, although the doctor had pulled a curtain around the bed.

"Are you okay?" Max demanded, standing close enough that no one could overhear their conversation.

Lucas shuddered. "No," he admitted with blunt honesty. "Christ, if I hadn't gone back inside . . ." He allowed his words to trail away, unable to allow the image of Mia lying dead on the floor to stain his mind.

It was unthinkable.

"I'm more worried about what would have happened if

you hadn't been with me," Max said, his expression grim. "The poison was clearly intended for both of you."

Lucas frowned. The killer might have been willing to poison both of them, but he was no more than collateral damage. It was Mia the mysterious stalker wanted dead.

And the bastard was obviously willing to go to crazy lengths to get the job done.

"It was bold," he muttered, wondering how many people had the nerve to break into a house in broad daylight.

"And sloppy," Max added.

Lucas glanced at his friend in confusion. "What do you mean 'sloppy'?"

Max folded his arms over his chest. "If you wanted to kill someone, would you crush up a bunch of pills and hope you could find something to toss them into?" he asked, his tone edged with disgust. "There was no way whoever did this could be certain that Mia or you would drink enough to do any serious damage."

"If I hadn't been there Mia might have died," he snapped.

Max shrugged. "Luck."

"Luck?" Lucas clenched his hands. He would never forget the feeling of helpless terror as he watched Mia tumble to the floor.

Max grimaced, no doubt sensing Lucas's distress, but he refused to back down.

"Think about it for a minute, Lucas."

"Think about what?"

Max held up one finger. "Tony was shot at close range in the middle of the street where the killer might easily have been caught on camera." He raised another finger. "If you're right about the first attempt on Mia's life, it was a bungled attempt to run her off the road. Something that had only a small chance of actually killing her." He raised a third finger. "And now a crazy scheme to poison her. It all seems so"—he gave a frustrated shake of his head—"amateurish."

Lucas made a sound of impatience. "Most murders are done by amateurs," he said.

Max shrugged aside his logic. "But this isn't the usual pissed-off neighbor, or gangbanger, or a botched robbery. If you want someone dead you usually take a little time to make a plan." He paused, as if debating his words. "This seems impulsive."

Lucas considered a long minute, forcing himself to put aside his anger and fear to actually contemplate the facts.

Max was right. Killing Tony on the street was either outrageously daring or downright rash. And the attempts on Mia's life spoke of a person who was frantic enough to risk being spotted.

So what could cause someone to be so desperate?

He stiffened as the answer came to him. "Or rushed," he breathed.

Max arched his brows before he gave a slow nod of his head. "Yes. A time limit. That makes sense."

The two men stared at each other, both silently shuffling through the various reasons Mia would have to be dead by a certain date. At last Lucas gave a shake of his head.

*Dammit.* They needed more information. Right now they were making wild assumptions that had no basis in fact.

"It still comes back to a connection between Tony and Mia," he said. It was the only thing they knew for certain.

Max hesitated, then, heaving a sigh, he shoved his fingers through his short hair. "You're not going to be happy with this question, but do you know if Mia has a will?"

Lucas clenched his teeth, holding back his urge to punch his friend in the face. Max was right. They needed to know if anyone benefited directly from Mia's death.

"No."

Max reached out to lay his hand on his shoulder. "You should find out."

Lucas parted his lips to agree, abruptly distracted by a

flash of movement as someone stepped into the hallway, only to turn and walk in the opposite direction.

"Damn," Lucas muttered, recognizing the tall, thin woman with suspiciously blond hair that she kept twisted into a fancy knot at the back of her head.

Vicky Fontaine.

Max gave his shoulder a squeeze. "Is something wrong?"

"Keep a watch on the door," he commanded. It didn't matter whether or not he had a nurse standing next to Mia. He wanted one of his brothers standing guard. "No one gets in or out unless they have a hospital ID."

"Where are you going?"

"To talk to an old friend," he muttered, shrugging off Max's grasp to jog down the hallway. Still, the woman he was chasing had nearly reached the elevators by the time he caught her. "Mrs. Fontaine."

The woman, who was wearing a dress that no doubt cost more than most people made in a month, slowly turned, revealing that she had changed remarkably little in the past fifteen years.

Her long, thin face had a few more wrinkles than the last time he'd seen her, and he'd bet his considerable fortune she'd had work done on her nose, but she still looked a decade younger than her fifty-plus years.

She might have been beautiful if it hadn't been for the gray eyes that were as hard as granite and the too-thin body that always made Lucas think of a praying mantis. He liked his woman warm and lush and filled with life.

The stray thought made Lucas recall the sight of Mia lying so pale in her hospital bed. Fury stabbed through him, even as he pasted a polite smile on his lips.

It was doubtful this woman would be involved in attempted murder, but for now everyone was a suspect.

"Can I help you?" The older woman widened her eyes as she belatedly recognized him. "Lucas St. Clair?"

"It's been a long time," he murmured.

She allowed her gaze to take in his unshaven face and hair that was tangled from the times he'd shoved his fingers through it.

"I didn't know you were back in town," she said. "Are your parents home?"

His smile never faltered despite the subtle dig. The woman had to know that his relationship with his family was strained.

Was she deliberately trying to annoy him or just being a bitch?

"No. They're still in Saint-Tropez."

"Ah." She peered down the length of her long nose. "Is there something you need?"

He managed to keep his smile intact. "I hope you aren't visiting a family member."

"No." She gave an elegant lift of one shoulder. "I'm on the board of directors for the hospital. I'm expected to make an occasional appearance."

"Of course," he murmured.

It was a perfectly legitimate reason for being there. And Lucas couldn't detect anything in her demeanor that would make him suspect that she had any other reason to visit the hospital.

Still, he wasn't done with his questions.

"If that's all," she murmured, her lips flattening with annoyance when he smoothly stepped between her and the elevators.

"I spoke to your lawyer yesterday."

She arched a perfectly groomed brow. "Why would you speak with my lawyer?"

"He was trying to pressure Mia Ramon to sell her father's land."

He carefully watched her expression, but it gave nothing away. Botox? Or simply nothing to hide?

"What business is it of yours?" she demanded.

"Mia asked me to handle her inheritance for her," he easily lied.

There was the briefest hesitation before Vicky responded. "I see."

"Can I ask what you want with the land?"

She lifted a thin hand that was shimmering with diamonds, including the outrageously large engagement ring that Paul had given her.

The husband was gone, but she wasn't about to toss away the pretty baubles he'd bought her. Not that Lucas blamed her. Paul Fontaine had always been a womanizing lowlife. She might as well get something out of her lousy marriage.

"I intend to clean it up so it can be turned into a protected wetlands," she said.

Lucas didn't bother to hide his disbelief. "Wetlands?"

She shrugged. "I'm told they're endangered."

"Philanthropy, Mrs. Fontaine?" he drawled.

A cunning glint entered the gray eyes. "You know how people like us enjoy having our names attached to good works," she said. "My grandfather built a library. My father added a wing on this hospital, and I'll have a nationally registered park."

Once again her words made perfect sense. Did he believe her?

Lucas wasn't sure.

Certainly his own parents gave obscene amounts of money to make sure their name was attached to fountains, gardens, buildings, and at least one petting zoo.

He'd have Teagan do some digging. He could at least discover if it was feasible to turn Mia's property into protected wetlands.

"Impressive," he assured her.

She glanced at the watch strapped around her thin wrist. "Now I really must go."

This time there was no stopping her as the elevator slid open and she brushed past him to step inside. Lucas waited until the doors closed before he hurried to the nearby emergency stairs.

Sprinting down the four floors, he waited in a dark corner of the lobby as the older woman headed out of the hospital. Predictably she had her vehicle parked in a handicap zone directly in front of the doors.

Lucas grimaced. A green Jag.

He'd had a ridiculous suspicion that she would be driving a black SUV.

Turning on his heel, he was on his way back to Mia's room when he realized that Vicky Fontaine didn't ask why he was there.

# Chapter Fourteen

Mia was done.

Well and truly done.

There was, after all, only so much testosterone a woman should have to endure.

First had been the doctor who'd adamantly refused to release her from the hospital. He'd insisted that she be monitored for twenty-four hours, despite the fact that she'd felt fine once the drugs were out of her system.

Then Max had stood a silent vigil outside the door to her room no matter how many times she pleaded for him to go to his hotel room and get some rest.

Next up was Detective Cooper, who'd spent over an hour grilling her on the who, the what, and the why someone wanted to kill her. She understood it was his job, but it didn't make the ordeal any more pleasant.

Then Lucas had arrived to take her home. Only he hadn't taken her to *her* home. Instead they'd driven to an elegant penthouse suite that overlooked the river.

His argument was that her house was a crime scene, but she knew he wanted her in a place that had 24/7 security. No one could get into the expensive building without showing ID to a guard. It no doubt cost a fortune, but Mia leashed her annoyance at his arrogant assumption he had the right to dictate where she lived.

She truly didn't want to return to her house. At least not yet.

So instead she'd walked through the large penthouse. A part of her grudgingly admired the soothing shades of gray and the two walls that were smoky glass from floor to ceiling. The kitchen was a chef's dream and there were two separate suites with private bathrooms attached.

Entering the largest of the bedrooms, she'd discovered Lucas had spent the night moving her clothing and personal items into the penthouse. She also discovered that his own belongings were tucked next to hers.

Not very subtle.

But when Lucas had dared to plant himself in front of her and flatly announce that she wasn't allowed to attend Tony's funeral, she'd reached her limit.

Standing in the middle of the bedroom that shimmered in shades of silver and gray as the late morning sunlight angled through the window, Mia planted her hands on her hips. "What did you say?" she demanded, her words a warning that he'd just treaded on her last nerve.

Lucas looked as if he hadn't slept all night. His silky hair was ruffled, his jaw was shadowed with whiskers, and there was a hint of weariness in his dark eyes. Still, he managed to look stunningly handsome.

How was that fair?

"I said you're staying here," he growled. "And that's final."

Mia judged the distance between them. She was pretty sure he was close enough for her to give him a black eye.

Then, with an effort, she resisted her more violent urges.

"I'm going to the funeral and there's nothing you can do to stop me," she informed him.

A slow, wicked smile curved his lips. "I can handcuff you to the bed."

A ridiculous thrill of excitement clenched her stomach before she was sternly trying to squash it.

"That's not funny," she muttered.

"No, but it is tempting." He stepped forward, his fingers tracing the curve of her neck as he studied her pale features. "How do you feel?"

"Fine." She slapped his hand away. She couldn't think straight when he was touching her. It was hard enough when his eyes were smoldering with a heat that made her blood melt. "You're not going to change the subject."

"Good." Without warning his arms wrapped around her waist and with one tug he had her pressed against his body. "I prefer not to talk at all," he rasped, lowering his head to bury his face in her hair.

She grasped his upper arms, swallowing her sigh of pleasure. For the past twenty-four hours she'd been so chilled she feared she would never feel warm again. No doubt a combination of her overdose and flat-out fear. Now she felt her muscles ease as the scent and heat of him wrapped around her.

"You're trying to distract me," she complained.

His lips skimmed over her brow and down her cheek. "You scared me," he admitted in a hoarse voice.

There was no doubting his sincerity. She could feel it in the tension of his body, and the rapid beat of his heart.

He'd truly believed she was going to die.

"I told you, I'm fine," she assured him.

He shuddered, nipping at her lower lip. "When I saw you collapse I thought I'd lost you." He pressed a hard, almost punishing kiss to her lips. "Christ."

She instinctively found herself trying to pull out of his tight grip. "Lucas," she breathed.

He gave her another kiss, this one softer . . . a gentle persuasion that made her shiver with anticipation.

"Just let me hold you," he huskily pleaded against her lips.

Silence filled the vast suite as he stroked his mouth over her cheek and down the curve of her neck. His touch was meant to be soothing, but as they stood in the middle of the room, Mia was acutely aware of the nearby bed. And just how much she wanted him to spread her over the silver comforter and make her forget the fact that someone was trying to kill her. The same someone who'd already murdered her friend.

And if it'd just been sex she might have given in to the impulse. She'd had one hell of a week. Why not enjoy a few hours of consensual pleasure?

But she could never have "just sex" with Lucas.

That was the reason she'd scrambled out of bed . . . when was it? Yesterday morning. God, it felt like a lifetime. And why she'd locked the door to the shower.

Just one night in his arms had already stirred up the emotions that she thought were buried and dead fifteen years ago.

With a sudden motion she was pulling out of his arms, a sharp pang of regret slicing through her.

"I truly am fine," she forced herself to say, her chin tilting. "And I am going to the funeral."

The sinful warmth was leeched from his eyes as he studied her obstinate expression. "Someone just tried to kill you," he growled. "Or have you forgotten?"

She flinched. "Of course I haven't forgotten."

"Then don't fight me on this." His breath hissed through his clenched teeth. "I need to know you're safe."

"You expect me to hide in this place until they catch Tony's murderer?"

His jaw tightened. "Yes."

"It could take days or weeks." She gave a frustrated shake of her head. "This case might never be solved."

He held her gaze, the force of his sheer willpower sizzling through the air. "We're going to catch whoever tried to poison you," he said. "I promise."

Mia grimaced. She knew that she was making this more difficult for him. For whatever reason, Lucas had proclaimed himself her protector. The fact that he considered he'd failed in his duty only intensified his need to keep her locked in a safe place.

Unfortunately for him, the mere thought of spending day after day trapped in this penthouse suite, no matter how elegant, sent her into a panic attack.

She not only had to keep herself busy, but she needed to feel as if she was a part of the investigation. It was her life in danger, after all.

If she was forced to sit around twiddling her thumbs, she'd go crazy.

"I can't put my life on hold," she said.

"Mia—"

"No." She interrupted his protest. "I've agreed to stay here, but I won't be a prisoner."

He heaved a rough sigh. "Have you always been so stubborn?"

She arched a brow. He had the nerve to call her stubborn? He could write the book on pigheaded obstinacy.

"Have you always been so bossy?" she countered.

As if realizing he wasn't going to win this battle, Lucas reached into his pocket to pull out his phone.

"Fine." He typed in a swift message. "I'll have Max take you to the funeral."

She blinked. She'd assumed he would take her. Now she had to hide her disappointment.

"You're not going?"

"Today is for Tony." He ran his fingers over his unshaven cheek. "Having a St. Clair attending the funeral would be an unnecessary distraction," he said. Mia wrinkled her nose, knowing he was right. Tony's family were simple people who would be self-conscious at having Lucas around. "I'll go to his graveside later to pay my respects," he promised.

She nodded, studying his beautiful face that was lined with weariness. He clearly needed to spend a few hours in bed, but she didn't believe for a second that he was going to stay home and take a nap.

"And you have other plans?" she demanded.

He shrugged. "I have a few things I want to check out."

"What?"

He turned to walk toward the closet, pulling out his leather jacket. "We'll discuss it over dinner."

Mia narrowed her gaze as she watched him smooth back his hair. "You're hiding something from me."

He turned to study her with a lift of his brows. "Don't you need to get ready?"

She did. She needed to take a shower and tame her hair before finding something to wear. But she couldn't help but worry that Lucas intended to do something dangerous.

"We're supposed to be partners," she reminded him.

He headed across the room. "We are. I promise we'll talk later. Max will be here to take you to the funeral in half an hour." He halted at the door, turning to send her a last warning. "Be careful."

Mia bit her lip, fear clenching her heart. "Lucas."

"Yeah?"

"If you get yourself hurt I'm not going to be happy."

There was a long, tense silence. Then, without warning Lucas was stalking back across the carpet and yanking her into his arms. Mia parted her lips in shock, unprepared for his fierce kiss that stole her breath and made her knees weak.

Clutching the lapels of his jacket, Mia felt her entire body dissolve beneath the scalding pleasure of his touch.

"I love you too," he murmured against her yielding lips.

Mia froze. *Did he really just say the L word?*

Before she could process what'd just happened, Lucas released her and was heading out of the room. She was still standing in the center of the floor when she heard the outer door close.

What the hell had just happened?

Had Lucas truly just confessed that he loved her? Or had he been teasing her to try and make her forget about her concern for his safety?

And if he was sincere, how did that make her feel?

She truly didn't know.

Joyous? Terrified? An intoxicating combination of the two?

With a shake of her head, Mia forced herself to concentrate on preparing for the funeral. Lucas had been right about one thing. Today was for Tony. She would worry about everything else after the funeral.

Taking a quick shower, Mia tucked her hair into a tidy knot at her nape and pulled on a black skirt and matching jacket. She took time to cover her pale face with makeup. It was inevitable that people would know she'd gone to the hospital, but she didn't want to attract unwanted attention by showing up looking like she was on death's door.

Precisely half an hour later she pulled open the door to the penthouse, not surprised to discover an unknown man standing beside the door. Lucas wouldn't have left her alone without making sure the penthouse was being watched by someone he'd personally hired.

She was equally unsurprised to catch sight of Max casually leaning against the wall near the elevators.

Although he couldn't have had much sleep, he looked edible in his gray slacks and dark cashmere sweater. His blond hair was smoothed from the square face that was more compelling than traditionally handsome, and his gray eyes darkened to smoke in the muted overhead light.

"Ready?" he asked.

She drew in a deep breath. Tony's death didn't seem real, which was only going to make the day more difficult.

But she couldn't hide in her penthouse and wish Tony was still alive.

This had to be done.

"Yes."

In silence they entered the elevator and rode down to the black-and-gold lobby. Crossing the marble floor, they waited for the uniformed guard to pull open the door.

Max hesitated, glancing up and down the quiet street before placing a hand on her lower back and escorting her to the waiting silver SUV.

Mia resisted the urge to roll her eyes at the sensation of being in a James Bond movie. It all felt so ridiculously unnecessary. Guarded doors. Companions with guns strapped to various parts of their bodies . . .

But then she remembered that someone had not only managed to sneak into her house and tried to kill her, but that Lucas was out there looking for the person responsible. She hoped he had a dozen guns with him.

And a flamethrower.

Brooding on the thought of Lucas in danger, Mia barely noticed Max driving them along the outskirts of town, heading toward the small church south of Shreveport. Tony would hate the thought of being surrounded by a bunch of people who turned their backs on him when he was alive, but the congregation would no doubt comfort his mother.

Mia remained lost in her dark thoughts as Max slowed the vehicle to turn onto a narrow dirt path.

Her companion abruptly broke the silence. "He's one of the good guys, you know."

Turning her head, Mia realized that Max was sending her concerned glances.

"Excuse me?"

"Lucas," Max clarified, clearly assuming that she was brooding on the man who'd crashed into her life like a wrecking ball. "He can be an arrogant ass—"

"No kidding," she muttered.

"But there's no one I'd rather have at my back."

Mia studied her companion's profile as he turned his attention back to the road. She drummed an absent finger on her leg, a voice in the back of her mind warning that she should ignore Max's soft words.

Unfortunately, the curiosity to know everything possible about Lucas was overwhelming.

"Is that why you're partners in ARES?" she asked.

Max's jaw tightened. "We're not partners. We're brothers."

His voice held the same fierce intensity as Lucas's when he mentioned the men who worked with him.

"Lucas is clearly closer to you than his own family," she said. "I suppose escaping from the Taliban together formed a bond that most of us will never understand."

Max shot her a quick glance. "Did he tell you what happened?"

She grimaced. She'd heard the edge of pain in Lucas's voice when he'd discussed his time in the Middle East, which was why she hadn't pressed him for more information than he was willing to offer.

"Just the basics," she said. "I don't think he likes to talk about that time."

"No." Max's hands tightened on the steering wheel, his knuckles white. "It's not something any of us want to remember." There was a long pause as he slowed to study the GPS. Mia, however, sensed that he was actually using the distraction to consider his next words. "You should know that he had the chance to walk away."

"I don't understand."

"His father is a very powerful man."

Mia released a sharp, humorless laugh. Just the thought of Senator St. Clair was enough to give her frostbite.

If Lucas's mother had been a controlling bitch, his father had been an intimidating, emotionless bully.

"Yeah, I know," she breathed.

Max turned onto a pathway that was even narrower, the trees draping over the top to form a canopy.

"Our captors negotiated with the bigwigs in the State Department to trade him," Max told her, wincing as his expensive vehicle jolted over the roots that bisected the road.

Mia could easily imagine the senator marching into the State Department and demanding that they interfere to rescue his son. Not out of love. But because he was the last St. Clair. A precious commodity.

"Trade him for whom?"

Max turned a corner and came to a halt at the sight of the small church with a muddy parking lot that was tucked among the cypress trees.

Putting the SUV in reverse, he made a U-turn and pulled onto a mossy patch of ground. Obviously he wanted to be ready in case they needed a quick getaway. Mia was okay with that.

She didn't think that the killer would be lurking in the church to attack her, but she didn't want to linger after the funeral to answer uncomfortable questions.

Switching off the engine, Max unhooked his seat belt and swiveled to face her. "It wasn't ever revealed who was supposed to be traded." He returned to their conversation, his expression shadowed as he thought back to the horror of war. "But Lucas assumed it was an Al Qaeda leader who was being held in one of our black sites." Mia could only guess that a black site meant one of the secret prisons used by US officials to interrogate prisoners. "Lucas refused to accept the deal."

Mia suddenly felt sick. Lucas could have been safe. He could have been home where he belonged. Instead he'd stayed in a place that still gave him nightmares.

"Why?"

Max turned his head to study the nearby trees, the tense

set of his shoulders revealing he was on high alert as his gaze scanned for any lurkers in the shadows.

"He said he wouldn't be responsible for releasing a terrorist back into the world. He couldn't live with himself if he discovered that the bastard later managed to pull off an attack and kill innocents."

She gave a slow nod. "I get that."

Max's lips twisted. "That wasn't the only reason he stayed."

"Why—" Mia bit off her words, suddenly recalling Lucas explaining how they'd gotten out of the prison. Each of them had a duty that had to be carried out. "The escape."

"Yep." Max held her gaze. "We'd already started our planning and the very foundation of getting out of the prison depended on Lucas talking the guard into giving him the keys to our cells."

"He wasn't going to leave you behind," she murmured.

"No."

Mia shivered. She couldn't even imagine what sort of courage it took to turn your back on the opportunity to walk away from hell. Who would have blamed him? Certainly not the men who'd shared his prison.

But he'd faced his worst fears and put the needs of his companions above his own.

"Why are you telling me this?" she demanded.

Max studied her with an unreadable expression. "Because I know he hurt you in the past."

Mia jerked with an unexpected pain. She should have suspected that Lucas would tell his friends about their painful history. It wasn't like it was a big secret. Still, the thought of having Lucas's friends knowing that she'd been found unworthy of the great St. Clair heir made her cringe with the humiliation that'd plagued her for fifteen years.

"Yeah, well, he wasn't quite so reluctant to walk away when I knew him," she said in harsh tones.

Something that might have been sympathy softened the gray eyes. "We all hopefully learn from our mistakes."

"Yes, we do." Her tight smile assured her companion that she'd definitely learned from her own error in judgment.

Max grimaced, but he refused to back down. "You can trust him, Mia," he assured her. "He won't walk away again."

She hunched a shoulder. That was the fear, of course.

She could make up a thousand reasons why she continued to battle against Lucas. Bitterness. Revenge. Indifference.

But the truth was . . . she was terrified he was going to hurt her again.

"How can you be so sure?" she asked, her voice a mere whisper.

"Because for fifteen years he's regretted losing you."

She gave a sharp shake of her head. "If he truly regretted his decision, he wouldn't have waited all this time to come back."

Without warning, Max was twisting to the side, reaching to grab a large manila envelope off the backseat. Then with a flick of his wrist, he tossed it into her lap.

"I think this will prove how much he cared."

Mia glanced at her companion in surprise. "What is it?"

"There's only one way to find out," Max said, his hand reaching out to lightly touch her cheek. "But don't forget what happened to Pandora. If you're happy with your life as it is, I would suggest that you toss the information in the trash."

Mia touched the envelope, an odd unease fluttering in the pit of her stomach.

It wasn't thick enough to hold more than a few pages, maybe a photo, but she still felt as if she had a live rattlesnake in her lap.

Did she open it or didn't she? Was she happy with her life?

Mia sucked in a deep breath, shoving the envelope into her purse. That was a question that was going to have to wait until after the funeral.

# Chapter Fifteen

Lucas parked at the Ramon Landscaping office building and walked the short distance to Mia's house. He didn't actually think he would be lucky enough to catch the killer lurking in plain sight. But he wanted to scope out the area on foot.

It'd been impossible to do any investigating yesterday. The house had been cordoned off as a crime scene as Detective Cooper had directed his men to collect the evidence. The man had grudgingly allowed Lucas to gather up Mia's clothes and toiletries, but he'd made sure Lucas was escorted from room to room until he was firmly shoved out the door.

Lucas had briefly considered making a phone call. One word to the state attorney's office and he'd have carte blanche to stay, regardless of Detective Cooper's "protocols." But there wasn't much he could do in the dark, and it seemed preferable not to piss off the authorities who were just doing their job.

Lucas had instead concentrated on finding a safe place for Mia to stay when she left the hospital.

Now he approached the house from the alley, pausing to determine how hard it would be to sneak through the yard and into the back door.

The answer was . . . that was easy as hell.

A car could use the alley to avoid the main street and park behind the garage or the neighbor's Dumpster.

It certainly wouldn't take an expert to sneak up to the house without being seen.

With a muttered curse he headed across the backyard, his eyes on the ground for any indication of tracks. Unfortunately the half dozen people who'd been wandering around yesterday had trampled the mud, so it was impossible to make out a specific set of footprints.

Halting near the house, he studied the best way to try and peek in.

From his position he couldn't see anything. He moved to the stairs that led to the small porch. His jaw clenched as he realized that he could easily see through both the kitchen and back door windows.

This was where the intruder had been standing the first night he'd been in the house. And where he must have been standing yesterday morning to make sure the coast was clear before sneaking into the kitchen.

Lucas's furious thoughts were interrupted as he caught a movement out of the corner of his eye.

There was someone creeping through the hedge toward the side of the house.

Keeping his gaze locked on the back door, Lucas loosened his muscles and concentrated on slowing his breathing. He wasn't as well-trained as Rafe or Hauk in hand-to-hand combat, but he could hold his own when necessary.

Focusing on his surroundings, he used his senses to make sure there wasn't more than one lurker in the area. Then, turning to jog down the stairs, he pretended he was headed for the garage before he was abruptly spinning to launch himself toward the intruder.

His shoulder connected with the man's head as he knocked

him backward. There was a low grunt as he landed on top of the stranger, knocking the air from his lungs.

Using his weight to pin the man to the ground, Lucas planted his forearm across the man's chest. Then, reaching to his side, he pulled out his gun.

There was a choked sound of fear as the captive began to struggle in earnest.

"Don't move," Lucas snapped, at last taking time to study the man beneath him.

He was older than Lucas had expected. The thin face was heavily lined with wrinkles and his body had the gaunt thinness of an addict. Drugs? Alcohol? Maybe both. His pale eyes were bloodshot and watery, and his teeth beginning to rot.

That didn't mean he didn't have a wiry strength as he tried to shove Lucas away.

"Get off me," the man rasped. "I'm calling the cops."

"Good," Lucas said, allowing his forearm to slide up so it was less than an inch from the man's throat. "We can tell them I caught you trespassing on Ms. Ramon's property."

The pale eyes darted to the side as he tried to come up with a lie. "I wasn't trespassing," he at last muttered.

"Don't screw with me," Lucas growled. "I'm not in the mood."

"I'm Carl Greene," he blubbered, confirming Lucas's initial suspicion. "I'm a neighbor."

"You're still trespassing."

"You don't have any proof."

Lucas shook his head. Was the man an idiot? He was clearly on Mia's property.

Still, if the man needed to be convinced to cooperate, Lucas didn't mind pushing his weight around. Or in this case, his name.

"Do you know who I am?" he asked.

The man scowled. "Why should I?"

"My name is St. Clair and I'm the son of a retired senator."

There was a flicker in the pale eyes that assured Lucas the man recognized the name. And the power behind it.

His features settled into a petulant expression. "Am I supposed to be impressed?"

With a cold disdain that would have made his father proud, Lucas stared down at the man. "No, you're supposed to realize that if it comes to the authorities believing my word or yours, you don't have a chance in hell of winning."

Carl didn't argue. He even stopped struggling to get away. Maybe he was smarter than Lucas first assumed.

"What do you want from me?" he demanded.

Lucas cautiously rose to his feet. He kept his gun trained on Carl, watching as the man scrambled upright and nervously tugged on his stained sweatshirt that looked like it'd been found in the trash.

"You've been watching Ms. Ramon?" he demanded.

Carl nervously licked his lips, his eyes darting to the side. "I've visited her once or twice to ask if she needed any help around the house," he said. "It's only neighborly."

Lucas snorted in disgust. There were few things that he hated more than a pervert who preyed on the innocent.

"And spent every other evening peeking out your window at her," he spat out.

Carl hunched a shoulder. "A man can do what he wants in his own house—"

"Shut up and listen," he interrupted.

The man flinched. He might be willing to creep through the dark, but he was a coward at heart. "What do you want?"

Lucas hesitated, carefully considering his words. The more time he spent with Carl Greene the less likely he appeared to be a suspect. After all, it seemed highly unlikely he had the ability or the motivation to track Tony to Houston and shoot him in the street.

Still, he had the proximity to Mia to easily sneak into her house, and no doubt a stash of prescription drugs that he could have crushed up and tossed in the coffee.

Lucas had to be certain he wasn't responsible.

"Someone tried to poison Ms. Ramon this morning," he abruptly revealed, closely watching the man's reaction.

"Poison?" There was genuine bafflement on the thin face. "That's why all those cops were here?"

"Yes."

There was a momentary surge of relief in the pale eyes that Carl swiftly replaced with concern. Lucas narrowed his gaze. The man had been worried that Mia had called the cops because of him, but there was no mistaking the fact that he didn't know anything about the poison.

Now the question was whether or not Carl had seen anything during his hours of peeking at Mia, to help find out who had been responsible for the poisoning.

"Is she okay?" Carl demanded. "I didn't see an ambulance."

"She's recovering," Lucas said.

The man glanced toward Mia's house. "Will she be home soon?"

Lucas folded his arms over his chest. Mia wasn't coming back here. Period. Even if he failed in all his attempts to convince her that her future was with him, this house was off-limits. Not only because Carl Greene was next door; there was no way in hell she could forget that someone had managed to sneak inside and tried to kill her.

He kept his thoughts to himself.

He instead turned the conversation in the direction he wanted. "I think you're missing the big picture here."

"What big picture?"

"There was an attempt on Ms. Ramon's life." Lucas allowed

a humorless smile to curve his lips. "Where do you think they'll look for the person responsible?"

Carl was stumped by the question. "How should I know?"

Lucas rolled his eyes. The man had clearly fried the majority of his brain cells.

"If I was a detective I'd start with the man next door who was accused of trying to kill his girlfriend." He spoke slowly, as if he was speaking to a child.

"How did you know that I . . ." Carl's eyes widened as he realized there was something more pressing to be worried about than how Lucas knew he'd tried to run down his girlfriend. "Shit. You ain't pinning this on me," he rasped, taking an awkward step backward.

Lucas shrugged. "You're the most obvious suspect. You live a few feet away, with easy access to the crime scene, and you have a history of violence toward women."

Carl raised an unsteady hand. "Why would I want to hurt her?"

"My guess is that she shut down your efforts to get to know her," Lucas said. Even though he didn't think the man was involved, he wanted him scared enough that he would cooperate when he got to the questions he needed answered. "That can piss off a man who thinks women owe him a good time."

Carl gave a panicked shake of his head. "Look, that thing with my girlfriend was a one-off. I was high on painkillers and she was a bitch," he babbled, sweat forming on his brow. "I never intended to hurt her. I just wanted to give her a scare."

"Where were you this morning?"

The man bristled with a combination of fear and anger. "Where the fuck do you think I was?" he snapped. "I have no money, no car, and no friends. I was here."

*Hmm.* No car. That meant he couldn't have been the one

who traveled to Houston or tried to run Mia off the road. Yet another confirmation he wasn't the one trying to kill Mia.

"Did you see anyone next door?" he asked.

Carl flattened his lips, clearly wanting to tell Lucas to go to hell. But he'd been spooked enough by the threat of being accused as a potential murderer to force himself to respond.

"You," he muttered.

"Anyone else?"

Carl gave a lift of one shoulder. "There was a man sitting in a car out front."

That had to have been Max. If there'd been anyone else his friend would have noticed.

"What about the backyard?"

Carl's brow furrowed as he tried to shift through his fuzzy brain for the memory.

"I saw a black SUV parked at the end of the alley," he at last admitted.

"Did you recognize the driver?"

The man gave a shake of his head. "I didn't pay attention. I've seen it there a few times, so I assumed it was a friend of Mia's."

"Ms. Ramon," Lucas snapped, as infuriated by the sound of Mia's name on the pervert's lips as he was by the knowledge that the SUV had been lurking behind Mia's house more than once.

"Fine," Carl conceded with a resentful glare. "Ms. Ramon."

Lucas tempered his burst of fury. He wasn't done with his questions. Which meant he couldn't break the man's jaw.

Not yet.

"How long was it there this morning?"

"It was there when I woke up."

"What time?" Lucas pressed.

"Five." Carl hesitated before giving a shrug. "Maybe five thirty."

"Did you see it leave?"

"No, but when I heard the cops coming I looked out and it was gone."

"You never saw anyone in the backyard?"

"Nope."

Of course he hadn't. Lucas swallowed a curse. Nothing could be easy. At least not when it came to discovering who was trying to hurt Mia.

Still keeping his gun pointed at Carl, he pulled out one of the business cards he kept in his jacket pocket. "If you see anyone, I want you to call me immediately," he ordered, shoving the card in the man's unwilling hand.

"Why should I get involved?" he muttered.

Lucas grimaced. Yeah. The man was a real winner.

"Because I'll give you a hundred bucks for any information that helps me track down the driver of the black SUV," he growled.

Greed sparked in the man's bloodshot eyes, assuring Lucas he would be getting a call if the SUV made an appearance.

"Okay."

Lucas took a step closer, ignoring the man's pungent scent. "I'll also give you a warning," he said, his voice hard. "The card I just gave you is from my new business, ARES Security. We're a group of highly trained, well-financed soldiers who enjoy hunting down bad guys."

Carl licked his lips, his expression wary. "What's that got to do with me?"

"I took precautions in the very unlikely event that Mia returns to this house," he smoothly lied. Mia was never coming back, but the man didn't know that. "I've placed a number of hidden cameras around the neighborhood. Cameras so small you would never find them."

Carl's gaze darted toward the light posts at the front of the house and then the large tree at the side of Mia's house. "That can't be legal," he said, his face draining to a strange shade of ash.

No need to ask if he believed Lucas's threat.

Lucas chuckled. "As I said, I'm a St. Clair."

"I still don't know what this has to do with me."

"If I catch sight of you creeping around the area, peeking into windows that don't belong to you, I promise you'll be very, very sorry." Lucas deliberately pointed the gun between the man's eyes. "Got it?"

Sweat dripped from the man's face as he hastily nodded his head. "Got it."

"Good boy."

Convinced he'd done everything in his power to protect the women who lived in the neighborhood, Lucas turned to jog back toward his car.

He wanted to be at the penthouse when Mia returned. The funeral was going to be rough on her. Probably rougher than she expected. He needed to be there to comfort her.

Reaching the end of the alley, he narrowed his gaze as he caught sight of a shadowed figure leaning against his car. Just for a second he considered circling around the building so he could sneak up from behind.

Then the figure turned and Lucas instantly recognized the large, heavily muscled man with dark caramel skin and golden eyes.

Moving forward, he smiled at his fellow ARES partner. "Teagan."

The younger man glanced toward the gun that Lucas still clutched in his hands. "Terrorizing the natives, St. Clair?"

"Me?" Lucas deliberately took in his companion's skull-shaved head and the tattoos that were revealed by the short-sleeved T-shirt tucked into his camo pants. "You look like a reject from a Vin Diesel movie."

Teagan heaved a faux sigh. "Men your age really should be wearing glasses."

Lucas chuckled, holstering his gun. "What are you doing here?"

"I think I have some intel that might help."

Lucas felt a surge of hope. If Teagan had driven all the way to Shreveport, it had to be important.

"What is it?"

Teagan nodded toward the restored Camaro parked near the exit of the lot.

"It's on my computer."

Lucas considered using Mia's office. He assumed most of the workers would be at Tony's funeral, so the chances of being interrupted were slim. But he couldn't shake the urge to return to the penthouse in case Mia needed him.

"Follow me," he abruptly commanded.

Without demanding unnecessary explanations, Teagan gave a nod and quickly crossed the lot and slipped into the Camaro. Lucas took a minute to instinctively glance around and make sure no one was watching before he slid into his own car and headed across town.

The Sunday traffic was light, and within half an hour, Lucas was opening the door to the penthouse to lead Teagan inside.

The younger man released a soft whistle as he crossed the living room to place his computer on a low coffee table.

"Nice," he murmured, settling on the edge of a gray sofa as he waited for his machine to boot up. "Did you have to dip into that trust fund to pay the rent?"

"It's mine, or at least it will be once the paperwork is done," he said, taking a seat next to his friend. The real estate agent hadn't been happy to be wakened in the middle of the night. At least she hadn't been happy until she realized Lucas was willing to pay full asking price in cash. "And no, I didn't use my damned trust fund."

Teagan stiffened, his expression suddenly unreadable. "You're moving to Shreveport?"

Lucas frowned at his friend's unexpected reaction. He assumed his partners would be happy as hell he'd found his true love.

Then realization slowly eased his confusion. Teagan was worried he was going to break up the team. The knowledge warmed his heart.

No one besides Mia had ever cared whether he was around or not.

"I intend to bring Mia to Houston, but I'll have to spend at least some time here," he told his friend. "I doubt Mia will agree to sell her company, which means she'll want to come back to check on things on a regular basis."

Teagan's expression softened, a hint of a smile touching his lips. "So it's like that," he murmured.

Lucas glanced around the penthouse, easily visualizing Mia standing near one of the glass walls as she savored the sunset. Or curled in one of the overstuffed chairs as she fell asleep watching TV.

A profound emotion clenched his heart.

"I hope so," he said, forced to stop and clear the lump from his throat. Feeling unnerved by the sheer strength of his need, he concentrated his attention on Teagan as he leaned forward and tapped on the keyboard. "What did you find?"

Teagan turned his head to meet Lucas's curious gaze. "Max said that you hadn't managed to locate any of Tony's associates."

"As far as I can tell he was a complete loner," Lucas said with a shake of his head. "No friends. No lovers. Not even a booty call."

Teagan returned to tapping on the keyboard. "That got me thinking."

"Miracles do happen," he teased.

Teagan reached out to smack Lucas on the back of the head without ever allowing his gaze to stray from the monitor. "Smart-ass."

Lucas smiled. As much as he loved having Mia back in his life, he missed the camaraderie of his friends. "It got you thinking about what?"

"The money trail."

Lucas frowned in confusion. "Max already gave it to me," he told his friend. He'd spent a few hours going over the financial report while he was waiting for Mia in the hospital. "The cash is going to be hard to trace."

Sitting back, Teagan turned to face Lucas. "Not necessarily."

"No?"

"As I was saying before I was interrupted, I spent some time on the computer searching through Tony's social media and e-mails," Teagan drawled.

Lucas felt like an idiot. It hadn't even occurred to him that Tony might have a Facebook page.

"What did you find?"

"Nada." Teagan swiftly squashed his flicker of hope. "I don't think he spent any time online."

"Great," Lucas muttered.

"I'm not done," Teagan chided.

"Of course not."

Teagan narrowed his golden gaze. "Do you want to hear or not?"

Lucas held up his hand in a gesture of peace. "Yeah, I want to hear."

"I finally tried to put myself in Tony's shoes." Teagan grimaced. "It wasn't hard. We both grew up poor and had to fight and claw to make our own way in the world. That sort of existence doesn't encourage us to embrace our fellow man."

Lucas's teasing smile faded as he studied his friend's grim expression. His own childhood had been a cold, lonely existence, but it couldn't compare to what Teagan had endured. If anyone would understand Tony's troubled life, it was the man sitting next to him.

"True," he murmured.

"We also both spent time in jail."

"Petty stuff," he murmured.

Teagan shrugged. "Jail is jail, which means to get out you have to convince someone to pay your bail."

Lucas considered the various possibilities. He'd never been in jail. Even when he'd been caught at a party with underage drinkers he'd been hauled home instead of to the station with the others.

No one wanted to make the phone call to Senator St. Clair to say his son was sitting in a cell. Now he tried to remember what his friends had told him when they'd been in trouble.

"I thought everyone called their mom?" he at last said.

Teagan shuddered. "Bro, *no one* calls their mom."

Okay. He'd clearly touched a nerve.

"What about one of his brothers?" he suggested.

Teagan shook his head. "As far as I can tell not one of them have a damned penny to share between them."

Yeah. That sounded about right. The Hughes boys might be hard workers, but they didn't make more than minimum wage. Plus they'd all started having kids before they were out of high school.

"So who did he call?" he asked.

Teagan nodded toward his monitor. "I did some digging

and came up with the name of Freedom Bail Agency. It's a local company."

Lucas tried to place the name and failed. "Should that mean something to me?"

Teagan turned the computer so Lucas could see the screen.

"No, but each of the bonds was secured by Vicky Fontaine."

# Chapter Sixteen

Mia stepped out of the side of the church and sucked in a deep breath.

*God.* She hated funerals. The hushed voices. The cloying scent of flowers. The heavy sadness that wrapped around her like a physical weight.

They all reminded her of the aching misery that had been her constant companion after her mother's death.

Now she halted at the edge of the crowd. People were busy filling their plates from the potluck lunch that'd been set out on long tables in the center of the small clearing.

Her eyes ached from crying and her entire body was still cramped from having the drugs forced from her stomach, but it was a relief to be able to suck some fresh air into her lungs.

She took another breath as Burt walked toward her, his blunt face blotched with tears.

"Thank you for coming, Mia," he murmured, his voice hoarse. "I know how much you meant to Tony."

She forced a sad smile to her lips, the memory of the carefree days when she and Tony had been kids playing together clenching her heart with a bittersweet emotion.

"I'm going to miss him." She glanced around, grimacing

at the handful of people who mingled near the food tables. Tony's family was there, of course. And Mrs. Hughes's friends from the church. But that was it. Just another reminder of how isolated Tony had become over the years. "He's been a part of my life for as long as I can remember."

Burt shoved his hands into the pocket of a suit jacket that had clearly been loaned to him by a friend who was two sizes smaller than him.

"I just wish we knew what happened," he muttered.

"The Houston detectives still don't have any clues?" she cautiously probed.

The last thing she wanted was to bring up the painful subject of Tony's murder, but she was desperate to know if the family had heard any new information.

"The Houston detectives don't give a shit," Burt said with a pained twist of his lips. "They think it was a drug deal gone bad. They ain't gonna waste any tax dollars trying to find who pulled the trigger."

She swallowed a sigh of disappointment. "We're going to discover who did this," she murmured, laying a comforting hand on his arm. "I promise."

Burt shook his head before he was squaring his shoulders and studying her with a worried frown. "I heard you had some sort of accident."

She lowered her hand, plastering a fake smile to her lips. In the South, everybody's business was everybody's business, but they were usually polite enough to take a hint when someone didn't want to talk about it.

"I'm fine."

He leaned closer, taking note of her pallor, which wasn't entirely disguised by her makeup, and the shadows beneath her eyes.

"Are you sure?"

"I'm sure."

Burt paused, as if trying to decide whether to let it go or

to ask the question that was trembling on the tip of his tongue.

"It wasn't St. Clair?" he at last demanded in gruff tones.

Mia blinked in confusion. "What do you mean?"

Burt hunched a shoulder. "I heard he was back in town. He wasn't responsible for putting you in the hospital, was he?"

Mia sucked in a shocked breath.

She knew that many families in the area resented the wealth and power of the St. Clair clan. And that they would love to believe they were inherently evil. But Burt couldn't possibly think that Lucas would ever hit a woman.

"Are you two back together?"

She blushed, her body tingling with the vivid memory of Lucas's touch.

"No." She struggled to pretend an indifference she was far from feeling. "He's just visiting for a few days."

Burt lifted his brows, not buying her act for a minute. "Visiting?"

She tilted her chin, her cheeks still burning. "Yes."

"Hmm."

Mia glanced away from Burt's knowing gaze, relieved to see Mr. Hughes waving a hand from the far side of the clearing.

She eagerly latched on to the distraction. "I think your father is trying to get your attention."

"Damn." Burt glanced over his shoulder, his big body tensing with an unexpected anger. "That bastard."

Mia frowned. The Hughes boys had never respected their father. He drank too much, he was lazy, and he'd cheated on their mother a dozen times. But they usually tried to keep their disdain behind closed doors.

"Is anything wrong?" she asked.

Burt gave a shake of his head, turning back to meet her worried gaze. "He's trying to get me to hustle everyone out so he can take Ma home."

Mia's heart clenched. Tony's father might be a waste of space, but Mrs. Hughes had always been a loving mother who'd done her very best for her boys. Her grief was painful to witness.

"This is a difficult day for her," she said in soft tones.

Burt snorted. "It is, but that's not why the old man is trying to get this over with."

"What's going on?"

"The cops stopped by this morning to say that we could get into Tony's condo," Burt confessed. "Now he can't wait to go there and start pawning off my brother's things."

Mia couldn't disguise her reaction. She had a sudden, vivid image of a vulture picking over a dead carcass. It was . . . horrifying.

"Oh," she breathed.

Burt heaved a sigh of resignation. "Nice, huh?"

With an effort, Mia dismissed the terrible thought. She didn't have the right to judge Mr. Hughes. Her own father had struggled with his demons.

"I'm sure he's just trying to deal with his grief," she murmured.

"You always think the best of everyone," Burt told her. Then, heaving a resigned sigh, he visibly squared his shoulders. "I need to go over there. There's no way in hell he's dragging Ma away until she's ready to go."

Mia reached out to grab his hand, giving it a small squeeze. "Take care of yourself."

Burt gave a slow nod. "You too, Mia."

Mia watched as Burt circled the small knot of people to lean down and speak in his father's ear. The older man flushed, his chin jutting out with stubborn fury.

No doubt the older man would do exactly what he wanted to do. . . .

Mia abruptly stiffened. *Crap.* She'd been so focused on

Burt's frustration with his father that she hadn't thought through his revelation.

Now she hastily turned to dart around the edge of the church, narrowly avoiding the two young boys who were sneaking a smoke out of sight of their parents. Avoiding a collision, she sent the boys a chiding frown before she was hurrying down the narrow lane.

Out of breath by the time she reached Max's SUV, she yanked open the door and climbed in.

Max closed the computer he'd been working on as he glanced at her in surprise. "Done already?"

"We have to go to Tony's condo," she told him, buckling her seat belt as Max turned to place his laptop in the back-seat before sending her a puzzled frown.

"Now?"

"Right now."

"Okay." He started the vehicle and headed down the narrow path. "We'll go back to the penthouse and call Lucas. He'll want to go with us."

"No." She leaned forward to type Tony's address into the GPS. "We have to go now."

Max instinctively picked up speed, bouncing over the deep ruts. "What's the hurry?"

"I just learned that Tony's father is anxious to get in and start selling off his son's possessions."

Max shot her a startled glance. "Today?"

She nodded. "As soon as he can get everyone to leave the funeral."

"Shit." He reached for his phone, which he'd left on the seat beside him. "I'll have Lucas meet us there."

"Just hurry," she muttered, ignoring her companion's clipped conversation as he spoke with Lucas.

She logically knew it was a long shot that they would discover anything that would reveal who'd killed Tony. After all, the cops had already searched the place. If there had been actual evidence they would have found it. But deep in her heart, she couldn't squash the hope that there might be something that was overlooked.

It helped to keep at bay the fear that whoever was stalking her was going to get lucky and kill her before they figured out the mystery.

Which meant they had to get there before Tony's dad managed to arrive with a moving truck and empty the place.

Max disconnected the phone and tossed it on the dash. "He's not happy," he informed her. "He wants you to go back home."

*Home.* Mia shuddered. It was a word that should inspire feelings of comfort, not fear.

The fact that someone had stolen that from her made Mia's dark mood even darker.

"The penthouse isn't my home. And I don't have to have Lucas St. Clair's permission."

"It's not about permission," Max said, generously over-looking her bitchiness as he turned onto a main road and headed toward Shreveport. "It's about keeping you safe. Not to mention the fact you just got out of the hospital." He sent her a worried glance. "You should be resting."

She blew out a sigh, reminding herself that none of this was Max's fault. His only sin was trying to help protect her.

"I need to find out who killed Tony," she said, her voice low as she tried to hide her fear. "No matter how much you and Lucas try to protect me, I won't be safe until the murderer is behind bars."

He kept his gaze on the thickening traffic. "You could try trusting us to handle the investigation. We're pretty good at it, you know."

She didn't doubt it for a minute. In fact, if she had to choose between the local detectives or ARES to solve the crime, she'd put her money on Lucas and his friends every time.

But that didn't mean she was willing to crawl into her bed and tug the blankets over her head until this was over.

Since her mother's death she'd had no choice but to take care of herself. Her father simply didn't have the tools to raise a daughter. Which meant handing over control of her life to someone else was more terrifying than hunting down a killer.

"I have no intention of deliberately putting myself in danger," she promised her companion. "But I'm not going to sit around and wait for someone else to solve my problems. It's not who I am."

No doubt sensing that her streak of independence went far deeper than just needing to be involved in the search of Tony's condo, Max gave a low chuckle.

"Lucas is going to have an interesting future."

Zigzagging his way through the traffic with a recklessness that earned him several honks and a dozen middle fingers, Lucas headed over the bridge into Shreveport. He was forced to slow his pace as he hit the residential section of town and weaved his way through the suburbs before he at last pulled into a parking lot.

At his side, Teagan gave a low whistle at the sight of the double-story brick condos that overlooked the nearby lake. "It's nice to have friends in high places," he murmured.

Lucas frowned, struck by his words. He'd seen the financial reports, but until this moment he really didn't consider just how generous Tony's benefactor had been. Now he truly allowed himself to take in the manicured grounds that surrounded the condos and the large pool next to the tennis court.

A long way from the swamps.

"Yes," he murmured, his mind churning. "You know, there can't be a long list of people in the area who can hand over a couple grand every month in cash."

"Drug dealers," Teagan suggested.

Lucas gave a shake of his head. It didn't feel right.

"It's possible," he said slowly. "But Tony couldn't be more than a middleman if he hasn't hit the radar of the local DEA." He nodded toward the elegant condos. "They'd have to be doing a substantial business to pay him for this place."

Teagan shrugged. "Maybe he was making meth in the bathroom for some extra cash."

Lucas snorted. Tony was a great guy but he wasn't the smartest tool in the shed. If he'd been making meth he would have blown the place up with his first batch.

Giving a shake of his head, Lucas was shoving open his car door when Max's silver SUV pulled to a halt beside him.

"Damn," he muttered, his gaze trained on Mia as she was climbing out of the vehicle.

Every fiber of his being vibrated with the need to toss her over his shoulder and carry her far away from the condo. Hell, he wanted to take her away from Louisiana.

Maybe they'd migrate to the Arctic.

A large hand suddenly gripped his upper arm, squeezing with enough force to jerk him out of his dark thoughts.

"Do you want some advice?" Teagan asked.

"No."

"You're getting it anyway." Teagan tightened his grip, making Lucas wince. "Don't try to keep her out."

His gaze never wavered from Mia as she walked toward the condo, her concentration on her purse as she searched for some missing item.

She was still dressed in the skirt and jacket that hugged her lush curves, with her hair tugged into a tight knot. His body instantly responded to her sexy librarian look. Hell, he was a male. And he'd fantasized about this woman for years. But it also reminded him that she'd just come from a dear friend's funeral.

"Easy for you to say," he muttered.

"Think about it, St. Clair," Teagan pressed. "We're all here to protect her. If you try to treat her like a helpless little woman who should stay home and wait for her man to save the day, she's going to rebel." He deliberately paused. "You don't want her going rogue."

Lucas grimaced. They were the same words he'd told himself over and over. It didn't make him like them any better to hear them from his friend.

"I hate this," he growled.

"We'll keep her safe," Teagan swore, climbing out of the car.

Lucas swiftly followed behind, his long strides allowing him to reach Mia's side at the same time that Teagan was taking her hand and smiling down at her with the dazzling charm that made women melt.

"Hello," the younger man murmured, lifting Mia's fingers to his mouth.

Lucas placed a possessive arm around Mia's shoulders, tugging her close to his side. Christ. It was a wonder he wasn't growling like a dog with a favorite bone. "Mia, this is—"

"Teagan," he smoothly interrupted. "You're even more beautiful than your picture."

Lucas reached out to grab Mia's hand, firmly pulling it out of his friend's grasp. "Back off," he warned.

Teagan laughed. "Hey. Women should always have choices."

Looking distinctly overwhelmed, Mia held up the key that she'd obviously been searching for when she was digging in her purse. "This should get us into the condo."

"We'll go through first." Max took command, plucking the key from her hand.

Mia's lips thinned, but she didn't protest when Max took the key from her fingers and headed toward the nearest condo. Unlocking the door, Max followed by Teagan slipped into the house and disappeared in the shadows.

Lucas stayed at Mia's side, his arm still wrapped around her shoulders. They didn't speak, but he counted it as a win that she didn't try to pull away.

In less than ten minutes Lucas received the text he'd been waiting for.

"All clear."

Gritting his teeth, Lucas led Mia into the condo, flipping on the light to reveal a large living room that was . . . beige. The walls, the curtains, and even the carpet. Beige. Beige. Beige.

There was a brown leather couch along one wall and a matching chair that was arranged to view the massive TV in one corner.

That was the only indication that Tony had even lived there.

"What are we looking for?" Teagan asked, glancing toward Mia.

She bit her bottom lip. "I really don't know."

Lucas gave her a small squeeze before he lowered his arm and turned toward his waiting friends.

"A phone. Receipts. Anything that might connect Tony to a partner," he said.

The men nodded before they headed up the carpeted staircase to the upper rooms.

Mia lifted her hand to press it against her temple. Lucas was instantly concerned. He'd known she was pushing herself too hard.

"Are you okay?" he asked, his hand lifting to touch her chilled cheek. "You look pale."

She dropped her hand, belatedly realizing she was giving away more than she intended.

"Just a headache. Nothing a couple aspirin won't cure."

His fingers trailed down to trace the line of her stubborn jaw. "The funeral must have been difficult."

She nodded, her eyes dark with pain. "It was."

"You meant a lot to Tony," he offered, understanding that there was nothing that would make Tony's death easier to accept. The only thing Lucas could do to help was track down the person responsible. "I think you were the only friend he could truly count on."

She released a shaky sigh. "I wish . . ."

"I know," he murmured as her words trailed away.

She closed her eyes before visibly gathering her composure and taking a step back.

"We should look around," she said in firm tones, turning to head toward the nearest doorway. "Tony's dad won't wait long to come and empty the place."

Lucas followed her into a room that looked like an office. Mia crossed directly to the desk in the center of the floor while Lucas chose the file cabinet near the window.

He frowned as he pulled open the drawers to find . . . nothing.

"There's nothing here," Mia muttered.

Lucas swallowed a curse as he turned to watch her straighten from the desk.

"Either Tony never bothered to use this room, or someone was here before us," he said.

"Detective Cooper?"

"Maybe." He glanced toward the window. The area was isolated enough to make it easy for someone to slip in and out unnoticed. "Or maybe the killer returned after he shot Tony and took everything that might name him as a suspect."

"Not everything," Max said as he stepped into the room.

Lucas moved forward, a flare of hope slicing through his frustration. "What did you find?" he demanded.

Max grimaced. "You have to see it to believe it."

Lucas arched a brow. That sounded ominous. Holding out his hand to Mia, he waited for her to join him before leaving the office and crossing the floor of the living room.

Max jerked his head toward the stairs as he moved to stand next to the front door.

Accepting that his friend would stay downstairs to keep watch, Lucas climbed the steps to the upper floor. Then, still holding Mia's hand, he walked into the nearest bedroom and glanced around.

There was more beige, and a leather chair that matched the one downstairs. There was also a king-sized bed with a tiger-striped cover that looked like it'd actually been bought by Tony. Along the far wall was a dresser with the drawers open to reveal that someone had searched through the folded jeans and T-shirts.

Lucas shook his head. It seemed impossible to believe that Tony could live here for so long and make so little impression on the place.

*Because it had never been his home*, a voice whispered in the back of his head. He'd obviously tried to leave behind his dirt-poor childhood, but he'd never been able to settle in a condo that was more suited to a middle-aged banker than a young bachelor.

The thought had barely formed when Teagan poked his head out of the walk-in closet and gestured for them to join him.

"What's going on?" Lucas demanded, stepping into the nearly empty space to discover that Teagan had pushed aside a hidden panel. "A secret door?"

His friend chuckled, squeezing through the narrow opening. "There's more than one secret."

Lucas joined Teagan in the cramped space, glancing in confusion toward the laptop computer that was set on a narrow shelf. "What is this?"

"I noticed a small hole in the wall," Teagan said, pointing up. "I wanted to see what it was for."

Lucas tilted back his head, looking at the small device that was mounted near the ceiling.

"A security camera?"

Teagan chuckled, reaching out to turn the laptop so Lucas could see the video that was currently playing.

"Not quite."

Lucas grimaced at the sight of a naked Tony writhing on top of some woman who was blocked from the camera.

"Christ," he muttered. Tony might not have bothered decorating his home, but he'd spent time and money to create his own private audiovisual playroom.

*Yeesh.*

"Lucas?" Without warning Mia was pushing her way into the room, giving a small sound of shock as she caught sight of the laptop. "We're supposed to be searching for some clue to Tony's murder and you're watching porn?"

Lucas tried to turn her away. "They're Tony's sex tapes."

"Eww. Seriously?"

Lucas waved a hand toward Teagan. "We can go through these later."

Teagan nodded, reaching into his pocket to pull out a thumb drive. Lucas rolled his eyes. Only Teagan would carry spare computer parts with him.

Sliding the stick into the USB slot, Teagan tapped the keys to start the backup. At the same time he began to turn the laptop away even as Mia lunged forward to grab his arm.

"Wait," she breathed, her eyes wide with shock. "Oh my God."

Lucas studied her in confusion. *What the hell?*

"Mia?"

"That's Vicky Fontaine," she rasped.

# Chapter Seventeen

Mia was absently aware of the two men regarding her with disbelief. No big surprise. The angle of the camera meant that the woman beneath Tony was almost completely hidden.

She could, however, clearly see the female hands that were grasping Tony's bare behind.

More importantly, she could see the obscenely large diamond that was catching the overhead light with every movement.

"How can you be sure?" Lucas demanded.

She leaned forward to point at the screen. "I'd recognize that ring anywhere."

Lucas made a sound of shock. "Can you zoom in?"

The large, frighteningly beautiful man who'd introduced himself as Teagan did something with the computer that enlarged the image of the woman's hand.

"God Almighty," Lucas muttered. "You're right. That's her ring."

Mia struggled to accept what she was seeing.

Tony and Vicky. He had to be twenty years younger than she was. Not to mention the fact that he was a boy from the swamps while she was the woman who swore she could trace her lineage back to French royalty.

It didn't make any sense.

Lucas frowned, looking equally baffled. "Can you tell when this was taped?" he asked his friend.

"December third," Teagan answered.

"That's just a few days before he was shot," Lucas muttered. "Are there any other videos?"

Teagan leaned over the computer, golden eyes narrowed as he concentrated on searching through the files.

"It looks like they go back at least five years," he at last said.

"Check out one of the older ones."

Teagan clicked on a file. Instantly the image of Tony in bed filled the screen. But this time the blond-haired woman was visible as she straddled Tony's naked body.

"Same babe," Teagan said, pointing to the flashing diamond on her hand.

Mia shivered. Tony and Vicky had been lovers for at least five years and he'd never said a word to her?

"I can't believe it." She shook her head. "Even seeing it on video doesn't make it seem real."

Lucas stiffened as a sharp whistle echoed from downstairs.

"Teagan," he said in warning tones.

"Got it." Teagan nodded, crouching down to allow his fingers to fly over the keyboard. Then, with a quick motion he was tugging out the thumb drive and slipping it into his pocket.

"What's going on?" Mia demanded.

"That's what I want to know, Ms. Ramon." The voice of Detective Cooper made Mia's heart miss a beat.

Turning, she watched as the lawman stepped into the closet. Belatedly she recalled the whistle. Max had been warning them that they were no longer alone in the condo.

"Detective Cooper," she murmured.

The detective was wearing dress pants and a white shirt and tie, but the jacket was missing. His hair was mussed and he needed a shave, but there was no mistaking the grim authority etched into his face.

"First, breaking and entering," he said in chiding tones, his gaze shifting to the laptop. "And now, tampering with evidence."

Lucas was instantly bristling with anger, his arm wrapping protectively around Mia's shoulders.

"A pleasure to see you too, Cooper," he drawled, his tone deliberately condescending.

Detective Cooper's lips thinned. Clearly working on a Sunday had put him in a sour mood.

Or maybe Lucas was responsible for the mood.

He was pretty good at pissing people off.

"What are you doing here?" the detective demanded.

Lucas shrugged. "I could ask you the same question."

Mia lifted a hand to press it against Lucas's chest, grimacing at the feel of his tense muscles. "Lucas," she murmured in a soft warning.

The lawman narrowed his gaze. "Would you like to have this conversation downtown?"

Mia hastily intervened. "We aren't breaking and entering." The last thing she wanted was Lucas spending the night in jail. "I have a key that Tony gave me when he first moved in, and the permission of his brother to be here."

"Why?"

Lucas once again was the one to answer. "She was hoping to find a small memento to remind her of her childhood friend."

The detective deliberately allowed his gaze to roam over the cramped space where the three of them were huddled together.

"And she just happened to stumble into a hidden room?"

"What are the odds?" Teagan mocked.

Mia swallowed a curse. Like things weren't difficult enough without Lucas's friends trying to annoy the detective?

"Burt told me the cops were finished with the condo," she said, hoping they could get out of the place without being shot.

Detective Cooper glared at Teagan before reluctantly answering her question. "We've completed our search."

"But you kept it under surveillance?" Lucas demanded.

The detective nodded. "We did."

Mia furrowed her brow. The cops had deliberately told Burt and his family the condo had been cleared, but they kept a watch on it? Why . . .

"This was a trap?" she breathed as realization hit.

Detective Cooper shrugged. "I was interested in who would show up."

She tilted her chin, angered that they'd been spied on like they were suspects.

"We have every right to be here," she stiffly informed him.

The detective nodded toward the panel that Teagan had pushed aside to reveal the hidden space. "Did you know about this?"

Mia gaped at the man in disbelief. Did he think she was some sort of pervert who liked watching her friend have sex?

"Of course not," she snapped. "I've never been here before."

Detective Cooper arched a brow. "So you won't mind handing over the computer?"

She jerked. So that was it. He thought she was on the sex tapes. And that she'd snuck in to erase the evidence.

"Now, look here, you—"

"She was a friend to Tony, not his lover," Lucas interrupted, tightening his arm around her shoulders.

Detective Cooper carefully studied her angry expression.

Was he trying to determine if she was lying or not? Apparently satisfied, he turned his head toward Teagan. "The computer."

Teagan leaned down to grab the laptop and with one graceful motion was stepping forward to shove it into the detective's waiting hand. "It's all yours."

"Shouldn't you be trying to discover who broke into Mia's house?" Lucas chided. "As far as I can tell, you haven't done a damned thing to locate the intruder."

Detective Cooper leaned forward until he was almost nose to nose with Lucas. "I'm a homicide detective, not a patrol officer."

Lucas refused to back down. "Someone tried to kill Mia. Are you trying to tell me it's not your case?"

"Do I tell you how to do your job?"

"You don't need to," Lucas snapped.

Without warning Teagan was grabbing Lucas by the arm and steering him through the narrow opening. "Yeah, I think that's our cue to take off."

The detective stepped back, his face reddened with annoyance. "Good choice."

"Come on, amigo," Teagan urged when Lucas tried to dig in his feet.

Mia did her own part by pushing at Lucas's back, managing to get him out of the closet and headed from the bedroom before he glanced toward his friend at his side.

"Did you get a copy?" he asked in a low voice.

Teagan patted his pocket. "Got it."

"Good."

They headed downstairs where Max was waiting along with three other men who were all dressed in suits with scuffed shoes. Detective Cooper's fellow officers.

The men of ARES, along with Mia, left the condo, not bothering to lock the door behind them as they headed across the parking lot.

"We'll meet back at the penthouse," Lucas commanded,

grabbing Mia's arm to firmly place her in the passenger seat of his car.

Teagan shrugged as he jumped into Max's SUV and they quickly pulled away.

Lucas started the engine, but instead of following his friends, he turned in his seat to study her with a worried gaze.

"You're shaking." He switched on the heater, then reached out to lightly touch her brow with the tips of his fingers. "Do you need to see a doctor?"

Mia instantly felt her shivers ease. It wasn't the warm air that was blowing out of the vents. Or even relief at being out of Tony's condo.

It was Lucas's gentle touch and the knowledge that someone actually cared whether or not she was okay.

"No. I'm fine." Her lips twisted in a wry smile. "It's just been . . . a shock."

"Yeah." Lucas glanced toward the condo. "When Teagan traced the money connection from Vicky to Tony I thought he must have been helping the woman with some shady business deals." He shook his head. "It never occurred to me that she was his sugar mama."

Mia studied Lucas's profile, her gaze unconsciously tracing the perfect line of his features.

"What money trail?"

"She paid his bond to get him out of jail when he was younger," he explained. "And now I assume she must have been giving him the cash for his rent."

Mia once again discovered herself floundering. She'd never actually considered who'd been responsible for getting Tony out of jail. Actually, it seemed that she hadn't given much thought at all to her friend and his hidden life.

"I had no idea," she rasped. "Why did they keep it such a secret?"

Lucas snorted. "Do you really think Vicky Fontaine would

want anyone to know that she was climbing between the sheets with Tony Hughes?"

Mia winced, vividly reminded that she'd been considered an embarrassment by the St. Clair clan.

"No. I suppose not," she muttered.

He frowned, as if sensing he'd managed to hurt her. "Mia—"

"Still, it's not like Tony to be able to keep his mouth shut," she interrupted, pulling away from his fingers, which were stroking down her cheek.

Now wasn't the time to rake over their past. They had to figure out if Tony's connection to Vicky had anything to do with his death.

Lucas allowed his gaze to roam over Mia's face, clearly wanting to press her for an explanation for her sudden retreat. Then, with a grimace, he let it go.

"Tony never gave any hint?" he instead asked.

"None." She glanced toward the nearby lake. This hushed, middle-class suburb was so . . . traditional. Not at all the sort of place where Tony would want to live. Which made her wonder if it'd been his choice or Vicky's. She wrinkled her nose at the thought of her childhood friend feeling trapped in a relationship where he was nothing more than a nasty secret. "I knew he worked for the Fontaines when he was in high school, and it's possible he did some handiwork for her even after he graduated, but he never talked about her," she said.

Lucas's jaw clenched, his eyes growing distant, as if he was recalling the past. "Damn."

"What?"

"After Tony was kicked off the football team everyone expected him to leave school, but instead some mystery donor arrived to pay his tuition so he could graduate with the rest of us."

She gave a slow nod. She'd gone to visit Tony in juvie,

expecting him to be devastated at the loss of his scholarship. He'd been so proud of attending Hale Academy with the rich kids.

But instead of being upset, he'd been cocky and defiant, and brazenly certain everything would work out.

"I remember," she murmured. "You think Vicky wrote the check?"

He held her gaze. "Who else would?"

She started to give a nod, only to freeze as the words truly sank in.

"They surely weren't . . ." She wrinkled her nose again. It was hard enough to imagine Tony and Vicky as lovers now, let alone when he'd been a wild teenager and she'd been a young, sophisticated pillar of society. "Together back then?"

"It happens."

Perhaps sensing she needed time to process the disturbing thought of Tony being seduced by the older woman, Lucas put the car in gear and pulled out of the parking lot.

Lucas opened the door to the penthouse. The scent of warm bread and corned beef teased at his nose, making his stomach rumble. Clearly Max and Teagan had made a pit stop at a local deli. A good thing. It'd been hours since his last meal and he was fairly certain there wasn't a damned thing to eat in the place.

On the point of leading Mia toward the appetizing aroma, he abruptly reached out to wrap an arm around her shoulder as she stumbled and nearly fell. Glancing down, he grimaced at the pallor of her face and the shadows beneath her eyes.

Of course she hadn't told him that she was clearly exhausted. He might have thought she was vulnerable.

And Mia Ramon could never be weak. At least not when he was around.

Careful to keep his tone light, he steered her across the living room toward the attached suite.

"You have to be exhausted," he murmured. "You should lie down for a while."

"I couldn't sleep. Besides, I'm fine," she predictably argued, only to ruin her stubborn insistence when her body trembled with weariness.

Resisting the urge to scoop her off her feet and tuck her in bed, he reached out to rub her bottom lip with his thumb. "Then at least take a hot bath."

She studied him with open suspicion. "What are you going to do?"

"We need to check through the computer files that Teagan managed to download." He gave a humorless laugh when she wrinkled her nose in disgust. He didn't blame her. The thought of spending hours watching Tony have sex with Vicky Fontaine was . . . disturbing as hell. "Yeah, you might want to give that a miss."

She flattened her lips. "You won't try to leave me out of the loop if you find something?"

He hesitated before he answered. There was a part of him that wanted to refuse. She'd been through enough. He wanted her to concentrate on regaining her strength while he figured out who was trying to kill her.

But Teagan's warning was still fresh in his mind. If he didn't include her in the investigation, she would go out on her own.

And that was unacceptable.

"No, I won't leave you out of the loop."

Perhaps sensing his reluctance, she narrowed her gaze. "You promise?"

"I promise." Leaning down, he pressed his lips to her brow, then, grabbing her shoulders, he turned her toward the bedroom. "Take your bath and I'll bring you something to eat."

There was a second when he thought she might continue her demands for reassurance before she wearily headed through the door. He waited until he heard the bathroom door close before he was jogging into the suite to the kitchen.

Teagan and Max were finishing up their dinner as he entered. Lucas's stomach growled as Max tossed him a sandwich, and quickly unwrapping it, he took a large bite of the toasted rye bread and the thick slabs of corned beef.

*Yum.*

"Did you convince her to rest?"

"Temporarily." He nodded toward the computer that Teagan had already set up on the kitchen table. "We need to get through those tapes before she joins us."

"On it," Teagan said, polishing off his bottle of water and moving to take a seat in front of the computer.

Lucas swiftly demolished his sandwich and reached into the fridge for a beer. Twisting off the top, he downed half the bottle in one long gulp as Teagan downloaded the videos.

Standing behind his friend's chair, he watched as the image of Tony's bedroom flickered onto the screen, but less than five minutes later he was sharply turning away to pace toward the glass wall that overlooked the river.

Darkness had descended, but the clouds had at last parted to allow the moonlight to shimmer off the water. With a small sigh, Lucas leaned his forehead against the window.

"Are you okay?" Max asked, moving to stand beside him.

Lucas shook his head. "Not really."

Max reached out to lay a hand on his shoulder. "Do you want to talk about it?"

Heaving a sigh, he turned to meet his friend's worried gaze. "Every time I think I might get answers I end up with more questions."

"That's not entirely true," Max argued. "We know that Tony wasn't quite the loner that we first thought."

Lucas released a sharp laugh. It wasn't that he'd ever believed that Tony lived like a monk, but he'd assumed his old friend must have used prostitutes when he wanted a little companionship.

Who the hell would ever have suspected he was conducting a secret affair with a woman twice his age?

"Craziness," he muttered, considering what they'd managed to discover during the day. "You know, Vicky Fontaine's name seems to be a recurring theme," he pointed out.

"True," Max agreed. "She was obviously Tony's lover."

Lucas nodded. "And Teagan discovered that she was his private ATM."

Max arched a brow. "Really?"

"Yep."

"And she wants to buy Mia's land."

"Desperately," Lucas agreed, trying to connect the dots in his mind.

Unfortunately, he still couldn't make sense of it.

At least not when it came to Tony's murder. Or why someone was trying to hurt Mia.

Granted, Vicky might have been furious if Tony had threatened to expose their love affair, but that was hardly a reason to kill him. And if she wanted Mia's land, then it wouldn't make sense to want her dead. It wasn't like Vicky would be in Mia's will.

Lucas frowned, belatedly recalling he hadn't asked Mia what actually happened to her property if she died.

"Is there any other connection?" Max asked as Lucas remained locked in his dark thoughts.

Without warning there was the scrape of a chair against the tiled floor as Teagan abruptly rose to his feet. "I might have something," he said.

Together, Max and Lucas rushed back into the kitchen, watching as Teagan shut down his computer and grabbed his leather jacket, which was tossed on the counter.

"What is it?" Lucas demanded.

"It's just a suspicion right now," Teagan warned, heading out of the kitchen and crossing the floor to the front door. "I'll know more when I run it through my equipment."

"You're leaving?" Lucas growled, following behind his friend.

"I need to get to Houston," Teagan said in absent tones, his mind clearly occupied with what he'd seen. "I'll be back when I manage to clean up the images."

Lucas muttered a low curse. "At least show me what you're looking at."

Teagan pulled open the door, glancing over his shoulder at Lucas. "Nope. I don't want to get your hopes up. It could turn out to be nothing."

Lucas clenched his hands at his side. It was that or give his friend a good shake.

"Dammit, Teagan—"

"I'll miss you too, sweetie," Teagan interrupted with a mocking grin. Then his attention shifted to Max, who'd moved to stand at Lucas's side. "Take care of him."

"You got it," Max promised.

With a nod, Teagan pulled open the door and disappeared from the penthouse.

"He's the most aggravating bastard I've ever met," Lucas breathed as the door snapped shut.

Max laid a hand on his shoulder. "And one of the best friends I've ever had."

A wry smile twisted Lucas's lips. "Amen."

# Chapter Eighteen

Taylor stood at her doorway, peering at the dark sedan parked next to her curb. She'd easily recognized the car. It belonged to Detective Cooper. Which was why her first instinct had been to call and make sure that Mia was okay the second she'd caught sight of the vehicle. Now that Lucas had promised Taylor that her friend was comfortably asleep in bed, her initial stab of fear had been replaced with a tingle of anticipation.

It was stupid.

She should go back inside and ignore the lawman. If the detective had a genuine need to see her, then he would have come to the door and knocked. Or more likely, he would have called and demanded that she drive to the station to answer questions.

Instead she found her feet moving forward, carrying her along the driveway and around the back of the car. She halted next to the driver's door, waiting for him to roll down the window.

"Detective Cooper," she murmured, barely able to make out more than a vague outline of his face and the fact he was still wearing his white dress shirt and tie.

Which meant he'd spent the day working.

"Brian," he softly corrected.

Her lips twitched at his stubborn insistence. "Brian."

"That's better," he murmured.

She leaned forward, trying to see his expression. "Justin told me there was some stranger lurking out here," she said. "I almost called nine-one-one."

"Next time don't hesitate," he chided. "You can't be too careful."

She rolled her eyes. There were occasions he was pure cop.

"I'll keep that in mind," she promised. "What are you doing out here?"

There was a long silence before she heard him heave a deep sigh.

"I don't know."

She frowned, sensing his tension. "Is something wrong?"

He scrubbed a hand over his face, his shoulders slumped. "Not really. It's just been a long, frustrating day and I . . ."

She studied his shadowed profile as his words trailed away. "And you . . . ?"

He turned his head to meet her searching gaze. "I wanted someone to talk to."

A dangerous tenderness threatened to melt her heart. There was something extraordinarily flattering about a strong, successful male seeking her out just because he wanted to talk.

Like she was special or something.

"Why didn't you knock on the door?"

His hands dropped, his gaze moving toward the door she'd left open to allow the soft light to spill across the front yard.

"Once I got here I realized that it was Sunday night and that you were probably enjoying a quiet evening with your family."

She studied him in confusion. "So you just decided to sit here in your car?"

"Yeah. I couldn't make myself go home." He hunched his shoulders. "Ridiculous, huh?"

"No. It's not ridiculous." Barely resisting the urge to reach through the open window and smooth his tousled hair, she instead grabbed the door handle and tugged it open. "Come inside."

He slowly crawled out of the car, his movements stiff, as if he'd been sitting for a long time.

"What about your family?" he demanded.

"We already had our dinner together," she assured him, wondering how he knew that she insisted they have a proper, sit-down meal on Sunday night. It was the one time during the week she could be certain they would be together. "Now my mother is at her weekly bingo game and my son is locked in his room. He's very vocal in his assurance that he can only handle a limited amount of enforced 'family time.'"

The detective allowed his head to tilt back to glance at the upstairs window that glowed with the light from Justin's computer game. "You're sure?" he pressed.

Was she?

There was a part of her that warned her this was a very bad idea. Not because she was afraid of Brian. He was a hero, not one of the losers she usually attracted. But because he made her think about dreams and wishes that she'd thought she'd managed to put in her past.

He remained perfectly still, allowing her the time to sort through her tangled thoughts.

"Yes," she breathed. "I'm sure."

In silence she led him up the driveway and onto the porch. Then, stepping aside, she allowed him to enter first, closing the door behind them.

With undisguised interest, Brian glanced around the small room with the worn couch and two recliners that were covered with blankets she'd crocheted when she'd been pregnant with Justin.

The walls were paneled, and the floor was original hardwood, making it darker than Taylor liked, but it was ruthlessly clean and filled with pictures of a family who openly loved each other. And to add to the coziness was a small Christmas tree that she'd decorated with Justin earlier in the day.

"It's not fancy, but it's home," she muttered, suddenly self-conscious.

She wished that she had taken time to brush her hair and change out of her jeans and oversized Tulane sweatshirt. She felt as frumpy as her house.

"It's nice." He turned, meeting her guarded gaze with a shimmering intensity that made her mouth go dry. "Comfortable."

She cleared her throat. How long had it been since she'd invited a man to the house?

Not since her horse patootie of an ex-husband had walked out.

"Would you like something to drink?" she abruptly demanded.

He tilted his head to the side, as if sensing her sudden unease. "What are you having?"

"Hot chocolate." She glanced toward the cabinet that held a couple of dusty bottles of whiskey. "But you're welcome to have—"

"Hot chocolate sounds perfect," he gently interrupted.

"Okay."

She waved a vague hand toward the sofa as she turned to scurry into the kitchen. She was anxious to put some space between them so she could regroup.

Was there anything more embarrassing than acting like a giggly teen on her first date?

But even as she crossed the linoleum floor, she felt the prickle of heat that meant Brian was only inches behind her.

Clearly he hadn't gotten the hint he was supposed to

stay in the living room while she regained command of her composure.

"Mmm." He sucked in a deep breath, moving toward the pot set on the ancient stove. "Made from scratch?"

Resigned to the fact that Brian intended to make himself at home, Taylor collected two mugs from the white-painted cabinets and moved to the stove.

Without her needing to ask, Brian lifted the pot and poured out the warm cocoa. Taylor reached for the marshmallows that she'd put into a bowl on the counter, tossing them into the mugs before she was carrying them to the small table near the window.

"My mother would consider it a blasphemy to use anything out of a package," she told Brian, watching as he took his seat and reached for one of the mugs.

"My mom's the same way."

Sliding into her chair, Taylor cupped the hot mug in her hands and studied her companion's face. His skin was pale, and there was a weariness etched into his features, but there was still a compelling vitality in the dark eyes and a steady strength in the hard line of his jaw.

A man's man, but with the protective instincts of a cop.

Dangerous.

"Does your mother live in town?"

He shook his head. "No, my family is from Texas, but since most of us have chosen to go into law enforcement I decided to migrate to Louisiana to avoid any talk of nepotism."

"Your father's a cop?"

"And my mother and brother and two uncles."

She blinked, unable to imagine a whole clan of policemen and women. That had to make family reunions interesting.

"Wow," she murmured.

"Yeah." He grimaced. "It's a little overwhelming."

"I think it would be wonderful to have a family tradition,"

she swiftly assured him. "Justin's father . . ." She halted, not wanting to discuss her ex with this man. "Let's just say that my son doesn't have the best footsteps to follow in."

Brian leaned forward, holding her gaze. "I'd say that he has the best footsteps in the world to follow in."

Heat stained her cheeks at the deep sincerity in his voice. She could go toe to toe with someone who tried to insult her abilities as a single mother, but she melted into a puddle of goo at any hint of approval.

"You said you wanted to talk." She hurriedly changed the direction of the conversation. "Did something happen with Mia's case?"

He took a sip of cocoa before answering. "Nothing I can share."

Taylor stiffened. "Okay."

He reached out to touch her arm, his eyes darkening with regret. "I really can't, Taylor. Not without risking the case if we ever make an arrest."

*Oh.* It wasn't personal. He obviously had a dozen rules and regulations when it came to his investigations.

Brushing aside her momentary pang of hurt, she concentrated on her friend.

"Can you at least tell me if you have any suspects?"

There was a brief pause before he shook his head. "Not yet."

She shivered, hating the thought of her friend in danger. "I wish there was something I could do to help."

He gave her arm a gentle squeeze. "We're doing everything in our power to keep her safe."

She allowed herself to become lost in the dark comfort of his eyes. The feel of his fingers seared through the heavy fabric of her sleeve, a delicious tension filling the air.

Then, just as swiftly as the magical moment was created, it was shattered as her sixteen-year-old son strolled into the kitchen.

The young man already topped six foot, but with a slender body that hadn't yet filled out. His hair was a dark brown and damp from a recent shower, and his thin face held the promise of the sculpted beauty of his father. The only decent thing Danny had ever given their son.

Clearly aware that there was a man in the house, Justin strolled nonchalantly toward the stove, shooting covert glances at Brian. "Is the hot chocolate ready?"

Pulling her arm away from Brian's hand, Taylor resisted the urge to jump to her feet. Why did she feel so weird?

It wasn't like there was anything going on.

Was there?

Waiting until her son had poured himself a mug of cocoa, she nodded her head in Brian's direction. "Justin. This is Detective Cooper."

"I know you." Justin blatantly inspected the male intruder, his expression unreadable. "You help with the Cajun Bombers."

Brian nodded. "When I have the time."

"Why are you here?" Justin bluntly demanded. "Is something wrong?"

"No, I just wanted to spend some time with your mother."

There was a startled silence. Taylor couldn't believe what he'd just said. Or what the words implied.

Justin, on the other hand, allowed a slow smile to curve his lips. "That's cool." Sauntering back across the floor, he sent Taylor a wink even as he spoke to Brian. "You should have some pecan pie. It's the best in town."

Taylor gave a slow shake of her head as Justin left the kitchen and the sound of his heavy footsteps pounding up the stairs filled the air.

What the heck had just happened?

Not at all rattled by the strange encounter, Brian leaned

back in his chair, his eyes dark with an unmistakable flare of desire.

"Why didn't I know there was pie?"

Taylor reached for her mug and took a deep, scalding drink of her chocolate. Oh Lord. She was in trouble.

The early morning sunlight was streaming through the window when Mia woke from a deep sleep. She blinked in confusion. Then, as her eyes cleared, she blinked again.

Was she still dreaming?

What else was a woman supposed to think when she opened her eyes to find she was lying naked in bed with a gorgeous male who was equally naked?

That was the stuff of fantasies, not real life.

Reaching out her hand, she touched the wide chest that was directly in front of her face. It felt solid enough. And warm. Yummy warm.

Her hand strayed over the silken heat, delighting in the hard muscles that tensed beneath her touch before she was stiffening in annoyance.

What was wrong with her?

She just woke up naked in bed with no memory of how she'd gotten there.

She should be thinking about kicking the aggravating man off the mattress, not how much she wanted to explore every delectable inch of him.

Planting her hand firmly against Lucas's chest, she gave him a sharp shake. "Wake up," she growled.

"Hmm." His eyes remained shut as he tightened his arms around her, tugging her against the searing heat of his body.

A shiver of pleasure raced through her at the feel of his erection pressing into her lower stomach. Unlike her, he obviously had no conflicting emotions about waking up with a naked woman in his bed.

"Lucas." She gave a push against his chest. "What happened?"

His lashes lifted far enough for her to catch a gleam of amusement in his astonishingly blue eyes.

"Nothing yet," he said in husky tones, tilting his head forward to brand a trail of kisses over her forehead and down her temple. "But that could change if you're feeling better."

She sucked in a deep breath, instantly saturated in the delicious scent of soap and warm, male skin. Had he showered just before coming to bed? Once again she was nearly overwhelmed by the vivid fantasy of tasting his body with her lips and tongue.

Curling her hands into fists to keep herself from smoothing them over his chest, she tilted back her head to avoid his kiss.

"Wait," she muttered.

Denied her mouth, Lucas contented himself with grazing his lips up and down the arched line of her throat.

"Haven't you heard the old saying 'to seize the day'?" he teased.

Mia trembled. How was she supposed to think when his touch was wreaking havoc?

"I don't think it's the day you want to seize," she muttered.

Scraping his early morning whiskers over her shoulder, he cupped her backside in his hands and tugged her even tighter against the hard length of his cock.

"Busted," he admitted with a low chuckle.

Her toes curled and her back instinctively arched in pleasure.

"Lucas, what happened last night?" she forced herself to demand, already feeling the urgency to shut out the world and drown in the sensations tingling through her.

After all, she'd decided she wasn't going to have sex with Lucas again, hadn't she?

He nipped the sensitive skin at the base of her throat. "I told you. Nothing."

She struggled to think through the fog of desire that was clouding her mind.

He was so big and warm and delectable. And his lips knew exactly how to make her quiver as they stroked down the line of her collarbone.

"I remember taking a bath and then nothing after that," she managed to rasp.

He smoothed one hand downward, grabbing the back of her thigh so he could tug her leg over his hip.

"You fell asleep in the tub," he explained, his lips twitching as she gave a tiny gasp at the feel of his arousal pressing against the point of her most intense pleasure. "I assumed you would be more comfortable in bed so I tucked you in and gave you a very chaste kiss on the forehead."

Last night's kiss might have been chaste, but the open-mouthed caresses he was spreading over the upper curve of her breasts now were anything but innocent.

Her nipples instinctively hardened, silently begging for his touch.

"You should have woken me up." She fiercely forced herself to concentrate on the point she was trying to make.

She did have a point, didn't she?

"Why?" Lucas asked, his tongue tracing the circle of her nipple.

"I . . ." She nearly forgot what she wanted to say as he at last closed his lips around the tip of her breast. Heat streaked through her, clenching her lower stomach as she pressed against the welcomed thrust of his cock.

"Yes?" he teased.

Her hands lifted to tangle in his hair, the jolts of intense excitement making her toes curl.

"I want to be a part of the investigation," she managed to murmur.

His sudden motion had her rolled flat on her back, pressing her into the mattress with the weight of his body.

"You are," he assured her, continuing to torment her nipple with tiny licks before he was sucking it deep into his mouth.

A small moan was wrenched from her throat. No one but Lucas had ever realized just how gloriously sensitive her breasts were. And how quickly she could become aroused from the feel of warm lips against her nipples.

Soon sanity was going to become a losing battle.

"Then tell me what you found on the computer."

He turned his attention to her other breast, clearly not in the mood to chat.

"Actually I'm not sure," he muttered.

Disappointment sliced through the dizzying desire, making her stiffen beneath him.

"Dammit," she snarled. "I knew you—"

He pressed his lips to her mouth to halt her furious words, waiting until she was melting beneath his kiss before he lifted his head to meet her angry gaze.

"I'm serious, Mia," he said in low tones. "Teagan muttered something about looking closer at one of the videos and then took off."

She stared up at his face, which was shadowed with an early morning beard and flushed with sleep. Even with his hair tousled he was still dazzlingly beautiful in the golden sunlight.

"Does he think it's a clue?" she asked, a small ray of hope flickering to life.

Right now it was easy to forget the world outside and the fact that someone might very well be trying to kill her. But she couldn't hide in the protection of Lucas's arms forever.

"Who knows?" His lips twisted into a wry smile. "The

last I heard he was driving back to Houston so he could run the data through HAL."

"Hal?" She furrowed her brow. Was that another ARES member?

"HAL 9000 from *2001: A Space Odyssey*. That's what I call his computer setup at our office. It looks like something out of the future," he explained, leaning down to press a light kiss to her lips.

Almost as if he couldn't keep himself from touching her. The thought made her heart clench with a joy that should have terrified her.

"He must have told you something," she breathed.

He traced his hands down the curve of her waist and over her hips. At the same time, he shifted his weight so he could settle between her legs.

"Teagan is a closet drama queen," he said, his lips skimming over her cheek. "He disappears with a vague promise of discovering new intel and then reappears with answers that always manage to dazzle us."

Her breath tangled in her throat as he kissed his way down her neck and into the valley between her breasts.

"I hope you're right," she choked out. She didn't know much about Teagan, but if he was anything like Lucas, she could at least be certain he wouldn't be satisfied until he achieved his goal.

"Haven't you learned by now that I'm always right?" he demanded, continuing to move down her body as he pressed searing kisses against her responsive flesh.

Mia squirmed beneath him, allowing her legs to part as he feathered kisses over the clenched muscles of her stomach.

"Do you want me to answer that?"

"Probably not." He tickled her belly button with the tip of his tongue. "There's nothing we can do but wait for Teagan to return."

She was melting beneath his touch, a dampness already forming between her legs as she ached for him to fill her.

"Then I should get ready for work," she said, even as she accepted she wasn't leaving this bed.

Not until Lucas finished what he'd started.

"No way," he retorted, tracing the slight swell of her belly with a reverent appreciation. She'd always loved the fact that Lucas vocally complimented her curves, claiming that no man liked a stick-figure in his arms. "You're staying home today."

She glanced down her body, mesmerized by the sight of him slipping off the end of the mattress as he tugged her legs over his shoulders.

"Says who?" she rasped.

He sent her a teasing smile before he turned his head to kiss the tender skin of her inner thigh.

"Don't you want to be here when Teagan returns?"

She released a choked groan, her heels digging into his back at the explosion of pleasure that rocketed through her.

He kissed each inch of her with a slow attention to detail that made her tremble with need.

"You could call me," she ridiculously suggested. As if she could go to the office and actually concentrate on work.

He slid his tongue through the damp heat between her legs. "Stay," he commanded.

"I'm not sure if this is a good idea," she gasped, her eyes squeezing shut as he dipped his tongue into the entrance of her body.

Her fingers tightened in his hair, her hips lifting off the bed as he pleasured her with his mouth.

Suddenly she couldn't remember why she was fighting this. It had something to do with the past. And protecting her heart . . .

But her body didn't care about that stuff.

It was ready, willing, and able to indulge in a few hours of fun.

Taking her to the very brink of an orgasm, Lucas planted a kiss on her inner thigh before he was moving back up her body.

"You're right," he husked. "Not a good idea. A *great* idea." He took time to kiss the tip of each breast before he was settling between her spread legs. "The best idea I've had in fifteen years," he assured her, gazing down at her with smoldering eyes.

Feeling as if she was spinning out of control, she said, "If this happens—"

"Oh, it's gonna happen," he insisted, trailing his tongue up the curve of her neck.

He was right. She was so close to climax she was fairly certain she would kill anyone or anything that tried to interfere. Still, she felt a cowardly urge to dismiss the intensity of her need.

"It's just a temporary madness," she breathed.

He lifted his head, his expression clenched with the effort of leashing his desire.

"This might be madness, but there's nothing temporary about it," he growled.

She rolled her eyes. Of course he couldn't let her hang on to her pretense this was a brief moment of insanity.

"Arrogant," she muttered.

"Yep." With a smile he leaned down to trace her lips with the tip of his tongue.

"That wasn't a compliment."

"If you can still talk, I'm not doing this right," he growled.

"I—"

Her words were cut short as he kissed her with a forceful purpose. Desire blasted through her, scorching away the flimsy barriers she tried to keep between them.

It'd been foolish from the beginning to think she could make love with this man without feeling utterly vulnerable.

That was how it'd always been between them.

Passionate. All-consuming. Irresistible.

Continuing to kiss her over and over, Lucas moved his hands to cup her breasts, his thumbs rubbing over her nipples until she was groaning with sharp-edged need to have him inside her.

"That's better," he teased with a smug contentment as she wrapped her legs around his waist.

"Like I said, arrogant," she muttered.

Lifting his head, he held her gaze as he reached to pull open a drawer of the nightstand beside the bed. Then, slipping on a condom, he entered her with one smooth thrust.

"Mia," he groaned in harsh pleasure, his eyes sliding shut as he slowly pulled out before surging forward.

Her hands moved to grasp his shoulders, the enticing tension building deep inside her as he continued to rock in and out of her as he pressed hungry kisses over her face.

But soon the slow pace wasn't enough. Mia was hovering on the edge of bliss, but before she gave in to her looming orgasm she wanted to smash through Lucas's fierce control.

She dug her nails into his flesh, angling her hips off the mattress as she met him thrust for thrust.

"More," she murmured.

A strangled groan was wrenched from his throat. "You're sure?"

"Yes."

Grabbing onto the sturdy headboard, he gazed down at her with passion-glazed eyes.

"Hold on, baby."

# Chapter Nineteen

Teagan stood behind the desk in his large office, leaning forward to study the computer monitor.

He had a chair, of course. One that'd been constructed to perfectly conform to his large body. Hell, he'd paid a small fortune to ensure that everything in his office was top of the line. But he'd been up for forty-eight hours, and it wouldn't take more than a few minutes in the buttery leather cushions to have him nodding off.

Planting his hands flat on the smooth wood, he impatiently waited for the program he was running to finish its latest polishing of the image he'd pulled from Tony's video.

At the same time, he listened intently to the approaching footsteps.

He already knew who was entering the door behind him.

"Have you had any sleep?" Hauk demanded, moving to lean against the edge of the desk.

Teagan straightened, glancing at his friend, who was wearing a tailored gray jacket and crisp white shirt with a burgundy silk tie.

It was his "meeting with a client" power suit.

Teagan, on the other hand, was wearing black jeans, a

gray Henley, and a pair of shit-kickers. No one was stupid enough to let him meet with clients.

"Not yet," he admitted, lifting his hand to scrape it along the whiskers that darkened his jaw.

"Go home," Hauk commanded. "Whatever you're looking for will be there tomorrow."

Teagan nodded his head toward the monitor. "Actually, I think I might have something."

Hauk arched a brow. "From the video?"

"Yep." On his drive to Houston Teagan had called Hauk to fill him in. "I had to enlarge the picture several times, which means that I'm still trying to sharpen the image, but you can start to see what she's handing him."

Hauk grimaced as he moved to have a clearer look at the screen. It wasn't a pleasant sight.

Tony was butt-naked and stretched across the bed with an equally naked Vicky Fontaine perched on top of him. But it wasn't their entwined bodies that interested him. Instead, he fast-forwarded to the point when the woman crawled off Tony. Then, rolling to the side, she reached for the purse that was left on a nightstand. Opening the bag, she pulled out a small object and tossed it onto Tony's bare chest.

Hauk leaned closer. "Is it a picture?"

"Not just any picture." Teagan tapped on his mouse, enlarging the image.

"Shit." Hauk turned his head to meet Teagan's steady gaze. "That's the picture of Mia."

"Yep."

When Teagan had first been skimming through the videos he'd thought the older woman had tossed a condom on Tony's chest. Her way of saying they weren't done. Teagan had made an effort to discover what it was only because he'd thought it was weird that Tony would jerk as if he'd been scalded when she made the move.

"Can you prove it was the one Tony was holding when he was killed?"

Teagan gave a lift of his hands. "Unfortunately, the video was grainy, and the efforts to enlarge the image have made it even fuzzier," he said. "I'm going to filter it a few more times to see if I can pick up the handwriting."

Hauk nodded, his brow furrowed as he turned to lean against the edge of the desk. "If it's the photo, it looks like Vicky Fontaine is involved in this mess."

Teagan gave a short laugh. "I'd say she's up to her recently lifted eyebrows in it."

Hauk looked confused. "Why would she want to kill her lover?"

Teagan had chewed over a dozen different explanations before realizing the most obvious. "My guess would be that Tony was going to Lucas to warn him that Mia was in danger."

Hauk arched a brow. "That makes sense," he murmured. "He was never the intended target."

"Not until he decided to talk to the wrong person."

Hauk glanced back at the screen. "The picture would imply that Mia is the one who's in danger." He returned his attention to Teagan. "Do we know why Vicky Fontaine would want to hurt her?"

"That's what Lucas is trying to find out," Teagan said. "So far we know the Fontaine woman wants to buy George Ramon's land. She claims it's to turn it into a protected wetland."

"Have you investigated the property?"

Teagan cocked a brow. Had his friend really just asked him if he'd done his research?

"From every possible angle," he said. "There are no hidden oil or natural gas deposits. There's no conservation group desperate to buy it to save some endangered toad. And there's no plan for any local businesses intending to expand in the area." He lifted his shoulder. "As far as I can discover it's just a patch of swampy ground in the middle of nowhere."

Hauk considered a long moment. "Maybe it isn't the land, but what's sitting on the land."

That had been Teagan's thought as well. "According to Lucas it was a bunch of junk," he told his friend.

"One man's junk is another man's treasure."

"True." Teagan had once known a man who'd stabbed his best friend for his lucky rabbit's foot. "It wouldn't hurt for Lucas to go out and have a look around. I'll say something to him when I finish cleaning up this picture and send it to him."

"Send it?" Hauk straightened, studying Teagan with a searching gaze. "You're not going back to Shreveport?"

"Not now." Teagan deliberately kept his tone light. "I have a few things I want to investigate."

Hauk narrowed his gaze. "What things?"

Teagan was prepared for the question. "I've already started with Paul Fontaine."

"Vicky's husband?"

"That's the one."

"Why?"

He tapped a finger on the edge of the desk. It was a long shot. The man had disappeared seventeen years ago. Which meant that there wasn't much chance it had anything to do with what was happening today.

Still, Teagan had a gut feeling. And that was something he'd learned never to ignore.

"The man skipped town with millions of dollars in pension funds," Teagan said.

Hauk shrugged. "Wasn't he already investigated?"

"He was, but I still think it's hinky," Teagan said.

"Show me."

Teagan led his friend to the long table set up next to the

edge of the room. There were a half dozen computers set up, all of them running separate searches.

Reaching the computer on the end, Teagan leaned down to type on the keyboard, pulling up the file he was running on Vicky's husband.

"This is Paul Fontaine." An image of a large man with a beefy face and short, black hair filled the screen. He looked more like a thug than a businessman. "His dad owned a chain of used car dealerships across the South."

"New money," Hauk murmured.

They'd both lived in the South long enough to understand the difference between someone who earned their fortune and someone who inherited a trust fund. Families like the St. Clairs would always consider themselves better than others because they came from a long line of wealth.

"Tarnished money," Teagan corrected. Which meant it was even worse than new money. "There were rumors he had some shady contacts, but he managed to get his son into the top schools."

Hauk leaned forward as Teagan pulled up another picture. This one of a young man standing in the middle of Branford Court.

"Yale." Hauk gave a low whistle. "Nice."

Teagan scrolled through the file to pull up the background he'd gathered on the man.

"At the age of twenty-four Paul moved to Shreveport, started his career as an investment banker, and married into respectability."

Hauk's lips twisted into a humorless smile as Teagan brought up a picture of Paul and Vicky standing in an elegant garden with a brick mansion in the background. The groom looked as if his cravat was about to strangle him while the bride had the grim expression of a lamb being led to the slaughter.

"I assume Vicky's family was in need of a cash injection?" Hauk asked.

"Yep." Teagan had discovered Vicky's father had mortgaged the family estate as well as quietly sold off the large art collection and the thoroughbred stud farm. "They were descending into shabby genteel status."

"So the daughter marries money, and the dutiful son marries a place in local society." Hauk shook his head. "The true American Dream."

Teagan shared his friend's disgust. When he'd been young he used to fantasize about buying a big house on a tree-lined street. From a distance those homes looked like they could offer a peaceful security that was agonizingly missing from the slums where he lived.

It wasn't until he was older that he realized what went on behind closed doors was pretty much the same no matter where you lived.

The only way to be safe was to learn how to take care of himself.

And that's exactly what he did.

"Paul's American Dream lasted until 1999 when he took off with millions of dollars that he'd embezzled from state pension funds," he said.

"No one knows where he went?"

Teagan shook his head. "I hacked into the old FBI files—"

"Shit, Teagan," Hauk interrupted. "Someday you're going to get yourself tossed in jail."

Teagan concentrated on finding the intel he'd downloaded. If he worried about getting caught every time he went digging for information, he'd never get anything done.

"It wouldn't be the first time," he muttered.

Hauk heaved a deep sigh. No doubt he itched to give Teagan a stern lecture. All his friends worried he would someday get into a mess over his head, but thankfully he'd learned that Teagan rarely listened to advice. No matter how kindly offered.

"What did you find?" he instead asked.

"There was an investigation started months before Paul took off," Teagan revealed. "He'd been dipping his fingers into his clients' accounts for years."

Hauk made a sound of shock as he swiftly skimmed through the financial report that Teagan pulled up. The banker had been ruthless in stripping his clients of their assets.

"Did Paul know his secret was out?" Hauk asked.

Teagan rolled his eyes. "The men in charge of the investigation were clearly rookies," he said. "They questioned his secretary, who agreed to testify against him, but they hadn't bothered to get an arrest warrant. Before they finally got one signed, sealed, and delivered, Paul had disappeared with over two million dollars in cash that he had stashed at his office."

Hauk straightened. "No one heard from him again?"

Teagan shook his head. This was where the story got hinky for him.

"His wife hired a private detective to hunt him down." It took a few minutes to click through the folders until he came up with the documents that had been handed over to the FBI by Vicky Fontaine. "She has pictures of him enjoying the sunshine on a beach in Bolivia," he said, at last finding the image of Paul wearing a bathing suit and dark glasses, sitting with an unknown woman near the water.

Hauk studied the image with a frown. "That's him, or he has a twin."

Teagan nodded. He'd run it through a face recognition program to be sure it was Paul Fontaine. He'd also researched the background to make sure it was actually a beach in Bolivia.

"Yeah. It's him."

"Who's the woman?"

"No ID." Teagan shrugged. He'd been unable to find any info on the dark-haired female who was seated at the table with him. "It was assumed she was some local beauty."

"What did the authorities uncover?" Hauk asked.

"Jack squat," Teagan growled. There was nothing that pissed him off more than shoddy work. "They wanted to hush it all up as quickly as possible, so the investigation was dropped just a few weeks after Paul disappeared."

"Hmm." Hauk studied him with a wary gaze. "You aren't planning a trip to Bolivia, are you?"

Teagan reached out to tap the monitor of the nearest computer. "An electronic trip," he said.

"What's that mean?"

"I want to backtrack Paul Fontaine's movements," he explained. "That might help me discover links to people who helped him escape, and if his crimes have anything to do with what's happening to Mia." He held up his hand as Hauk arched a brow. "I know it's a long shot."

Hauk smiled. "Actually I was going to ask where you're going to start."

Teagan's tension eased. He occasionally forgot the amount of trust his friends placed on his hunches. And in his ability to turn a gut feeling into tangible evidence.

"If he traveled out of the country he had to have plane tickets and a passport," he said.

Hauk folded his arms over his chest. "With two million dollars you can buy a new identity," he pointed out. "Not to mention the fact that security wasn't nearly as tight before 9/11."

Teagan agreed, but the days of being able to fade into the

mist were long gone. "No one disappears completely," he assured his friend. "Not unless they're dead."

"Okay." Hauk gave a slow nod. "What else are you investigating?"

Teagan grimaced. "I want to know who benefits if Mia dies."

Hauk shoved his fingers through his hair. Neither of them wanted to consider Lucas's reaction if something happened to Mia. "Does she have a will?"

"Yeah. Most of her property is connected to her business, which she makes monthly payments on."

"The loan she got from Lucas?"

"Yeah, although I don't think she knows that yet," Teagan said.

Hauk made a choked sound of surprise. "So if she dies he gets everything?"

"Not everything," Teagan corrected his friend. "She has a traditional loan on her new office building and house. Plus, the land that belonged to her father will go to a charity that helps foster children."

"Ah." Hauk studied Teagan's tense features. "What do we know about the charity?"

"Not enough. I'm going to do some digging today."

There was a pause before Hauk nodded his head. "I think it's a good lead to follow."

Teagan narrowed his eyes. "Do I hear a 'but'?"

Hauk stepped toward him. "What's the real reason you're staying in Houston?"

"I've just told you—"

"Teagan." Hauk's expression was suddenly hard with warning.

Teagan swiftly considered their options before muttering a low curse. Hauk might not possess Lucas's ability to read people, but he obviously sensed that Teagan was trying to hide something.

"I know you found another note," he at last confessed.

Hauk jerked in surprise. "How . . ."

His words trailed away as Teagan nodded toward the computer at the end of the table.

On the screen was an image taken of Hauk as he entered the building an hour ago. He was wearing a soft cashmere coat over his suit, and his blond hair was ruffled from the wind.

More importantly, he was hastily shoving a white piece of paper in his pocket as he flicked a wary glance toward the surveillance camera that covered the front of the building.

"Shit. I was afraid I might have been seen."

Teagan rose to his feet, not a bit happy his friend had tried to keep the latest threat from him.

He got Hauk's desire to go Lone Ranger on this. Whoever was stalking him had made it a personal fight and Hauk wanted to be the one to solve the mystery.

But Teagan wasn't going to let the stalker prod Hauk's pride into doing something stupid.

"Where did you find it?" he demanded.

Hauk's jaw clenched, his body tense with a fury that smoldered just below the surface. Whoever was leaving the notes had been screwing with Hauk's mind for weeks, and it was clearly wearing on his nerves.

"In the trunk of my car."

Teagan's brows snapped together. The stalker had the cojones to break into Hauk's car?

"How?"

Hauk lifted a hand. "I don't know. I haven't had a reason to open the trunk for a couple of weeks, so it's impossible to pinpoint where or when it was put there."

*Shit.* Teagan scrubbed his hand over the bristle of his shaved head. "Have you read it?"

"Yeah."

Of course he had. Teagan gave a shake of his head.

"Max specifically told you not to disturb the note if you got another one." He sent his friend a chiding frown. "He's going to kill you when he finds out you might have destroyed potential evidence."

Hauk's lips twisted in a humorless smile. "He's going to have to get in line."

Teagan grimaced. He hated the knowledge they were at the bastard's mercy. Unfortunately, until he made a mistake, there wasn't a thing they could do to stop him.

"What'd it say?"

"My day of retribution is coming."

# Chapter Twenty

Lucas sat at the kitchen table, his laptop open in front of him although his gaze remained locked on Mia as she scurried through the suite like a butterfly caught in a windstorm.

It'd been that way since she'd wiggled out of his arms earlier that morning and insisted they had to go to the grocery store. Lucas had urged her to remain in bed and call for something to be delivered. If she wanted to expend her restless energy he had a much better way than slaving away in the kitchen.

Mia, however, had been insistent, and within a couple hours they had the cabinets and fridge full, and a huge pan of homemade lasagna and garlic bread filling the air with a tantalizing aroma.

Resigned to the fact that he wasn't going to convince Mia to return to bed, Lucas was surprised to discover a strange sense of satisfaction in sitting down with her to eat a meal that she'd cooked for the two of them. It was . . . comforting. Like they were a real couple just enjoying a lazy day at home.

They were just finishing lunch when Teagan sent him a text that said he was sending an e-mail that would help in their investigation. Lucas had rolled his eyes at the vagueness of the text, but knowing Teagan wouldn't be sending anything unless it was important, Lucas had called Max to ask him to come over.

Ten minutes later the sound of a buzzer echoed through the suite and he hurried to open the front door before Mia could do it.

The security in the building was top notch, not to mention the fact he had hired a full-time guard to keep watch on the door, but nothing was perfect. He wasn't going to take any chances with the woman he loved.

"Max," he murmured as he stepped back and waved in the tall, blond-haired man. "Come in."

Max shrugged out of his coat and tossed it on the hall table, revealing his black slacks and white cashmere sweater.

Lucas had chosen a pair of jeans and a pale blue sweater. Mia had a far more casual style when she was away from work, and he was determined to make her feel comfortable.

The last thing he wanted was any reminder that they'd been raised on opposite sides of the river.

"Damn," Max breathed, heading straight for the kitchen. "Something smells good."

Mia was instantly on her feet, eager to do something. "I made lasagna and garlic bread," she said. "Do you want some?"

Max offered his most charming smile. "I wouldn't say no."

Lucas heaved a mournful sigh. "Be careful, Mia," he teased. "The men of ARES are like strays. Once you feed them they'll never go away."

She sent him a frown. "So I've noticed."

Max pulled out a chair and took a seat at the table. "Don't listen to him, my dear. Lucas has always been selfish."

"Because it's my lasagna and I don't share," Lucas informed his friend, taking his own seat.

"See?" Max demanded. "Selfish."

Mia rolled her eyes. "Is it a rule that all men must stay perpetually twelve years old?" she demanded.

"A rule?" Max arched a brow. "Actually I believe it's a law. What do you think, Lucas?"

Lucas pretended to consider the question. "Yep, it's a law," he finally announced.

"Good grief." Without warning Mia gave a burst of laughter. "I'll get you some food."

Both men watched in silent appreciation as Mia buzzed around the kitchen to pile a plate with more food than any one man could possibly eat.

"I like her," Max announced in low tones.

Warmth flooded through Lucas. "Me too."

Still speaking in a soft voice, Max glanced toward the nearby laptop. "What did Teagan find?"

Lucas shrugged. "He promised to e-mail it to me, but I haven't received anything yet."

"He's not coming back to Shreveport?" Max demanded in surprise.

"Not unless we need him."

"What happened?"

"He didn't say, but I'm guessing it has to do with Hauk," Lucas admitted, knowing the only thing that could keep Teagan from being in the thick of the action was worry that Hauk might be in danger.

"Thanks," Max murmured as Mia set the plate in front of him, along with an ice-cold beer. "Does he need me to come back to Houston?"

"No." Lucas was acutely aware of Mia frowning as she sat on a stool next to the breakfast bar. "He said Rafe was coming in today."

"Good." Max dug into his food.

Mia, of course, wasn't so easily satisfied. "If you need to go—"

"No," Lucas interrupted. If Hauk was in immediate danger Teagan would have asked them to come back.

Mia grudgingly conceded defeat, and a silence filled the

kitchen as Max swiftly polished off the enormous amount of food. At last finished, he settled back in his chair with a deep sigh.

"This was delicious," he complimented Mia. "I can't remember when I last had a home-cooked meal."

Instantly Mia was hopping off her stool and moving to collect the empty plate.

"I should make some chocolate chip cookies," she said as she headed toward the sink.

"Mia, relax," Lucas commanded.

"I can't." She rinsed off the plate before putting it into the dishwasher and turning to meet his worried gaze. "I've worked since I was ten years old. Just sitting around is making me nuts."

On the point of suggesting they rent a movie, Lucas was distracted when his computer gave a loud *ding*.

"At last," he breathed, leaning forward to pull up the e-mail that had just hit his in-box.

Max moved his chair to see the screen while Mia leaned over his shoulder.

"What is it?" she demanded, her voice edged with raw frustration.

It took a tense moment for the e-mail to load, the three of them barely daring to breathe.

"What the hell?" he muttered, peering at the screen in confusion.

At first he couldn't imagine why Teagan had sent them the video of Vicky Fontaine perched on top of Tony. They already knew that they were lovers. Then Lucas's brows arched as the woman reached into her purse and tossed something onto Tony's chest.

Curious, Lucas clicked on the next file Teagan had e-mailed, his brows drawing together at the fuzzy image. It wasn't until it at last began to clear that he realized it had been taken from the previous video.

But it had been enlarged so all that was visible was the square piece of paper she'd put on Tony's chest. . . .

"It's the picture they found on Tony when he died," he breathed, clearly capable of making out Mia's dark hair as well as the threat that had been written across her face.

Mia's hand landed on his shoulder, her fingers digging painfully into his flesh, although he doubted she was aware of what she was doing.

"My picture," she breathed.

Lucas nodded, reaching to hit a button on the keyboard that allowed him to zoom out enough to show the female lying beside Tony in the bed.

"Vicky Fontaine," he growled. "She gave the picture to Tony after they had sex."

"Why?" Mia questioned. "Why would she want me dead?"

Lucas surged upright. Vicky Fontaine was at the center of the mystery. Now they at last had the proof they needed to confront her.

"I intend to find out," he assured Mia.

Max nodded as he moved to stand at Lucas's side. "I'll drive."

Mia studied the two of them with a stubborn expression. "I'm going with you."

Lucas stiffened. Why was he surprised? He should have expected Mia to want to be in on the action. She seemed to have no sense of self-preservation. But he still found himself caught off guard.

"No way," he snapped before he could find a more politically correct way of urging her to stay at the penthouse.

She planted her fists on her hips and leaned forward. Never a good sign. "That's not your decision."

He swallowed a sigh. "Mia, there's a good chance this woman has tried to have you killed more than once. Now you want to waltz into her house like nothing's wrong?"

Mia refused to back down. "She's not going to do anything with the two of you with me."

"I'm not willing to take the risk."

He thought he heard Max mutter a word beneath his breath. Something that sounded remarkably like "idiot," but Lucas's focus remained on Mia's flushed face.

With a visible effort she swallowed her angry words and instead forced herself to try and use reason with him.

As if he could be logical when it came to keeping her safe.

"The only time I've been in danger is when you weren't with me," she smoothly pointed out.

His brows snapped together. How could he argue? She'd been alone when someone had tried to run her off the road.

And again when someone had tossed drugs into her coffee. If he hadn't been out front with Max, no one would have dared to enter the house.

"That's not fair," he muttered.

She shrugged. "It's true."

"Fine." He nodded toward his friend. "Max can stay with you."

"No way," Mia snapped. "You aren't going to see that witch alone."

"Mia—"

"You can take me with you. Or I'll go on my own." Mia met him glare for glare. "You choose."

Max loudly cleared his throat. "That's what they call a rock and a hard place, my friend," he said.

Like Lucas didn't already know that Mia had his balls in a vise? Turning his head, he sent his friend a frustrated frown. "Thanks a lot."

Max shrugged as Mia circled around his rigid body.

"I'll get my coat," she said.

* * *

In the end, they'd decided to take two cars. Max in his SUV, and Lucas and Mia together in his car.

Mia's stomach was tied in a knot of nerves by the time they'd driven across Shreveport and turned onto the private lane that led to Magnolia Court. Thankfully the wrought-iron gates that protected it were open and they had no problem following the tree-lined driveway to park in front of the mansion.

Even draped in the chilly December rain, the house was stunning.

Built in the Tudor style, it had steeply slanted roofs and dark half-timbers with creamy stucco in between. There were mullioned windows and herringbone brickwork that made the place look as if it should be the home of a British aristocrat. The same Old World elegance had been lavished on the surrounding grounds, which were divided into gardens with handcrafted marble fountains.

Climbing out of the car, Mia joined Max near the covered porch as he released a slow whistle.

"Nice place," he muttered.

Mia nodded. She'd been here a few times when she helped her father, but she'd never been inside the main house. Daughters of the gardener weren't exactly on the guest list.

"It belonged to Vicky's parents," she muttered, ignoring Lucas's searing gaze as he swiftly joined them. She understood that he wasn't happy with her. But there was no way in hell she could sit at home and wait for them to find out why Vicky Fontaine wanted her dead. "She moved back here after her father died."

Max nodded, glancing toward the sunken garden at the side of the house. "I'm going to have a look around," he announced.

Mia sent him a startled glance. "You're not going in?"

"I need to make sure I can call for backup in case the two of you don't come out."

Mia grimaced. "Oh."

Max shifted his attention to Lucas. "And to keep an eye out for Detective Cooper," he murmured. "He has the same video we do. Eventually he's going to be knocking on Mrs. Fontaine's door. If he finds you inside, he's not going to be happy."

Lucas nodded. "Keep your eyes open."

Mia impulsively reached out to lay her hand on Max's arm. They'd known each other less than a week, but she already felt as if he was one of her most trusted friends. She couldn't bear it if something happened to him because of her. "Be careful."

Leaning down, he brushed a light kiss over her cheek. "Always."

He turned to casually stroll along the edge of the house, no doubt intending to do a thorough search of the outbuildings. She was discovering the men of ARES Security had a very loose interpretation of the law.

With a small sigh, she forced herself to turn toward the large house. Inside was Vicky Fontaine. The woman who potentially wanted to kill her.

It still seemed impossible to believe.

The aloof, arrogant woman seemed barely capable of dressing without a servant to help her. Could she really have tried to run her off the road? Or snuck in her house and put drugs in her coffee?

Mia gave a shake of her head, glancing toward her grim-faced companion. "Let me talk."

"Why?"

"You'll be able to read her better than I can," she said.

That had always been Lucas's gift. His ability to understand what people were saying with their bodies, not with their mouths. The skill would have given him a tremendous advantage if he'd continued on with his career as a diplomat.

He cocked a dark brow. "Read her?"

"You'll know when she's lying." She stepped back, resisting the urge to press her hand against her stomach. It felt like someone had released a hundred butterflies inside her. "Besides, you might have a chance to look around if I keep her distracted."

His eyes narrowed. "Now, what's the real reason?"

She released her breath on a low hiss. There was no point in trying to lie. She was terrible at it.

"You can be . . ." She struggled for the right word.

"Arrogant. Bossy? Annoying?" he suggested.

"All of the above," she agreed in dry tones. "But I was about to say that you're intimidating. If Vicky feels threatened, she'll call for her lawyer." Mia deliberately paused. "Or the cops."

"Fine." Taking her arm, Lucas steered her toward the door. "You take the lead."

Mia didn't think for a second that she'd managed to sway Lucas. Like most men, he assumed he was always right. Which meant he had his own reason for letting her think that she was in charge.

Too nervous to try and figure out Lucas's devious plotting, Mia squared her shoulders and prepared for the upcoming encounter.

The first hurdle was actually getting in to see Vicky Fontaine.

Pinning a smile to her face, Mia allowed Lucas to lead her up the stairs and across the porch where the short, well-rounded housekeeper was already pulling open the door. Mia instantly recognized her. Louisa Sharp. Her hair had gone gray and her face was lined with age, but she was the same servant who'd been with Vicky's parents when Mia had gone to the estate to help her father.

"Mia?" the older woman murmured in surprise, her gaze flicking toward Lucas. "Mr. St. Clair."

"We're here to see Ms. Fontaine, Louisa," Mia said.

The housekeeper nervously glanced over her shoulder before returning her attention to Mia. "She's not here."

Mia's smile remained in place as she brushed past the housekeeper and into the wide foyer with a black-and-white tiled floor and large chandelier.

"That's okay, Louisa, this will only take a minute," she murmured, her pace never slowing as she headed toward the arched opening that led into a long library.

The room was beautiful. There was a line of mullioned windows that overlooked the side garden, with towering shelves stuffed with leather-bound books and an open-beamed ceiling. At the far end was a large stone fireplace with a wooden mantel that was decorated with holly and the traditional red stockings.

There was also a large Christmas tree in the corner, with matching silver bulbs and a twinkling angel on the top. And an antique nativity scene that was placed next to a heavy walnut desk.

All very festive.

At her entrance a tall, slender woman rose from a leather wing chair. Her thin features hardened with annoyance as she lifted her hand to touch the blond hair that was smoothed into a tidy knot at the base of her neck.

"Hello, Vicky," Mia murmured.

"Mia." Silvery-gray eyes, as hard as granite, swept over her before moving toward the man who'd halted just behind Mia's right shoulder. "Lucas. I'm not sure how you managed to get in here, but I was just leaving."

Mia deliberately glanced toward the magazine that Vicky had just tossed aside and then the cheery fire. They both indicated a woman who intended to spend the afternoon at home. "This will only take a minute."

Vicky shook her head, her diamonds flashing as she straightened the cuffs of her black designer dress. "You'll have to make an appointment. My schedule is filled for today."

Vicky stepped forward, clearly intending to leave the room. They had only a few seconds to keep her from disappearing.

"I know that you and Tony were lovers," she bluntly announced.

Vicky froze, her face wiped of all expression. "Excuse me?"

Mia tilted her chin. "I said—"

"I heard what you said," Vicky snapped. "I just don't understand why you would say it."

"Because it's true."

The older woman flattened her lips, her icy composure once again intact. "If Tony told you that absurd story, then you're a fool to believe it."

Mia gave a slow shake of her head. The woman was a remarkable liar. Cool. Collected. Absolutely convincing.

"I saw the videos."

"Videos." A flicker of alarm deep in the gray eyes. "What videos?"

"Of you and Tony," Mia pressed.

"That's . . ." Vicky licked her dry lips. "That's a lie and if you insist on repeating it I'll have you sued for defamation of my character."

Lucas placed a protective arm around Mia's shoulder. "It's no lie," he said, his voice filled with an authority that made Vicky pale to a strange shade of ash. "We have the videos."

With jerky steps Vicky paced toward the fireplace, her hands clenched. There was a long silence as she stared down at the flames, no doubt considering the implications of having her secret affair revealed.

Or maybe she was considering how she could turn the situation to her advantage.

Vicky was nothing if not clever.

At last she spun back around, her expression one of icy disdain. "I will not admit nor deny my private relationship with Tony. Quite simply, it's none of your business," she informed them.

Mia's fear was abruptly forgotten beneath a surge of anger. Whether the woman was innocent or guilty, she'd been Tony's lover for years.

Hadn't she felt anything for him?

"It is if your personal relationship has something to do with Tony's death," Mia accused, her voice harsh.

"How dare you?" The woman sucked in an outraged breath, pointing toward the door. "Get out."

Without warning Lucas pulled out his phone, pulling up the image Teagan had sent to them. He turned the screen toward Vicky.

"You gave Tony this picture of Mia," he said. "The words at the bottom say 'Kill her or else.'"

The gray eyes flickered, an indefinable emotion rippling over her face before she was sending Mia a narrow-eyed glare. "Don't do this."

Mia frowned. Was that a threat? "I'm not stopping until I find out who killed my friend," she told the woman.

Vicky made a sound of impatience. "He's dead. Let him rest in peace."

Mia shuddered, once again reminded that she might be in the presence of a killer.

It was a chilling thought.

"Why?" she demanded. "Because you might end up in jail?"

A humorless smile curved her lips. "Because you're not going to like the answers."

Lucas gave Mia's shoulder a small squeeze, almost as

if he was trying to warn her of something. Mia, however, refused to glance in his direction. She'd spent her childhood being bullied and intimidated by women like Vicky Fontaine.

Never again.

"You know what I don't like?" she demanded between clenched teeth. "The fact that my friend is dead. And that someone is now trying to kill me."

"You can't think that I . . ." Vicky allowed her words to trail away, her eyes widening with a faux disbelief as she released a shrill laugh. "You really are out of your mind."

Mia felt a strong urge to slap the mocking smile off Vicky's face. No, that wasn't right. She actually wanted to punch her so hard she broke that perfect nose.

It wasn't that Mia was a violent person, but the woman's mocking pretense that she didn't know anything about Tony's death was truly pissing her off.

"Why did you give Tony that picture?" she demanded.

The faux amusement was wiped from Vicky's thin face as she abruptly moved toward the desk in the corner. "I'm done talking," she warned. "Get out before I call my security and have you thrown out."

Mia parted her lips, but before she could speak Lucas was stepping forward, his expression sending a tiny chill down Mia's spine.

She'd never seen him look so dangerous.

"Perhaps you'd prefer if we call the sheriff's office?" he drawled, pressing his thumb against the screen of his cell phone. "I'm sure they'd be interested in what we discovered."

Vicky jerked toward Lucas, her hand held out. "Wait."

# Chapter Twenty-One

Lucas studied the older woman as she took a cautious step forward.

Her resemblance to a praying mantis was only intensified in the shadowed room with the flickering flames behind her, but that wasn't what made Lucas shudder.

Mia was right when she'd said he could read people. It'd been a necessary talent, being raised in a house where displeasure was expressed by the lift of a brow, or a turned back when he entered a room.

And he knew without a doubt that Vicky Fontaine was cunningly leading them into a trap.

It wasn't anything overt that she'd done. In fact, she'd reacted just as he'd expected when Mia had accused her of sleeping with Tony. She'd been outraged, even a little shocked that anyone would think she would sleep with the younger man.

She'd expected it to work. After all, she'd gone to great lengths to ensure the affair was kept secret.

But after discovering they not only had proof that the older woman had been sleeping with Tony, but that they had video evidence she'd given him the picture of Mia with a demand for her death, she'd only briefly shown a flicker of panic. Then, with a skill he could only admire, she'd smoothed her expression and squared her shoulders.

Almost as if she had prepared for this precise moment.

With seeming nonchalance, he took a step back, making sure he could keep an eye on the door as well as the bank of windows. He wasn't going to let anyone sneak up on them.

Unaware of his growing unease, Mia glared at the older woman, her face flushed with anger. "Wait for what?" she demanded.

Vicky pretended to hesitate, her expression regretful even as her eyes remained as hard as granite.

"I didn't want to have to do this," the older woman murmured, turning to head across the room.

Immediately Lucas was moving to block her path, his hand on his gun, which was holstered on his belt. "Hold on," he growled. "Where do you think you're going?"

Vicky came to a reluctant halt, peering down her nose as if Lucas was a piece of fungus that had suddenly appeared in front of her.

"You said you wanted the truth." She waved a jeweled hand toward the nearby desk. "I need to open my safe."

Lucas took a slow step backward. "Do it."

"Thank you," she drawled, sweeping past him with her chin tilted in the air.

Lucas followed behind her, his hand remaining on his gun. He didn't trust this woman as far as he could throw her.

She halted in front of a glass case filled with rare books that was placed behind the desk. Her slender fingers ran over the top edge, as if searching for something. For a second nothing happened, then there was the faint sound of a *click* and the entire case slid to the side to reveal an opening cut into the floor.

Vicky gracefully bent down, her hand reaching into the dark space.

Lucas stepped forward, his gaze narrowed. "Be careful," he warned. "No one wants any unfortunate accidents."

"There's no need for threats," she chided, pulling her hand out of the hidden safe to reveal two large manila envelopes.

Straightening, she crossed directly toward Mia, shoving one of the envelopes in her hand.

Mia frowned, staring down at the envelope as if it might bite her. "What is it?"

A hint of mocking resignation touched the older woman's face. "The answers you claim to want."

Lucas was swiftly moving to Mia's side, a sudden fear sizzling down his spine. Vicky might try to pretend she'd been forced into handing over the information, but Lucas sensed that beneath her submissive facade she was buzzing with anticipation.

This was exactly what she wanted.

"Mia, wait," he murmured in warning.

Mia shook her head, stubborn to the end, as she opened the flap and reached her hand inside.

"No. I want to know," she said.

She pulled out what looked to be a half dozen black-and-white photos. Instantly her face drained of color and she swayed as she shuffled through the stack. "Oh my God," she breathed.

Leaning forward, Lucas yanked the pictures out of her hand, his brows drawing together.

The first image was fuzzy, making Lucas suspect a cheapy disposable camera had been used. But it'd at least been taken during the day, giving plenty of light. Which meant there was no mistaking what he was seeing. It was an open trunk of a silver car, and inside the trunk was a body stuffed at an awkward angle.

Swiftly he moved to the second photo. This one was just as fuzzy, but it had been zoomed in to capture the image of a middle-aged man with a square face and salt-and-pepper hair. His eyes were closed and his lips slightly parted, almost as if he was asleep. Lucas, however, wasn't fooled. He'd seen death too many times during his tours in Afghanistan.

He was looking at a corpse.

Shuffling to the next picture, he released his breath on a hiss. He recognized the blunt features and heavy jowls.

Paul Fontaine.

The man who everyone assumed was sitting on some exotic beach with a few million dollars he'd stolen from the state pension funds.

The vague fear that had been sending chills down Lucas's spine now settled like a lead ball in the pit of his stomach.

There was no way in hell Vicky would have shared these pictures unless she could use them to her advantage.

But how?

Lifting his head, he met the icy-gray gaze with a fierce scowl. "What the hell are these?" he demanded, waving the pictures in her direction.

"I think it should be obvious," Vicky said, a hand lifted to her throat. The perfect pose for a tragic widow. Lucas wondered if she'd practiced it in the mirror. "Pictures of my husband."

"He's . . ." Mia's words faded, her face still pale.

"Dead," Vicky helpfully supplied.

Coldhearted bitch.

Mia made a sound of distress. "You killed him?"

Vicky widened her eyes with faux shock. "Of course not. Why would I kill my husband?"

Lucas gave a sharp laugh. "I can think of several million reasons why."

With a lift of her shoulder, Vicky crossed toward a table set beneath one of the windows. Lifting a crystal decanter, she poured herself a glass of wine before turning back to meet his unwavering gaze. "I think I should start from the beginning," she murmured.

"We're listening," Lucas said, assuming she'd deliberately chosen not to offer them refreshments. Sort of a nonverbal way to assure them they were unwelcomed guests.

He was betting that Vicky Fontaine didn't do anything without a purpose.

"It was no secret that I married Paul because he promised to rescue my parents from bankruptcy." Her gaze moved toward the framed portrait above the mantel. It was an oil painting of a handsome older couple whom Lucas vaguely remembered as Vicky's mother and father. They had been exactly like his own family. Pampered. Entitled. Incapable of change. Vicky turned back to Lucas, her lips twisting into a humorless smile. "I was young and gullible enough to view my husband as some sort of knight in shining armor rushing to my rescue."

Lucas felt Mia move to stand beside him. He desperately wanted to put his arm around her, but he needed to keep his hand free so he could pull his weapon if necessary.

"I assume the fairy tale didn't last?" he asked.

"No." Vicky took a drink of the wine, genuine disgust darkening her eyes. "Paul and I were two very different people." Her revulsion for her dead husband was one thing she didn't have to fake. "Naturally, we started to drift apart. He had his life, and"—she paused, as if trying to find the proper word—"interests. And I had mine," she at last finished.

"And a seventeen-year-old boy was one of those interests?" Mia snapped.

Vicky glared at the younger woman, clearly unaccustomed to being treated with anything but deference from those she considered beneath her.

"Don't take that tone with me, Mia Ramon," she snapped.

Predictably, Mia refused to back down. Once she might have wilted beneath the woman's disdain, but she'd matured into a person who refused to be bullied.

"I'm not one of your servants, Vicky Fontaine." Mia gave a toss of her head, her passionate nature a direct contrast to the older woman's frigid composure. "I will speak however I want."

A cruel amusement tightened Vicky's thin features. "We'll see."

Lucas stilled. The mocking words had held a threat that made him instinctively step toward Mia. Shit. He was certain she was playing a game with them, but he couldn't figure out what it was.

"You became Tony's lover?" he demanded, his gaze locked on the older woman.

Vicky took another sip of wine, slowly turning her attention toward Lucas.

"I was lonely and isolated, and Tony was often at the house," she said, her voice lacking any hint of apology. "We drifted into an affair."

"He was just a boy—"

Lucas interrupted Mia's angry accusation. "You paid for Tony's tuition?"

"Yes," Vicky admitted. "His family was worthless. He didn't have anyone else whom he could depend upon."

"And his rent?" Lucas pressed.

"Yes."

Mia muttered a curse as she glared at the older woman. "Did he know you killed your husband?"

Drinking the last of her wine, Vicky calmly set aside her empty glass. "I didn't kill my husband."

"Right." Mia gave a sharp laugh of disbelief. "Then who did?"

"Tony did," Vicky smoothly announced, sending Mia an icy smile. "And your father."

A shocked silence filled the library.

So that was it. The cunning woman intended to pin the

blame on two men who were dead and unable to deny her accusations.

"You lying bitch," Mia breathed, lunging forward as if she intended to physically force Vicky to take back her ugly allegations.

With a swift movement Lucas turned to block her path, his hands gently grasping her shoulders.

"Mia," he murmured softly, his gut twisting as he felt her trembling beneath his hands.

No big surprise. Who wouldn't be upset to have someone claim her father was a murderer? And if it was just some random woman saying it, he'd let Mia beat the hell out of her.

But Vicky Fontaine was a powerful member of local society, with enough money to hire an entire team of lawyers. She was also a cunning enemy who'd clearly spent a lot of time plotting her strategy if anyone discovered her husband was dead.

"Let me handle this," he commanded in a low voice.

Mia's cheeks were flushed, her eyes smoldering with fury. "She said—"

"I heard what she said," he soothed.

She trembled, sucking in a deep breath as she visibly struggled to control her emotions. "My father would never kill anyone," she protested in soft tones.

His hand cupped her cheek, his thumb brushing her lower lip. "I know, Mia."

Something that might be relief eased her trembling. Damn. Had she actually been worried he might believe Vicky's accusation against her father?

Granted, he'd never liked George Ramon. The man had been a drunk, a sketchy gardener, and a lousy father, but he'd never been violent, not even when he was completely plastered.

Mia parted her lips, but before she could speak there was

the sound of approaching footsteps that had him spinning around to face Vicky.

"I have proof," the older woman said, her tone smug.

Lucas moved to block her from reaching Mia. Not only to ensure the woman couldn't touch Mia, but to keep the younger woman from going nuclear and doing something that might mean having to bail her out of jail.

"Show me," he commanded.

Vicky came to a halt, her expression mocking as she took in his protective stance.

"Fine." She nodded toward the stack of photos he still held in his hand. "Turn over the last picture."

Lucas briefly considered crossing the room to toss the pictures into the fire. He and Mia had come there for answers, but suddenly the photographs seemed to pose a threat to Mia and her happiness.

Only the knowledge that Mia would remain in danger if they didn't halt the killer made him turn over the pictures to glance at the backs.

Lucas frowned as he found the picture and skimmed the block-style letters that looked like they'd been formed by a five-year-old. Or a man who was barely literate.

"Lucas." Mia touched his arm, her voice unsteady. "Let me see."

Knowing she wouldn't let it go, he reluctantly tilted the picture to the side so she could see the words.

"'I have your husband's body hidden where you'll never find him. I want fifty thousand dollars in cash left on my doorstep before sundown tomorrow,'" she read out loud.

"I'm sure you recognize your father's handwriting," Vicky drawled, making Lucas wish he didn't have a rule against hitting women.

Instead he sent the coldhearted bitch a fierce glare. "Did you pay him?"

"Of course," Vicky murmured. "I was terrified he intended to kill me as well."

Bullshit. Lucas gave a shake of his head, shifting his attention to Mia, who looked as if she'd been hit by a truck.

"Is this your father's handwriting?" he asked in a gentle voice.

She licked her lips, a pulse at the base of her throat racing as she struggled to contain her volatile emotions.

"How can I be sure?" she muttered. "Anyone could forge this note."

Vicky gave a flick of her hand, the diamonds glittering in the firelight. "Play stupid if you want," she taunted, the confidence in her voice assuring Lucas the photos and the note were real. "I'm sure the investigators could prove whether or not it's a forgery."

Grudgingly accepting that Vicky held the upper hand, at least for the moment, Mia wrapped her arms around her waist. "Why would my father or Tony want to hurt Mr. Fontaine?"

Lucas covertly tucked the pictures in his jacket pocket. He'd have Max run a few tests on them later. For now he concentrated on Vicky's polished performance as she gave a soulful shake of her head. The bitch had truly missed her calling. She should have been on stage.

"It's partially my fault, I suppose." There was a dramatic sigh. "Tony was so young and passionate and not overly bright. He somehow convinced himself that if he could get rid of Paul, we could be together." She paused, giving a tiny shiver. "I never dreamed he would do anything like that."

Lucas couldn't deny the charges against his old friend. Tony had always been a victim of his emotions. And unfortunately, he hadn't been particularly intelligent. But that didn't make him a killer.

In fact, Tony would never have the brains or backbone to plot a cold-blooded murder. He could, however, be easily persuaded to do anything to earn the approval of someone he loved.

"You're saying Tony killed Paul so the two of you could get married?" Lucas asked, his voice edged with disbelief.

Vicky shrugged. "That's exactly what happened."

Mia stepped around him, ignoring his warning glare. "You said my father was involved," she reminded Vicky.

"He was there," the older woman said, an emotion that Lucas couldn't define searing through the gray eyes. "Tony needed his assistance to move the body."

"No way," Mia breathed. "My father hated Tony. He would never have helped him."

"According to Tony your father was desperate for money," Vicky said.

Lucas wasn't impressed with the claim. It'd been no secret that George Ramon had struggled to make a living.

"Tony paid him?" she demanded.

"Of course not." Vicky gave a sharp laugh. "Tony was constantly broke, but he assumed he would have access to my bank accounts after we married." She gave a laugh that was like sandpaper against Lucas's nerves. "When I made it clear I didn't have any interest in making our relationship legal, he informed your father he couldn't come up with the money." She deliberately held Mia's angry gaze. "That's when your father arrived at my office and shoved the envelope in my hands. What choice did I have but to give him the fifty thousand dollars in cash he demanded?"

Mia stiffened, and Lucas knew she was thinking about the cash that'd been stuffed in the hope chest her father had given to her.

*Damn.* He didn't believe Vicky's story. At least not entirely. But it was growingly obvious that she'd spent the past seventeen years creating a story that not only covered her ass, but squarely laid the blame on other people.

"Why didn't you go to the cops?" he demanded.

Vicky turned away, pacing back to the table to pour herself another glass of wine. Lucas studied her seeming display of unease.

Just an act?

Or a tool to give herself time to think of her answer?

"When Tony confessed what he'd done I was in shock," Vicky at last murmured, slowly turning to meet his suspicious gaze. "A part of me felt responsible for what'd happened. After all, if I hadn't allowed my loneliness to lead me into an affair with Tony, Paul might still be alive." She flicked her gaze toward Mia. "And naturally I was scared of what your father might do."

Lucas spoke before Mia could. "And that's the only reason?"

Vicky swirled the wine in her glass, her lips pursed. "I'm not an angel."

"No shit," Mia muttered.

Lucas gave her arm a small squeeze, keeping his gaze trained on the older woman. "You were happy to have your husband dead?"

"Not happy," she protested, sending him a chiding frown before her gaze lowered and her expression hardened. "But our marriage had become a nightmare. Paul drank too much, he spent outrageous sums of money, and he preferred spending his nights with cheap whores instead of his own wife."

Lucas had heard his mother discussing Paul Fontaine and his unsavory habit of spending nights in seedy bars. Having her husband the subject of constant gossip must have brutalized Vicky's pride.

A very real motive for wanting him dead.

Of course, there were easier ways to deal with a husband who turned out to be a drunken sleazebag.

"Why not divorce him?"

Vicky hesitated, no doubt deciding whether or not to

answer Lucas's question. Finally she lifted her lashes to reveal eyes that were hard with a hatred she couldn't disguise.

"He held the mortgage to this estate," she admitted, her head turning toward the portrait over the mantel. "He threatened to have my parents thrown out. It would have destroyed my father to be publicly humiliated."

Lucas's lips twisted. He didn't doubt that the older couple would have preferred death to the horror of being thrown out of their beloved mansion by their own son-in-law.

"So you said nothing?" he asked.

She shrugged, trying to look repentant. "I know it was wrong."

Accepting that she'd rehearsed her story often enough that she wasn't going to be rattled by his obvious questions, Lucas abruptly tried to catch her off guard.

"What about the pictures of your husband in Bolivia?" he demanded. "There's no way in hell Tony could have come up with those."

Wine sloshed from Vicky's glass as she gave a sharp jerk, but with a speed that was chilling, she was rapidly regaining control of her nerves. She even managed to paste a stiff smile on her lips.

"No, Tony was able to hide in the condo when it became public knowledge that Paul was missing. I, however, wasn't so fortunate. A week after he didn't show up for work, his office called the authorities. I was forced to deal with the mess." She carefully set aside her glass, perhaps sensing that Lucas intended to keep her rattled. "It was sheer luck that I'd had a private detective following Paul for months before he disappeared, even when he'd left the country on a supposed business trip. When the cops arrived and started asking questions, I panicked." She gave a lift of her shoulder. "Before I knew what I was doing I was giving them the pictures the investigator had taken."

Lucas resisted the urge to roll his eyes. He doubted this

woman had ever panicked in her life. In fact, he was fairly certain that he'd never met a person so deviously capable of thinking on her feet.

Without a blink of her eye, she'd confessed that her husband had been dead for the past seventeen years. Then promptly pinned the murder on her lover and George Ramon. She even managed to absolve herself of the cover-up by saying she'd simply freaked out and used her husband's serial infidelity to explain his disappearance.

It was all so smooth.

Which meant trying to force the truth from her was going to be next to impossible. The only thing he could hope was to keep her talking long enough she made a mistake that gave her away.

"And the cops were satisfied?" he demanded.

Vicky lifted her hand to study her manicure, her expression unreadable. "Hardly satisfied, but the investment bank where Paul worked wanted it all hushed up."

"Yes." He folded his arms over his chest. "The investment bank."

She lifted her gaze. "Do you have a point?"

He arched a brow. Clearly the woman surrounded herself with lackeys who had no choice but to allow themselves to be bullied and intimidated by this woman.

He, thankfully, wasn't one of them.

"According to the official report your husband managed to pilfer millions of dollars," he said. "What happened to the money?"

Vicky didn't miss a beat as she waved a dismissive hand. "Paul was a gambler," she said, her voice edged with contempt. "And like most things, he wasn't very good at it."

Lucas tried to imagine Vicky and Paul seated at their dining table, the air thick with mutual hatred as they silently wished each other dead.

The mere thought was enough to make him shudder in horror.

"You're saying your husband wasted millions at the poker table?" he demanded.

"It wasn't just his gambling," she clarified. "There were also risky investments, his expensive cars, and of course, his lavish trips with his whores. It all added up."

Lucas glanced around the room, which was perfectly restored with all the modern conveniences while keeping the impression of Old World charm.

He had a vague memory of visiting when he was young. It'd been one of those endless fund-raising parties for his father's reelection, which meant they all had to play the happy family. The party had been held in a side garden, but like most kids, Lucas had an insatiable curiosity, and the fact that he had been warned to stay out of the house only ensured that he'd crept inside the minute his parents' backs were turned.

There'd been nothing particularly shocking, but even his youthful eyes had noticed the shabby emptiness of the rooms, including this library.

Nothing at all like the glowing beauty that now filled the home.

"And renovations on this estate?" he asked.

"No," she denied. Too quickly. "Unlike Paul and my father, I happen to possess a talent for business. Once Paul was . . ." She hesitated, as if searching for the word.

"Dead?" he helpfully supplied.

"Gone," she corrected, her lips flattening at his blatant expression of disbelief. "I sold our house and used the funds to make my own investments. They've paid out nicely."

*Yeah, right.* Lucas didn't doubt that she was more capable than her husband of managing her fortune. Unlike Paul, she would never toss away millions on gambling or lavish vacations with expensive women. But he was fairly certain her seeming business acumen came from the missing funds that'd been stolen from the investment bank and not some hidden talent for finance.

"Your husband's secretary claimed he kept two million dollars in a safe in his office," he said.

The older woman gave a sharp bark of laughter. "Ginger Albee said a lot of things, most of which were lies."

Lucas arched his brows. No need to ask Vicky what she thought about her husband's secretary. "Why would she lie?"

Vicky abruptly paced across the floor to straighten the carved pieces of the nativity scene. Was she hiding her expression, or giving herself time to think of her next lie?

Impossible to say.

"She didn't want to admit that she'd been sharing my husband's bed from the day he hired her, or that he was paying for her apartment as well as buying her a new car every year," Vicky at last claimed.

"What would it matter?" Lucas moved to the center of the room. He didn't want to give Vicky an open pathway to the door. Not that he thought she was going to make a run for it, but better safe than sorry. "I doubt Paul Fontaine's habit of sleeping with other women was much of a secret."

She turned to send him a narrow-eyed glare. "Ginger was beautiful, but she wasn't very bright. She might have thought the investment bank would demand she pay back the money that Paul spent on her." She shrugged. Lucas studied her with open suspicion. "Or more likely she stole whatever cash was in the office and laid the blame on my missing husband," she added. "All I know is that his safe was empty when I went through his things."

"Hmm." Lucas gave a slow shake of his head. She truly was masterful. Now she'd managed to pin the theft of millions of dollars on the hapless secretary. "You seem to have an answer for everything."

She sniffed. "I don't have answers, I have the truth."

Yeah, and pigs could fly. He faced her squarely, knowing it was time to pull out his ace in the hole.

"There's still one thing you haven't explained," he drawled.

She smiled, revealing her utter lack of fear. The sight pissed him off.

Oh, he wasn't a bully. He didn't get a kick out of terrifying females. But he needed to find a way to rattle this woman, and the fact he hadn't managed to do it was annoying as hell.

"What's that?" she demanded.

"The picture of Mia you tossed on your lover's chest."

# Chapter Twenty-Two

Mia was barely aware of Lucas's continued inquisition, her mind reeling with Vicky Fontaine's shocking accusations.

It couldn't be true.

Could it?

Okay, her father had a habit of drinking too much after her mother's death. And he wasn't the hardest worker, which meant there never had been enough money. . . .

*The money.*

With a shudder Mia was blasted with the memory of finding the fifty thousand dollars that had been hidden in the bottom of the hope chest.

She'd told herself it had to be a part of her mother's life insurance policy, which her father had mentioned when he'd first learned he was sick. He had, after all, made vague promises that she would have what she deserved after he was gone. And it would be just like the paranoid man to hide her inheritance in a chest rather than put it in a bank where it could be kept safe.

Now, however, she couldn't shake the fear that she'd deliberately stuck her head in the sand.

She hadn't wanted to question the notion that George

Ramon would actually purchase life insurance for his young, seemingly healthy wife. He hadn't even believed in health insurance. It'd been easier to bury the past along with her father.

Her cowardice had come back to bite her in the butt.

Nothing could make her believe her father was an accomplice to murder, but how had Vicky managed to get her hands on her father's handwriting? There'd been no mistaking the childish block letters, no matter how much she might have protested anyone could have scrawled the note on the back of the picture.

And how could the older woman have possibly known about the fifty thousand dollars?

There had to be an explanation. But what?

She was jerked out of her brooding thoughts when she heard Lucas mention the photo with her name on it.

As disturbed as she was by the slander against her father, she was far more troubled by the knowledge someone wanted her dead.

"Ah." Vicky flicked a glance toward Mia. "The picture."

Not for first time since entering the mansion, Mia had to battle back the urge to slap the condescending smile off the older woman's face. "I suppose you have some sort of story that explains wanting me dead?" she asked, her voice edged with barely suppressed fury.

Vicky pretended to be startled by the accusation. "It wasn't me."

Mia rolled her eyes. "Of course not."

"If you don't want to hear my explanation, leave," the older woman snapped.

Lucas shi.ted to stand at Mia's side, his arm wrapping around her shoulder. Mia wasn't sure if it was meant to be soothing or a warning that they wouldn't get anything from Vicky if they were thrown off the estate.

"We're all ears," he drawled.

There was a long pause, as if Vicky was considering whether or not to answer. Mia wouldn't have been surprised if she'd decided she'd had enough.

In fact, Mia was astonished the older woman was willing to talk to them at all.

She could easily have ordered them to leave the minute they'd stepped into the house. Instead she'd allowed herself to be pumped for information.

The question was why?

Because she was truly innocent? Or because she was eager to pin the blame of Tony's murder on someone else?

"A few weeks after George's death I received a phone call from Tony," Vicky eventually said.

"Was that unusual?" Lucas asked, his expression impossible to read.

It was the same expression he'd been wearing when he told Mia he was leaving Shreveport and wasn't coming back.

"I preferred that we speak during our scheduled visits," Vicky explained. "As I've said, I didn't want people to know about our relationship."

Mia made a sound of disgust. "Nice."

Vicky narrowed her gaze, but before she could respond Lucas smoothly distracted her. "What did Tony want from you?"

With a glare at Mia, the older woman slowly turned her attention to Lucas. "He said he'd gotten on the wrong side of some drug dealers."

Lucas frowned. "I thought Tony was only a casual user."

Vicky shrugged. "Maybe, but he liked to make extra money by transporting"—she curled her lips, as if disgusted by her lover's illegal activities—"packages from Texas or Florida to Shreveport. I warned him that it was too dangerous, but he refused to listen." She shook her head in resignation. "Eventually his habit of playing with fire got him burnt."

Mia flinched. She'd known that Tony had friends in bad places. And that he probably made some extra money doing things that were shady. But that was yet another thing she preferred not to dwell on.

Dammit. She should have taken more time to find out what was going on with her friend. It might not have changed anything, but she wouldn't now be plagued with guilt. "What happened?" she demanded.

Vicky's gaze remained locked on Lucas. "During his last trip the people who were supposed to give him the drugs instead beat him up and robbed him." She gave a delicate shiver. "He was not only injured, but he had to come home without the drugs or the money. His contacts weren't happy."

"How much did he lose?" Lucas asked.

"Twenty thousand dollars."

Mia sucked in a shocked breath. Tony had been busted four or five times and never had more than a dime bag of weed on him. "That's a lot of money," she muttered.

Vicky gave a stiff nod. "Enough to make the dealers threaten Tony's life. They wanted their money back. Tony asked me to help." She gave a small shrug. "I refused."

Mia's lips parted in fury. This woman had used Tony when it suited her. But she couldn't do anything when he needed help?

But before she could speak, Lucas was asking the question trembling on her lips.

"Why would you refuse?"

"To be honest, I could tell that Tony was on a downward spiral," Vicky said, no hint of remorse in her frigid tone. "He was drinking too much and constantly stoned. I was considering ending our relationship."

Lucas gave a sharp laugh. "Yeah. We could tell by the tapes just how eager you were to end the relationship."

Instead of being embarrassed by the reminder that they'd seen her in the sex tapes, the older woman managed to look even more arrogant. Tilting her chin, she peered at Lucas down the length of her nose. "He begged me not to leave him, and I felt guilty enough to give in to his pleas."

"So you gave him a pity fuck, but not the money?" Lucas mocked.

Vicky flushed, but Mia was guessing it was from anger, not shame.

"No. I should have." Lifting a hand to her lips, Vicky gave a delicate sniff. "He might be alive today if I'd agreed."

Mia ground her teeth. She wasn't fooled for a second. Vicky Fontaine had about as much feeling as a spitting cobra. "So what does any of this have to do with me?"

Vicky's gaze lowered as she brushed an imaginary piece of lint from the cuff of her dress. "Tony was desperate," she said, speaking slowly, as if giving herself time to consider her words. "He told the thugs who demanded the money that he was going to come into a fortune once your father died."

"My father?" Mia blinked in disbelief. "That's ridiculous."

Vicky lifted her head, squarely meeting Mia's suspicious glare. "I think he was hoping your father had the money he'd blackmailed from me still hidden somewhere in his cabin. After all, everyone knew George Ramon was paranoid of banks. If he could find it, he could use it to pay off his debt." She gave a lift of her shoulder. "If nothing else, it gave him time to come up with another plan. But then your father passed away."

Lucas's fingers tightened on Mia's shoulder and she abruptly remembered the lighter they'd found at her dad's house. It proved that Tony had been there, but not when or why he would go to the cabin.

Was it possible that he'd been searching the property hoping to find the fifty thousand dollars?

"I presume the dealers wanted their money?" Lucas said.

"Exactly," Vicky agreed. "Tony was forced to confess that

the money he'd hoped to get his hands on was now out of his reach."

Mia narrowed her gaze. The woman never missed a beat. It was truly a masterful performance.

Lucas looked as skeptical as Mia felt. "The drug dealers didn't believe him?" he mocked.

"Actually, they did," Vicky retorted in icy tones, her gaze shifting to Mia. "And since Tony had claimed that he was an heir for your father, they naturally assumed if you were gone he would finally get his hands on the money."

Lucas frowned. "That's a hell of a leap."

"I doubt if any of them have more brains than Tony did," Vicky said. "Whatever the explanation, when I went to visit Tony he revealed the picture of Mia he received with the demand that she be killed."

Mia shook her head. She'd seen the image that Teagan had sent to Lucas. "The picture was in your purse."

"I'd barely walked through the front door when he shoved the picture into my handbag and begged for my help."

Lucas released a sharp laugh. "And that led to sex?"

"I knew I was going to refuse." Vicky flicked a cold, dismissive glance over Mia. "No offense, but I wasn't about to put myself in the position of being blackmailed by a gang of thugs who considered me their personal bank." The older woman ignored Mia's grimace as she continued. "Plus I intended to end my relationship with Tony that night. I was trying to soften the blow."

Mia didn't believe her for a minute. It was like Vicky kept putting puzzle pieces together, but none of them fit into a clear picture.

Still, she couldn't call her a liar. Not when the only other person who could tell them what had actually happened was dead.

Seemingly agreeing with her logic, Lucas didn't bother to press the older woman. Instead he turned the conversation.

"Why did Tony go to Houston?" he abruptly asked.

Vicky paused, her arms folding over her waist as she searched for her answer.

"I don't know," she at last conceded. "I remember he spoke about you and the fact that you'd opened some sort of detective agency in Houston."

"Security," Lucas growled.

Vicky waved away his correction. "Maybe he was hoping you could help him. Tony had a habit of getting in trouble and expecting someone else to clean up his mess."

Lucas lifted his brows. "You aren't suggesting that I shot him?"

"It's certainly more likely than your obvious assumption that I'm involved," Vicky responded, refusing to be intimidated. Then, sucking in a deep breath, she continued in a controlled tone. "But I was about to suggest that the dealers followed Tony to Houston and shot him before he had a chance to speak with you."

Mia made a sound of frustration. There was something deeply annoying about hearing Tony's name on this woman's lips.

They might have been lovers, but it was obvious that Vicky hadn't felt anything for the younger man. In fact, Mia was convinced she'd only used Tony for sex. And maybe murder.

She shuddered as she forced herself to meet the icy-gray gaze. "That doesn't explain why someone would want to kill me."

Vicky shrugged. "The dealers might have been afraid that Tony said something to you that would tie them to the murder. It was no secret that the two of you were close."

"If that was true they'd shoot me, not try to poison me," Mia countered. Who'd ever heard of a gangbanger tossing pills into a coffeepot?

Vicky narrowed her gaze. "Then it must be some other enemy. You father was hardly a pillar of society—"

Mia abruptly snapped. In the past six months she'd lost two of the most important men in her life, and this ghastly woman was doing her best to shred their memories.

She was done playing nice.

"Don't you dare say another word about my father," she shouted, lunging forward.

With a speed that caught Mia off guard, Lucas was suddenly standing in front of her, blocking her path.

"I think that's enough for now," he murmured in soft tones.

"More than enough," Vicky snapped, moving to the desk to grab her cell phone. "Either you leave now or I call and report you for trespassing."

Lucas never turned his gaze from Mia's flushed face, his hand reaching up to tuck a curl behind her ear. "We're not going to get any more today," he murmured.

"But—"

Her words were cut short as he pressed a finger to her lips.

"We'll discuss this later." He brushed the back of his fingers over her cheek. "Trust me."

Catching sight of the grim determination etched onto his face, Mia gave a grudging nod. He wasn't giving up.

Or at least, he'd better not.

Still standing in front of her, Lucas turned his head to glance toward Vicky. "Thank you for your time."

Vicky remained by the desk, glaring at Mia over Lucas's shoulder. "I'd like to say it was a pleasure, but we all know it wasn't."

Grabbing Mia's arm, Lucas steered her toward the door. "We'll let you know if we have more questions," he told Vicky.

"Next time you want to speak with me, call my lawyer."

\* \* \*

Lucas clenched his teeth, refusing to slow as he tugged Mia out of the house and toward his car.

Mia was clearly close to a meltdown. Hardly surprising when Vicky was accusing her father of being an accomplice to murder.

He wanted her away from the venomous atmosphere that swirled through the house.

Pulling her to the side of Max's SUV so they were out of sight of the front windows, Lucas sent a text to his friend before meeting Mia's worried gaze. "Are you okay?"

She shivered, wrapping her arms around her waist. "You don't believe her, do you?"

Lucas paused, sensing how important his answer was to Mia. "I think she's a very clever, very dangerous woman," he said, choosing his words with care. "She mixes in just enough truth to make her lies plausible."

Mia bit her bottom lip, her expression brittle. "Tony wouldn't have killed Paul Fontaine."

Lucas wasn't nearly so certain. Tony was physically strong, but he rarely made the effort to think for himself. He preferred to be told what to do and when to do it.

"He wouldn't have plotted the murder, but he could have been persuaded to do it by someone he loved," he said.

She frowned. "Vicky?"

"We just witnessed that she's a master manipulator," he pointed out with a small shudder. He felt contaminated from his time with Vicky Fontaine. When they got back to the penthouse he was going to take a long, hot shower. "It would have been easy to convince Tony that she was in a terrible marriage and the only way to get out was to kill her husband."

Mia flinched, knowing he was right but still wanting to

cling to the belief that her friend would never take the life of another.

"He wasn't a violent man," she muttered.

"He didn't initiate fights," Lucas agreed, reaching out to cup her cheek in his palm. "But if he thought someone was trying to hurt you, he would have beat the hell out of them."

She blinked back sudden tears, as if reminded of a time when Tony had stood up to a bully for her. "True."

"If Vicky told him Paul was abusing her, Tony would have rushed to the rescue."

"I suppose," Mia grudgingly conceded, her jaw hardening with a stubborn expression. "But my father would never have agreed to help."

Again Lucas hesitated. He wanted to assure her that she was right. That there was no way George Ramon was involved. Only the fact that there was someone out there who wanted to hurt her forced him to press the issue.

"Fifty thousand dollars is a lot of money," he said, holding up his hand as her lips parted in protest. "Wait, Mia. I don't mean your father would kill for his own gain. But I think he understood on some level that he'd failed you after your mother died."

Pain flared through her eyes as his words struck a raw nerve. "What's your point?"

He stroked his thumb over her chilled cheek, hating the fact that she was so obviously upset.

"It's possible he wanted to do something to make up for his inability to be the father you needed," he suggested in gentle tones. "If he could give you financial security after he passed, it might help ease his sense of failure."

She shook her head, her brow furrowed. "He wouldn't kill anyone, not even for me."

"No, but he might be coerced into covering up a crime."

She stepped away from him, as if needing the distance to regain command of her shaken composure.

"If Tony was Vicky's lover and he agreed to murder her husband for her, then who shot him in Houston?"

It was a question that continued to nag at Lucas. "I think he was coming to me because he knew you were in danger," he said. "And whoever gave him that picture of you followed him to Houston to stop him from talking to me."

"Drug dealers?"

He gave a slow shake of his head. "If it was drug-related Tony would never have allowed them to get close enough to shoot him at point-blank. The only way they could have killed him would be to do a drive-by."

"A horrible thought, but true," she muttered. "Besides, it's ridiculous to believe that they would be trying to kill me."

"No, but Vicky is cunning. She creates one distraction after another to keep the blame from landing on herself."

"There has to be some way to prove she's involved."

"Did I just hear you say the lovely Ms. Fontaine is involved?" Max drawled as he suddenly stepped around the front of the SUV.

Resisting the urge to grab Mia and pull her close against him, Lucas forced his attention toward his friend.

Quickly he gave a condensed rundown of what they'd discovered, including the fact that Paul Fontaine was dead, and Vicky's attempt to pin the murder on Tony and George Ramon.

As he listened, Max studied Mia's pale face, no doubt sensing her brittle distress. It wasn't until Lucas finished speaking that Max turned his attention back to him.

"She can't believe that lame-ass story will hold up in court?"

Lucas shrugged. "I doubt that she's worried about her story. She has the sort of money and power to ensure that her lawyers will keep her off any witness stand."

Max grimaced. "True enough."

"Did you find anything?" Lucas asked.

"The stables have been closed and it looks like the pool hasn't been used in years," he answered.

Lucas shrugged. "Not surprising for a woman living on her own. I doubt they've kept horses here in the past fifty years. And Vicky doesn't strike me as the sort of woman who likes to lie around the pool."

"True," Max agreed.

"What about the rest of the outbuildings?"

"The greenhouses have recently been restored." Max nodded his head toward the far end of the house. "And the garage looks as if it's in decent shape."

"Did you check the vehicles?" Lucas demanded, his lips twitching as Max cocked a brow. Of course his friend would have done a thorough search of the garage. "What did you find?"

"A Jag and a more mundane Taurus."

Disappointment flared through Lucas. Why couldn't anything be easy? "That's it?" he asked.

Max flashed a secretive smile. "Nope."

Lucas stared at his companion, waiting for him to continue. When Max simply smiled, Lucas muttered a low curse. "You're as annoying as Teagan."

Max snorted. "No one is as annoying as Teagan."

"Okay. That's true," Lucas conceded. "Tell me what you found."

Max glanced around, making sure there was no one close enough to overhear his words. "I went to the side driveway where the employees park their cars."

"A black SUV?" Lucas demanded.

"Yep." Max gave a nod of his head. "I asked the gardener about it and he said it belonged to the housekeeper."

"Louisa?" Mia's eyes widened with confusion. "Why would she try to hurt me?"

"It probably wasn't her," Max assured her. "The gardener

admitted that most of the servants leave their keys in their cars in case they need to be moved for a delivery."

Lucas moved to the back of Max's SUV, studying the end of the house. There was a large, screened-in porch that looked as if it was rarely used. If Louisa was busy working, she wouldn't be able to see that her vehicle was missing. In fact, she'd probably have to actually go outside and look to notice if it'd been moved.

"So anyone could have borrowed it," he murmured.

Max moved to stand at his side. "Yes."

Lucas released a slow breath. Mia wasn't going to like what he had to say, but it was increasingly obvious that Vicky Fontaine was deeply involved in Tony's murder, as well as trying to hurt her.

He was done screwing around.

"It might be time to turn over what we've learned to Detective Cooper," he told Max.

As expected, Mia sucked in a harsh breath as she hastily stepped forward to grab his arm. "Wait."

He frowned down at her strained expression, knowing that she was going to try to convince him not to contact the cops. "Mia."

"Please, listen," she pleaded.

He heaved a sigh. He was going to regret this. "What?"

"We don't have any real evidence," she said softly, glancing toward the house with a tiny shiver. "And Vicky has enough money to hire an entire string of lawyers who will be happy to smear Tony's name, along with my father's."

He pressed his lips together. He understood her reluctance. He truly did. But he didn't give a shit about the reputation of George Ramon, or even Tony.

Not when Mia was in danger.

"If it keeps you safe I don't care," he said.

"But we can't be sure it will," she pressed. "Can we?"

He swallowed a curse. She was right about one thing. They would never get Vicky convicted of a crime without some sort of evidence.

"Do you have a better idea?" he demanded.

She gave a slow nod. "I want to go to my father's house."

# Chapter Twenty-Three

Mia unconsciously dug her fingers into Lucas's arm, willing him to agree.

She knew he probably thought she'd gone over the edge. After all, they weren't a part of the police department, and if Vicky Fontaine was responsible for Tony's death, they needed to let the officials deal with her.

But a small, selfish part of her couldn't bear the thought of the older woman spewing her lies. And not just because it would destroy her father's reputation.

She wanted to at least make an effort to find the truth.

Lucas studied her with a frown. "Why do you want to go to your father's house?"

"When I was young, my father only had one rule," she said, her voice not entirely steady.

It'd been a long, stressful afternoon.

"What was his rule?" Lucas asked.

"I wasn't allowed into the small shed that he built near the edge of the swamp."

"Did he say why?"

Mia gave a lift of her shoulder, still vividly recalling her father's long lecture after he finished building the shed.

"He claimed he kept poisons out there to kill the bugs and rodents around the house."

Lucas studied her, no doubt wondering why it would be a big deal. Most parents had places they made off-limits to their kids.

Mia, however, had been raised by a father who rarely remembered she was in the house, and certainly he'd never been concerned she might get into something that might hurt her. Not when he had guns, and pills and alcohol in easy reach.

"You didn't believe him?" Lucas asked.

She shook her head. "No. I woke up late at night to see him walking down to the shed with a lantern. I knew there had to be something out there he wasn't telling me about."

"Did you go look?"

She gave a sharp laugh. Was he serious?

"I was a lonely adolescent girl who lived in the middle of nowhere," she reminded him. "Of course I looked."

"What did you find?"

"Nothing at first." She instinctively stepped closer to Lucas, recalling her fear as she'd waited for her father to pass so she could sneak down to the edge of the swamp. "The shed was empty except for a shelf with the cans of pesticides and a small table and chair in the middle of the floor."

Lucas looked as confused as she'd felt. "Did he go there to drink?"

"He drank everywhere," she said, her voice suddenly harsh. "It wasn't like he tried to hide it from me."

His hand lifted to touch her cheek in a familiar gesture of comfort. "So what did he do in there?"

"I followed him one night and watched through a crack in the door." At the time her heart had thundered so loud she thought it might give her away. Her father hadn't been abusive, but he had a fiery temper that she tried to avoid. "I could see him standing on the chair so he could reach into the rafters and pull out a large silver box."

Lucas's fingers traced the curve of her throat. "What was inside?"

"I couldn't see at the time, so I went back the next night to take a look." A bittersweet pain tugged at her heart. "They were letters to my mother."

"Old love notes?" Lucas asked in confusion.

That had been Mia's first thought as well. But as she'd skimmed through the letters she'd realized they were about recent events.

"No." She grimaced. "He wrote to her as if she was still alive."

"What did they say?"

"Sometimes he wrote about his day. Sometimes he pleaded for her to come back." A tiny quiver raced through her body. Her father's mourning for his dead wife had been like a raw, open wound that refused to heal. "I only read a few. They were too painful."

Sympathy darkened Lucas's blue eyes. "And you think he might have written something about the murder?"

"If my dad was really involved with Paul Fontaine's death, he would have confessed to my mother."

Lucas's jaw tightened, as if he was battling against the urge to ignore the potential treasure trove of clues.

"Do you think the letters are still there?"

Mia shrugged. She hadn't thought about her father's private stash for years. Which was why she hadn't looked for them when they'd been at the house the last time.

"Unless my father got rid of the letters. I doubt anyone else knows about them."

Lucas muttered a low curse, lifting a hand to shove his fingers through his hair. "I suppose it wouldn't hurt to look through them," he reluctantly conceded.

Mia released a breath she hadn't realized she was holding. "Thank you."

Lucas was an idiot.

They knew Vicky was involved in the mess, but there was a very good chance she wasn't working alone. Who knew who else might be involved?

But he also understood Mia's fierce need to do everything in her power to clear her father's name. They might not have been close, but he was the only family she'd ever really had.

Standing a few feet away, Max cleared his throat, his face carefully devoid of expression.

A good decision. One smirk at the way Mia had so easily manipulated him and Lucas would punch him in the face.

"What do you want from me?" his companion asked.

"I want you to keep an eye on Vicky Fontaine," Lucas told his friend. "If she leaves the house I want you to follow her."

Max scowled. "I don't like the thought of you being without backup."

Lucas glanced toward Mia, silently weighing the danger before returning his gaze to his companion. "It's only for a couple of hours."

Max flattened his lips, but he didn't bother to argue. He was well aware that once Lucas made up his mind, there was no way to change it.

"Keep your cell phone handy," he instead commanded.

Lucas nodded. "I will."

"And your gun."

"Always," Lucas promised, glancing toward the heavy gray sky that promised rain. "Can we take your vehicle? Mine wasn't built for the back roads."

"Sure."

The two men quickly switched keys, and Lucas reached out to grab Mia's arm.

"Let me know if the Wicked Witch leaves her lair," he told his friend, tugging Mia toward the passenger door of the SUV.

"Do witches live in lairs?" Max called out, leaning against the hood of Lucas's car. "I thought that was vampires."

Lucas rolled his eyes, helping Mia climb into her seat before rounding the hood and opening the driver's side door. "Just be careful," he told his friend.

Max gave a small salute as Lucas slid into his seat and started the SUV.

Trusting Max to keep watch, Lucas headed toward the nearby highway. He flipped on the heater as a cold drizzle began to fall from the thick clouds, and covertly glanced toward Mia, who was huddled in silence.

He didn't try to distract her from her brooding.

She'd endured one shock after another over the past couple of days. She needed the opportunity to process her thoughts.

Besides, he didn't have any words of comfort.

He was willing to give her the next hour or two to go through her father's letters. After that, they were driving straight to the Caddo sheriff's office.

ARES Security might have better resources than the local law department, but they didn't have the ability to make arrests. He wanted Vicky Fontaine too worried about being tossed into a jail cell to try and hurt Mia.

The road to the small cabin had turned into a muddy mess, and by the time they parked in the front yard, which was now a bog, Lucas was relieved the SUV had four-wheel drive.

Lucas felt a tiny chill inch down his spine as he studied the house, which was surrounded by shabby outbuildings and piles of weed-covered junk. It was a depressing sight under the best of circumstances. In the gathering gloom, it was downright scary.

Like something from a horror flick.

All they needed was a man in a hockey mask wielding a machete.

"Wait until I do a sweep," he murmured, pulling out his gun as he pushed open the door of the SUV and climbed out.

Not waiting for Mia's protest, he headed directly toward the house, peeking in the windows to ensure there was no one inside before he headed toward the sheds. Finding nothing, he did a quick circle of the mounds of abandoned cars and junk before returning to the SUV and opening Mia's door.

"Which shed?" he asked when she slid out of her seat to stand beside him.

He wanted to look through the letters and leave. The place was giving him the creeps.

"Follow me," she said, heading directly toward the far shed, nearly hidden beneath the Spanish moss that draped from a nearby tree.

"Careful," he murmured as she grabbed the rusty doorknob to pull open the door.

She sent him a startled glance. "I thought you already searched."

He grimaced, holstering his gun as he pulled out his phone and hit the flashlight app.

"For bad guys, not snakes," he said, allowing the light to fill the dark space.

As Mia had warned, the shed was virtually empty except for the small table and chair, both of which were covered in layers of dust. There were no windows, but there was a stray shaft of gray light that filtered in from a hole in the sagging roof.

On one wall was a shelf with old canisters, and in a corner was a pile of empty whiskey bottles.

It didn't look as if anyone had been inside for years, but he still continued to swing his phone from side to side, allowing the light to dance over the floor before moving up to the open rafters.

Only when he was certain there weren't any creepy crawlies about to leap out of the shadows did he allow Mia to step inside.

She flashed him a wry smile. "Such a hero."

He followed behind her, setting the phone on the table to allow the light to spread through the small space before he turned toward his companion.

Reaching up, he framed her face in his hands. "I need to protect you."

She stilled beneath his gentle touch, her expression instantly wary.

"I've been taking care of myself for a long time."

"Too long." The familiar pang of regret sliced through his heart. If he'd taken Mia with him when he'd left Shreveport, she might not be in danger now. "I want it to be my turn."

She licked her lips, reminding him of just how good that sweet mouth felt as it'd skimmed down his naked body.

A delicious tingle warmed his blood.

"Lucas, now isn't the time," she protested.

He bent down until they were nose to nose. He knew this woman better than anyone else.

Which meant he was well aware that she was already considering just how the news of her father's potential involvement might impact her future.

And the future of others.

"I want to say this now," he insisted, savoring the warm scent of her skin. "It doesn't matter what we find or don't find in this shed. I don't care if your father was involved in Paul Fontaine's death."

She trembled beneath his touch. "You should. Your family—"

"I don't give a shit about the people who gave birth to me," he interrupted, brushing his mouth over her parted lips as she gave a small gasp at his blunt words. "I know that's harsh, but they're toxic, and until they change, I can't have them in my life."

Her expression eased with sympathy. At one time she might have believed the image of the perfect family that his parents had loved to portray, but she'd witnessed firsthand the emptiness behind the facade.

"I get that," she murmured.

"The only people who matter are my brothers at ARES," he said, pressing another light kiss against her lips. "And you."

She pulled back, her features tight with strain. "Being seen with the daughter of a potential murderer isn't going to help your business," she pointed out in grim tones. "How could your customers ever trust you?"

His lips twisted, wondering who Mia assumed came to ARES Security for help.

Parents of missing children? Women with cheating spouses?

The usual customers couldn't afford the fee just to get through the front door.

"The sort of clients who seek out our services don't give a crap about our private lives," he assured her in low tones. "They need the best and that's what we are."

"And your friends?" she stubbornly demanded.

"They would lay down their lives for the woman I love," he assured her without hesitation.

A hint of vulnerability softened her eyes before she was once again seeking a way to put barriers between them.

"Even if we did . . ." She briefly faltered, as if struggling with the mere thought they could put aside the past and become more than enemies. "Start a relationship," she at last said. "Have you considered the fact that we live hours away from each other?"

His lips twitched. Did she have to sound like she was being tortured when she said the word "relationship"?

"I'm aware we have hurdles in our path," he conceded. "And I think we can work past them."

"Hmm." Her eyes narrowed. "Are you assuming that I'll drop everything and move to Houston?"

Lucas bit back his curse, silently reminding himself that Mia was being deliberately provoking.

It was her go-to option. How else could she push him away?

"I'm assuming we'll negotiate a compromise that will make both of us happy," he said, proud of his mild tone. "That's what grown-ups do."

She frowned, realizing that he'd stolen her thunder.

After all, he wasn't demanding that she walk away from her life, or sacrifice everything to be a couple.

All he was asking was a chance to see where this might lead.

"I don't know," she hedged.

His fingers threaded through her hair, his gaze skimming over her pale face. "Just answer one question."

"What?"

"Do you love me?"

She flinched at his unexpected words. "I—"

"Tell the truth, Mia," he commanded.

There was a slight pause before she heaved a small sigh. "Yes, I love you."

Joy seared through him as he pressed a soft kiss to her forehead.

"That's all that matters."

# Chapter Twenty-Four

The thickening darkness outside the shed finally had Lucas lifting his head and stepping back. Dusk was swiftly creeping in. He didn't want to be there once night had fallen.

"Okay, let's get this done," he murmured, gingerly stepping onto the chair.

"Be careful," Mia muttered as the chair wobbled beneath his weight.

Well aware the chair might split in two at any moment, Lucas reached through the open rafters. He could see a dark form that he was hoping was the case that held the letters.

"I think I have it," he said, coughing as a cloud of dust and cobwebs landed directly in his face. "Stand back," he warned Mia. "The rafters are rotted and there's no telling what will come down when I pull the case out." Waiting until he heard Mia stepping back, he ran his hand over the smooth object until he found a handle. Wrapping his fingers around it, he gave a hard yank. The case slid through the rafters at the same time as a portion of the roof tumbled down, hitting him on the head. "Damn."

Jumping off the chair, he rubbed the bump even as Mia scurried forward to brush the dust from his face.

"Are you okay?"

"Fine," he murmured, relieved when he pulled his hand down to discover there was no blood. He might have a concussion, but he wasn't going to bleed to death. He was taking that as a win. "I have a hard head."

"Amen," Mia muttered, moving back as he placed the case on the table.

Lucas ignored her taunting, instead concentrating on the object he'd just pulled from the rafters.

It was made of metal and the size of a large briefcase. The sort of case that people bought to protect important documents.

Sliding the two levers on the front, he frowned when nothing happened.

"It's locked."

Standing at his side, Mia pointed toward the tiny combination lock.

"Try two-four-eight-four," she said.

Leaning forward, Lucas used his thumbnail to turn each tumbler to the numbers Mia suggested, then, pressing the levers, he heard a click as the top sprang open.

Straightening, he sent Mia a questioning gaze. "How did you figure it out?"

She shrugged. "It's my parents' anniversary."

Of course. Lucas resisted the urge to roll his eyes. He admired George's devotion to his dead wife, but if he'd truly cared about her, he wouldn't have allowed his grief to lead him to the bottle. Instead he would have poured his heart and soul into making sure his young daughter was given a safe, stable home that was filled with love.

That's what her mother would have wanted.

Keeping his thoughts to himself, Lucas tugged open the lid of the case and pulled out a thick stack of papers.

He pressed them into Mia's hand. "Here, you start with these."

For once, Mia didn't argue. She quickly began to scan

the short notes that were written in awkward block letters, placing the ones she'd read on the table before moving to the next in the stack.

"He loved her so much," she murmured on a soft sigh.

Lucas began to sort through the remaining pieces of paper in the case.

"I doubt my parents have ever written a letter to one another," he admitted.

Mia lifted her head, studying him with a searching gaze. "Their marriage isn't a love match?"

He released a short burst of laughter. He'd never seen his parents hold hands, let alone kiss. If it wasn't for the fact that they'd managed to have two sons, he would have assumed they'd never bothered to climb into the same bed.

"More like an uneasy truce to combine two powerful families," he admitted with a wry grimace. "I'm not sure if my mother is capable of loving anyone."

Pity softened her features. "And your father?"

"He loves himself," Lucas said, returning his attention to the stacks of paper still in the case.

He worked hard at not thinking about the Honorable St. Clair and his insatiable ambition that'd driven Lucas's older brother to suicide. No doubt a psychologist would have a field day with him.

But, hey . . . pretending his father didn't exist worked for him.

Skimming through a dozen letters, Lucas was reaching for more when he caught sight of the compartment built into the inner side of the lid. Curious, he reached inside to pull out a large manila folder.

"Was this in there before?" he asked.

Mia gave a slow shake of her head. "I don't remember it."

Flipping open the folder, Lucas stiffened in shock at the sight of the grainy photos stacked inside.

The first few were exact duplicates of the ones that Vicky

had shown them. Clear proof that the older woman hadn't lied about where she'd gotten them. And a surprising revelation that Mia's father was smart enough to keep copies.

As he flipped through them, however, he realized that there were more than just the ones Vicky had shared with them.

"Shit," he breathed.

Mia dropped the letters, holding her hand out. "What is it?"

He offered her the folder. "Look."

In silence she studied the pictures, her eyes widening as she reached the last few.

"Oh my God." She held up a picture that revealed a large, dark-haired man standing over a body that was crumpled on the ground. "That's Tony with a gun. He really did kill Paul."

"It looks bad," Lucas agreed.

Mia studied the fuzzy image. "I assume that's Paul Fontaine on the ground."

Lucas nodded, wishing the picture was clear enough to reveal the background. All he could determine was that there was a large brick structure that might be a house. He hoped Max would be able to magnify it enough to give them a clue where the picture was taken.

"That's my guess," he murmured.

Mia shuffled to the next photo, her breath hissing between her teeth.

This one revealed Tony still holding the gun, but there was a blond-haired woman bending over the dead man on the ground, as if studying the bleeding hole in the center of his chest.

"Vicky," Mia breathed.

"Yes."

Mia shivered. "She was there."

"She was an accomplice, if not the actual killer," Lucas

agreed, reaching out to tap the pictures. "And now we have proof."

Mia nodded before she was fanning the pictures out on the table, her expression brittle as she studied each of them in the light from Lucas's phone.

"There's none of my father," she at last said, her relief a tangible force in the thick air.

"No."

Lucas stood at her side, trying to imagine the distance and angle of the photographer from Tony and Vicky. If someone wanted to take decent pictures of the horrifying scene, they would have stood considerably closer. And they would have chosen to stand on the other side of the body so the sun didn't create a glare. Most importantly, they wouldn't have allowed thin branches of some sort of bush to create strange crisscross patterns in several of the photos.

Which told Lucas that whoever took the pictures was hiding in a bush and shooting the scene without Tony or Vicky being aware he was there.

"Is it possible my father wasn't even there?"

Lucas reached his hand back into the compartment in the lid of the briefcase, searching for any other hidden treasures.

"Actually, I would guess that he was the one taking the pictures," he told Mia.

She wrinkled her nose. "Why would he do that?"

Not about to suggest that the older man might have stumbled across the scene and hoped to blackmail his wealthy employer, Lucas abruptly pulled his hand out of the briefcase and held up the small cassette tape he'd found at the very bottom of the compartment.

"This might tell us," he said, a sense of triumph flaring through him.

There was no guarantee that there were answers on the cassette, but he had a good feeling. Why else would it have been hidden with the pictures?

"A tape?" Mia asked in confusion.

"It looks like it's from one of those mini cassette recorders," Lucas said.

Mia confirmed Lucas's suspicion the tape belonged to George Ramon. "My father used to have one. He said it was easier to make notes by recording them instead of having to write them out. There might be one inside the house."

Lucas battled against his urge to rush into the house and play the cassette. If it was connected to the murder, it was seventeen years old.

Not only would the tape be fragile after all that time, but the heat and humidity of Louisiana might have warped the plastic. They would have to take extreme care not to destroy the thing before they could ever discover what was on it.

"We should get this to Max," he forced himself to mutter. "He'll be able to take it to his lab in Houston."

Mia frowned. "Why Houston?"

"He has equipment there that can play the cassette without the risk of doing something that might damage it," Lucas said, not bothering to tell her that she was going to Houston at the same time. She would find out soon enough. "Once we have a copy of the tape, we're handing over everything we have to the cops."

Mia gave a reluctant nod, gathering the pictures and putting them back in the case. Lucas dropped the tape inside and closed the lid, hearing a distinct *click* as the locks tumbled into place.

The incriminating evidence was no doubt the reason Vicky had been trying to get rid of Mia. She had to know that Mia would eventually go through her father's belongings and find it.

Now that they had what they'd come for, he was anxious to get the hell out of there. The sooner they could hand over the case to the cops, the sooner he could be certain Mia was no longer in danger.

Grabbing the handle of the case, Lucas was reaching for Mia's hand when there was the sound of footsteps just outside the shed. With a swift motion, Lucas was pulling his gun and shoving Mia behind him.

Prepared to shoot whoever stepped through the narrow entrance, Lucas was caught off guard when the door suddenly slammed shut.

He frowned. Had he imagined the footsteps? Could it just have been the wind?

Motioning for Mia to stay where she was, Lucas cautiously moved forward, his gun still in his hand when he reached out the other one to grab the knob.

It turned easily in his hand, but when he tried to shove the door open, it wouldn't budge. Shit. Something was blocking their one and only way out of the shed.


Max was sitting in Lucas's sports car just outside the gates of Vicky Fontaine's estate.

He'd fully intended to remain in the driveway after Lucas had driven away, but the gardener had approached just a few minutes later to inform him that Vicky was threatening to call the cops if he didn't leave.

He didn't have the authority to stay. And the last thing he wanted was to find himself hauled down to the Shreveport police station. Not when Lucas might need him.

Thirty minutes later, he was nearly crawling out of his skin.

He was usually a man who understood patience.

His approach to life was exactly like his approach to science. Slow, methodical, and always striving for perfection.

But he couldn't escape the strange premonition that Lucas was in trouble.

Slipping out of the car, he avoided the cameras that monitored the gate and strolled along the quiet street. He shivered as the icy drizzle dampened his hair and the breeze tugged at his coat, but he kept his pace casual as he headed around the hedge that separated the large estate from the neighbor.

He'd noticed a gap in the bushes when he was doing his earlier search.

Picking up his speed, he was careful to remain in the shadows as he moved along the hedges and darted through the narrow gap. Once through, he came to a halt as his phone vibrated.

He pulled it from his pocket, hoping it was Lucas. Instead Teagan's name flashed across the screen. He hesitated before connecting the call and lifting the phone to his ear.

Teagan wouldn't contact him if it wasn't important.

"Hey, bro," Max murmured, his voice pitched low as his gaze remained locked on the large Tudor house. The lights were beginning to be turned on in various rooms, but he couldn't see into the windows from his position.

He needed to get closer.

"Are you with Lucas?" Teagan demanded with his usual blunt style.

"Nope." Remaining close to the hedges in case he needed to make a quick exit, Max headed toward the side of the house. "He took Mia to find some old letters at her father's property. What's up?"

"I need to talk to him, but he isn't answering his phone."

Max's unease intensified. "How long have you been trying?"

"Not long," Teagan admitted. "Five minutes or so."

Max clenched his fingers on the phone. He wasn't going to overreact, dammit. There were a dozen reasons why Lucas wasn't answering.

"It's a remote area," he told Teagan, choosing the most obvious explanation. "The reception is probably sketchy."

"Maybe." Teagan's concern hummed in his voice. "I think you should check it out."

"Yeah, so do I," Max muttered, angling toward the long bank of windows that lined the north wall of the house. Before he took off he wanted to make sure that Vicky was occupied with whatever kept rich old ladies busy on chilly evenings. "As soon as I see what's going on with the Wicked Witch."

"What the hell are you talking about?"

"I'm supposed to be keeping a watch on Vicky Fontaine," Max said, his thoughts distracted as he stepped onto one of the stone urns that were handily placed at each corner of the home. They offered a perfect position to peer through the windows.

Of course, if one of the servants happened to catch sight of him, he'd no doubt be arrested as a creeper.

"Why?" Teagan demanded.

"It's a long story." Max frowned, scanning the large library for some sign of life. Nothing. "Did you find out something you want me to pass along to Lucas?"

"It's possible," Teagan hedged.

Max jumped off the urn and headed toward the back of the house. "Tell me."

"I came up with a dead end on Paul Fontaine," Teagan said.

Max grimaced, recalling Lucas's revelation that Paul Fontaine had been murdered and stuffed in a trunk.

"Probably because he quite literally is a dead end."

There was a startled pause as Teagan absorbed the news that Fontaine was dead. "No shit?" he at last said.

"Lucas saw the pictures."

"Pictures?" Teagan made a sound of disbelief. "What the hell happened?"

Max eased his way along the back of the house, trying

to stay out of the line of sight of the long greenhouse where he could see the silhouette of the gardener.

"Tony, as well as George Ramon, was implicated, but we're still working on the truth," he said.

"Tony Hughes? The dead guy?"

"That's the one."

Max reached the windows that looked into the kitchen. The housekeeper was busy preparing dinner. That meant Vicky had no intention of going out. At least not for a while.

A portion of his sizzling tension eased, although he couldn't dismiss the lingering knot of anxiety in the pit of his gut.

"Hmm," Teagan breathed.

Max stepped beneath a brick arbor that led to the rose garden to finish his conversation with Teagan. He was out of sight of the kitchen windows, and yet close enough to keep an eye on the garage in case Vicky decided to go for an unexpected trip. It also had the benefit of giving him a brief respite from the pesky rain.

"What's on your mind?" he demanded, knowing Teagan well enough to sense when something was bothering him.

"Just trying to put this puzzle together," the computer guru said.

"You and me both, bro," Max said, shaking his head in frustration. Teagan was right. It was like a puzzle where they had a few of the pieces, but nothing fit together. "So what did you discover?"

"Since you and Lucas are searching for any enemies who might want Mia dead, I decided to start from the other end."

Max frowned. "What's that mean?"

"I wanted to see who would gain from Mia's death."

Max grimaced. He knew it was an important question. Hell, he'd urged Lucas to find out if anyone benefited after she was rushed to the hospital. But it didn't make it any easier to think of someone deliberately plotting her murder.

He'd known the young, vulnerable woman only a short time, but she was already a part of the ARES family, as far as he was concerned.

"She has a will?" he asked.

"Yep."

"And?"

"She carries a large amount of debt on her business and her home," Teagan revealed. "If she died, most of her property would become the property of the loan company."

Max shivered as a strong gust of wind whipped through the arbor. "You mean Lucas," he said, referring to the dummy company that their friend had set up to ensure Mia could get the funds she needed for her expansion.

"Exactly."

"So that rules out money as a motive."

"Not entirely."

Max frowned. There was no way Teagan was implying that Lucas would want Mia harmed. Which meant there must be some collateral that wasn't a part of her business. "Does she have a life insurance policy?"

"Nope. But she did inherit her father's land," Teagan said.

Max didn't often question his friend. Teagan was a research god. But it seemed hard to believe anyone would be willing to risk killing Mia for a patch of swampland overrun with rusty cars and rotting sheds.

"According to Lucas it's not worth much," he told Teagan. "Unless there's a hidden treasure beneath all the junk."

"I don't know about any treasures, but if something happens to Mia the land goes to a local charity," Teagan retorted.

"Not surprising," he murmured. "I don't think she has any close family. What do you know about the charity?"

"It's for wildlife conservation."

Max's lips twitched. It was doubtful any other charity would be interested in the land.

"That makes sense, but I don't understand why you think this has anything to do with someone trying to hurt Mia."

"Three weeks ago the charity received a large influx of cash. In gratitude the board of directors chose a new chairman." There was a long pause. "Or in this case, a new chairwoman."

Distracted by the sound of the greenhouse door being opened and shut, Max leaned to the side, watching as the gardener walked toward the side of the main house. Clearly he was done for the day.

Max wished he could say the same.

Dark was closing in and it was damned cold.

"Lucas is right," he muttered. "You are a drama queen."

"Hey," Teagan protested. "At least make me a king."

Max rolled his eyes. "What does the damned charity have to do with Mia?"

"The new chairwoman is Vicky Fontaine."

Max stiffened. "Why the hell would she be interested in wildlife conservation?"

"My guess is that there's something on that land she wants," Teagan said. "Desperately."

"Dammit, what are we missing?" Max growled. "First she tried to hound Mia into selling the property, and now she's elbowed her way into control of the charity that will gain ownership of the land if Mia dies."

"I don't know what she wants," Teagan admitted, "but I don't like the thought that Lucas is out there without backup."

The nagging unease abruptly exploded into outright fear. Still clutching the phone to his ear, he darted out of the arbor and headed toward the side of the house.

He'd agreed to keep an eye on Vicky Fontaine because Lucas asked him, but he hadn't actually thought she personally was a danger. He assumed she had an accomplice. He'd been prepared for her to call for her partner in crime to come over so they could plot their next move. Or for her to try and slip away so she could meet her accomplice in some secret location.

Now he realized he'd failed Surveillance 101. Never assume a damned thing.

Sprinting around the corner of the house, he muttered a string of curses as he discovered the black SUV was missing.

"What's wrong?" Teagan demanded.

"That bitch managed to slip past me."

"How?"

"There must be a side exit," Max growled, not bothering to take the time to discover how Vicky had left the estate unnoticed.

Instead he jogged down the driveway and out the front gate. He didn't give a shit if he was caught on the security cameras. All that mattered was getting to Lucas and making sure he was okay.

As if reading his tension, Teagan muttered a curse. "I don't like this, amigo."

Max slid into the sports car and switched on the engine. "Me either."

"It might be time to give Detective Cooper a call."

Putting the phone on speaker, Max tossed it into the passenger seat and put the car in gear. Pressing on the gas pedal, he took off with a squeal of his tires.

"And say what? That I suspect one of his most reputable citizens might or might not be trying to kill Mia? It's not like I have any actual proof. I'll go out and warn Lucas that Vicky is on the move."

"Do you know how to get there?" Teagan demanded. "Lucas told me it's in the middle of nowhere."

Max weaved his way through the elegant neighborhood, headed back to the interstate. It didn't matter whether or not he knew how to get to the property; his first problem was finding a vehicle that could navigate the muddy roads.

"I'll get there," he promised his friend.

Clearly sensing that Max needed his full attention on the thickening rush hour traffic, Teagan heaved a frustrated sigh. "Call me when you find him."

"You got it," Max assured his friend, darting around a delivery truck.

"Max, you have an hour to contact me," Teagan warned. "After that I'm calling Cooper and telling him to get his ass out there."

"Love you too," Max muttered, reaching over to disconnect the call.

He had enough to worry about without Teagan's nagging.

# Chapter Twenty-Five

Taylor moved across the office to retrieve the winter coat she'd worn over her tailored skirt and bright Christmas sweater.

It'd been a long day of doing her work as well as taking on a portion of Mia's usual tasks. She knew her friend well enough to realize that Mia wouldn't give herself time to recover if she thought the business needed her.

Besides, Taylor couldn't deny a renegade pleasure in making the decisions. She didn't have Mia's experience in landscaping, but she did have a talent for organization.

Now she was ready for an early dinner with Justin and her mother, followed by a hot bubble bath.

Lost in thoughts of what she needed to pick up from the grocery store on her way home, Taylor didn't hear the door open. It wasn't until she turned from the coatrack that she realized she was no longer alone.

"Oh." Pressing a hand over her racing heart, she frowned at her unexpected visitor. "Detective Cooper. You startled me."

His lips twitched. "My name is Brian, not Detective Cooper," he gently reminded her.

Her gaze skimmed over his brown hair, which had been

ruffled by the breeze, and the dark suit, damp from the drizzling rain.

A growingly familiar warmth filled her heart at the sight of him, even as she had to bite her tongue against the urge to chide him for not wearing a warmer jacket.

It wasn't her place to fuss over him.

"I was just getting ready to lock up," she murmured.

With a frown he glanced at the watch strapped around his wrist, as if he had lost track of time. "I didn't know it was so late." He lifted his head, his gaze straying toward the closed door to Mia's office. "I need to speak with Ms. Ramon."

Taylor clenched her teeth at the stupid disappointment that flared through her. Good Lord. Had she assumed he'd come by to see her?

Taylor jerked on her coat, pasting her professional smile on her lips. She was such an idiot when it came to men.

"She isn't here," she said, brushing past her companion as she headed to her desk.

"Do you know where I can find her?" he asked.

"I assume she's with Lucas at his penthouse." Taylor pulled open her top drawer to grab her purse and keys. "She didn't come into the office today."

"I tried to call her cell phone, but she isn't answering," Brian said, his brows drawn together.

She closed the drawer and moved around the desk. "Did you try Lucas?"

"He didn't answer either."

She shrugged. "Maybe they're occupied."

Brian pressed his lips together, looking all cop as he placed his hands on his hips, revealing the gun holstered beneath his jacket. "I really need to find her, Taylor."

She stilled. There was no missing the edge in his voice. "Has something happened?" she demanded.

He paused, as if considering whether or not he was going to answer her question.

Then he folded his arms over his chest. "I want to know why she didn't tell me that Tony was Vicky Fontaine's lover," he said in clipped tones.

Taylor blinked. It took her a minute to realize exactly whom he was talking about.

"Tony Hughes? And Vicky Fontaine?" she said in slow tones. Brian nodded and Taylor gave a sudden laugh. Raunchy, barely educated Tony being involved with the classy Vicky Fontaine was . . . ridiculous. Not to mention the fact that Vicky had to be at least twenty years older than Tony. "No way. I don't know who told you the two of them were lovers, but they were messing with you."

Brian looked anything but amused. "I have evidence."

"Seriously?" She lifted her hand as his scowl deepened. She didn't know what was going on, but it was obvious Brian was worried about something. "Sorry. I just can't imagine the two of them together."

He gave a small shudder. "Consider yourself fortunate."

Taylor arched a brow. Exactly what sort of evidence did he have? Considering the various possibilities, she abruptly gave a shake of her head.

She needed to concentrate on what was important.

"What does their relationship have to do with Mia?"

"She deliberately hid the fact that Tony had a romantic relationship," he accused.

Taylor shook her head. "She didn't hide anything. Mia didn't know about the relationship."

"How can you be so sure?" he demanded.

Taylor shrugged. "She would have told me."

His lips parted, but before he could speak, the door to the office was yanked open and a tall, blond-haired man charged into the room.

Taylor instantly recognized him as Lucas's friend from Houston. Max Grayson. She'd briefly spoken to him when she'd visited Mia in the hospital.

A tiny shiver raced through her. He was gorgeous, but he had the same air of danger that sizzled around Lucas.

"Good, you're still here," he said in rough tones.

Taylor studied him in confusion even as she felt Brian move to stand at her side. "If you're looking for Mia, she isn't here," she said.

Max flicked a glance toward her companion, his expression hardening before he returned his attention to Taylor. "I'm here for you."

Taylor widened her eyes, not sure if she was more surprised by Max's words, or by the sensation of Brian wrapping a possessive arm around her shoulders.

"Why?" the lawman demanded.

Max ignored Brian's question, his gaze remaining fixed on Taylor's face. "Can you take me to George Ramon's property?"

Brian tightened his fingers on her shoulders, his body stiff as he glared at the taller man. "I asked you a question."

Gray eyes narrowed with a smoldering impatience. "I'm talking to Taylor." His gaze moved back to her. "Unless he speaks for you."

"He most certainly does not," Taylor said in emphatic tones.

She didn't know what was happening between her and Detective Cooper, but she didn't allow anyone to speak for her. Not ever. "Is something going on with Mia?" she asked.

Max hesitated, clearly unhappy with Brian's presence. Then he gave a resigned shake of his head. "She went to her father's house with Lucas. I need to make sure they're okay."

"Why wouldn't they be?" Brian demanded.

Taylor sent the detective an annoyed glance. "Brian—"

"No," he interrupted, his expression stubborn. "St. Clair and his friends have been interfering in my investigation since they arrived in town."

Max folded his arms over his chest. "All we're doing is

trying to keep Mia safe. Something that doesn't seem too high on the priority list for the sheriff's office."

Brian jutted a stubborn chin. "We do what we can."

"Which isn't enough," Max drawled.

Sensing a brewing battle, Taylor stepped between the two men, her gaze locked on Max. "Why do you think she's in danger?"

He held her worried gaze. "We have reason to suspect that Vicky Fontaine is responsible for her husband's murder, and that she—"

"You have evidence she murdered her husband?" Brian interrupted with a snap. "Why didn't you come to me?"

Max visibly struggled to maintain a hold on his temper. "Because we don't have evidence," he said between clenched teeth. "And if we'd come to you, the bitch would have lawyered up and pinned the blame on Tony Hughes and George Ramon."

"Vicky killed her husband?" Taylor breathed, feeling as if her head was spinning.

She'd never liked the older woman, but she would never have dreamed she would actually be capable of murder.

Max shrugged. "More likely she convinced Tony to do it."

Taylor frowned. *Why would Tony help . . . ? Oh yeah, he was Vicky's lover.*

Giving a shake of her head, she tried to focus on the fact that Max feared her friend was in danger. "So how does this connect to Mia?"

"We're not sure, but we think it has something to do with her father's land," he said. "If Mia dies, it goes to a charity that Vicky recently became chairwoman of."

Brian stepped forward. "How do you know her husband is dead?"

Max glared at the lawman. "I don't have time for this." He turned his head toward Taylor. "Are you going to take me or not?"

Taylor nodded, but before she could speak, Brian was headed toward the door.

"I'll drive you there." He sent Taylor a warning frown. "You go home."

Taylor scowled. "If my friend is in trouble, I need to help her."

Brian moved with unexpected speed, framing her face in his hands as he stared down at her with a burning gaze. "Your son needs you to stay safe," he murmured, shocking her speechless as he leaned down and pressed a soft kiss to her parted lips. "*I* need you to stay safe." Another lingering kiss that sent shock waves of pleasure through her. "Go home, Taylor."

Too astonished to protest, Taylor watched as the men left the office.

What had just happened?

Mia winced as Lucas ran across the cramped space of the shed and smashed his shoulder into the door.

It was the third time he'd tried to force their way out. And the third time he'd done nothing more than send a ton of dust falling from the rafters.

Not to mention the fact he would no doubt be black-and-blue in the morning.

"Stop. You're going to hurt yourself," she pleaded as he backed across the shed preparing to once again ram the door. Moving forward, she blocked his path. "Please, Lucas."

"We have to get out of here," he growled, reaching into his pocket to pull out his phone. He scowled, clearly still unable to get service. "Worthless."

She laid her hand on his arm, noting his tension in the clenched muscles that felt like granite beneath her fingers.

"Max knows we're out here," she reminded him. "He'll eventually come looking for us."

He grasped her hand, giving her fingers a squeeze. "Mia, the door didn't close on its own."

"The wind—"

"No," he cut her words short, his expression hard. "Someone is out there."

Her heart thudded with a sudden fear, her eyes widening as she caught the unmistakable stench of smoke.

"Do you smell that?" she asked.

Lucas turned toward the back of the shed, where flames were licking along the bottom of the wooden planks. Someone was trying to burn the shed. With them stuck inside.

"Shit," Lucas breathed.

For a stunned second they both froze, trying to comprehend the fact that they were trapped inside a burning building. Then, taking command of the situation, Lucas was moving to grab the chair and pull it toward a far corner.

Mia watched in confusion as he stepped onto the chair and held out his hand. "Come here."

She crossed to stand next to him. "What are you doing?"

He pointed toward the rafters. "If I lift you up, you should be able to crawl through the hole in the roof."

Angling back her head, Mia studied the spot where the shingles had rotted away to leave a gaping space. It would be tight, but she could probably wiggle through.

Or at least she could if she was willing to selfishly escape while letting Lucas stay stuck in the burning shed.

"I'm not leaving you," she snapped.

He glared down at her, his expression grim. "It's not about leaving me, Mia. If you don't get out of here, we both die."

He was right, of course.

Someone had to get out to open the door.

"Fine," she grudgingly conceded, climbing onto the chair.

"Take this," Lucas commanded, pulling the gun out of its holster and shoving it into her hand. "Once you get out I want you to take the vehicle and go for help."

She carefully placed the gun in the pocket of her coat, knowing she would need both hands to climb out.

"Sure," she muttered.

As if sensing she had no intention of leaving until she was confident he was safely out of the shed, he grasped her shoulders. "I mean it, Mia," he said between clenched teeth. "Whoever is out there wants you dead. If they manage to kill you, then I die too." He lowered his head until they were nose to nose. "You're our only hope."

A shiver inched down her spine, but she sternly squashed her terror.

Now wasn't the time to worry about the horror of someone wanting to kill her. All that mattered was getting out so she could save Lucas.

"Got it," she assured him.

Ignoring his scowl that warned he wasn't fooled for a minute, she reached up to grab the rafters, giving a hard pull as he wrapped his hands around her waist and lifted her upward.

Shards of decayed wood bit into her fingers even as there was a sharp pain as her hair caught on a nail, but she didn't hesitate as she wiggled through the rafters. The smoke was already thickening in the cramped space. She had to get out and get the door open.

Swinging her legs up, she wrapped them around the rafters so she could use them as leverage as she reached to shove her hands through the hole in the roof. She ignored the blood that dripped from her fingers as she braced her palms on the rough shingles that'd once protected the roof and pressed herself up and through the narrow opening.

Immediately she was wrapped in the icy drizzle that continued to fall, but she didn't care. Instead she sucked in deep breaths of the frigid air, trying to clear her lungs of the smoke that was now billowing through the hole.

*Damn.* She could already hear Lucas coughing. She had to hurry.

"Don't hesitate to shoot," he called out as she pushed herself completely through the opening and perched on top of the sagging roof. "I don't care who it is."

Inching toward the side of the shed, Mia tried to avoid the spots that were the most rotted. She couldn't help either of them if she ended up falling back into the shed.

She was near the edge when there was the rustle of footsteps coming around the corner of the shed. Mia tried to scoot back. The dusk had thickened enough that she might be able to avoid being seen.

A shadowed form stilled, and Mia knew she'd been spotted. Scrambling forward, she leaped off the roof seconds before the sound of a high-pitched *bang* splintered the air.

*Holy crap.* Someone was shooting at her.

Darting into the nearby underbrush, she crouched down as she listened to the footsteps search around the cabin before heading toward Max's SUV, which Lucas had left parked near the road.

Clearly the person was hoping she was going to try and make a run for it.

Instead, Mia silently made her way along the edge of the bog, using her memories to lead her to the flat-bottom boat her father always kept tied to a tree. Precious minutes passed before she at last found it bobbing at the edge of the water. Trying to avoid making any sound, Mia reached over the edge of the boat to grab the two buckets stashed in the back. Her father used them to bail out the water that leaked in whenever he went fishing.

Keeping crouched low, she filled the buckets with water and hurried back to the shed. The rain had thankfully picked up, helping to battle the fire that was slowly crawling up the back of the shed. Combined with the damp wood and the water Mia tossed from the buckets, the flames sputtered and died a smoldering death.

For once, she fully appreciated the soggy Louisiana weather.

On the point of making her way back to the front of the shed, Mia froze in her tracks at the sound of a female voice calling out her name.

"Mia." There was a pause as footsteps cautiously headed toward the shed. "It's Vicky Fontaine. I was driving by and I thought I smelled smoke."

Mia's heart pounded. Vicky Fontaine. Somehow she'd already suspected the bitch had followed them. Unfortunately, she didn't know if the older woman was alone.

Pressing herself against the charred wall of the shed, she pulled out the gun and clicked off the safety.

It was too dark to see more than just a few feet in front of her. Which meant her only hope was to keep Vicky and her potential accomplices distracted until Max came to check on them.

Or until she could get Lucas free.

"You smelled smoke so you decided to shoot me?" Mia demanded, moving to the edge of the shed.

Peeking around the corner, she thought she could see someone standing near the clump of cypresses that gave her a perfect view of the shed's only door.

Dammit.

"Someone was shooting at you?" Vicky's voice held a faux concern. "Come out so we can call the police."

Mia rolled her eyes. Did Vicky think she was an idiot?

"I know it was you," Mia said. "You killed your husband and now you're trying to kill me."

"I told you, it was your father and Tony who murdered Paul," Vicky called out, leaning to the side as if trying to get a glimpse of Mia.

Or an open shot.

"I saw the pictures," Mia informed the woman.

There was a short pause, as if Mia had managed to catch the older woman off guard.

"Of course you did," Vicky at last said. "I showed them to you."

"Not those pictures." Mia glanced over her shoulder, making sure no one was sneaking up from behind. "I'm talking about the ones that show you kneeling beside your husband's body to make sure he's dead."

Even from a distance, she could hear Vicky's muttered curse of disbelief. "That's impossible," she at last said.

Mia shivered. Vicky had seen the snapshots. No doubt her father had included them when he'd given her the others.

"Did you forget to share those photos with me?" Mia demanded. "Or did you destroy your copies?"

"Honestly, I didn't think George Ramon had the brains to keep the pictures," Vicky at last admitted.

Mia frowned. She'd assumed Vicky had followed them to the remote property because she knew her father had evidence she was involved in the murder of her husband.

Now she didn't have any idea why the woman had tried to burn them in the shed. Or seemed determined to lure Mia out in the open so she could shoot her.

"Clearly you underestimated my father," she taunted.

"Your father was a cowardly drunk who peeked through windows and lurked in the shadows. If it hadn't been for Tony, I would never have allowed him on my property."

Mia squashed her flare of anger. The woman was hoping to provoke her into doing something stupid.

"He managed to outsmart you," she instead taunted.

"Even fools get lucky once in a while," Vicky snapped.

Lucky. Mia stiffened, struck by a sudden realization.

Vicky was right. It'd been hard to imagine that her father would have been waiting in the bushes with a camera to take pictures of the murder. Now she abruptly recalled that he occasionally used a disposable camera to photograph a few of the gardens he worked on, for new brochures or to show potential clients.

It was quite possible that it'd been nothing more than a coincidence for her father to be at Vicky's mansion with a camera on the day of the murder.

Mia grimaced. It still troubled her that her father hadn't gone to the authorities with the photos, but George Ramon had been fiercely suspicious of anyone connected to the government. And, as painful as it might be to admit, her father wasn't above taking advantage of a situation.

"I don't consider it luck that he was forced to witness you murdering your husband," she said.

Vicky's short, humorless laugh echoed through the thick silence that shrouded the area. "He managed to make a small fortune off that murder."

Mia ignored the insult. Her father was dead. Nothing could hurt him now.

She was far more concerned with Lucas. The fire was out, but the shed had been filled with smoke. Was it enough to hurt him?

And where the hell was Max? He'd promised to keep an eye on Vicky. Surely he couldn't be far behind her?

"What about Tony? Did you pay him off?" Mia demanded, sensing the woman's growing impatience. Soon she was going to decide that she was done talking.

"Tony was in love with me," Vicky drawled. "He would do anything I asked."

Mia flinched. There were many reasons to hate the older woman, but the top of the list was the way she'd used and abused a young, vulnerable boy.

"Not anything," Mia said with utter confidence. It was now obvious there was no mysterious drug cartel demanding her death. It'd been Vicky Fontaine who wanted her dead, and she'd done her best to try and manipulate Tony into doing the dirty deed. The older woman had clearly overestimated her power over her lover. Or perhaps she'd just underestimated Tony's loyalty to his friend. "He wouldn't kill me."

Mia's words clearly hit a raw nerve.

"I'm done with this," Vicky snarled, her shadow moving as she lifted her arm. "Show yourself."

Mia made a sound of disbelief. Was the woman so arrogant that she believed she could toss out orders and have them instantly obeyed?

"I don't think so."

Without warning there was the sound of gunshots. Mia instinctively crouched down, covering her head as she pressed against the shed. It wasn't until the loud blasts stopped that she sucked in a deep breath and glanced around the corner.

She half expected to see Vicky running in her direction. Instead she was still standing in the shadows of the cypresses, her gun pointed at the shed.

What was the woman doing? Either she was a terrible shot or she . . .

Mia's breath suddenly tangled in her throat, her heart forgetting to beat as she leaned far enough to catch a glimpse of the small holes in the side of the shed.

The bitch hadn't been shooting at Mia. She'd been firing bullets through the rotted planks of the shed.

"Stop," Mia called out, her voice high with fear.

"Afraid I'm going to kill your precious Lucas?" the older woman mocked, firing more bullets into the shed. "Come out or I'll keep shooting until your lover is dead."

"You're crazy," Mia cried, pressing her ear to the rough wooden plank, trying to hear Lucas.

Had he been overcome with smoke? Hit by a bullet?

"I'm not crazy, just tired of trying to kill you," Vicky corrected her, the scrape of metal warning Mia that she was reloading her gun.

"You tried to run me off the road," Mia said, dropping to the ground as she crawled toward a nearby barrel. Vicky was right about one thing. Enough was enough. She had to end this before the woman managed to hurt Lucas. First, however, she needed a better angle. "And you put the drugs in my coffee."

"Yes. But you refused to die." The older woman's voice held disgust for Mia's refusal to bite the dust. "This time I'm not leaving until I'm certain you're dead."

Mia shook her head. The woman really was crazy.

"It doesn't matter if I'm dead or not," she warned, her fingers tightening on the gun in her hand. "Lucas's partners already know about the pictures." Mia didn't bother to share the fact they hadn't been able to tell Max they had proof that Vicky was involved. "It's too late."

"It's not too late. Once I'm done with you and Lucas, I'll get rid of the pictures." There was a hint of panic in Vicky's voice, the sound of her approaching footsteps making Mia tense with determination. "Without evidence no one can prove that Paul is dead. And they certainly can't pin the blame on me."

"It's over, Vicky," Mia prodded. "Give it up."

"No." Vicky continued to move forward. "I won't let you destroy me."

Reaching the back of the shed, the older woman shot toward the dark shadows where Mia had so recently been huddled.

Mia's mouth went dry.

This was it.

Now or never.

Squashing her instinctive horror at deliberately harming another human being, she rose to her feet and aimed her gun. Then, as Vicky turned to shoot her, Mia squeezed the trigger.

There was an explosive flash of light from the muzzle of

her gun, followed by a recoil of energy that jerked her arm back. Mia hurriedly bent low as she prepared for Vicky to return fire.

Instead there was a sharp cry of pain as Vicky toppled forward, landing on the muddy ground with an audible thud.

Clutching her gun in a tight grip, Mia inched her way around the barrel. She half expected Vicky to leap to her feet and start shooting. Instead she remained unmoving as Mia made a wide circle around the corner of the shed. Once out of sight of the woman, Mia darted toward the front of the small structure to discover a crowbar had been wedged between the door and the jamb.

It was no wonder they hadn't been able to get out.

Now she hurried forward, grabbing the bar and tugging with all her might. The slick metal made it almost impossible to get a good grip with one hand, but she wasn't willing to put away her gun. Not when Vicky might rise from the mud like a vampire and try to finish what she'd started.

Giving one last tug, the crowbar at last came free, slipping through her hand as the door swung open.

Swiftly stepping into the shed, it took a minute for her eyes to become accustomed to the thick gloom. Inching her way forward, she at last caught sight of Lucas's body stretched on the wood-planked floor.

"Oh my God, Lucas."

Dropping to her knees, Mia reached to carefully turn him onto his back. His low groan assured her that he was still alive, but that didn't ease her panic. It was too dark to see if he'd been seriously injured.

"Lucas," she breathed, pressing her lips to his forehead as she tried to clear the fog of panic from her mind.

She could have a breakdown later. Right now Lucas needed her.

Concentrating on the best way to get Lucas out of the

shed and into the SUV, Mia nearly missed the sound of a branch cracking as someone neared the shed.

With a surge of adrenaline she was on her feet, the gun pointed toward the open doorway.

"Stop or I'll shoot," she warned.

"Mia, it's me," a male voice called out. "Max."

"Oh, thank God," Mia breathed, her knees going weak as the large man cautiously stepped into the shed. "Lucas is hurt."

Using the flashlight on his phone, Max swept it over Lucas's body. "I don't see any blood," he reassured Mia, bending down to place his fingers against Lucas's throat. "And his pulse is strong."

Mia bit her lower lip, relief searing through her. "He must have been knocked out from the smoke."

Max straightened, reaching out to gently take the gun from her shaky hand. "He's going to be fine."

She nodded, wondering why she couldn't stop shaking. Was she in shock?

"Vicky—" She started to warn Max, only to bite off her words when he held up his hand.

"Don't worry," he murmured. "Detective Cooper has her cuffed."

A combination of relief and smoldering frustration churned through her. She wanted to be sure the older woman could never again try to hurt her. But at the same time, she really didn't want to live with the knowledge she'd killed a woman. Even if it was in self-defense.

"She's alive?" she demanded.

Max grimaced. Clearly he wasn't torn. "Unfortunately. The bullet went through her shoulder. Cooper called for an ambulance."

Mia nodded, wrapping her arms around her waist. She felt chilled to the bone.

"Vicky killed her husband," she managed to say between chattering teeth. "Or at least, she convinced Tony to kill him."

"We know." Pulling off his jacket, Max wrapped it around her shivering body. "The detective parked down the road so we could sneak up without alerting Vicky. We heard everything."

She blinked, her fear easing as she heard the whine of sirens as the ambulance raced down the road.

"It's over?"

Max nodded. "Yeah, it's over."

As if capable of hearing their words, Lucas heaved a soft sigh. "Mia," he breathed.

# Chapter Twenty-Six

Lucas had had enough.

He'd spent the night in the hospital to ease Mia's concern that he wasn't suffering any lingering effects from the smoke he'd inhaled. But now the sun was up and his patience was at an end.

He'd nearly lost Mia yesterday. He needed to have her in his arms.

Coming out of the bathroom attached to his private hospital room, he ignored the older nurse who was glaring at him. He was showered and dressed in the black slacks and white shirt that Max had dropped by last night. Now he grabbed his few belongings and shoved them into a small leather bag.

Bustling around like a fly who couldn't decide where to land, the nurse at last reached to take his bag forcibly from his hand. "Mr. St. Clair, I must insist that you get back in your bed," she muttered. "You haven't been officially released."

Lucas planted his fists on his hips. Usually he preferred to use his skills at negotiation to get his way. He'd been born with position, money, and power. Then he'd been trained to become physically superior to most people. It would have been easy to evolve into an arrogant bully.

Today, however, he wasn't in the mood to play nice. Not when he didn't know where Mia was, or why she hadn't come to see him.

"You can insist all you want, but I'm getting out of here," he growled. "Tell the doctor to get his ass in gear so he can sign me out."

The nurse pressed her lips together, looking as if she wanted to put him across her knee and give him a good spanking.

"The doctor is very busy."

Lucas reached to snatch the bag out of her hand. "Then I'll leave without his approval."

"Let me handle this." A soft voice interrupted the brewing argument and Lucas swiftly turned to watch as Mia stepped into the room.

Instantly the tension that felt like steel bands wrapped around his chest eased. His gaze ran a greedy path over her beautiful face, which was framed by the dark curls left free to tumble over her shoulders. He allowed his attention to stray lower, taking in the cherry-red sweater and the faded jeans that hugged her lush curves with mouthwatering perfection.

The nurse gave a loud sniff. "He is very stubborn."

Mia's lips twitched. "Yeah, I know."

"Just hit the buzzer if you need me," the nurse said as she conceded defeat and headed out the door.

Mia shook her head. "The poor woman is just trying to do her job," she softly chided. "And you were supposed to stay in bed until the doctor is sure you're not going to have a reaction to the smoke you inhaled."

Lucas tossed his bag on a nearby chair as he strolled forward, framing her face in his hands. "I wanted to find you."

She stilled, sensing the smoldering frustration that had forced him from his bed despite the nurse's shrill protests.

"I promised I was coming to pick you up this morning," she said.

"I know, but . . ." His words trailed away as he realized where they were.

Mia frowned. "What?"

He heaved a resigned sigh. The sterile hospital room wasn't the setting where he'd planned to share his most intimate desires, but he didn't want to wait.

He'd wasted fifteen years. He wasn't wasting another second.

"I was afraid you would disappear," he admitted with blunt honesty.

"Disappear?" She looked confused. "Why would I do that?"

He gave a lift of his shoulder. He'd tossed and turned all night, terrified that he was too late for a second chance with this woman.

"It's what I did to you. Now I know how you must have felt." His thumbs brushed her cheeks as he savored the feel of her satiny skin. "The thought that you might walk away and leave me behind . . ." He sucked in a deep breath, a shudder of horror racing through him. "It's unbearable."

She reached up to place her hands against his chest. "I'm not going anywhere, Lucas."

"Neither am I," he swore, holding her gaze. "I called Hauk this morning."

"Why?"

"I told him that I was leaving ARES."

"Leaving ARES?" Her lips parted, her eyes darkening with shock. "I don't understand."

Neither had Hauk. The man had refused to accept Lucas's resignation, at first pleading for him to reconsider, before he was ordering him to return to Houston so they could talk in person.

"Your life and business is here," he said. "So this is where I want to be."

Her expression softened, but before she could respond, the door was pushed open and Max strolled into the room.

He was wearing a leather coat over his gray suit and his hair was ruffled from the stiff breeze. He brought with him the scent of fresh air that Lucas longed to breathe.

He'd had enough of the stench of disinfectant to last a lifetime.

Max silently took in the sight of Lucas wrapping a possessive arm around Mia's shoulder before he glanced toward the bag already packed and waiting on the chair. "I can't believe you're still here," he said in way of greeting.

Mia rolled her eyes. "Don't encourage him."

Lucas smiled. Max knew him well enough to suspect he wasn't going to wait for some damned doctor to tell him when he could leave. "Have you talked to Detective Cooper?" he demanded.

When Lucas had awakened in the hospital it'd been Max who'd told him Vicky had been arrested, and that the authorities had the evidence that George Ramon had kept locked in the silver case.

He'd also promised he would keep them updated on what was happening with Vicky Fontaine.

The younger man gave a dip of his head. "I did."

Lucas tugged Mia closer, knowing this was going to be difficult for her.

"Did he let you listen to the tape?"

Max grimaced. "After some convincing."

Lucas wondered exactly what convincing Max had been forced to use. But before he could ask, Mia was asking the question that'd no doubt been preying on her mind.

"Was it my father's?"

"It was," Max said, his tone gentle.

"What did he say?" Mia asked.

"He talked about witnessing Tony shoot Paul Fontaine and Vicky helping to load the body in the back of a black Mercedes." Max met Lucas's narrowed gaze. "He also claims that he saw them with stacks of money that Vicky hid in a large bag."

Lucas arched a brow. "So Paul did have the two million."

"Yeah." Max nodded. "Seems like she decided to kill two birds with one stone. She got rid of her unwanted husband and got a fortune to continue to live in the style she assumed she deserved."

So had Vicky convinced her husband to embezzle the millions of dollars over the years? Or had she taken advantage when she caught sight of him with the last two million in cash he managed to squeeze out of the accounts before he was murdered?

They would probably never know.

"Anything else?" Lucas asked.

Max hesitated, glancing toward the woman at Lucas's side. "It's not pretty."

"Mia—" Lucas started, only to be interrupted by his stubborn companion.

"No." Mia tilted her chin, her expression resolute. "I need to know."

The two men exchanged rueful glances before Max continued his revelation of what he'd learned. "Your father wasn't a fool," he told Mia. "He knew that if he used the pictures to blackmail Vicky he would be putting his life at risk. She'd already had her husband killed. There was nothing to keep her from killing him and destroying the photos."

Lucas arched a brow. He hadn't actually considered how simple it would have been for Vicky to rid herself of George Ramon.

"Makes sense," he murmured. "What did he do to protect himself?"

There was another short pause before Max answered.

"He followed Tony into the swamps where he dumped the car. Then, after Tony left, he used his truck to pull the car out and took it to his own property," he explained. "On the tape he gives the directions to finding it."

Mia gave a soft gasp, her face draining of color. "There was a dead body on the property?"

Max nodded. "Sunk in the bog out back."

"Oh my God," Mia breathed, squeezing her eyes shut in horror.

Lucas sympathized with her distress. It wouldn't be pleasant to know that she'd been living at a place where there was a dead man rotting in the trunk of his car. Still, he couldn't deny that George was far more clever than he'd ever suspected.

"Creepy, but smart," he said. "Vicky had done everything in her power to convince people her husband had run off with the money. She couldn't have his dead body showing up. It would have been easy to convince her to pay George the money he wanted."

Mia instinctively pressed closer to Lucas, although she maintained a rigid control over her emotions. Her courage would never fail to amaze him.

Although he intended to have a long conversation with her about her decision to stay and put out the fire rather than simply disappear into the bogs. Vicky would never have been able to hunt her down.

"I still don't understand why she wanted me dead," she said.

Max gave a lift of his shoulder. "After your father passed away she must have feared you would try to do something with the property."

Mia bit her lower lip. "I did contact a recycling center about hauling off the cars and tearing down the old buildings."

"That would have spooked her," Lucas said. "She would be desperate to find Paul's car before someone else could."

"That's why Tony's lighter was out there," Mia murmured.

Lucas nodded. He could easily imagine his old friend returning night after night to search the property, only to come up empty. And when he couldn't find the Mercedes he must have gone into the house to search for some sort of clue. Or maybe he just went inside to get out of the cold and have a smoke.

"Next, Vicky tried to buy the land," Lucas said. "She had to have been out of her mind with frustration when you wouldn't sell."

Mia wrinkled her nose, but it was Max who spoke.

"Frustrated enough that she managed to find out that you had a will that endowed your father's land to a wildlife conservation group if you died," he muttered. He'd revealed the night before that Teagan had discovered Vicky's connection to the charity that Mia had chosen to leave the land to in case of her death. "It was simply a matter of giving a big enough donation to be named chairwoman."

Mia shivered. "The power of money."

"Exactly," Max agreed.

Another shiver shook Mia's body and Lucas lowered his head to press a comforting kiss to the top of her head.

"So she really was trying to kill me," Mia breathed.

"First she tried to convince Tony to get rid of you," Max said.

Lucas sent up a silent thank-you to his dead friend who'd refused to give in to his lover's urgings, and had instead traveled to Houston to seek Lucas's help. Even if he'd never made it to the ARES office, he'd alerted Lucas that Mia was in danger.

"Did she admit to shooting Tony?" Mia asked.

Max made a sound of disgust. "She's lawyered up, but my bet is on Detective Cooper," he said.

"Which one?" Lucas demanded, remembering the older detective who worked in Houston.

"Both." Max allowed a wry smile to touch his lips. "The cops are already swarming over the Fontaine estate, searching for the gun that shot Tony, as well as questioning her staff. Eventually they'll get the evidence they need to prove she was responsible."

Lucas nodded in agreement. Detective Cooper was like a bloodhound. Solid, stubborn, and ruthless when he was on the hunt.

He wouldn't quit until he had Vicky on trial for murder.

Suddenly tired of the bitch who would hopefully spend the rest of her life rotting in jail, Lucas abruptly turned the conversation. "Are you headed back to Houston?" he asked his friend.

Max narrowed his gaze, his jaw tightening. "Not until we have a little chat."

Lucas frowned before realizing why Max suddenly looked like he'd swallowed a lemon. "You've spoken with Hauk?"

"He said you're staying in Shreveport," Max growled, his voice harsh with displeasure.

Lucas shrugged. "I am."

Max parted his lips to argue, only to snap them shut when Mia held up a slender hand.

"Can Lucas and I have a few minutes alone?" she asked, meeting Max's glare without flinching. "Please?"

"Fine," the blond-haired man muttered, pointing a finger in Lucas's direction. "But I'm not leaving town until we talk."

Lucas sighed as his friend reluctantly left the hospital room and closed the door behind him.

"And you call me stubborn," he muttered.

Turning until they were face-to-face, Mia laid her hands on his chest. "They're your friends," she murmured in soft tones. "They aren't going to accept your resignation, you know?"

Lucas ignored the small pang at the thought of leaving ARES and the men who'd become family to him.

If that was the price he had to pay to have Mia back in his life, there was no contest. Nothing was more important than this woman.

"They'll have to."

She smoothed her hands over the clenched muscles of his chest, sending tiny darts of pleasure through him. "I thought we were going to find some compromise."

His blood heated as he became increasingly distracted with the thought of having her naked in his arms. How long would it take to get from the hospital to the penthouse? Twenty minutes?

"All I want is to have a place in your life," he assured her, bending his head to press his lips to her forehead before trailing a path of kisses down to the corner of her mouth. "It doesn't matter to me if that's in Houston or Shreveport, as long as we're together."

"I don't see why we can't do both." Her hands skimmed upward so she could wrap her arms around his neck. "I spoke to Taylor this morning and she's agreed to become an office manager."

Lucas lifted his head, struggling to concentrate on her words. "What's that mean?"

Mia shrugged. "She'll deal with the day-to-day customers and take over the accounting."

He studied her lovely face with a searching gaze. "You're okay with that?"

"Yeah," she said without hesitation. "She has the talent to take on more responsibilities, and even if she ends up getting married, I think she'll be happier being in charge."

Lucas blinked. His need to get this woman naked really was clouding his mind. He didn't have a damned clue what Mia was talking about.

"Taylor is getting married?"

She frowned in disbelief. "Surely you've seen the way Detective Cooper looks at her."

He shook his head. "I've been a little preoccupied."

She sighed at his lack of insight but, seeming to accept that he'd been obsessed with his need to protect her, she didn't press.

"I'll still need to come to Shreveport to oversee the contracts and to design the landscapes for any new clients," she continued. "But she can handle the day-to-day business, while Sonny can supervise the staff. We can spread our time between here and Houston."

A fierce joy clenched his heart. She'd accepted that they belonged together.

Everything else was just icing on the cake.

"What made you change your mind?" he asked.

Pulling out of his hold, she reached into her back pocket and retrieved several sheets of paper that had been folded in two.

"This." She shoved the papers in his hand.

"What is it?" he demanded.

"The loans you made to me so I could expand my business."

Surprise streaked through him as he glanced down at the papers in his hand.

"How?" He gave a sharp shake of his head. "Never mind," he muttered, accepting that one or more of his interfering friends had decided to stick his nose in where he didn't belong. "It had to be Max. Or was it Teagan?"

"It doesn't matter," Mia said, obviously not about to narc on who was responsible.

Not that Lucas was going to demand an answer. She was right. It didn't matter. His friends might be a pain in his ass, but they'd only wanted to help.

Wrapping her in his arms, he buried his face in the silken strands of her hair.

"I felt that I'd lost my chance to be with you," he admitted, "but I wanted to make sure you could follow your dreams."

"You never stopped caring."

"Never," he said in fierce tones.

She snuggled against him, her cheek pressed over the steady thud of his heart.

"That's all I ever needed to know."

Please turn the page for an exciting sneak peek of
Alexandra Ivy's next novel of romantic suspense,

**PRETEND YOU'RE SAFE,**

coming soon wherever print and eBooks are sold!

*First came the floods. And then the bodies . . .*

Jaci Patterson was running late.

It all started when she woke at her usual time of four a.m. Yeah, she really and truly woke at that indecent hour, five days a week. On the weekends, she allowed herself to sleep in until six. But this morning, when she'd crawled out of bed, she discovered the electricity was out.

Again.

The lack of power had nothing to do with the sketchy electrical lines that ran to her remote farmhouse in the northeast corner of Missouri. At least not this time. Instead, it could be blamed on the rains that had started the first day of March and continued to hammer the entire Midwest for the past three weeks.

When the lights at last came on at five, she had to rush through her routine, grateful that she'd baked two dozen peach tarts and several loaves of bread the night before.

As it was she'd barely managed to finish her blueberry muffins and scones before she had to load them into the back of her Jeep. Then, locking her two black Labs, Riff and Raff, in the barn so they didn't destroy her house, she headed toward Heron, the small town just ten miles away.

Predictably, she'd driven less than two miles down the muddy lane that led to the small farm that'd once belonged to her grandparents, when she discovered the road was blocked. *Crap.* Obviously the levee had broken during the night, releasing the swollen fury of the Mississippi River.

It was no wonder her electricity had gone out.

Grimacing at the knowledge that her bottom fields, along with most of her neighbors', were probably flooded, she put the Jeep in reverse. Then, careful to stay in the center of the muddy road, she reversed her way back to the lane. Once she managed to get turned around, she headed in the opposite direction.

The detour took an extra fifteen minutes, but at least she didn't have to worry about traffic. With less than three hundred people, Heron wasn't exactly a hub of activity. In fact, she ran into exactly zero cars as she swung along Main Street.

She splashed through the center of town that was lined with a small post office, the county courthouse that was built in the 1800s, a bank, and a beauty parlor. Farther down the block was a newly constructed tin shed that housed the fire truck and the water department. On the corner was a small diner that had originally been christened the Cozy Kitchen, but had slowly become known as the Bird's Nest by the locals after it'd been taken over by Nancy Bird, or Birdie, as she was affectionately nicknamed.

Pulling into the narrow alley behind the diner, Jaci hopped out of her vehicle to grab the top container of muffins that were still warm from the oven. Instantly, she regretted not pulling on her jacket as the drizzling rain molded her short, brown hair to her scalp and dampened her Mizzou sweatshirt and faded jeans to her curved body.

With a shiver she hurried through the back door, careful to wipe the mud from her rubber boots before entering the kitchen.

Heat smacked her in the face, the contrast from the chilled wind outside making the cramped space feel smothering.

Grimacing, she walked across the floor to set the muffins on a narrow stainless-steel table that was next to the griddle that was filled with scrambled eggs, hash browns, sausage, and sizzling bacon.

The large woman with graying hair and a plump face, efficiently flipped a row of pancakes before gesturing toward the woman who was busily washing dishes. Once the helper had hurried to her side, she handed off her spatula and made her way toward Jaci.

Nancy Bird, better known as Birdie, was fifteen years older than Jaci. When she was just seventeen she'd married her high school sweetheart and dropped out of school. The sweetheart turned out to be a horse patootie who'd fled town, leaving Birdie with four young girls to raise on her own.

With a grim determination that Jaci deeply admired, Birdie had bought the old diner and over the past ten years had turned it into the best place to eat in the entire county.

At this early hour her clients usually consisted of farmers, hunters, and school bus drivers who were up before dawn.

"Morning, Birdie." Jaci stepped aside as the older woman efficiently began to place the muffins on a large glass tray that would be set on the counter next to the cash register. Many of the diners liked to have a cup of coffee and muffin once they were done with breakfast.

"Thank God you're here."

"I'm sorry I'm late. The electricity didn't come on until almost five."

Finishing, Birdie grabbed the tray and bustled across the kitchen to hand it to her assistant.

"Take this to the counter," Birdie commanded before turning back to Jaci with a roll of her eyes. "The natives have been threatening to revolt without their favorite muffins."

Jaci smiled, pleased by Birdie's words. She'd learned to bake at her grandmother's side, but it wasn't until she'd inherited her grandparents' farm that she considered using her skills to help her make ends meet.

Leaning to the side she glanced through the large open space where the food was passed through to the waitresses.

She released a slow whistle. The place hadn't changed in the past ten years. The walls were covered with faded paneling that was decorated with old license plates and a mounted fish caught from the river. The floor was linoleum with a drop ceiling that was lit with fluorescent lights.

There was a half dozen tables arranged around the square room with one long table at the back where a group of farmers showed up daily to drink coffee and share the local gossip.

At the moment, every seat was filled with patrons wearing buff coveralls, camo jackets, and Cardinal baseball hats.

"Damn, woman. That's quite a crowd," she said, a rueful smile touching her lips. The rains meant that no one was able to get into the fields. "At least someone can benefit from this latest downpour."

Birdie sucked in a sharp breath, her hands landing on her generous hips.

"I hope you're not suggesting that I'm the sort of person who enjoys benefiting from a tragedy, Jaci Patterson," the older woman chastised. "People want to get together to discuss what's happened and I have the local spot for them to gather."

Jaci blinked, caught off guard by her friend's sharp reprimand. Then, absorbing the older woman's words, she lifted a hand to her lips.

"Tragedy?" she breathed. "Oh no. Has something happened?"

Birdie's features softened. "You haven't heard about the body?"

"Body?" Jaci felt a tremor of unease. She'd already lost her father to a drunk driver before she was even born, and then her grandmother when she was seventeen. Her grandfather had passed just two years ago. She still grieved for them. "Like I said, the electricity went out last night and as soon as it came back on I started baking. Has someone died?"

"I'm afraid so."

"Who?"

"No one knows for sure yet," Birdie told her.

Jaci frowned. What was Birdie talking about?

"How could they not know?"

"The levee broke in the middle of the night."

"Yeah, I figured that out when I discovered that the road was closed . . . oh hell." She tensed as her unease became sharp-edge fear. The levee had broken before and flooded fields, but her closest neighbor had recently built a new house much closer to the river. "It didn't reach Frank's home, did it?"

Birdie shook her head. "Just the back pasture."

"Then what body are you talking about?"

"When Frank went to move his cattle to higher ground, he saw something floating in the middle of his field."

Jaci cringed. Poor Frank. He must have been shocked out of his mind.

"Oh my God. It was a dead person?"

"Yep. A woman."

"He didn't recognize her?"

Birdie leaned forward and lowered her voice, as if anyone could overhear them with the noise from the customers, not to mention the usual kitchen clatter.

"He said it was impossible to know if she was familiar or not."

"I don't suppose he wanted to look too close," Jaci said. If she'd spotted a body in her flooded field she would have jumped into her Jeep and driven away like a maniac.

"It wasn't that. He claimed the woman was too . . ." Birdie hesitated, as if she was searching for a more delicate way to express what Frank had said. "Decomposed to make out her features."

"Decomposed?" A strange chill inched down Jaci's spine.

"That's what he's saying."

Jaci absently glanced through the opening into the outer room where she could see Frank surrounded by a group of avid listeners.

When Birdie had said a body, she'd assumed that it had been someone who'd been caught in the flood. Maybe she'd fallen in when she was walking along the bank. Or her car might had been swept away when she tried to cross a road with high water.

But she wouldn't be decomposed, would she?

"I've heard that water does strange things to a body," she at last said.

Birdie tugged Jaci toward the back door as her assistant moved to open the fridge. Clearly there was more to the story.

"The body wasn't all that Frank discovered."

Jaci stilled. "There was more?"

"Yep." Birdie whispered, as if it was a big secret. Which was ridiculous. There were no such things as secrets in a town the size of Heron. "Frank called the sheriff and while he was waiting for Mike to arrive, he swears that he caught sight of a human skull stuck in the mud at the edge of the road." Birdie gave a horrified shudder. "Can you imagine? Two dead people virtually in his backyard? Gives me the creeps just thinking about it."

Jaci's mouth went dry. "Did Frank say anything else?"

Birdie shrugged. "Just that the sheriff told him to leave and not to talk about what he found." Birdie snorted. "Like anyone wouldn't feel the need to share the fact they found a dead body and a skull in their field."

A familiar dread curdled in the pit of her stomach.

She was being an idiot. Of course she was. This had nothing to do with the terror of her past.

Still . . .

She couldn't shake the sudden premonition that slithered down her spine.

"Is Mike still out at Frank's?" she abruptly demanded, referring to the sheriff, Mike O'Brien.

"Yeah." Birdie sent her a curious glance. "I think he was waiting for the Corp of Engineers to get out there so they could discuss how long it would take for the field to drain." She wrinkled her nose. "I suppose they need to make sure there aren't any other bodies."

More bodies.

A fierce urgency pounded through her. She might be overreacting, but she wasn't going to be satisfied until she spoke to Mike.

"I need to go."

"You haven't had your coffee," Birdie protested.

"Not this morning, thanks, Birdie."

"Okay." The older woman stepped back. "I'll get your money and—"

"I'll stop by later to get it." Jaci turned to pull open the back door.

Instantly a chilled blast of air swept around them.

"What's your rush?" Birdie demanded.

"I have some questions that need answers," she said.

"With who?" Birdie demanded, making a sound of impatience as Jaci darted into the alley and jogged toward her waiting Jeep. "Jaci?"

Not bothering to answer, Jaci jumped into the vehicle and put it in gear. Water trickled down her neck from her wet hair, but when she'd gone into the diner she'd left the engine running with the heater blasting at full steam.

Which meant she was a damp mess, but she wasn't completely miserable.

Angling the vent in a futile effort to dry her soggy sweatshirt, Jaci stomped on the accelerator and headed back toward her house. This time, however, she swerved around the barrier that blocked the road, squishing her way through the muddy path that led along the edge of Frank's property.

It was less than ten miles, but by the time she was pulling her vehicle to a halt, her stomach had managed to clench into a tight ball of nerves.

It didn't matter how many times she told herself that this had nothing to do with the past, she couldn't dismiss her rising tide of fear.

Ignoring the avid crowd of onlookers that were gathered at the edge of the field, Jaci skirted around the wooden barrier, her gaze skimming over the sluggish brown water that had surged through the broken levee. Massive logs and plastic bags that had once been filled with sand swirled through the field. But no body.

Thank God.

"Jaci." A male voice intruded into her distracted thoughts as a skinny man dressed in a dark uniform that was covered by a clear raincoat stepped in front of her.

She forced a smile to her lips. "Morning, Sid."

The young deputy nodded his head toward the flooded field, trying to look suitably somber.

"I guess you heard the news?"

"Yep." Jaci's gaze moved over the deputy's shoulder, landing on the man who was pacing along the edge of the road with a cell phone pressed to his ear.

Sheriff Mike O'Brien.

Only a couple years older than Jaci's twenty-seven years, he was wearing a crisp black uniform with a star on his sleeve that indicated his elected status. Beneath his shirt he was wearing body armor that emphasized his broad, muscular frame. He had light brown hair that he kept cut military short beneath his black ball cap, and a square face with blunt features and eyes that were an astonishingly bright shade of green.

He was the sort of solid, dependable man that Jaci had always told herself that she should want. Which explained why she'd dated him for several months after returning to Heron.

Unfortunately, they just hadn't clicked. At least not for her. Mike continued to ask her out. She didn't know if he was truly smitten with her, or if she was a convenient date.

After all, Heron wasn't overrun with eligible women.

"I think half the town is here to gawk." Sid once again interrupted her thoughts, his chest puffed out. It was a rare treat to have so much excitement. Jaci, however, was intent on reaching Mike. She stepped around the barrier, neatly avoiding Sid's attempt to grab her arm. "Hey, wait," he commanded.

She marched forward, the mud threatening to suck off her rubber boots.

"I need to speak with Mike," she said, battling her way toward her friend.

Sid made an effort to block her path. "The sheriff closed

off this area. He said he didn't want no one here disturbing things until he finished up."

She darted around him. She was nothing if not determined. "I'll just be a minute."

"But—"

"Don't worry, Sid," she called over her shoulder. "I won't disturb anything."

Realizing he was going to have to physically wrestle her to the ground if he hoped to stop her, Sid returned to his post beside the barrier.

"He's going to put my balls in a vise," he groused.

Jaci concentrated on the increasingly marshy ground in front of her. Even before the breech in the levee the soil had been eroded by the pounding rains. One misstep and she could find her foot being caught in a hidden cavity. The last thing she wanted was to fall on her ass.

Or worse, twist an ankle.

Thankfully Mike was distracted by his phone call. Which meant that he didn't have a chance to flee before she was standing directly beside him.

Belatedly realizing he was no longer alone, Mike abruptly turned to scowl at her with blatant annoyance.

"Shit." Shoving his phone into his pocket, he planted his hands on his hips. "I told Sid not to let anyone through," he growled. "I've already ran off Nelson when I caught him creeping around, snapping pictures with his expensive camera, and Andrew drove his tractor down here to have a look before I could have the field blocked off."

Jaci pressed her lips together. Mike was referring to Nelson Bradley, a local celebrity who was a famous photographer. He'd recently returned to Heron to open his own gallery. And Andrew Porter, a local farmer who cash-cropped Jaci's land.

"I'm not just anyone," she argued.

"No? And why is that?" he demanded. "Just because we dated doesn't give you special privileges."

She jerked at the unexpected attack. Was he being serious?

"I'm not here because we dated."

He paused, sucking in a deep breath. Clearly he'd had a stressful morning with a day stretching ahead that probably wasn't going to be any better.

And to top it off, the chilled drizzle was threatening to become yet another downpour.

"If you're worried about your land, I'll have Sid drive out and check it out," he at last managed, his temper still evident as he glanced toward the breech in the levee. "At least I will once the damned Corp of Engineers gets here."

Jaci gave an impatient wave of her hand. Did he really think she was interrupting him just to get someone to check a few muddy fields?

"I'm not worried about the land. I'm worried about the dead woman."

"Oh." His expression softened. "It's okay, Jaci. She was no one local."

"You're sure?"

He grimaced. "As sure as I can be considering how decomposed the body was." With a shake of his head he pulled out his phone that was buzzing. "I have a lot on my hands right now. You need to go home. I'll stop by later."

She clenched her teeth. A part of her wanted to turn and walk away. Why not accept that this was nothing more than a tragic accident that had nothing to do with Heron? Or her.

God knew she had enough to worry about.

But if she'd learned anything over the past eleven years, it was the fact that nothing, absolutely nothing, was worse than not knowing.

"How was she killed?" she demanded.

There was a short silence as Mike studied her with a

searching gaze, clearly sensing her unease. Then, he reached out to brush her bangs off her wet brow.

"What's going on?" he asked, his voice gentle as he ignored his buzzing phone.

She bit her lower lip before she reluctantly revealed her worst fear.

"What if it's starting again?"

"Starting again?" He wrinkled his brow, seemingly baffled by her harsh question. Seconds later, realization hit and the green eyes narrowed with frustration. "Jesus Christ, Jaci. Don't do this to yourself."

She hunched her shoulder. "I can't help it."

He reached to cup her cheek in his palm as he towered over her. He wasn't more than six foot, but she barely topped five foot two, which made it easy for him to play the overprotective lawman.

Something he enjoyed.

"Listen to me," he ordered. "This has nothing to do with your crazy theories in the past."

A familiar sense of aggravated fury pounded through Jaci. She was used to having her fears dismissed as being "crazy." Hell, the previous sheriff told her that she was being "hormonal."

No one wanted to listen to her fears.

Maybe not that surprising.

She'd just turned sixteen when she'd received the first golden locket. She'd found it on the porch swing when she'd come home from school. At first she assumed that it was a belated birthday gift from her grandparents, but when she opened it up, she'd found a lock of blond hair wrapped with a piece of ribbon that was smeared with blood.

It'd freaked her out enough to insist that her grandmother call the cops. They'd dismissed it as a prank. And Jaci had tried to do the same. There were plenty of bullies at the small school that would delight in terrorizing her. Including her half brother, Christopher.

But the second locket arrived only a few months later. This time the hair was dark, but it was once again wrapped in a bloody ribbon. Once again Jaci had taken it to the sheriff and once again she'd been dismissed.

For the next two years she'd continued to receive the lockets. Sometimes it would be up to six months apart, and sometimes it would be only weeks. But while she was increasingly convinced that the hair in the lockets belonged to women who were being hurt, if not actually killed, no one would believe her.

In fact, it'd become a joke to everyone but her grandparents.

They were the only ones who'd offered her sympathy, even if they didn't entirely accept her belief that there was a maniac in Heron who was killing woman and leaving bits of them in golden lockets on their porch.

The terror had finally stopped when she'd traveled to attend college at Mizzou. And thankfully, there'd been nothing since her return to Heron two years ago.

But now . . .

She shivered. "And how do you explain a dead woman and skull stuck in Frank's field?"

His jaw tightened, his expression guarded as he slid into cop mode.

"There's a thousand potential explanations, and none of them have anything to do with a killer."

"A thousand?" She arched a brow. "Really?"

"Most likely the body came from someone who fell overboard. Or it could have been a victim who was dumped upstream and floated down here." He stepped back, waving a hand toward the muddy water. "Chicago is notorious for getting rid of problems by tossing them in the river."

He was right. Despite the danger, there were always

people who took boats onto the water during a flood. Either because they had no sense, or because it was their job.

And it was also true that she'd been hearing stories about bodies floating down from Chicago her entire life. Not that one had actually been found as far as she knew, but it was an urban myth that everyone was happy enough to believe.

She still wasn't satisfied.

"What about the skull?" she pressed.

Mike rolled his eyes. "Dammit. Is Frank telling everyone in town?"

"Yes."

Mike heaved a resigned sigh. "Look. The most reasonable answer is that both of them were accidental drownings. The recent floods would have churned up a lot of unpleasant things that were hidden at the bottom of the river." He shrugged. "Or it's even possible that the waters disturbed a cemetery and swept a few of the graves down here."

Okay. That actually made sense. A portion of her tension eased.

"When will you know?"

"The body and the skull has already been picked up by the coroner," he said. "He'll drive it down to the medical examiner in Columbia to do an autopsy. Until then, this place is off-limits to everyone. Including you, Jaci." He pointed a finger at her. "Got it?"

"Fine."

Turning, she stomped her way back through the mud.

"I mean it, Jaci," he called from behind her.

"Whatever," she said, cutting along the edge of the field. She'd wasted enough time.

She still had deliveries to make. Not to mention doing her daily grocery shopping, stopping by the bank, the post office, and the vet to get cream for Riff's ear infection.

Later she could worry about dead bodies and strange skulls.

\* \* \*

*The breath was yanked from his body as he watched Jaci Patterson walk away.*

*Oh. It was glorious. The white-hot excitement that made his heart pound and his cock jerk to attention.*

*It felt like he was standing in the center of a lightning storm.*

*How long had it been? Eight years? Maybe nine.*

*Too long.*

*He'd tried to replace her. After all, she'd abandoned him just when he was about to take their relationship to the next level.*

*But while he'd found a fleeting satisfaction with other players, no one had ever given him the same thrill as sweet, sweet Jaci.*

*He hid a smile, conscious that there were dozens of upright Heron citizens who could witness his every expression.*

*It was so ironic.*

*When he'd received the call that the floods had exposed his burial grounds, he'd panicked. The bodies had the potential to attract attention that could ruin everything.*

*Now he forgot his unease.*

*Okay, there might be a brief spark of interest, but it would quickly be forgotten. Especially if the majority of his victims had been swept downriver.*

*And any hassle at dealing with nosy neighbors, and even a potential investigation, was mere nuisances when compared to the dazzling burst of pleasure as he watched the anticipation that was etched on Jaci's beautiful face.*

*She remembered their game.*

*And she was already eager for it to begin again.*

*Just as he was . . .*